Purcell Station

A novel

By
Dale Glenn

First published by Dog Ear Publishing
4010 W. 86th Street, Ste H
Indianapolis, IN 46268
www.dogearpublishing.net

ISBN: 978-1-4575-1968-0

This book is printed on acid-free paper.

This book is a work of fiction. Places, events, and situations in this book are purely
fictional and any resemblance to actual persons, living or dead, is coincidental.

Printed in the United States of America

Dedicated to:

The Glenn and Huffman families

In memory of Nola, George and Joe Glenn

PROLOGUE

Now there are some things we all know, but we don't take'em out and look at'm very often. We all know that something is eternal...it ain't houses, it ain't names, it ain't the earth, it ain't even the stars.... Everybody knows in their bones that something is eternal, and that something has to do with human beings

—Thornton Wilder in *Our Town*

The trains are gone now. Gone from the small towns they used to connect, dropping off passengers, the mail, the daily newspapers. They gave way to the modern highway and the two car garage, the way Grandpa's horse gave way to his '37 Chevy. The only ones left are the freights and the Amtraks that zip through small towns with barely a whistle, ignoring them like jet planes on their fly-overs.

Gone too are the free shows on Saturday night, skinny dipping in the river, the baseball games at the Sand Bowl, bomb shelters, post-war patriotism and parades, and the secrets that only the natives knew. Gone are the front porches where neighbors met nightly, having given way to fenced-in, backyard patios. And where are the soda fountains, the pool room, and the softball games in the vacant lot and the kids who hung out there?

They're gone too.

But some things are permanent. I see it clearly now, but I didn't at the time, when I spent the summer in Purcell Station, among the people that would open up new worlds and shape me—a boy of twelve, scared of growing up until I realized I was almost there. Looking back, twelve was the magical year, that transient point in the journey where a young man finally gets it: when he understands who he will become. Those lessons in life, handed to me by those who were living them, remain universal and timeless.

Maybe that's what Wilder meant when he wrote: *The whole story of thousands of years; Greece, Palestine, the Magna Charta, the French Revolution, is the story of a boy growing up, learning to straighten his shoulders.*

So here is how it happened, as best recalled from the journals of my mind. I've tried not to embellish, but time may have frayed the pages a little, so I cannot guarantee its accuracy. I can, though, vouch for its authenticity.

CHAPTER 1

We were running fast, past the smoke and factories of the city, into the open countryside. It was quiet now, but back at the station it was a different story. The crowd and commotion and crush of people made me wish I could find Mr. Simmons and go back home. But I knew I couldn't. There was no one there.

I woke up early this morning anxious about leaving and worrying about what was going to happen next. My heart was still pounding minutes ago when I boarded the Pullman at Union Station in Indianapolis and found a seat all alone, hoping no one would sit next to or across from me. I didn't want to have to talk or answer any questions about how old I was, or why I was alone, or explain what happened to my father. I just wanted to get through the summer without any more bad news.

I'd never been on a train alone or away from home before, so I sat there all nervous, watching people come down the aisle looking for seats. I was in the back, near the rear door, and when I heard the conductor call, "All aboard," I thought I was home free. But at the last minute a woman carrying a little boy shuffled up the steps and stood over my shoulder, eyeing the empty seats across from me.

I felt a rumble and the train lurching forward, and the next thing I knew they were sitting there staring at me. She was a fancy-looking lady in high-heeled shoes, blue suit, and hat perched on the side of her head. She sat with the little boy, about three, on her lap.

I caught her glancing at me as if she was sizing me up, like noticing my pants were too long and my shirt collar too big, but she didn't say anything. Mom always got my clothes a little big now that I was growing so fast.

I didn't want her to ask where my parents were and have to explain what happened, so I looked away. Across the aisle and up a row, a man in a dark suit sat facing me, reading a newspaper. I could only see the top of his head. His hair was combed back and parted in the middle. He'd been reading the paper since we'd left the city. His suit and tie and newspaper made him look pretty important.

I heard something across the aisle. A serviceman in a brown uniform was sitting alone, snoring. He wore one of those hats like the cooks wear at the White Castle in the city, the kind that unfold and sit slightly cockeyed on the crown of the head. Only his was brown. His chin was drooping and every once in a while his head would jerk, and he'd look around to see where he was. I figured he was on furlough from the war in Korea. He looked to be about eighteen or nineteen—probably enlisted right after high school. That's what my Uncle Jake did. He joined the Navy at age seventeen.

Just then the conductor came by and took my ticket out of the holder on the back of my seat. He stood tall and stroked his moustache as he studied my destination.

"Terre Haute, huh?" he said as he peered over his spectacles, those half -moon kind, resting halfway down his nose.

"Yes sir." I was afraid he was going to ask what I was going to do there. I didn't want to get into that.

"Your name's Garrett?"

"Yes sir."

"And you got on in the city. You traveling alone?"

"Yes sir."

"You look kinda young for that. Your first time?"

"Yes sir." Before they left for Cleveland, Mom had gotten me a ride down to Indianapolis with Mr. Simmons, the shop teacher at the high school. He was going down there anyway to visit the Army surplus depot at Fort Harrison and said he would see that I got downtown to Union Station and got on the right train.

"You look like you ought to be in school."

I glanced at the lady across from me. She looked like she was wondering the same thing. "We get out early," I said.

She raised an eyebrow

"So kids can help with the planting," I added.

"A country boy, huh?" he asked as he checked the ticket of the soldier across the aisle. "You people must be quick to get it all done by May. City folks go to school into June. What grade you in?"

"I finished seventh last week."

"Pretty young," he said, stroking his chin. "Well, we'll keep an eye on you. If you need anything just let me know. The restroom's up front. It'll take another hour and a half to get to Terre Haute."

"Thanks," I said, but the conductor was already checking the ticket of the lady across from me. I heard her say she'd gotten on in "Bala'mer." I think she meant Baltimore.

By the time he finished working his way up the aisle marking tickets, I began to get sleepy. I didn't get much sleep last night. I woke up hearing the painful moaning, and then the light went on in their bedroom, and I heard talking. There was movement and more talking, then after a while, silence, and I fell back asleep until the next time. And the next time it woke me again, and this went on until Mom got me up to get dressed, before they left for Cleveland where Dr. Spellman is supposed to work miracles.

I flinched when the conductor called out, "Next stop, Greencastle."

The train came to a stop and I looked out the window. I saw people moving both directions, some getting aboard and others carrying luggage off to waiting cars. A mail man loaded a bag onto a cart and pushed it to a waiting truck.

Soon the whistle sounded and we picked up speed again on our way to Terre Haute, where I would switch trains. There was some history there—family history—where something important happened. Without sounding too obvious, I'd asked Mom to tell me the story again and where it happened, and afterward, when she wasn't around, I wrote down the address.

Within minutes, the little boy across from me began thrashing around and stretching his arms. He opened his eyes and yawned.

"Where are we, Momma?" His mother lifted him off her lap and sat him beside the window. "We're in the country, Hon. See all the farms? Over there's a silo."

There was that accent again.

"Where?"

"Over there. See that big, tall round thing?" A red silo stood beside a barn and next to a row of cattle feeders.

"What's it for?"

"I think they put corn or hay in it," she said.

Before I could stop myself, I blurted, "It's used to store fodder for cattle."

Immediately, I knew it was a mistake. She turned and looked at me, and I felt myself blush. I didn't want to talk, so I stared up the aisle, as if I was studying something really interesting. She didn't seem to notice my mind was busy.

"You must be a farm boy."

"Not really, ma'am." I looked down at my feet. "My grandpa was though."

"Are you traveling alone?" I figured she already knew. The conductor asked me the same question earlier.

"Yes ma'am."

"Are you going far?"

"I'm getting off at the next stop to switch trains." I didn't tell her what else I planned to do there.

"Are you going to visit family?"

"My grandparents. I'm spending the summer."

"Oh, how nice. Where do they live?"

"A small town. Most people never heard of it...place called Purcell Station."

Just then I heard a sharp rustling of paper and saw the man reading the news eying me over the top of his paper. His eyes were fixed on mine, but his expression was blank, like something was on his mind. He stared so long I wondered if I'd said something wrong. Then he lowered his paper, and I thought he was going to stand up or say something; instead he just stared. I glanced away; then looked back again. He was still staring. I felt myself shiver. Then he gradually raised his paper and disappeared behind it, as if nothing had happened.

For several minutes I sat there looking out the window, afraid to look back. I stayed that way until we were slowing down again. I was anxious to get off. The man was making me nervous, but there was also something I had to do in Terre Haute. I'd heard about it in stories and I'd pictured it in my mind. Now I wanted to see it for real. I didn't tell Mom what I wanted to do, and it wasn't part of her instructions, but I figured she would understand. I just hoped I'd have time.

Soon, the conductor came in and called out, "Next stop, Terre Haute."

We came to a stop and I stood, reached for the overhead shelf, and pulled down my suitcase and a small sack. When I turned around the man with the newspaper was gone.

I lugged my suitcase through the aisle and then down the steps and entered the depot. It was busy. I looked up at the high ceiling and tall windows and thought of the courthouse back in Wabash where voices echoed off the walls and high heeled shoes clicked on the marble floors. It even had the same smell, like a place old and used.

I found the schedule of departures and looked for a south-bound local. There were two of them. The first one left in ten minutes and the second one at 3:35 p.m. I moved into the line and waited. It was when the man at the head of the line bought his ticket and turned to leave that I saw his face. It was the man on the train with the newspaper! Slowly, I ducked behind the lady in front of me and stared straight ahead. I thought he glanced my way, but I wasn't sure. I was afraid to look. He disappeared in the crowd heading out to the tracks.

When I reached the ticket window a man in a green visor was sorting bills and placing them in the money drawer without looking up.

"What can I getcha, young man?" he asked.

"I'd like a ticket to Purcell Station, please."

"You too?" He looked up. "Must be a popular place.

Me too?

"Which train? The 1:42 p.m. or the 3:35 p.m."

"The 3:35."

"You sure? You got time to board the 1:42."

"Thanks, but I'll take the 3:35." I figured that would give me enough time.

"Okie dokie, that'll be $1.75. You gotta be careful traveling alone at your age."

"I know. I've been told. Is there a place I can leave my suitcase for a while?"

"Got some lockers over there," he said, pointing across the room. "You can put it in there for a nickel."

I paid for my ticket and wedged my suitcase into a locker. From my pocket I took out a rumpled piece of paper and glanced at the hand-printed words. I then stuffed it back in my pocket, grabbed the sack lunch Mom had given me, and stepped out into the bright sunshine and the fresh spring air.

I saw a porter standing on the curb with someone's luggage. "Excuse me, sir. Could you tell me where Thornton Street is?" I asked.

"Thornton? Thornton. Sure kid. It's in that direction," he said, pointing east. "Lemme see. Go about five blocks that way and turn left two blocks."

I thanked him and then crossed the street. I was getting hungry. Mom had packed a paper sack with a sandwich and an RC Cola. Heading east, I unwrapped the sandwich, opened the RC, and hurried off toward Thornton Street.

After a few minutes I took out the piece of paper and checked the address again. The campus was behind me. The stories I'd heard placed the house about eight blocks from the college. Finally, I reached Thornton Street and stopped. I looked up and down the street. The homes were large, two-story, either brick or limestone with big front yards. They were nicer than any I'd ever seen. Old oak trees lined both sides of the street.

As I approached the 900 block my stomach began to churn. I tried to imagine what kind of people lived here. Reading the house numbers, I knew I was getting close. Then I saw "942" on the front porch of a large, red brick house. I stood there, frozen, thinking about all I had heard about it, and for a moment I forgot about my father and the Cleveland Clinic.

Then, checking to see if anyone was looking, I took a seat on the curb across the street, to picture how it all began, twenty years ago, the way my mother had described it in the stories at bedtime, when a man she didn't know knocked on the door.

The Dubois family was pretty well off, she told me, at least more than most families living in the Depression. Mr. Dubois was a certified public accountant working for the Hulman Company, famous for manufacturing

Clabber Girl Baking Powder. He wasn't rich, very few people were in the 1930's, but he wasn't poor either. He had a wife who also had a part-time job as a receptionist for a law firm, two small children, and a Labrador retriever. They had a family sedan, a black Model A Ford which he drove to work, after dropping his wife off at the law firm. The Dubois' liked to socialize and go to their country club and go out at night. And when they did, they certainly had the means to hire help, usually girls from the college, to take care of their two kids.

And that's where my mother came in.

CHAPTER **2**

I sat staring at the house across the street, thinking about the years my mother lived there, knowing how it almost didn't happen. The stock market crash and the Depression left people in hard financial times, including her father. He was a working man of German descent who'd gained quite a reputation as a house painter and paper-hanger; things people could do without in the Depression. Furthermore, he didn't see the need. "Girls don't need college. All they need is to find the right guy and get married, raise a family, and be a good mother and wife," he had said many times.

But she wanted something more, and if it hadn't been for Mr. Francis, her English teacher and next door neighbor, she may never have gotten to college. He arranged for her to get a scholarship that paid her tuition, and through a mutual friend, arranged for her room and board to be provided in turn for helping the Dubois family with their children.

When she arrived at State College and saw how big it was and realized she didn't know anyone, she almost went home. She told me once how scared she was then, a seventeen-year old girl from a small town, away from home for the first time.

But that's not all she told me.

I've heard the stories on how it began—different versions depending on who was doing the telling. How a strange man had walked up to the porch and knocked on the door one afternoon while she was home alone, and how she almost didn't answer the door but eventually did, looking startled and afraid. How he introduced himself as Edward Gentry, and said he was a friend of Victor Hollister and that Victor had asked him to check on her and to see that she was okay.

A month before, Victor and Edward had hopped a freight train to North Dakota looking for work in the wheat fields. They ended up in Fargo. For more than a week they searched for work and were about to give up when they met a rancher who had a place outside Fort Ransom. He said he had enough work for one of them, more or less permanently, but not both. When the wheat harvest was over, he needed a hand to help with his cattle operation.

They told the rancher to give them a minute and they walked around the corner of a vacant building to decide what to do. They discussed whether they should move on west to Bismarck and keep looking or give up and go home. After giving it some thought, Edward turned to Victor and said, "You take it. You need it worse than I do. I can always go back to school."

"Aw, I don't know about that. Are you sure?"

"Positive," said Edward. "I've been thinking. I can go home and sell a load of corn that I have stored in the crib for emergencies. That'll get me my first semester's tuition. I'm sure I can get my job back cooking in that greasy spoon off Wabash Avenue. I'll get my meals free, and my wages will pay my board. I can make it on that. You take this job. It's all you got going for you right now."

Victor hesitated, shifting on one foot then another. Edward looked at him and said, "What's the matter?"

"I don't know what to do about Leah," he said.

"Who's Leah?"

"A girl I've been seeing.

"Since when?

"We just met last spring. Lives over in Purcell Station. She's going to college up in Terre Haute this fall."

"How come you've never mentioned her?

"Because you were away at college. Besides she's about the prettiest girl in Purcell Station, and I've tried to hide her from the competition."

"You didn't need to worry about me," Edward said. "I don't have any money for girls."

"Well, anyway," said Victor. "I don't know how she's gonna take the idea I've gone off to North Dakota and stayed. I sorta led her to believe I'd be back by the end of summer. She's kinda nervous about going away. Never been out of Purcell Station overnight…says she doesn't know anybody up there." He paused, looking down at his feet. "I'd told her I'd come up and see her every once in awhile…check on her to see how she's getting along."

Edward put a hand on Victor's shoulder. "Look, if you take this job, and I go back to school, I'll be at Terre Haute, too. If it'd make you feel any better, I'd look her up and tell her you asked me to check on her."

"Would you do that?" Victor looked up. "That'd make me feel a little better about things. I could write and explain it all—tell her who you are and that you're helping to look out for her."

"I'd be happy to," said Edward. "Consider it done."

Victor let out a sigh like a great weight had been lifted from his shoulders. They walked back to the rancher and Victor told him, "If it's still offered, I'd like to take the job. Edward here says he'll go on back home. He thinks he's got something going back there."

So, Victor got the job and Edward got the responsibility of seeing after a girl he had never met.

Victor's letter of explanation never reached Leah. It arrived in Purcell Station the day after she left for school, and her mother just figured she could wait until her first trip home to get it. So it was a surprise when Leah opened the front door that fall afternoon after her classes were over and a stranger stood there smiling.

The stranger was surprised, too, when he saw the pretty, dark haired girl with big brown eyes standing behind the screen door. He had no idea Victor had this much taste.

"Hi! My name's Edward Gentry," he said smiling. He was tall and had dark hair combed back in the style of the day.

"Who do you want to see? The Dubois' aren't home," she said, as she hooked the screen door.

"I'm looking for Leah Halderman, and I'm willing to bet that's you."

"How did you know my name?"

"Victor sent me to look after you. Didn't you get his letter?"

"What letter?" she asked.

"You didn't get a letter from him explaining that he got a job and would be staying up in Fargo and that I, Edward Gentry, a gentleman and a scholar and his friend from back home, would be looking after you and seeing that you were okay?"

"No, I didn't. And I think you just might be making this whole story up." She was sensing this "gentleman" might be a little too slick. "How do I know you're telling me the truth?" she asked.

"Don't I have an honest face?"

"Not really," she said. "Are you from New York or someplace?"

"Now is that a way to treat an old country boy? If I'm a friend of Victor's, don't you think we grew up pretty close together?"

"And where might that be?" She decided to test him.

"Well, if you looked real hard, I bet you could stand atop the hill in Purcell Station and look west and pick out my family's farmhouse on the horizon. About three miles as the crow flies, but worlds apart."

"And why do you think we'd be worlds apart?"

"Because you people are city folk. We're just proud country folks."

She laughed for the first time and answered, "City? A population of five hundred, maybe, double that if you counted stray dogs."

"But we're just poor dirt farmers. We even had our own high school because you city people didn't want to rub elbows with us dirt folk."

Leah laughed at the absurdity, but she was beginning to relax with this country boy from the Wabash bottoms.

"Would you like to sit down on the porch swing?" she asked as she unlocked the screen door and came out on the porch.

"I was beginning to think you were never going to ask," he said, taking a seat beside her on the swing.

They spent the better part of the afternoon talking and swinging and drinking iced tea. By the time Edward excused himself to leave, the sun was fading in the west and Edward had a date with Leah Halderman for Saturday night. They went to the Sweet Shop on Wabash Avenue and then for a walk through campus, stopping to sit on a bench in the old quadrangle to watch the strollers pass by. At eleven o'clock, the chimes in the Union Building rang and Leah said she had to get home. They walked hand in hand to her place on Thornton Street then they said goodnight. It was the first college boy she dated. It was also the last.

I heard a noise and looked up to see a street sweeper coming toward me. I quickly got up off the curb and stepped back as it passed. The driver waved, as if he was sorry he had made me move. I figured it must be getting late, so I turned and looked one last time at the front porch where my mother and father first met. The wind gusted, briefly moving the porch swing, and although it was empty, I imagined them sitting there, gently swinging where it all began twenty years ago.

I'd lost track of time. I was a long way from the station, and I didn't want to miss my train. I headed west, looking for the street I took getting there. Instead, I found myself on a busy street where traffic picked up and people looked like they had places to go. Nothing looked familiar. The buildings were different—run-down and shabby. Some were empty. I passed a tavern with neon signs in the window. It was dark inside. A country song from the juke box blasted when someone opened the door and came out. I kept going, past boarded up windows, then a homeless mission and more taverns. I was starting to panic.

Up ahead I saw a group of men standing on a corner. Some were leaning against a car parked along the curb. Two other men stood next to a building that looked like an old hotel and they were talking to a woman sitting in an open window. As I got close I saw that she wasn't very well dressed; in fact, she was barely dressed at all. She was leaning out of the window and nearly out of her dress, and I wondered if she knew she was showing herself and if someone should tell her. They were arguing about something, and then the men walked over to another window and started talking to another woman who wasn't very well dressed either.

I ducked my head and pretended I didn't see them.

"Move it, kid." It came from one of the men standing by the car. I didn't bother to look over, but I figured it was meant for me since I didn't see any other kids. I picked up my pace and kept my head down.

Down the street I slowed to catch my breath, wondering how much time I had. I saw an old man sitting in a vacant doorway drinking something from a paper sack. A chain of a pocket watch hung from his belt loop.

I came closer. "Excuse me, mister, could you tell me what time it is?"

He looked at me like I had aroused him out of a dream, and then eyed me as if I might be trying to rob him. Or maybe he was going to rob me. Finally, he pulled out his watch and mumbled, "Quarter past three, more or less."

"Thanks." I stepped up the pace. What if it was more? I couldn't be late. My grandparents were expecting me in Purcell Station by late afternoon.

Going west I figured I had to come across the railroad tracks sometime, and when I did I saw the station just to the north. I ran to the platform, checking the clock tower above the station. It was 3:32. I found a porter and asked if the 3:35 southbound local was in yet.

"It's right over there, on track No. 2. Leaving in about three minutes."

"Thanks, I'll be right back," I panted. "Don't let'em leave!"

The porter chuckled.

I ran into the station, sprung open the locker, grabbed my suitcase, and hurried out to track No.2. Hopping aboard just as the train lurched forward, I lifted my suitcase up to the overhead rack and found a seat where I would be alone. We were already moving, heading south on the last leg to Purcell Station.

CHAPTER 3

T he land was flat now. The river lay to the west, too far away to see but close enough to know that we were traveling through the lowlands of the Wabash bottoms. I was alone, no one near me, and when the sun came through the window and warmed my lap, I put my head back and closed my eyes. It had been a long day since Mom got me up this morning and then the two hour drive down to Indianapolis with Mr. Simmons. It was catching up with me.

I woke when I heard the conductor call out the next stops for Sullivan, then Oaktown, but fell back asleep again until I heard, "Next stop, Vincennes," the last stop before Purcell Station. We cruised through the north side of the old city and past homes built a century ago.

We eased into the station and came to a stop. The conductor said we'd be here a while, so I decided to get out. As I stepped onto the platform I saw several military men, probably home on furlough from Korea. One of them was buying a newspaper from a boy hawking them in front of the depot.

My father once told me that when he was a young boy back in the Depression there used to be a lot of train traffic in Vincennes since major railroads crossed there. Because of that it became a popular place for panhandlers and young boys looking to make some money. One of them was a little red-headed kid who would stand on his head or do somersaults in front of a crowd and then pass a hat. He eventually went on to Hollywood and became famous. His name was Red Skelton.

I looked around to see if another boy had taken Red's place, but I didn't see any. The conductor yelled, "All aboard," and I hurried to my seat. I was eager to get to Purcell Station. There were just ten miles to go.

Southbound out of town, the land was as flat as a table top, dark and rich, stretching all the way to the Wabash River. That's why the Gentrys settled here.

As a young man in 1889 my father's father migrated to Knox County from Switzerland County, just across the state line from Cincinnati, carrying all his earthly possessions in a wagon pulled by two teams of oxen. He had heard about the rich soil of the Wabash Valley, and when he arrived he found a farmer who needed a team of oxen, and Grandpa happened to have an extra. He traded the two oxen for eighty acres of the farmer's land. By the time the Depression hit, his farm had grown to over 500 acres, and his family had grown to seven children.

We were slowing down now, and I was getting anxious. Out the window I saw the water tower and the words "Purcell Station." By the time the conductor came through and announced our stop, I was up and pulling my suitcase off the overhead rack. Moving up the aisle I looked out at the depot, searching for anyone waiting for me. Descending the steps, the platform was empty, but around the side of the building a man in a cap and vest was lifting a mail bag onto a cart. He looked up and saw me, then my suitcase, and said, "Your name wouldn't be Gentry, would it?"

"Yes, sir."

"You're Minnie Halderman's grandson, aren't you?"

"Yes, sir. Name's Garrett."

"Hi, Garrett. I'm Taylor Barth, the stationmaster. They told me they were expecting you. I figured they'd have someone here to pick you up, but something must've come up. It's not like them to just not show up. I'd offer you a ride, but I can't leave the station."

"That's all right. Thanks, anyway."

"Well, if you'll wait here a moment, Bud Tate, the postmaster, will be here to pick up the mail bag. He'd be glad to give you a lift. That's a long hill to be lugging that suitcase up."

"That's okay, thanks. I'll walk. I've been riding all day."

"Okay, but it's kind of treacherous." He smiled.

I walked around to the front of the station and took a long look up Main Street.

The town of Purcell Station sat on a hillside sloping down to the railroad tracks. A bend of the White River came up from the south and then curved west where it met up with the Wabash twenty miles below. Across the street from the depot stood the Purcell Hotel, providing room and board to what Grandpa says are "traveling salesmen, medicine men, and circuit rider preachers." The water tower and the Civil Defense Air Tower stood at the top of the hill, standing guard over the town below.

Taking a deep breath, I picked up my suitcase and lugged it across Depot Street and up Main. My grandparents lived in the middle of town, then two blocks south. My suitcase would be getting pretty heavy by then.

I started up the hill and hadn't walked more than a block when I saw them coming. A pack of five mangy dogs came running toward me, barking and sniffing like I was a slab of fresh meat. I stepped up my pace and kept going, trying to ignore them, when one started nipping at my pants leg. When he bit into the fabric and started pulling, I kicked and shook my leg to dislodge my pants from the grip of his jaw. By this time the other dogs sensed the kill and started nipping at my other leg, creating quite a scene. A car drove by, slowed down, and drove off. Just then a piercing cry came from behind a white picket fence next to the sidewalk.

"Whup! Killer! Stop! No! Git back! Git in here!"

I looked up and saw a little old lady in a long, flowered dress. She was carrying a broom, and as she approached the fence and threw open the gate, she swung the broom at the dog who must have been Killer. He stopped barking, turned away with his tail between his legs, and walked silently through the gate and into the yard. The others, at the sight of the broom, stopped barking; then stood looking at the broom lady for a moment before trotting down the street and out of her reach. I figured they'd met her before.

"Are you okay?" asked the lady. She had her hair done up in a bun and wore high heeled boots. The sleeves of her dress were rolled up as if she had just done a tub of laundry.

"I think so," I said, still shaking from the attack.

"I'll shoot that dog someday. Someone must've left the gate unlocked and he got out again. He's not the smartest dog on the block, but he's smart enough to push the gate and see if it is unlocked."

She straightened up and looked me over. "My name's Muldoon. They call me Lady Muldoon, after that famous lady. Real name's Tilley. You okay? Your pants leg torn? You're new here, aren't you?"

"I'm all right. Thanks. Just a little shook up. I'll be okay." I wasn't sure if that answered all her questions.

"Let me take a look at that ankle." I pulled my pants leg up so she could see. "Looks like he broke some skin. Let's go in and clean that up and put something on it."

I followed her into the house, leaving my suitcase in the yard. Killer was sitting on the front porch. We looked at each other, and I gave him a wide berth as he emitted a low growl. I wasn't sure he was through with me yet, but figured I was safe with Lady Muldoon and her broom.

In the kitchen she washed off the small break in my skin, dabbed it with iodine, and put a Band-Aid on it. As she was washing her hands, she looked back at me and studied my face for so long it made me look away. Finally, she said, "You aren't from around here, are you?"

"No, ma'am," I answered.

"Did you just get off the train?"

"Yes, ma'am." I figured I'd beat her to the next question. "I came to spend the summer with my grandma and grandpa."

She studied my face some more, searching for clues.

"Why, you must be Leah Marie's boy!" she said.

"You know my mother?"

"Everyone in Purcell Station knows your mother. She was one of the nicest girls in town. Prettiest, too! Still is, although she doesn't get back here much anymore."

She was smiling now, as though the thought of my mother brought back good memories. "My son went all the way through school with her. Like about every other boy in town, he was sweet on her, too. They all tried to get her attention, but she'd have no part of that. She was too busy for boys."

She stood up, nodding for me to follow, and led me into the living room. I thought she was seeing me to the door, but instead she stopped and pointed. "See that piano over there?"

It was an old upright, like the one in Grandma's parlor.

"She sat there one night and played it for over an hour and never had a sheet of music in front of her. My, she could play. She used to play piano up at the Baptist church all the time. Those Baptists, they like their music. She could sing, too. She sang a solo at Moon Mullins's funeral, and the tears just flowed. People crying all over the place, even though nobody liked ole Mullins. His wife thought they were cryin' over him, and that made her feel good, because she thought he never had any friends. She got that right."

Lady Muldoon was just getting warmed up. She asked me to take a seat on the sofa, and I did, figuring this might take a while.

"She wasn't much interested in sports, but one time the boys dared her to take a turn at bat up at the Sand Bowl, that's what they call the ball park behind the school. A bunch of classmates were playing ball after the senior picnic. My boy, Harold, was one of them, and they dared some girls to join the fun, calling them sissies and such to rile them up. Well, after that went on for a while, Leah Marie grabbed a bat and walked up to the plate. The boys had Ace McCauley pitching, and he was a good one. Cocky, too. Played for the high school team. Well, your mom stepped in, and old Ace lobbed a few easy ones, and she swung and missed, and the boys were all laughing.

"Ace was feeling pretty cocky now, and the boys were all hollerin' and carrying on, so he throws another one and Leah swings. She must've hit it dead center, 'cause it hit ole Ace right in the belly button. The boys got real quiet all of a sudden, but the girls were laughing and hooting and hollering. Leah just dropped the bat, turned, and walked away. The boys all yelled at her to come back and let Ace throw some more pitches, but she just walked away. The boys didn't like it much, but it was hard to be too mad at someone they all wanted to go out with."

Lady Muldoon smiled as she finished this story and said, "You'd better get on your way. I'm sure Minnie and Conrad are anxious to see you. You tell 'em I said hello."

"I will, and thanks for calling off the dogs, and for telling me those stories."

"Don't worry about Killer. He's a good dog until he gets out with those strays up the street. Most of 'em are good one to one. It's when they run in packs they get a bit nasty sometimes. Harold used to take to shootin' em with a BB gun. They got a little smarter after that."

"Thanks. I'll be on the lookout." I looked for Killer but didn't see him, so I picked up my suitcase, opened the gate and headed up Main Street.

CHAPTER **4**

Up the hill, I passed Maddie's Café and saw the sign for Smokey's Pool Room. A group of older boys was standing at the curb in front, smoking cigarettes. I thought about crossing the street, but just then one of them looked at me and must have said something because they all turned to look. It was too late to cross over, so I went ahead, knowing it was a mistake. I figured my suitcase would tell them I was new here.

I barreled ahead, and when I got up close I tried to ignore them by looking in Smokey's window and pretending to be interested in what was going on inside. Some men were playing at the two pool tables in the front. I hesitated, as if I might go in and take up a cue stick and join them. This must have interested one of the boys who looked over his shoulder and said, "You lookin' for a game?"

"What?" I couldn't tell if he was being mean or friendly.

"You heard me," he said. It wasn't friendly.

"Not really. Just lookin."

A muscular boy in bib overalls stepped out of the crowd and stared. "You a pool shark or something?" He had a pack of cigarettes twisted in the sleeve of his tee-shirt. His thick arms looked like a blacksmith's.

"No. I play some, though," I lied. I could feel my face getting hot.

He looked me over and then studied my suitcase.

"Look at him." He was pointing as if they couldn't see me otherwise. "He must be a pool shark. Got his suitcase and all, traveling around looking to con us country boys out of our money." They all thought this was funny, and I felt myself blushing. I looked around to see if anybody might be coming to my rescue. Nobody was.

"What you doin' here if you ain't looking to shyster us?" said a pudgy, red-headed boy with freckles. His sunburned nose and cheeks were peeling. He stepped toward me as he spoke, and I got the feeling he was showing the other boys how tough he was, although he didn't look tough.

"Just visiting family. I just got off the train." My voice cracked, and I felt a shiver down my spine. I wished I'd crossed the street when I had the chance.

The muscular boy in overalls stepped close and looked down at me with a smirk. He held his cigarette between his thumb and index finger and slowly raised it to the corner of his mouth. Squinting into my eyes, he took a long drag and exhaled, blowing perfect circles of smoke in my face. I turned away and coughed just in time to sense the redheaded boy circle around behind me and disappear.

"Whatta you think we oughta do about it, Jesse?" asked one of the boys standing in back. He was smiling. They all were.

I took it Jesse was the one blowing smoke in my face. He was grinning like something was about to happen. I watched, expecting movement and ready to flinch if I saw a hand come toward me. Just then Jesse stepped up real close, getting nose to nose, and pushed me backwards. I fell over the redheaded boy who had knelt down on all fours behind me. Somersaulting, my feet flew up and I landed hard on the sidewalk. I felt the back of my head hit the concrete.

The boys all thought that was funny and doubled up laughing so hard the men in the pool room came over to the door to see what the commotion was.

I sat there, stunned. My head was spinning. I reached around and felt a knot rising on the back of my head. My heart pounded, and my face felt hot. The boys were all pointing and laughing.

Just then the screen door of the pool room swung open and a man yelled, "What's going on out here?" He was short, stocky and bald. He was smoking a cigar.

"Nothin,' Smokey. This here boy just fell over and bumped his head. Must've fell over that suitcase there," said the redheaded boy, trying hard to be serious.

"Likely story, Pee Wee," Smokey said. "Ya'all think you're pretty tough when ya have your buddies around. Now just clear out of here and be on your way, and leave this kid alone."

The gang looked at Jesse, who waited just long enough to let everyone know he would leave on his own sweet time. Finally, he flipped his cigarette butt in the street, exhaled, and turned slowly up the street, giving me one more smirk to let me know I hadn't seen the last of him.

"You okay?" asked Smokey.

"I think so," I said, rubbing the knot on the back of my head.

"Let me take a peek." He parted the hair, and I flinched as he hit the soft spot.

"Just a little bump on the noggin. The skin's not broken. You want me to put some ice on it?"

"No. It'll be okay."

"Is that your suitcase? Don't guess I know you. You new here?"

"I'm here to stay with my grandparents, Minnie and Conrad Halderman."

"Connie Halderman? Known him all my life. So, you're his grandson?"

"Yes, sir." I'd never heard him called Connie before.

"He's the best painter and paperhanger in this part of the country. Too bad about his stroke. How long you here for?"

His stroke? What stroke? I wasn't sure what a stroke was, but I didn't want to let on.

"I'm spending the summer."

"The whole summer?"

"Yes, sir. My father's going to Cleveland to the hospital there and will be laid up for a while. Mom's going to be with him. They didn't think Cleveland was a place they'd want me spending the summer."

"Leah Marie? I know your mom. She married that Gentry fella down in the Wabash bottoms, didn't she?

"Yes, sir. Edward. His dad's E.E. Gentry.

"Right. I guess about everybody around here knows both trees you came from: The Gentrys and Haldermans."

I told him I'd better be going. I thanked him and as I turned to go up the street, Smokey said, "Nice meeting you. If you ever have any more trouble with those hoodlums, just let me know. They act tough when they're in a pack, but it's all bluff."

I wasn't so sure. Jesse looked like someone I'd take seriously when it came to trouble. Anyway, I thanked Smokey again and walked up Main Street. I passed Danny's Barber Shop, Brockman's Grocery, and a vacant lot where I saw a group of men and boys playing softball. I watched for a second and then moved on before my suitcase caught their attention. At Dub's D-X station I turned and headed toward Grandma's house.

I came up the alley and saw the tunnel. I'd named it that when I was three and looked out the back door at the grape arbor running from the porch to the alley. In the growing season it is dark inside and looks like the tunnel the trains run through over by French Lick. My parents had taken me on a train ride there when I was three.

At the end I stopped and looked through the arbor at Grandma's porch. I remembered my Uncle Jake in his Navy dress whites coming down the tunnel, surprising my grandmother just as she walked out the back door. A big smile on his face, Jake had picked her up and swung her in a circle, and she'd cried at the sight of her youngest son home on furlough.

I remembered my uncles, aunts, and cousins all coming through the tunnel to the alley after Sunday dinner to watch me, at age nine, throw the ball to my catcher, Uncle Wilbur. He had a way of making my pitches pop, sounding like they had more zip than they really did, prompting Grandpa to proclaim to everyone assembled that, without a doubt, I would be in the big leagues someday, and my relatives all nodded their heads in agreement. I became the artist performing his craft so some day they would all be able to say they knew the kid back when.

Later, when nobody was around, I asked my mother if Grandpa really thought I could make the big leagues, and she said, "No one ever made it if they didn't think they could." And we let it go at that.

I turned around. Across the alley stood Grandpa's red barn. It had once housed a team of horses before Purcell Station had cars. Up above, it had a hay-mow my cousins and I used to play in, and before that, my mother and her brothers. We would climb up to the loft, grab hold of a rope, swing down, and land on a pile of straw. The horses were gone now, having moved on about the same time Grandpa bought his 1937 Chevy.

I picked up my suitcase and walked through the tunnel toward the back porch. The back door was always unlocked. Only salesmen and strangers used the front door. If they were fortunate enough to be asked in, they were offered a seat in the parlor. Cookies and iced tea awaited whoever came in the back door.

I peeked in the screen door and yelled, "Anybody home? Grandma, I'm here!"

I got no answer. I started in, but just then Louise Francis from next door came running across the driveway all out of breath.

"Garrett?"

"Hi, Mrs. Francis."

"Good to see you." She gave me hug and then with a serious look said, "I've been waiting for you. I am supposed to tell you that your grandmother is at the hospital in Vincennes."

"Hospital? Is she okay?"

"She's fine. It's your Grandpa. He had a mild stroke last night. They took him to the hospital shortly before midnight. They didn't have any way of getting ahold of your parents before you left."

"Is he okay?"

"They think so. They're hoping they can release him in a couple of days. Your grandma should be home any time now. Biff Overmeyer went to get her. She told me to tell you she's sorry she wasn't at the station to meet you, but she should be home soon. She wants you to take the back room, and make yourself at home. Just let me know if you need anything."

I thanked her and said I would.

The back porch led to the kitchen. Inside, I saw my old wooden high chair still sitting in the corner where they'd left it the day I outgrew it. The windows over the sink looked out across the driveway at the Francis' house. An ice box stood on one side, a wood burning stove on the other. An oak pedestal table stood in the middle of the room and on it a white cloth covered a plate of cookies and a crock of tea.

I picked out a cookie and poured a glass of tea. Then I opened the bottom door of the ice box, took a pick, and chipped off two pieces of ice. I dropped one in my tea glass and held the other one to the bump on the back of my head. I sat down, closed my eyes, and nearly drifted off to sleep. Then I heard a dog bark.

I heard Mrs. Francis yell, "Poop Deck! Poop Deck! Get over here." Poop Deck was the Francises' long, low-slung beagle that had seen his better days. He'd get riled when a chipmunk or squirrel invaded his space, but most of the time he'd lie under a shade tree and sleep.

I went in the bedroom, put my suitcase on the bed, and looked around. It was my mother's old bedroom. The oak dresser, the Jenny Lind bed, and the bedside table were all just as they had been the day she left for college twenty years ago. There were two windows, and between them sat an oak library table that served as mother's desk where she studied to become the valedictorian of her class.

I was asleep on the bed when Grandma got home. A small puddle of water was all that was left of my ice pack. It was nearly 7:30 p.m., and the sun was sagging quickly over the Wabash bottoms in the west.

"Hey there, young man," she greeted me. "Are you ready for some supper?"

I stirred and shook my head, then pulled the pillow over the melted ice. I didn't want to explain the bump on my head.

"Hi, when did you get home?" I rubbed my eyes and saw her small frame standing beside the bed. Her grey hair and the lines in her face revealed a lifetime of hard work. She was in her seventies now.

I struggled to my feet and gave her an awkward hug.

"Oh, about an hour ago." Her voice was strained and thin. "I'm glad you're here; I was worried about you. How was your trip?"

"Long. I guess I didn't realize how tired I was." I yawned.

"I figured you needed your sleep so I didn't wake you. Sorry I wasn't here when you got here."

"That's okay. Mrs. Francis told me everything. Is he going to be okay?"

"The doctor thinks he's gonna be able to come home soon. The question is how much the stroke will affect him afterward."

"What could happen?"

"Well, he might not be able to walk as well, and his speech could be slurred. We'll just have to wait and see. It's in the Lord's hands now, so we'll see what He has in store for us."

Grandma was an elder in the General Baptist Church over on Main Street next to Dub's D-X station. She also served as superintendent of the

Sunday School that preceded the sermon every Sunday. It was her faith that got her through the Depression and the "Big War" that her two older sons had fought in.

We sat down to eat, and I waited for Grandma to say Grace. She thanked the Lord for this food, for my safe trip to Purcell Station, and she asked for His care in restoring Grandpa and my dad to good health. As soon as I heard "Amen," I dug in. It had been eight hours since I'd eaten my sack lunch in Terre Haute.

"Tomorrow, Mr. Overmeyer will be giving me a ride to the hospital on his way to work. I'll have to leave here before 8 a.m. and stay most of the day until he gets off," Grandma said. "You can go with me, but the hospital has a rule that no one under fourteen can visit patients. You'd have to wait down in the lobby."

"How about if I just stay here?"

"That's what I thought you'd say. I asked Louise next door if she'd look after you and make you some lunch, and she said she'd be glad to. I hate leaving you alone, but I didn't anticipate this happening either."

"Don't worry. I'll find something to do. Do you still have that old basketball and baseball mitt out in the garage?"

"I don't know, but you can look. But if you run out of things to do, Jimmy Brockman across the street may invite you into the shack. There's plenty to do there."

"What's the shack?"

"I'm not sure. He and his daddy don't allow females in there."

After supper, I stretched out on Mom's old bed, my mind racing about all that had happened: the strange acting man on the train, the house in Terre Haute where my parents met, the stray dogs and Lady Muldoon, the bully Jesse, and Grandpa's stroke. Then I thought about home and Somerset and my father and why he was in a hospital in Cleveland.

CHAPTER 5

Somerset

People call it an artist colony because Somerset is like a picture on a postcard. They say it could have been in New England, with its church steeples sticking out over the tree line and houses with white picket fences. Instead it was in Northern Indiana, snuggled beside a bend of the Mississinewa River just east of the Francis Slocum State Park. The area was so remote the natives of nearby towns joked, "You can't get there from here."

It is here that my parents came to teach at Somerset Junior-Senior High School after discovering the village one summer on a family trip to the state park. We arrived at the end of World War II, and like most people we struggled to make ends meet; so when the school year ended, Dad, like most teachers, needed a summer job. He'd worked on the railroad the previous summer but found out they weren't hiring this time around. He had just about given up hope when Mr. Chase, the school principal, came to the rescue. He knew somebody. That connection landed Dad a job at a factory in Marion, just twenty miles south.

On May 5th Dad showed up for work on the dock of the electrical plant in Marion. After eight months of teaching mathematics, he said he was looking forward to a summer of mind-free physical labor. He figured working in the shipping department of the electrical plant would be right up his alley.

That same day Mom started summer classes at Manchester College, a small liberal arts college on the north side of the county. She wanted to finish her bachelor's degree so she could upgrade her teaching license. She worked it out so she would be in class three hours a day, and during that time I would go with her. She assured me I would find a lot to do on the college campus. We hitched a ride with another teacher, Mrs. Winthrop, who was also working on her degree.

I was excited. When we got to the campus, Mom pointed out the building where her class met and then showed me the Student Center, the library, the gymnasium, and the outdoor basketball courts. She explained she would be done at 12:00 and to meet her in front of the Student Center. "Just remember, I'll be right there in Room 114 if you need me," she said.

"I'll be fine," I assured her. "I think it's kinda neat here."

I browsed the Student Center and walked around the campus. Then I entered the gymnasium and wandered the hallways, looking at the pictures and trophies of past teams. I saw the old leather helmets and canvas pants of the football teams and the baggy woolen uniforms of the baseball teams.

Finally, I moved into the gym itself and watched a pickup basketball game. When it ended I went back to the car, got my basketball, took it to an outdoor court beside the gym, and began shooting baskets. Soon, three college boys came up and started shooting on the other court. When one of them looked at me and yelled, "You want to play? We need a fourth," I was excited.

I joined in and they were nice enough to let me score some easy baskets. We played for the next hour, until I heard the chimes of the chapel, and I knew my mother's class was ending. I found the quadrangle in front of the Student Center and sat down on the wall to wait. When I saw her coming I jumped up and greeted her, telling her about my exciting morning.

"It sounds like you had a pretty good day. Does that mean you'd like to come back tomorrow?"

"I can't wait. There's a lot of stuff to do here, isn't there?"

"Didn't I tell you that?"

"I think this might turn out to be the best summer ever."

"I was thinking the same thing," Mom said.

The accident happened, not in a fiery crash or a free fall, but on a loading dock at the plant in Marion where Dad started working the day before. He was moving heavy cartons on the loading dock with two co-workers, Hoyt and a guy they called Luger. They were tipping a large container up to let a forklift slide under it when the operator of the lift began raising it up before it was secured. The men tried to get the operator's attention, waving and yelling, but by the time he heard them, the load was about four feet up and it was too late. It slid off to one side and fell on Hoyt, pinning him under the carton. Dad bent over, straining to lift the weight off the fallen man's legs and managed to free him enough so that Luger could pull him out from under it. As he did this, he felt something like a bolt of lightning shoot up his spine, and he fell to the dock in intense pain. As he lay tossing on the dock, his legs began to feel numb, and soon he lost all sensation from his waist down.

They rushed him by ambulance to the hospital where doctors put him through a series of tests and x-rays. They tried to contact Mom, but we had no telephone, so the hospital called the Wabash County sheriff's office, and they sent an officer to tell us what had happened. When he pulled into the driveway and came to the door, Mom answered. "What is it, officer?"

"Are you Leah Gentry?"

"Yes. Has something happened?"

"They asked me to tell you that you need to go to the hospital in Marion."

"What is it? Edward? What happened?"

"He had an accident at the plant. He's in the emergency room," said the officer. "Do you have a way to get there?"

"I don't have the car. Edward drove it to work. Maybe I can get Phil Hedrick to take me." The Hedrick's owned the general store on Main Street.

Phil Hedrick told Mom I could stay with them as long as needed. I was worried and wanted to see Dad, but Mom assured me she would call the Hedricks as soon as she got any information. When she called, she had a lot to tell me.

When they arrived at the hospital she found him asleep, but as she tiptoed toward the bed and leaned in to hear him breathing, his eyes opened and he moaned.

"Edward, it's me. How do you feel?"

He forced a faint smile and mumbled something Mom didn't understand.

"Don't try to talk now. I just want you to know that I'm here and I'll stay here as long as you're here. I left Garrett with the Hedricks."

He nodded. It was obvious he was heavily sedated. When he finally dozed off, Mom walked down to the nurse's station and asked if she could talk to the doctor.

"Doctor McClennen is making his rounds, but when he comes in, I'll tell him you're here," said the nurse.

Mom thanked her and returned to Dad's room. She walked to the window and stared out. She wondered what was in store for them now. She was saying a silent prayer when she heard footsteps, and a man in a white coat with a stethoscope around his neck entered the room.

"You must be Mrs. Gentry." he said. "I'm Doctor McClennen." He extended his hand.

"Yes, Leah. Nice to meet you."

He looked at Edward, who was still asleep, and then back at Mom. He spoke quietly. "Your husband did a valiant thing, and it may have saved a man's life, but the downside is it put him at risk."

"What kind of risk?"

"We won't know for some time if it's permanent. Right now, he has no feeling in his legs."

The words leaped out. She stared at the window and then felt herself get weak in the knees.

"His records show he had surgery once before," said the doctor, looking at a file lying on his lap, "and I'm afraid he's going to have to have it again. But it will be a different type this time and a little more serious."

"Serious? How serious?" Mom asked.

Dr. McClennen looked up from the chart. "There are only two hospitals in the United States that perform this surgery, but I think it's important he try it if he is to have normal function again."

Mom heard the last few words and began to shiver. Tears welled up in her eyes.

Dr. McClennan walked over to her and put his hand on her shoulder. "I'm recommending he be transported to the Cleveland Clinic in Ohio. I know a surgeon there, a specialist by the name of Dr. Spellman, who's one of the best. I have sent other patients to him with similar circumstances, so I know his work. I'm sorry if I made it sound so negative, but it is a serious operation."

Mom wiped her eyes. "I know. It's just that it's so overwhelming."

"Well, we're going to try to fix it, and we'll think positively." Dr. McClennan went on to tell her the operation would mean that Edward would not be able to be moved for some time. He would have to convalesce there in Cleveland. It could take several weeks.

Mom realized her summer had changed its course. When Dr. McClennen finished talking, she tried to think and get organized. She used a hospital phone to call Mrs. Winthrop and tell her she would be withdrawing from her summer classes at Manchester. She spent the night in Edward's room at the hospital and the next day called the college to withdraw. Finally, she called her mother in Purcell Station. I would have to spend the summer there. Dad would enter surgery in one week and remain in traction for another five to six weeks. Rehab would take even longer.

Within two days, Mom had everything organized. She got me a ride to Indianapolis with Mr. Simmons, and gave me money to purchase train tickets at Indianapolis and Terre Haute. She helped me pack and made me a sack lunch. Taking Dad to Cleveland in an ambulance was too expensive, so Mr. Hedrick loaned Mom his station wagon and Dr. McClennan showed Mom how to support his back with pillows and make him comfortable lying in the back. Once situated, they stopped by home to get clothes for the long summer ahead.

When the station wagon was loaded, I stood where Dad lay resting and squeezed his hand. He turned to face me and grimaced.

"You going to be okay?" I asked.

"Uh-huh. How about you?" His voice was weak and strained.

He closed his eyes and drifted off. The pain medicine was working. I stepped back. I could feel a lump rising in my throat.

I heard a car coming. As Mr. Simmons turned in the driveway, Mom gave me her last thoughts. "Help Grandma and Grandpa out. I'll call them on the Francises' phone once a week and let you know how your dad is doing and find out how you're doing. Purcell Station may not be Manchester College, but there're a lot of nice people there. I don't think you'll be bored for a minute."

Mr. Simmons was waiting. I climbed in the front seat, waved to Mom, and watched as the house disappeared in a plume of white dust.

CHAPTER 6

I slept until late morning and only woke up then because Louise Francis came to the back door, knocked, and then yelled my name. She hadn't seen me and was worried. I quickly got up and assured her I was okay.

When she left I dressed and, having held it for fourteen hours, went to the outhouse back by the alley. Since it was daylight, I had to go inside. It was a different story at night since the outhouse had no electricity. When my uncles were young they started using the alley behind the outhouse at night, claiming it was too hard to hit the hole inside in the dark. When Grandma found out and didn't object, they figured she was just happy she wouldn't have to experience a wet seat.

When I was five and old enough to go by myself, I joined them in this male ritual before bedtime, lining up and watering the back side of the outhouse. Uncle Jake became so good he could spray his name on the wall in script, although by the time he got to "e" the "J" was already washed out. Once, when we were home for Christmas and there was snow on the ground, Jake spelled out his name in the snow, and it stayed there until the spring thaw.

After breakfast I found Uncle Jake's old basketball in the garage under the work bench, all dusty and flat. The leather was dried out and scuffed, like it had played its last game too many years ago. Jake and his brothers had broken it in during their youth, used it up, then joined the war, leaving it to lie idle in a wooden box in the garage. It would take some time and muscle to restore it, but I had all summer.

The pump was hanging on a hook above the tool bench. The garage was dark inside since it had no electricity and only one window. The dirt floor was made up mostly of sand, and as I walked in, I kicked up clouds of dust that made me cough and my eyes water. Judging by the dust on the tools, it looked like years since anybody had used the garage, except when Grandpa backed his 1937 Chevy out and drove downtown. He was in his late seventies now, and with his failing eyesight and balance problems, Grandma kept harping on him to give it up. Now that he had suffered a stroke, I figured she'd win that argument.

The goal was a homemade metal ring bolted above the garage door. Years ago Grandpa had it welded over at Willie Lickert's blacksmith shop out of steel rods Willie had rescued from a hay baler.

The sun was bearing down directly overhead when I began shooting baskets in the driveway. The big maple tree between the house and garage wouldn't offer any shade until late afternoon. An hour in the hot sun just about did it for me, but as I was lining up my last shot, I saw Mr. Francis pull into his backyard and get out of his car. Taking his fishing gear and bucket out of his trunk, he glanced over, saw me, and waved. I went on shooting, feeling his eye, and after watching me miss a couple of shots, he came over.

"Let's see that again," he said. "I want to see what they've been teaching you up north." Grandma must have told him I'd made the seventh grade team last winter.

I stepped up and let fly a shot that hit the rim and bounced off.

"That's okay, but it's going to be hard to get that shot off when someone's guarding you," he said. "Let me show you another way."

I handed him the ball and stepped aside. After all, he had some history. As coach of the Purcell Station High School Aces, Mr. Francis had etched his name into Indiana legend when at the age of twenty-seven he'd lead the Aces to the championship of the Wabash Valley tournament. The tournament, the largest intra-state high school tourney in the nation, started out with over a hundred teams from Indiana and Illinois, all located along the Wabash River, which separated the two states.

Everybody in Purcell Station knew the story by heart, how the local boys won the regional round at the Vincennes Coliseum in front of 6,000 fans, advanced to the finals at State College in Terre Haute, and defeated Clinton, Sullivan, and the local Terre Haute Gerstmeyer Black Cats—all schools five times larger—for the championship. The exciting final game was won on a center court shot at the buzzer by little Spud Dugan.

When the team arrived back in Purcell Station at midnight, the whole town turned out and lined Main Street. The team and cheerleaders rode on the fire truck to a bonfire at the Sand Bowl behind the school. Players made speeches, and when it was Mr. Francis' turn, he referred to the Bible story of how David slew the giant, and how the local boys brought down the mighty giant schools to the north. From that moment on, the boys and Mr. Francis became household names for generations to come. Now he was offering to help me learn a new shot.

"Hold the ball like this," he said, demonstrating the position. "Now, with your hand under the ball, bend your elbow while pushing the ball up, flipping it off your fingers."

I tried it just as he described and followed through.

"Now, bend your knees, place the ball over your head, jump, and release the ball at the top."

It felt awkward, taxing all my energy just to get the ball up to the goal. My shots were falling short, but I was getting the rhythm down better each time.

"Keep working on it. It takes time to master the jump shot. Next year, everybody will be shooting it."

I tried it several more times until Mr. Francis said, "Well, I have to go clean those fish so Louise can fry them up for supper. Keep practicing. You might get good enough to play for Coach McCracken up at Indiana University some day." He smiled.

I kept working on my new jump shot until darkness came and Grandma came home. She gave me an update on Grandpa's condition and said she hoped he would be able to come home tomorrow. She told me I could go back out and shoot until she got supper ready.

When I came in for supper, I told her how Mr. Francis had been teaching me a jump shot.

"Well, nobody knows basketball better than Coach Francis," she said. "He's also a good teacher, or at least that's what your mother said. He was young, smart, and handsome when she was in school. He's still smart and handsome, just not so young anymore." She dished out a helping of ham and beans and put it on the table.

"When he won that big tournament, most people thought he walked on water. Your mom didn't really care about that, but she loved his English classes. Claims he inspired her to become a teacher. You know what I think?" She was smiling. "I think she had a crush on him."

I gulped down half a glass of iced tea. "Do you really think so?"

"Well, I thought so at the time. You know, if it weren't for him, your mother wouldn't have gone to college. I don't suppose your mother and father would've met then, either."

"I know." I was glad Mr. Francis lived next door.

I was shooting baskets at the garage the next afternoon when a black Packard sedan drove into the driveway and a round-faced, heavyset man got out and opened the door to the backseat. I recognized him as Rollie Brockman, the neighbor across the street and part owner of Brockman's Grocery. Grandma got out of the other side and came around, and then I saw Grandpa, slowly rising out of the backseat. I hurried back to the car, held out my hand to help, and said, "Hi, Grandpa, welcome home."

He had lost weight since I'd last seen him at Christmas, and his grey hair was now white and thinner. He looked frail and hesitant.

"Hey there, young man," he said weakly, giving me a gentle hug.

They helped him out and held him until he found his balance. He steadied himself, and I took a hold of his arm to lead him into the house. Rollie was on the other arm. Grandpa started to take a step but waited and looked at me for what seemed to be several seconds.

"What's your mother feeding you?"

"I don't know. Meat and potatoes, I guess."

"If you keep it up you'll be taller than me. I didn't say smarter, just taller."

I didn't want to think about that. Over the past year I had already grown taller than Grandma and was closing in on Grandpa. I'd always looked up to him. I wanted him to stay taller a while longer.

We walked him gently up the steps to the front porch and into the parlor where he sat down on the sofa. Rollie, backing out the front door, said, "If you need anything—a ride someplace or anything—you know where I'll be."

"Thanks," said Grandma, "You've been a big help already."

She then took off Grandpa's shoes and put house slippers on his feet. He was wearing his painting uniform, tan cotton pants and matching shirt. Once settled, she walked him into the dining room, which was not a dining room at all but the room where most of the living took place. It held a sofa, Grandma's oak rocking chair, a recliner for Grandpa, and two stuffed chairs. An RCA radio sat on a table by the window. It was their connection to the outside world.

Grandpa sat in his chair and leaned back, lifting his feet to the footrest.

Grandma brought him a large class of iced tea and asked if he was hungry. He took the tea and after a long sip told her, "No, just tired."

"Well, we'll leave you alone and let you take a nap. When you get hungry, just call me, and I'll have supper ready."

Grandma nodded at me and motioned toward the kitchen. I followed her and let the swinging door to the kitchen close behind me.

"We need to let him rest. He's worn out just getting dressed and coming home."

"Is he going to be okay? Will he get any better?"

She walked over to the icebox and opened the door, fidgeting for something long enough to think about my question. Finally, she turned around. "He may, or he may not. You never know with a stroke. He's slurring some of his words, and you've probably seen how slow he's walking, shuffling his feet. We may have to get used to that. He's not getting any younger, you know."

I sat looking at the floor. I didn't want Grandpa to age. I thought about the time in the alley when he was watching me throw pitches to Uncle Wilbur and saying how I would someday pitch in the big leagues. People still talk about what a good painter he was and how at the age of sixty-five, he climbed a scaffold and painted the steeple of the Methodist Church, some thirty feet in the air. It was hard to see him now so frail.

Grandma must have sensed my mood; she quickly changed the subject. "Tomorrow is a big day in Purcell Station. It will be a good time for you to get out and explore and make some friends."

"What's special about tomorrow?"

"It's Saturday, when everybody comes to town, and at night there's a free show over at the vacant lot on Main Street. You should go and have a good time."

CHAPTER 7

Grandma was right; it was busy on Saturday afternoon. Farmers were in town shopping for feed and supplies at the co-op elevator down by the railroad tracks. Their women and kids came to stroll Main Street, browse in the stores, and huddle with friends on the sidewalk.

I wandered into and out of the Purcell Drug Store and saw kids crowded around the soda fountain. Going on down the street to Maddie's Café, I saw an older crowd, mostly farmers. They sat around in the booths drinking "Maddie's Famous Coffee, Guaranteed to Get Up and Walk." At least that's what the sign said above the counter. A few of the younger ones played the pinball machine by the back wall. I stood over by a booth where three farmers were talking about their melon fields.

"Next week should be about right for settin'em out," said a man in bib overalls. I heard one of the others call him Tip.

"Well, it ain't easy to get good help any more, and the weather forecast doesn't look too good—no rain in the forecast," said another man. Other farmers huddled around, nodding their heads. They all agreed the outlook looked pretty grim.

Up the street, Slinker's General Store had some serious shoppers looking for bargains on shovels, dog food, salt blocks for their cattle, and remedies for gout. The largest store in town, it was stuffed with so many goods there was little room to walk around. The store's motto, written above the front door, stated, "If We Don't Have It, It Ain't Worth Having." I'd heard Grandpa once say, "If it ain't worth having, they got it."

I walked through the aisles which were so narrow I almost had to turn sideways. Grandpa once told me how Boots Slinker always prided himself on knowing where everything was located and handling every request himself, at least until one day a stranger came in asking for a snipe harness. Slinker, scratching his head, looked puzzled for a moment; then he nearly went berserk shaking down every corner of the store looking for a snipe harness, until a group of locals over by the cash register burst forth with such laughter that he realized he'd been duped.

By sundown the boys at Tulley's Tavern had already staked out their places at the bar, judging by the number of cars and trucks parked outside. Located a block from the Purcell Hotel, this newest business in town was a sore spot with Grandma. When it was proposed a few years back, the women at the Baptist Church combined with the Methodists and Nazarenes to fight this "sin center." Grandpa told me it was one of the few times the women at the three churches ever agreed on anything. They got a petition up against the tavern and stirred up quite a fuss, but in the end it failed to make a difference.

They blamed it on the Catholics. The figuring was the Catholics out numbered the Protestants by rounding up all those farmers over around Saint Mary's and getting them to sign a counter-petition. Whatever the reason, the temperance movement failed, the tavern opened, and the Baptist, Methodist, and Nazarene women never lived it down.

Of course, the Lutherans took their share of the blame, too. Neither they nor the Catholics had a church in Purcell Station, but both had congregations out east and north of town, respectively, so they became good targets for anyone looking to place blame on "outside forces."

The free show started at dusk every Saturday night from May, when school let out, until Labor Day. It took place on the vacant lot on Main Street between Brockman's Grocery Store and Dub's D-X station, where I'd seen the softball game the day I arrived.

Local businesses stayed open late on these nights, hoping to cash in on the large crowd. Dub's D-X station's pop machine got a good workout. Across the street, the Baptist church set up a popcorn popper in the front yard and sold five-cent bags of hot, buttered popcorn. Brockman's Grocery stayed open to allow visitors the opportunity to visit its popular candy display.

My walk up Main Street ended in front of the viewing area, which was filled with people talking and laughing and kids and dogs running everywhere. The Purcell Station Community Band was playing a John Phillip Sousa march from a little stage in front of the movie screen. It was their job to entertain while the sun was setting before the movie could start.

Looking around, I noticed there must have been some unwritten rule about where people sat. Families with little kids already in their pajamas settled onto blankets with their stuffed animals and pillows. They probably lasted through the cartoons and then signed off minutes into the main event. The older adults staked claims to the raised sidewalk seats, getting there early and staying put, or they brought lawn chairs and sat in front of the sidewalk. Older kids, those weaned from the apron strings but not too sophisticated to watch the show, sat in clusters down in front, far away from their parents. Teenagers huddled in groups on Main Street, sitting on the fenders of parked cars and as far away from the screen as possible.

Not sure where I fit in, I hung around the back, standing first on the sidewalk and then finding a seat on the running board of a Mercury sedan, a safe distance from the older kids. At dark Dub closed his gas station and turned off the lights so they wouldn't interfere with the movie. A few men still sat on his liar's bench out front and talked in muffled voices. The only light left on was the street light on the corner.

After the cartoons, the Movietone News, a newsreel of last week's world events, drowned out cries of the babies that were still holding out before falling asleep. Once, the black and white picture hit a few jumpy spells. The film slipped in the projector, causing the image to blur and then stop. Flash lights came on at the projector table. It was then I noticed Rollie Brockman, Grandma's neighbor, was the operator, although he was receiving plenty of help from a number of volunteers. Once he got it going again, some of the crowd applauded.

It was quiet once the babies fell asleep and the feature got underway, except for a couple of old-timers heard snoring in their lawn chairs in the back. The teenagers were another story.

About halfway through the movie I heard a loud commotion from down the street. It came from a dark area near the drugstore. It caused Rollie Brockman to turn and look, but he kept the projector running. He must have figured it was nothing.

I decided to take a better look. I crossed the street, and crept into the shadows of parked cars, past the drugstore, and stopped behind a pickup truck. In the middle of the street stood a crowd of older kids. They were in a circle and yelling at someone. I climbed up in the back of the pickup truck to get a better look, hiding behind the cab so they couldn't see me.

From the street light on the corner I could see a large, dark man in bib overalls standing in the middle of the circle, saying something I couldn't understand. He wore a straw hat pushed back on his forehead, showing a round face, dark whiskers, and eyes that bugged out in fear. His jaw bulged with a chaw of tobacco.

A muscular boy in a red shirt had his back to me, but I could hear him yelling at the man. I couldn't make it out, but whatever it was it drew a good laugh from the crowd and they all started howling. Then the boy yelled again, and I heard it this time: "Hey, Spooky! You stink like Schuler's pigs, ain't that right, Spooky?" This got the crowd more riled up with laughter, and they joined in on the taunting. "Spooky Man stinks! Spooky Man stinks!"

Just then another boy stepped up into the man's face and said, "You smell, old man. You smell like horse sh…."

"Le…le…leave m—me…alone." the man stuttered. His face was red, and he strained to get the words out. But the boy in the red shirt had his audience with him now, and he was enjoying their attention.

"Spit it out, old man. Come again? What'd you say?" The boy posed with his hands on his hips in mock anger. "You gotta problem with me, Spooky?"

The crowd snickered, and the boy turned to them and grinned. With the mob behind him, he brought his fists up and started sparring and shadow boxing, poking his knuckles into the ribs of the man he called Spooky Man, playfully slapping him in the face. The man stood there all puffed up, trying to talk, but the words wouldn't come, and the circle of kids laughed when all he could do was stutter.

At that moment the boy in the red shirt pushed him backward into another boy who pushed him back into another boy. This went on as one after another took turns pushing him, bouncing him against the circle of the crowd like a cue ball. As this was happening, the boy in the red shirt turned at an angle where the street light shined on his face, and a chill went up my spine. It was Jesse!

By now the man had had enough. He was crouching, huffing and snorting like a mad bull. Following their leader, the herd mocked and jeered the outnumbered man, getting courage from each other. Someone yelled, "Look! Spooks, el Toro! Spooks, el Toro! Look at the bull!" The mob joined in chanting, "Spooks, el Toro, Spooks, el Toro!"

This prompted Jesse to take off his red shirt, puffing out his chest and flexing his muscles. He faced Spooks, held his shirt to his side like a matador, and yelled, "Charge!" The crowd picked up the chant and added, "Charge! Jesse, el Matador! Jesse el Matador! Charge!"

His eyes wide in fear; his shoulders slumped, Spooks stood dazed, looking at his tormentors. Jesse started flapping the shirt and swinging it down to his side as a matador does in coaxing the bull to make a pass. The crowd loved this move and his prancing and showing off, and they stepped up their jeering. Just as Jesse held the shirt up again to entice the raging bull, a boy pushed Spooks into the shirt as Jesse pulled it aside and yelled, "Ole!"

Spooks stumbled, falling face down in the street. The crowd roared, and Jesse stood over him, placing one foot on Spooks' back in triumph. Stunned, Spooks started to get up but fell, then struggled to his knees. His face was bleeding where his nose and cheek had scraped the street. Looking frightened and angry, he pulled himself up again and managed to get on his feet. Blood was dripping down his face and into his mouth. He tried spitting it out and wiping it with his bandana but only smeared it over his face.

Jesse said, "Here, cover that ugly mug of yours. We don't want to see any blood." He took his red shirt and threw it over Spooks' head. Then he took hold of Spooks' bib and started turning him around and around. Under the cloth and unable to see out, Spooks got turned around until he was wobbling and weaving and losing his balance. Then he fell over, slumping to the ground once more.

Jesse stood over his body, posing in triumph, announcing, "The mighty Spooks hits the dust." Again the mob cheered.

I saw the lights and heard something coming. A pickup truck came roaring down the street and screeched to a stop beside the crowd. A door slammed and a voice from the back of the circle yelled, "That's enough, Jesse, you coward! Let him alone!"

The laughing stopped, and the crowd hushed. They looked at Jesse. Their look told me nobody talked to Jesse like that. Two days before I'd seen how kids followed him, afraid they'd be next if they didn't. I remembered what Lady Muldoon said about the pack of dogs and how they get courage from the pack, picking on someone who couldn't fight back. Mrs. Muldoon was right, but who would call Jesse a coward? And the voice...it didn't sound like an adult.

Jesse snorted. "Who said that?" Everyone looked through the darkness, trying to see who would be that foolish.

"Get your friends and get out of here. You're all cowards." It came from behind the mob. They turned to see a person in the shadows standing on the running board of the pickup. Jumping down and into the darkness, a solitary figure strutted into the middle of the now-quiet mob.

They parted, staring to see who was so brave. Into the circle and under a beam of street light entered a guy in bib overalls and a baseball cap pulled down over his eyes. He was smaller than Jesse, and I wondered who would be so foolish to take on such a bully. I strained to get a good look and then I saw what looked like a blonde ponytail hanging out the back of the baseball cap.

It was a girl! She walked directly toward Jesse, standing tall with her hands on her hips, getting into his face.

"So, you're a real tough guy, picking on Spooks. Who you gonna pick on next? A girl? Try me."

Jesse glanced around the quiet crowd. They were looking at him waiting to see what he was going to do about this. But he only stood there, breathing heavily and staring back at the girl in the ponytail. He said nothing.

"You're a big man, picking on Spooks in front of all your bootlickers. He never hurt anybody. He's as gentle as a lamb, but I guess that's why you pick on him. You know he won't fight back."

Then she turned to the crowd. "And you're not any better. You're all afraid of him." They looked at each other without saying a word. Some looked back at their leader, expecting him to say something, but there was nothing to see.

Jesse stood there as the crowd broke up and walked away. Two of his friends walked over to him. I recognized the pudgy one as the boy who'd knelt behind me so Jesse could push me. He leaned in to Jesse and said, "Come on, let's get out of here." Jesse just stared straight ahead, his temples pulsating, the anger building up inside of him.

The blonde girl reached down, helped Spooks up, and wiped his bloody face with a handkerchief. Then she walked him across the street toward the truck. She opened the passenger door, helped him in, then got in on the other side and drove off.

The crowd wandered back down the street just as the movie was ending. Standing in the back of someone's pickup truck, I glanced at Jesse, who was still standing alone where he had just been embarrassed in front of his followers. I didn't want the owner of the truck to find me standing in it, so I got down and walked into the crowd and back to Grandma's house, wondering what I'd just witnessed.

I could see a light still on in the kitchen. I entered the back porch and closed the door quietly so not to wake Grandpa. In the kitchen Grandma was waiting at the table, working a crossword puzzle.

"Hi, Grandma!" I whispered. "Why are you still up?"

"Well, it's something I always did when my own kids were out at night. I just like to know you got home safely."

"Purcell Station's pretty safe, isn't it?"

"Most of the time. We've got our hoodlum element, though. It's not as safe as it used to be."

I wondered if she was referring to Jesse and the gang I had already encountered.

I pulled up a chair and sat down. "Grandma? Do you know a boy they call Jesse?"

"Why do you ask?"

"Well, I saw him tonight being really mean to a man."

"What did he do?"

"He teased a guy they call Spooks. He taunted him and called him names and poked and shoved him and treated him awful."

"Did he have a group of his buddies with him?"

"Not only them, but a bunch of other kids, too."

"That's gotta be Jesse Sprowl. Sounds like him. He's a mean one, just like his daddy. They live down across the tracks by the bend in the river, hid way back in the woods where nobody goes. His gang follows him around, raising a racket and keeping Marshal Hopper on their tail. He's been up to no good ever since he quit school back in the winter."

"What makes him that way?"

"Probably a lot of things. His daddy's always getting drunk and causing trouble. And there're some cousins down in Patoka who aren't anything to brag about, either. Tell me what happened."

I went on to tell all about the scene on Main Street while the movie was going on. How awful Jesse treated the man they called Spooks and how, out of nowhere, a girl came into the crowd and put Jesse in his place, shaming him.

"Not many in this town would do that. What'd she look like?"

"She had blonde hair and a ponytail. She's pretty. And she seemed to have a lot of confidence. She drove right into the crowd in an old pickup truck."

"That's what I thought. That's Skipper Manion."

"A girl named Skipper?"

"That's not her real name. It's a nickname. You're gonna have a nickname if you live in Purcell Station very long. Her real name's Danielle."

"How'd she get the name Skipper?"

"I guess she was such a rambunctious little girl, always bouncing and jumping around, that her daddy called her Skip. Anyway, he wanted a boy and Skip sounded like a boy. As it was, she turned out to be a pretty good tomboy."

"What I don't understand is how she just walked into that crowd and told Jesse off, and he stood there and took it. Everybody else acted afraid of him."

"Well, you just have to know the Manions to appreciate it. Jack Manion owns the Chevrolet dealership over on Main Street. He also owns a lot of melon ground, not to mention the biggest house in town, up at the top of the hill. Comes from a family people almost worship around here. He hires a lot of people at his garage and farms. But, in spite of his money, he's one of the nicest people in the whole county. His wife and kids are, too. They're all smart, capable, but humble, too. Skipper's older brother plays baseball down at Vanderbilt, and Skipper can do about anything she puts her mind to."

"But why did Jesse let her embarrass him in front of all his friends?"

"Those weren't his friends. Except for a few toadies who hang around him, the rest were scared of him. They're afraid they'll be next, so they all just go along and laugh to stay on his good side. I bet not one of them tried to stop him, did they?"

"Not until Skipper came along. I don't get it."

Grandma smiled and suppressed a yawn. "I have a theory that she knows something on him, but it's only a guess. I figure it'll all come out some day."

She got up, tucked her house coat around her waist, and said, "We should hear something from Cleveland tomorrow." In all that had happened I'd almost forgotten about my father's operation.

CHAPTER 8

Cleveland

Leah Gentry had learned to drive at the age of twenty-five after giving birth to Garrett. It was not something she really wanted to do. When Edward suggested she learn, Leah protested, "I can't see myself going anywhere without you, so why do we both need to drive?"

"What if I'm hurt or sick and need to go to the hospital? How would we get there if you couldn't drive?" he said. So Edward taught her to drive out on a remote gravel road in their 1939 Mercury.

What he didn't teach her was how to drive in Cleveland, Ohio. They left Indiana on U.S. Route 24 after Leah managed to negotiate the streets of Fort Wayne with knuckles clutched to the steering wheel and a spine so rigid it never touched the back of her seat. In eastern Ohio, near Napoleon, they took Route 6 on through Bowling Green to Sandusky. There, on the outskirts of town, the traffic began to pick up, and Leah's nerves intensified. It was only sixty-five more miles to Cleveland, and she was getting anxious. She had no idea how she was going to find the Cleveland Clinic once she got there.

Between Sandusky and Cleveland the highway followed the shores of Lake Erie. The wind had shifted in the early May morning and was coming off the lake from the northwest, causing Leah to chill. Edward, resting on the cushions and pillows they had fixed up for him in the back, moaned and wrestled around a few times but never complained. Thinking he might be cold, Leah found a rest stop and pulled over to get a sweater out of the back and an afghan to throw over him. When she covered him, he asked her to rearrange the pillows, taking some out and placing them behind the front seat and out of the way.

By noon they were in the outskirts of Cleveland, approaching Lakewood. Traffic was picking up, and Leah clutched the steering wheel again. When they got downtown the traffic was heavier. The buildings were closer together and all looked alike to Leah. She had never driven in such a big city. Staying on Highway 6 and following the directions Dr. Spellman's office had given her, she found East Ninth Street and turned right.

Immediately, she heard the siren of an ambulance approaching from behind. She pulled over and let it pass and had a sudden impulse to follow it, thinking it might lead her to the hospital. She thought better of it when she realized the speed it was going. Pulling back out into traffic, she went a block before having to stop at a red light. While idling she reached over in the vacant front seat, picked up her handwritten map, and read the directions. Just as she did a horn blew behind her, and she looked up at a green light. *These city people sure are impatient*, she thought.

Edward was stirring in the back, which meant he was in pain again. Around them cars were swerving and changing lanes and revving their engines at stop lights. Leah felt a drop of sweat trickle down her cheek. The tall buildings were blocking the breeze from the lake, and she had to crack the windows to let in some air. She could hear the noise of the traffic now and felt it closing in. She gripped the steering wheel tighter.

Just as she approached an intersection as the light turned green, a car from the right came screeching through the intersection, running a red light. Leah saw it and slammed on her brakes. She managed to miss it, but the car on her left didn't. It smacked into the errant car broadside and spun it around. Leah's sudden stop threw Edward forward against the extra pillows Leah had placed there outside of Sandusky.

Leah turned and screamed, "Oh, no! Edward!"

His eyes were closed, and his grimace told her what she was afraid to know. "Edward?"

He lay still, breathing heavily. He tried to say something, but Leah couldn't understand a word of it.

"Are you okay?"

Edward lifted his hand and nodded.

"I'm sorry. A guy ran a red light. I tried to stop. I just missed him," she said, wiping the sweat from her forehead.

Just then, a siren got her attention, and she saw the flashing lights of a police car stop in the middle of the intersection. Instantly, an ambulance followed. Emergency workers jumped out and started tending to the driver of the battered car. The driver's side was caved in, and they were having trouble getting the man out. Finally, they took him out the other side and placed him on a stretcher and into the ambulance. They then tended to the driver of the other car, who was walking around with a bloody face.

Leah was looking at both drivers and thinking how close she'd come to being hit when she was interrupted by a voice.

"I said are you people okay?" It was a policeman leaning into her open window.

"Oh, I'm...I'm sorry. I'm just a little upset. It happened so fast."

"Are you okay?" he repeated. "I don't think you hit anything, did you?"

"No, we're lucky. Just a little shaken, I guess. My husband's going to have surgery and that's why he's lying in the back. He says he's okay."

The policeman leaned back and peered into the window. "You sure? We can get him an ambulance if he needs one."

Leah looked at Edward who shook his head "no." "Thanks, but we're almost there," she said.

"Well, as soon as we clear the debris off the street, you may go." The policeman stepped back to rejoin the others.

He had taken three steps when Leah called out, "Oh, sir! Excuse me."

"Yes."

"I have a problem."

"Ma'am?"

"Could you tell me how to get to the Cleveland Clinic? I seem to be lost."

The policeman stepped back to the open window and pointed straight ahead. "Just go six more stoplights ahead, and turn left on Euclid Avenue. You can't miss it."

Six blocks later, Leah saw not just one building, but several. It was the biggest hospital she had ever seen. She found the admissions entrance and managed to get Edward through the red tape and into a room on the fourth floor.

For the next two days doctors put Edward through a series of tests. Among other things, they wanted to see if his heart was able to withstand the five hours of surgery. By the end of the week, they reviewed the results and pronounced him surgically ready.

Leah spent the day of his surgery wandering. At five o'clock, Dr. Spellman found her pacing the floor of the surgical waiting room and called her into his office, where he detailed the operation, explaining that everything looked good so far, but that a long and difficult rehab was in store for him. He explained that Edward would be in recovery for the next twenty-four hours and would be monitored closely. but she would be able to see him after that. She thanked him and relaxed for the first time since they'd left home.

Early Sunday morning, she went down to the chapel for services, thankful for the operation's success, and that afternoon she went to see Edward. She found him asleep, so she left the room and took the elevator down to the cafeteria. She got something to eat and took a seat next to a large window overlooking a courtyard. The tulips and daffodils were in bloom, and Leah couldn't help but think about home and the grape arbor and everything that must be in bloom there.

She finished her lunch and walked down the hall to the lobby. There in a corner she found a booth. She took a dime from her purse, sat down, and dialed the phone of Don Francis in Purcell Station, Indiana.

CHAPTER 9

Sunday morning I awoke when I heard Grandma stirring in the kitchen, and I could smell bacon frying on the stove. When I came into the kitchen, Grandpa was sitting at the table glancing over the *Sunday Commercial* and drinking a cup of coffee.

"Hi, Grandpa," I greeted him. "Are you going to church with us today?" I already knew the answer.

He glanced over at Grandma and said, "Not today. I'll let your Grandma stand in for me."

It was a source of contention between the two of them that Grandpa didn't go to church. It had been that way for over forty years, and I didn't expect it to change today, but I thought I would put him on the spot a little because I knew how much it bothered Grandma.

The first church bell rang at 9 a.m., as I was finishing up breakfast. Grandma had made strawberry pancakes and fried up a batch of bacon, and I was washing them down with orange juice she'd just squeezed. I just had enough time to get into my good pants and shirt to get there by the last bell.

It was no secret that Grandma was one of the four or five people who'd held the church together through the World War, when all the young men were overseas and many women were off working in munitions plants. Now that it was over and families were together again, the membership was growing. She not only taught the adult class, she organized Vacation Bible School, and served as Sunday School superintendent.

We walked through the tunnel and down the alley to Fourth Street where the Baptist church sat on the corner across from Dub's D-X station. Along the way I asked, "Does it bother you about Grandpa?"

"You mean his not going to church?"

"Yeah."

"You know what I think? I believe the Lord watches over him and knows there'll be a day when your Grandpa comes to church, at least spiritually, if not in person.

"Why? He hasn't gone all these years."

"Because sooner or later, if they have *it* in their heart, they all come home."

"What is *it?*"

"I can't explain it, but I know it when I see it. It's something you feel, deep down in your bones. It's spiritual, and the church is at the center of it."

"Do you think Grandpa has *it?*"

"I think he has a lot deeper well than he lets on," she said, "just like your Uncle Grant."

"What about Uncle Grant?"

"He went to church all his life, until he was eighteen. When he turned eighteen, he announced he was no longer going to church, and he quit. I didn't say anything. After all, he was a young man then, so I let him make his own decision. The day he said he wasn't going anymore, he looked at me like he expected me to argue with him."

"What did you do?"

"I just looked him in the eye and said, "You'll be back someday.""

"Did he come back?"

"Just as soon as he got home from the war. He married your Aunt Marie and settled down and rejoined the church. That was right before he moved to Texas to join his brother Wilbur in the oil fields."

We passed Dub's D-X station where a group of men were sitting out front on the liar's bench. The station was a small, square building with a roof on the front that extended out over two gas pumps. The liar's bench was actually two benches, one on each side of the front door, where the old-timers sat to whittle and tell stories. Above the door was a sign that read, "Woodrow Walden, Proprietor." They called him Dub for short.

On Sunday mornings, Dub's was a place where all the men who didn't go to church sat and watched those who did. The Baptists were across the street, the Methodists around the corner, and the Nazarenes two blocks up Main, so they had a good view of who the pious people were.

They gave us the eye, spitting tobacco juice on the gravel drive as we walked by. The smell of cigar smoke filled the air, causing Grandma to exaggerate a cough, designed to show them her disapproval. As we climbed the church steps and entered the door, I began to get nervous. Grandma had told me I'd be in the junior-senior high class, and I didn't know anybody in there yet. She also told me to sit somewhere in the middle while she went down in front to get ready to lead the service.

As soon as I entered, I noticed the back pews were already occupied. A group of teenagers filled the last two rows, except for a large, older man next to the window that overlooked the D-X station across the street. The man had his arm resting on the windowsill, and he was fanning himself. I couldn't see his face because he kept looking out the window.

I went down the middle aisle a few rows, found an empty pew, sat down, and looked straight ahead. I got the feeling people were looking at me since I was probably the only strange face there. When the music started, Grandma asked the congregation to stand and turn to a page in the hymnal, and the organ played the introduction to "Bringing in the Sheaves."

Bringing in the sheaves, bringing in the sheaves,
We will come rejoicing, bringing in the sheaves.

Just as the last chorus ended, I sensed someone coming down the aisle and stopping next to my pew. I moved over, and then glanced back and was startled to see a pretty girl with long, blonde hair in a blue flowered dress. My heart jumped as she sat down, smiled, and whispered "Hi, I'm Skipper."

"What did you talk about in your Sunday School class today, Garrett?" Grandma asked while fixing dinner. She had given me a knowing smile last night when I asked her about the girl who had helped Spooks. But that girl had on bib overalls, work boots, and a pony-tail sticking out of a baseball cap. I was having trouble believing the girl in the sun dress with blonde hair and the whitest teeth I'd ever seen was the same girl.

Grandma must have guessed I had trouble concentrating in class with Skipper Manion sitting beside me.

"We heard the story about the Good Samaritan," I said, not remembering the details and hoping she wouldn't ask. Trying to head off any more questions, I asked, "What did your class talk about?"

"We read the passage about the Good Samaritan, too, and talked about how there are Good Samaritans living right here in Purcell Station."

"There are?"

"Why, yes. You told me about one last night. I used it as an example. About Skipper and how she rescued Spooks during the free show."

For the rest of dinner I asked Grandma so many questions about Skipper I felt embarrassed. After it was over I helped her clear the table and do the dishes. Grandpa got up from the table, shuffled off to the sofa in the dining room, and was soon heard snoring away in his afternoon nap. We were finishing up in the kitchen when Louise Francis came running over to the back door.

"You have a phone call. Long distance from Cleveland," she said.

The Francises had one of only two telephones on the block, so whenever Grandma needed a phone, Louise told her she could use theirs. Grandpa figured part of that was because they were good neighbors and the other part was because Louise liked to eavesdrop.

Grandma hurried over to take the call and I tagged along behind, partly to see inside the Francises' house. People said their floors were so clean you could eat off of them. Taking my shoes off, I entered the back porch and then the kitchen where the phone hung from a wooden box on the wall.

Grandma answered while I checked out the hardwood floor. "Hello, this is Minnie."

There was a brief silence and then the sound of coins dropping. "Leah, is that you? I can barely hear…is that you?"

"Yes, can you hear me?"

More silence followed.

"That's nice…good. How is he doing?"

Grandma listened for nearly a minute, and then she said, "That's good… good news. My prayers have been answered. We'll keep our fingers crossed.

I'll be sure and tell everyone. Yes, Garrett is doing fine. He's eating well, and he went to the free show last night and church this morning. Yes….he's standing right here. Would you like to talk to him?"

She handed me the phone. "Hi, Mom. Is Dad okay?"

She explained that the surgery and the post-op had taken up most of the day and that Dad has been in recovery all night and a good part of today. She said he would be assigned a room this afternoon, and she would be able to visit him there. It might be a while before we knew how successful the operation would be.

Maybe she didn't want me to worry, so she changed the subject. "Are you finding your way around town?" she asked.

"Yes, I've met some people already."

"Oh? Who?" She wanted to know.

"I met Lady Muldoon just as soon as I got off the train, and her dog and his friends. She told me some stories about you. She thinks you're pretty special."

"Maybe I've got her fooled." She laughed. "Who else did you meet?"

"I met a guy named Jesse…and his friends."

"Not Jesse Sprowl?"

"I think that's his name. Why?"

"Well, just be careful. He's not someone you want to be friends with."

"I've already found that out. And I met a girl named Skipper. She sat beside me in church this morning. I think she was sitting in back with the other older kids and saw me sitting alone."

"That sounds just like something she'd do. You'll like her."

"How do you know so much about her?"

"That's something to save for another day. This call is long distance and I don't have much more change. I need to go now. Take care of Grandma and Grandpa, be good, and have a good time, okay?"

"Okay, Mom, love you."

Louise wanted to know all about Dad's operation, and Grandma obliged. When Grandma was out of details, we thanked her for use of the phone and went home. That evening, when the sun went down and the lights came on I looked out the kitchen window at the Francises' house and saw Louise talking on the phone. I figured by morning everybody in Purcell Station would know all about my father's back.

After supper, Grandpa sat in the dining room by the radio and listened to the St. Louis Cardinals play the New York Giants in a night game from the Polo Grounds. The Giants' center fielder, Willie Mays, had homered, and the Cardinals were answering with the bases loaded with Stan Musial at bat.

Harry Caray, the Cardinals' announcer, was getting worked up. "The bases are loaded. Musial digs in...Liddle takes the sign...the pitch...there's a looong drive down the right field line....It could be....It might be...foul!"

Grandpa interrupted. "This pitcher for the Giants, Don Liddle, used to pitch here. Played for Mt. Carmel, just across the Wabash in Illinois."

"Really? A big league pitcher played here?"

"Yep! He wasn't the only one, either. Turley, who pitches for the Yankees, played here, too. And you've heard of Gil Hodges, the Dodger first baseman. He played here, too. Raised up the river in Petersburg, although people down in Princeton say he's from there."

"Do they still play baseball here?

"Every Monday and Friday night over at the Sand Bowl behind the school."

"Here's the pitch...Musial swings...a hot shot down the line...one run is in...two runs are in...Schoendienst stops at third, and Musial's on second with a stand-up double. Ho...lee... cow!"

Harry's excitement sent a tingle running down my back.

"We've had a few local boys make the minor leagues. Had a good pitcher when your mother was in high school, guy named Ace McCauley. Signed right out of high school with the Cincinnati Reds."

"Did he play in the big leagues?"

"Nope. Made it to Double -A and blew out his arm."

"Whatever happened to him?"

"He got drafted in the war and got killed in Germany fighting Hitler.

"Did he like my mother?" I remembered Lady Muldoon saying he did.

Grandpa was staring straight ahead at some imaginary point on the fireplace, thinking about Ace. "They all did," he said.

I thought about that a while and then I changed the subject. "Do you think we could go to a game sometime?"

CHAPTER 10

The lights came on in the Sand Bowl before the sun went down, while the visiting Elberfeld Tigers were taking batting practice. Grandpa and I shuffled the four blocks from his house in record slow time. Since his stroke, his steps had slowed and taken on the look of someone walking on ice for the first time. I offered to hold his arm, but he had too much pride for that, so we shuffled along like those slow dances at school sock hops. Along the street, people fell in alongside of us, slowing their pace out of respect.

"Is that your grandson?" asked Tip Albee. I recognized him from Maddie's Cafe on Saturday night.

"Yep. Name's Garrett," said Grandpa. "He's spending the summer with us."

"How old are you, Garrett?"

"I'm twelve."

Tip looked at me like he was sizing me up, but he didn't say anything.

Grandpa paid the man at the gate fifteen cents for himself and ten cents for me, and we went in and placed two cushions we'd brought from home in the second row behind the Purple Aces dugout.

The Sand Bowl was one of the best baseball fields around, sitting half way up the hill and behind the school. At night its lights could be seen all the way to Illinois—ten miles as the crow flies. The stands were made of concrete covered with a wooden roof, and under the roof was a booth for the official scorer and the announcer. A concession stand sat behind it.

After batting practice ended the teams lined up along the foul lines as a girl from the high school choir sang the National Anthem. When she finished, the public address announcer gave the starting lineups, and thinking the voice sounded familiar, I looked up in the booth and saw Rollie Brockman.

Tip Albee and a group of farmers sat to our right, and between pitches, they talked about the coming melon season, the price of fertilizer, and the need for good hired help.

"I see Johnnie's throwing his ace tonight," Grandpa said. He was referring to the manager, Johnnie Coleman, and his star pitcher, Wilson Barnes. "Barnes played at Purcell Station High School three years ago before going off to college at Hanover. You shoulda seen him in high school. Teamed with Patrick Manion. They were quite a battery."

"Manion? Is he any relation to Skipper?"

"Yep. Brother. He's a pretty good catcher."

"Is he catching tonight?"

"Nope, not here anyway. He's up at Falmouth, playin' in the Cape Cod League. Played at Vanderbilt last year and got a chance to go to the Cape," Grandpa said. "It's the best summer league in the country up there."

"Is he good enough to play for the Cardinals?"

"Never know. There're lots of scouts at the Cape Cod League."

Tip jumped in, "He had an offer from the Reds last year, but it wasn't enough money. Least that's what I heard."

Purcell Station is located half way between St. Louis and Cincinnati, dividing the loyalties between the Reds and Cardinals. Some pretty good arguments got going at Danny's barber shop over which team was the best.

When the Purple Aces came to bat and the first two batters got on base and the third popped up, Rollie got the fans on their feet cheering for the cleanup hitter, Mac "Truck" Gorman.

"Truck once played in the Cubs farm system," Grandpa informed me. "He could hit the ball a country mile, but he set a record for strikeouts, so they released him."

"Why did he come back here?" I asked.

"Because he still has the dream."

Just then I heard a crack of the bat and the crowd yelling. I looked up in time to see a fly ball disappear over the fence in left field, landing on the railroad track. Truck circled the bases in a slow trot.

The next batter swung at the first pitch, and a foul ball popped up and headed in our direction. Grandpa yelled, "Heads up!" It landed in the row behind us and bounced high up off the concrete seats. "Grab it!" Grandpa said.

I jumped up just as it came down and bounced into my hands. I heard some fans clap as I quickly sat down.

"Take that over to the concession stand and turn it in. They'll give you a pop and sack of popcorn," Grandpa said. "That's how they get the foul balls back."

I waited until the fans' attention was back on the next pitch; then I climbed the bleachers to go to the concession stand in back. As I got there a group of boys was standing at the counter, so I stepped up behind them to get in line. They were talking loud and I heard some swearing and then they all laughed. Then one of the boys turned around and saw me holding a baseball.

"Whoa, what we got here?" he said. He must have been sixteen or seventeen and had a tee shirt that showed off his arms. The others all turned around, and that's when I saw Jesse. I'd avoided him since that first day and sure didn't want to see him now. He must have remembered me from Smokey's, because he cocked his head and grinned and started toward me. Then he saw the ball. I dropped it down to my side and tried to hide it, but it was too late. He reached out to grab it, but before he could take it, I heard a voice from behind me.

"Garrett! I didn't know you were here." It was Skipper. She was with two other girls.

"Oh, hi!" I said.

"I see you got a baseball. Here, I'll take it around back so you won't have to wait in line. My mom's working in there tonight."

I felt the stares of Jesse and his friends as I handed Skipper the ball and followed her to the back of the stand.

"Wait here. I'll be right out."

She returned with the R.C. and a sack of popcorn, plus one for her and her friends.

"Garrett, this is Ginny Bonhomme," she said, nodding to a dark haired girl. "And this is Sarah Begley. Garrett is here for the summer, visiting his grandparents, the Haldermans."

Turning back to me, she asked, "You wanna sit with us? We're over there." She pointed to the back row behind home plate.

I quickly accepted and went down to tell Grandpa.

I spent the rest of the game talking with Skipper and her friends, pausing to cheer a hit or a rally and then picking right up where we left off. They asked me a lot of questions: why I was here, where I was from, and how old I was. I found out Skipper and her friends were fifteen and going to be sophomores in the fall.

The game ended much too soon. When Grandpa came back to get me, Skipper said they come to all the games and asked me to join them next time. I told her I would. I felt safe from Jesse with Skipper around.

When Grandpa and I got home about 10 o'clock, Grandma was waiting up.

"How was the game?" she asked.

"It was great," I said. "We won 5 to 3 and Mac 'Truck' hit a homer. There were supposed to be some big league scouts there, and did you know some major leaguers used to play here? And Wilson Barnes pitched and may have a chance to sign with a big league team?"

"No, I didn't know all that. It sounds as if you had a pretty good time."

"Oh, I think he did, but he didn't tell you all of it." Grandpa paused for effect. "I'm not sure he saw all of the game."

After getting his licks in trying to embarrass me with his version of my night with Skipper and her friends, Grandpa shuffled off to bed. I pulled up a chair at the kitchen table across from Grandma. She offered me a cookie and a glass of milk.

The cookies were still warm. I took a bite and poured the milk.

"Grandma, tonight I found out Skipper is fifteen years old. But the other night when she saved Spooks, she was driving a truck, and she put Spooks in it and drove him home. She's not old enough to have a license, so how'd she get by with that?"

"Well, she's been driving since she was about nine, so she's got plenty of experience. She only drives when she needs to. As long as Marshal Hopper doesn't mind, why should anyone?"

"Do they let other kids drive?"

"Depends. You see, there are rules, and there are Purcell Station rules. People around here all know each other. If she was out joy-riding that would be different, but she's not. So people here cut her some slack. If you're being responsible, people don't necessarily care if you have a piece of paper saying you're legit. Heaven knows some people who have that piece of paper don't have any business driving."

"Does Purcell Station have other rules, too?"

"That depends on whether the good it does overrides the bad. Sometimes people here look the other way. You'll probably figure that out."

CHAPTER 11

The push mower was rusty and needed oiling. I took a long-necked oil can and oiled the reel and the wheels, and pushed it back and forth a few times. The grass had not been mowed since Grandpa went in the hospital, and it was getting out of hand. When I started, it was just past 8 o'clock. When I finished, it was nearly 10 o'clock, and the sun was bearing down and sweat was soaking my shirt, but I didn't mind. It felt good to work hard.

When I finished I washed up, put on a clean shirt, and headed downtown. I'd been thinking about looking for a job. I liked the idea of hard work, and a little extra money sounded good. I thought it might also help my grandparents out.

As I turned the corner at Dub's D-X station, a pickup truck wheeled in and stopped next to the gas pumps. I recognized the driver as he got out.

"How'ya doing, Tip?" one of the men on the liar's bench said. They couldn't see me, but I could hear them. "You got yer melons in?"

"Nope, that's why I'm here. I'm tryin' to rustle up some help. About all able-bodied men and boys are taken, 'cept those who have an aversion to work," he said, looking down the street in the direction of Smokey's Pool Room. "Don't reckon there's anybody there or down at Tulley's that has any interest in makin' honest money." Smokey's hosted a running poker game most nights and well into some mornings. The same could be said for Tulley's Tavern, except they played right out in the open. Tulley prided himself in flaunting the law, such as it was in Purcell Station.

"Maybe if you paid them a decent wage, they'd come work for you," said Elwood Warner.

Elwood conferred upon himself the title of Honorary Mayor and kept office hours on Dub's liar's bench every afternoon and evening. Mornings he slept in, having stayed up half the night watching the card players at both local establishments. He never played himself, not for real, anyway, just imaginary money he'd play in his head looking over someone's shoulder. He always said he broke even that way.

"I don't figure fifty cents an hour for twelve hours is that bad. When's the last time you made six bucks a day?" asked Tip.

"I saw Petey Laudermilk make that much in three minutes last night," Elwood said.

"Yeah, well, he probably lost twice that much the next three minutes, too."

"Reckon you're probably right. But he didn't have to bend over and lift anything, either," said Elwood, drawing a laugh from the men sharing his bench.

Dub came out from under a car on the grease rack and asked Tip if he wanted any gas.

"You can fill'er up and check the oil," said Tip. "And if you know anybody who can spare me a couple of week's work, I'm in the market."

"I'll keep my ears open," said Dub.

Tip walked around the gas pump to see how much he owed for the gas. It was then he saw me.

"Why, hi ya, young man." Then he paused, "Garrett, right?'

"Hi, that's right."

"Did you have a good time at the ball game last night?"

"Yes, I...."

"I reckon you did. I saw you made some friends—some pretty nice friends, looked to me." He glanced at the other men and winked.

I felt myself starting to blush. Tip must have noticed. "Nah, I didn't mean to embarrass ya. I was only teasing. What I'd really like is for you to come work for me. I need some help for two weeks, at most. Just long enough to get my melons in. You look like you'd be a good worker."

"I don't know much about melons," I said.

"You can learn on the job. Not that much to it once you get going."

"When do you need to know?"

"I'm gonna start tomorrow morning. You could let me know tonight. I start you out at 40 cents an hour until I see what you can do and then 50 cents when you prove yourself."

That sounded fair. It was a lot more than I was making. I hurried home, excited to run the idea past Grandma and Grandpa.

They must have sensed my enthusiasm. "It's a good honest day's work," Grandpa said. "It never hurts a young man to find out how hard something is."

"And Tip's a pretty good guy to work for," said Grandma. "He'll treat you right." We agreed it'd be a good experience, so Grandma went over to the Francises' house to call Tip.

"Have ya thought about how you're going to get there? It's pretty far out," said Grandpa.

I hadn't.

"Come out here and let's see what we can rig up." Grandpa shuffled through the tunnel and into the side door of the garage. Feeling his way around in the dark, he reached up on the wall and took down an old bicycle. When we got it outside in the light we saw it had some problems.

"Looks like a fixer-upper," Grandpa said.

He went back into the garage and came out with some tools, an oil can, and a wire brush. I scrubbed the bike and oiled it. Grandpa hooked up the chain and fastened the handlebars. We aired up the tires.

"There, that's as good as it's gonna get," Grandpa said. I climbed aboard and started coasting down the driveway and into the street. I circled past the Francises' house and then back up the driveway.

"How's it ride?" he asked.

"A little creaky, but okay."

"Well, it won't win any beauty contests, but it's transportation."

I decided to try it out. I rode to the water tower at the top of the hill and down to the train depot at the bottom. When I came back up Main Street I stopped to watch the softball game in the vacant lot, and I noticed a wheelbarrow sitting on the sidewalk. It had a license plate attached to the front. It read, "TT 3849," and the year was 1950. I looked around to see who it might belong to, but there was no one close.

As I watched the game I saw Skipper standing on the mound, and several boys were scattered around the infield and outfield. She lobbed a pitch toward the batter, and when he swung he hit a ground ball that rolled past several fielders all the way to the sidewalk where I was standing. Skipper saw me and yelled, "Hey, Garret! Come on down."

When I jumped down off the sidewalk onto the field all the kids were yelling at a big man lumbering around the bases. It was Spooks.

When he crossed home plate Skipper introduced me to all the guys and explained the rules. A boy threw me a mitt and I took a place in the outfield watching Skipper as she lobbed slow pitches to the younger boys and faster pitches to the older ones. Since everyone got a hit, they begged her to keep pitching.

When the game broke up, Skipper followed me to the sidewalk where I'd left my bike. Behind her came Spooks.

"You got a nice hit there, Spooks," she said.

"Yeah, I m—made a h—home run." He gave her a tobacco-toothed grin, then a bunch of boys surrounded him, slapping him on the back, and walking with him down the street.

I stood there talking to Skipper, telling her about my new job. She told me she'd worked for Tip, and I'd like working for him too, but she warned me to be ready. "It's hard work," she said.

My alarm went off at 5 a.m. Grandma was standing over the stove frying eggs and browning bread on the stove top for toast. From the dining room I could hear the radio playing Grandma's favorite gospel music. Each morning at 5:15 she tuned in to station 1420 to listen to the Melody Masters Quartet. I think it was her way of waking Grandpa and at the same time giving him a dose of the religion he missed on Sundays.

"I've packed you a sack lunch," she said.

"Thanks, I'm getting kinda nervous. I hope I do okay."

"You just do what Tip tells you to and give him a good day's work. You'll do fine."

The Melody Masters were winding down their last song and signing off when Grandma said, "Just a minute. You'll need a hat to keep the sun off your face or you'll get sunburned."

She handed me a straw hat with a red band around the crown. "This belonged to your uncle Wilbur when he was working for Tip. Looks like it'll fit."

It was a little loose, but my ears kept it from falling down over my eyes.

I pedaled north out of town on a blacktop road, past fields of melons, tomatoes, and sweet potatoes. The sun was rising to my right to a clear blue sky. The morning air brushed my shirt and sent the tail flapping in the breeze. A pickup truck came up behind me with its headlights still on and tooted to let me know it was passing. In the back sat three boys not much older than I. I figured they were heading off to work the fields too.

About two miles out I stopped under a sycamore tree and got out the directions Grandpa had drawn to Tip's farm. It showed Graveyard Hill on the right and a white frame house about a half mile ahead. I figured that was Tip's.

I parked my bike under a shade tree and entered the packing shed where a group of men and boys sat on a flatbed wagon. Tip saw me. "Morning, Garrett. You can put your lunch in the ice box over there."

I felt the others looking at me.

"Boys, this is Garrett. He's joining us today, just learnin' the ropes, so you all make him feel welcome and help him get started." Tip then told us to hop on the wagon and they would take us to the hot beds to load up the first set of boxes. One of the boys on the wagon held out a hand and pulled me up, and I sat down on the edge, dangling my feet over the side like the others.

The hot beds were covered with glass panels that slid open so the plants could be watered and then covered again to keep out the frost. Inside were rows of plants in four-inch wooden boxes filled with sand. Tip pulled the wagon between two beds. He got in one bed and the other man in the other, and they started handing boxes to the rest of us. We lined them up in straight rows on the wagon until it was full.

It took over an hour to load the wagon, and when we finished we climbed on the wagon to ride to the back forty. A guy named Jack pulled the tractor in the lane between the rows and set the speed. The rest of us carried the boxes out to each row and set them in the soil and covered the dirt in around them. It was hard keeping up with the pace of the tractor, and after a few minutes I stopped to look up and this pause caused our side of the wagon to get behind. I heard Tip yell, "Gotta keep up, boys. Can't fall behind the other side."

We made it to the end of the field; then stood under a shade tree while Jack turned the tractor around. I learned it did no good to look up every once in a while to see how far we'd come. It was better just to keep my head down and do my job and then be surprised when we came to the end of the row. When we got back to the other end we'd run out of boxes, so Tip told us to climb aboard and we headed back to the hot beds to reload.

It was after 10 o'clock when we got the next wagon loaded and Tip gave us a water break. Under the shade tree beside the house we found our cups and filled them up. Water never tasted so good and cold. I filled my cup again and gulped it down, then poured a third cup over my head and let it roll down my face. I sat down, leaned against the base of the tree, and closed my eyes. I let my muscles relax and my mind go blank, wishing I could take a nap.

A few minutes later Tip snapped, "Okay, men. Up and at'em."

The next two hours dragged on before we emptied the wagon and headed back to the hot beds. It was approaching noon now, so Jack pulled the wagon under the packing shed roof where a little breeze swept through the opening and gave us some relief from the heat. We sat down at the picnic table Tip had set up and ate in silence, too tired to talk, when all too soon Tip came out and yelled, "Okay, gang! Just six more hours, and we'll have 'er licked."

The afternoon sun bore down even heavier and the wind died down, trapping the sun's heat in the sand. By four o'clock I ached from lifting, carrying, and bending over. It was nearing six when we reached the end of the field and Tip said, "Take 'er in and put her away, and we'll call it a day, men." We left the field, and Jack pulled the tractor into the pole shed and turned it off. I welcomed the silence after the constant roar the past twelve hours. As I climbed down off the wagon, Tip called me over.

"That's a pretty good first day for a young boy who didn't know anything about melons."

"Thanks. I didn't know if I could make it."

"Well, you did and tomorrow you'll get that raise."

On the fifth day the rains came. It had not rained in twenty-two days, and the soil was dry and crusty, threatening to stunt the young melon plants before they could get a good start. The farmers and their wives—the ones who went to church, anyway—had been praying for rain for over two weeks, and they were overjoyed and thankful for their good fortune.

It started at 3 o'clock in the morning, and when I awoke at five, it was pelting the tin roof on my back bedroom so hard I didn't need an alarm. I rolled over and looked at the still-dark sky and saw a bolt of lightning. A crack of thunder pierced the silence, and I knew I was home free. From my open window on the leeward side, I could smell the cool, fresh air, and so I pulled the sheets up over my shoulders and lay there thanking my good fortune and falling back asleep.

It was nine o'clock before I awoke again and slipped sheepishly into the kitchen. My grandparents were early risers and had little use for sloths that slept past six. I was expecting some sort of comment from Grandpa, who was known for snide remarks about laggards. I found him in the dining room reading the newspaper, his chin was resting on his chest. He was snoring. As I reached down to unlodge the paper from his hand, he jerked awake and shook his head.

"Well, youngster you going to sleep all day?" He peered over his bifocals to bring me into focus.

"No, but it looks like you might," I said.

"I was just resting my eyes. You get my age, and your eyes get tired."

I let him think I believed him.

The rain was still coming down and looked as if it might continue for a spell.

"Not much to do here when it rains, is there?" I asked Grandma.

"There is if you use your imagination. This past winter the town board voted to fund a new library. They took a lease on the vacant store next to the bank and asked for people to donate their old books. I thought you might want to go down there and browse around."

"I'll give it a try. What do I need to do?" I'd been checking our biographies of famous Americans at the county seat back home.

"You'll need a card, so just tell Miss Perkins who you are and give her my name. But don't get your hopes up too high. It's probably nothing like your library back home."

It was in an old dry goods store that had closed years ago. It was a white frame building with windows across the front and a recessed front door that rang a bell when someone entered. I set off the bell and walked to the back of the room. A lady wearing glasses with the top half missing and attached to strings looping around her neck stood behind a counter.

"May I help you?" she asked.

"Yes… well, no, I just want to look around."

"Well, take your time. The children's books are along that shelf." She pointed to the wall to my left. I started over there and then stopped, wondering why she thought I belonged in the children's department. "You're new here, aren't you?"

"Yes, my grandmother, Minnie Halderman, told me to get a card."

"Oh, you're her grandson. I heard you were in town. I'm Miss Perkins. Welcome to Purcell Station. You go ahead and look around. I'll get you a card."

I made sure she saw me walk over to the adult nonfiction section where I found biographies. After browsing for a few minutes, I narrowed it down to either Teddy Roosevelt or Stonewall Jackson. I chose Jackson on the basis of his nickname.

"That's a good choice," said Miss Perkins. "I think you'll like that." She handed me a card.

When I got back I climbed the maple tree beside the driveway and sat down on a board I'd nailed between two limbs. I did this last Sunday when Grandma and Grandpa were taking a nap. I'd found a piece of corrugated roofing in the barn and nailed it above for a roof. Another board below the seat served as a foot rest. I stayed there with my book, hearing the rain against the tin roof, until Grandma called me for lunch.

As we were sitting around the kitchen table, I was explaining the origin of Jackson's nickname when we heard a knock on the back door.

Grandma looked up. "Come in, Jimmy. We've missed you around here." It was Jimmy Brockman from across the street.

"I've been gone, visiting my cousin Sam in Louisville. We're working on a new contraption."

"You're always working on a new contraption. We're just finishing lunch. Would you like something to eat?" she said.

"No thanks," he said. "I came over because I heard there was a stranger in town."

"Well, you heard right. Jimmy this is Garrett, Leah's boy."

"Hi, Garrett. I heard you were in town. Not many strangers ever come here, so I imagine about everybody's heard about you by now."

I shook his hand. "Hi. I've heard a lot about you."

Jimmy stood over six feet tall and had an angular, lean frame, not like his father Rollie, who was short, heavyset, and round-faced. Grandma had already told me Jimmy ranked number one in the junior class at Purcell Station High School and was known as a bookworm and a tinkerer who always had some new scientific project going on. People figured he'd probably end up as a famous inventor someday.

"Would you like to have a seat?" Grandma asked.

"No, I need to get back to the shack. I'm in the middle of something. I thought Garrett might want to come over and see what's going on."

Grandma looked at me. "I bet he would. How about it, Garrett?"

"You mean it?" I'd heard about the shack. I knew it was a real privilege to be invited in.

"Sure," said Jimmy, "but Minnie, I want you to tune your radio dial to 910. I've got a surprise for you."

"I'm never surprised by anything you have up your sleeve, but I'll play along. You boys run along, and have a good time."

Jimmy and I crossed the street and opened the gate of the picket fence surrounding Brockman's yard. Between the garage and house I stopped and stared at the fish pond with the colored fish swimming around green lily pads. Above it stood a rock formation with waterfalls cascading down the rocks and into the water. Old elm and maple trees shaded the backyard, and lilac and spirea bushes gave it privacy, color, and scent. We walked on a curving brick path through shrubs and trees until we came to a white building with a green tin roof. The door was partially hidden with a lattice overgrown with ivy. It stood in the back corner of the Brockman property inside a high wooden fence that was also covered with ivy. Beyond the fence lay nothing but forest and meadows sloping down to the river half a mile away.

Jimmy opened the door and let me in. "You'll have to excuse the mess. I just never got around to cleaning it up."

It was dark inside, and when Jimmy flipped on the light I was startled. Across the room sat an old, badly worn easy chair, reclining with the footrest still up. It had white fiber stuffing peeking out the arms, and a spring was sticking out of the seat.

Jimmy must have seen me stare at it. "That's Dad's chair. He says it's comfortable. He sits there to read or listen to his music with his headphones."

I looked around the room and noticed a work bench that ran the length of the south wall. On it were tools, technical manuals, and electronic equipment. Above it rested a shelf that wrapped around the entire room at various levels. It had a hinge that raised and lowered it over the door, and at some points it was higher than at other points. I walked over to get a closer look and saw it held rails for a miniature train.

"That's my model train track," said Jimmy. "I can put the shelf down over the door and run the train all around the room. That tank in the corner is where it stops for water to make its steam." On the north wall the ledge was wider. "Here's a double track along here. It's called a switch. That's where one train sits while another train passes or meets it."

There were miniature trees, a depot, and other buildings beside the switch yards to resemble a small village. "I made these out of balsa wood, the kind model airplanes are made of. Here, I'll show you how it works." Jimmy lined up one engine with coal cars and a caboose and started running it counterclockwise. He set up another engine with a string of passenger cars and began running it at a different speed. Sitting at the control panel, he pulled the levers, allowing the coal train to move over and let the passenger train pass. I watched as Jimmy maneuvered the trains. This went on for several minutes when Jimmy said, "Whoa! I almost forgot. I told your grandma to tune in to her radio. I bet she's been waiting."

He walked over to the table under the double windows, took a seat in front of a microphone, and flipped a switch. Behind it rested a box with dials and needles showing readings of various numbers. He turned a knob, and one of the needles started jumping back and forth.

"What's that?" I asked.

"That's frequency modulation. It's warming up. Pretty soon we'll start broadcasting over the air."

"You mean you can broadcast, like a radio station?"

"It is a radio station."

"Really? What do you use it for?"

"Whenever I get a notion I play music, give some local news, a little weather, some sports scores, or whatever I want to talk about."

"Who listens to it?"

"Mostly people here in town. I only have enough power to cover that and a few hundred yards beyond. That's probably good, though, since I don't have a license."

"How'd you know how to put this stuff together?"

"I read a lot of books and manuals and things like that. Dad helped me find the equipment and put it together."

"What if you get caught?"

"That would be a problem. I don't think it would happen though. People around here aren't going to tell the FCC. They have their own secrets, so they're not about to turn each other in. As long as I don't carry over to the highway where they can pick it up on their car radios, I should be safe. That's a mile away and out of my range. Hold on a minute."

He put on a set of earphones and turned some more dials and a squeaking noise came over the amplifier. He turned another dial and it went away. He pulled the earphone off his right ear and said, "Go over to your grandma's and see if she's listening. I'm ready to go on the air."

I ran back through the floral backyard and across the street. Entering the kitchen, I announced, "Get the radio tuned in. Jimmy's going on the air."

Grandma was already sitting in her rocking chair by the radio.

"I've been waiting, and all I've heard is static. When's he coming on?"

"He said right away...I just heard..."

Then it came on. "Jimmy B. here, broadcasting from our studios in the Shack Out Back, in beautiful Purcell Station, the backbone of the nation's breadbasket, the crossroads of America. Hello to all the Purple Aces Tribe out there, and welcome to Tea Time Tunes on this beautiful, misty afternoon."

I looked at Grandma and shivered with goose bumps as Jimmy continued his rant. He continued, "I'm going to dedicate this song to a special person, the "*materfamilias*" of Purcell Station, Mrs. Minnie Halderman." The familiar sounds of "A You're Adorable" filled the air"

"'A' you're adorable, 'B' you're so beautiful, 'C' you're a………"

"What's a '*materfamilias*,' or whatever he called you?" I asked Grandma.

"Oh, that's just Jimmy being Jimmy. He's always got his nose in a book, and he comes away with this high falootin' vocabulary. I think it's like a matriarch—a woman who heads a household."

"Then that's an honor, right?"

"I suppose."

Just then, the background music stopped and Jimmy's voice came on in the middle of the song as he sung his own solo of the chorus before returning it to the sound-track.

Grandma noticed my surprise. "That boy sure has a great imagination. There's never a dull moment. You better go on back over there and see what you can learn."

I opened the door to the shack and found Jimmy sorting through a stack of records, lining up his playlist for the afternoon. I pulled up a stool and watched as he introduced the next number and spun the record on the turntable. When he turned off his microphone, he turned to me and asked, "How'd you like to come with me to the baseball game tonight and keep my scorebook?"

"Why do you have to keep a scorebook?"

"Because I'll be broadcasting the game, and I need some help keeping the book. It's hard to talk and write at the same time. Besides, I need to break you in as my backup, in case I have to go to the restroom or something."

"You mean you're broadcasting the Purple Aces game? On your station?"

"You got it. How about it? You in or not?"

"Gee, I don't know."

"Great. Now, I need to show you how to record a game."

CHAPTER 12

The rains ended on Friday, but the baseball game was called because more than four inches of rain fell, turning the Sand Bowl into mud and postponing my debut on the radio. On Saturday morning I was in Brock-man's Grocery, browsing at the candy counter, when Tip Albee came in and told me we wouldn't be able to get back in the fields until Tuesday. I sensed his disappointment and tried to hide my joy. Not having to work meant I'd be able to help Jimmy Brockman cover the game Monday night.

I spent the morning helping Grandma set out tomato plants and three rows of potatoes in the garden behind the barn. The strawberries were starting to come in, so we picked a small box and washed them for lunch. When we finished I shot baskets out in the driveway. I was hop-ing Mr. Francis might be looking out his kitchen window.

On Saturday afternoon I found Grandpa sitting in the swing on the front porch listening to the Cardinals. The volume was turned up loud enough that Louise Francis next door was keeping track of the score while sweeping the dirt path between her house and the outhouse. I backed into the swing and plopped down next to Grandpa.

I sat and listened to the game until I got restless, then told Grandpa I was going over in town. I took the long way to Main Street, circling up the hill past Skipper's house, hoping I might get a glimpse of her, but I didn't. I coasted all the way down the street, past the afternoon crowd on the liar's bench and the drugstore, where more people were loitering.

I continued down the hill to the depot. Parking my bike across the street, I sat down on the top step of the hotel. I was in the shade of the porch, and it felt good to be out of the sun. The rain had cleaned the air and settled the dust. I leaned back on my elbows and stretched, breathing in the smell of the lilacs surrounding the porch. I closed my eyes.

In the distance I heard the whistle of a train coming down from the north, and I saw Bud Tate arriving with a fresh mailbag, so it had to be a passenger train. As it came closer the crossing lights blinked, and the hum of the engine grew louder until it came to a stop at the station. It wouldn't be stopping unless there were passengers.

As Bud Tate grabbed the mail bag and flung it into his truck, I saw a girl stepping out of one of the cars. She was carrying a bag and smiling, and then she was waving at me. It took a moment, but then I realized it was Skipper. I ran over to meet her.

"Hi, Garrett!" She was all dressed up in a blouse and skirt. I was staring, thinking how different she looked without her overalls and work boots. "What're you doing down here?"

"Just riding my bike," I said self-consciously. "What're you doing on the train?"

"I've been up to the city to get some books at the library. Here, look at this." She held up a book, and I read the title: *Of Mice and Men.*

"Why didn't you get it here?"

"They don't have it here. Some people think it's too controversial. Miss Perkins doesn't like anything that might stir people up. It's got some bad language and violence, but it's a classic. It's written by John Steinbeck and it teaches people how to have empathy for people who are different."

"How do you know what it's about?"

"Because, I've already read it. I got it for someone else. Someone who needs it."

I started to ask, but Skipper was putting the book back in her bag and saying, "Would you give me a lift to my house?

"You mean ride double?" I asked.

"Yeah, I'll put my books in the basket and ride on the cross bars."

In the hot sun it wasn't easy riding double up Main Street, especially when the men at Dub's hooted and hollered as we passed, but when Skipper asked me if I'd like to join her at the free show it made it all worthwhile.

"Good. You can sit with Ginny and Sarah and me," she said.

We didn't watch the show. After darkness came and the movie started, Skipper and I rested our heads on the pillows she brought from home and we talked. The movie was an action film and just noisy enough to drown out our voices. I told her about my father's accident and about my trip down here on the train and taking the side trip to see the house where my parents met. She liked that. I told about how the man on the train with the newspaper stared at me and made me nervous when I mentioned Purcell Station. She thought that was odd, but one of the things she talked about was also strange: a secret hideaway she knew about down the river and another one up at a place called Taber Hill. She said there was something going on there that was a mystery. "People don't like to talk about it," she whispered.

I wanted to ask her more, but the lights at Dub's came on and the movie ended. She promised to tell me about it another time.

CHAPTER 13

I was excited about the baseball game. Jimmy picked me up in his father's Packard at 6:30 sharp, and we drove over to the Sand Bowl. He parked in back of the bleachers, and we unloaded the equipment and carried it up the ladder to the broadcast booth.

Jimmy hooked up the microphone and the amplifier and tested them for a connection. The Petersburg Saints had arrived and had started tossing balls around down along the first base line. Just as Jimmy finished checking the equipment I heard the roar of a motorcycle coming from behind the bleachers. It was Rollie, Jimmy's father, the public address announcer. He shut off the noisy cycle and approached the ladder leading up to the broadcast booth.

The ladder was fastened to the back wall, and extended up through the floor of the booth. The opening was small, and for Rollie that was a problem. When confronted with questions about his heft, he admitted to two hundred-fifty pounds, but it was compounded by his height; he stood five feet eight inches. There had been some talk about making the opening larger, but there was equal talk of Rollie losing some weight, so nothing had been settled at that point.

Rollie tossed his helmet up through the opening to Jimmy and then started climbing the ladder. When his head poked through the floor, he lifted his arms up through the opening and used his elbows to help lift his body upward. Jimmy grabbed his shoulders, and down below two men who had done this before each grabbed a leg and pushed. Rollie took a deep breath and yelled, "Liftoff!" The men pushed, and Jimmy pulled until Rollie's massive midsection squeezed through. He climbed the rest of the way up, smiled at me, and said, "I don't have as much trouble going down. Gravity sets in."

Everybody liked Rollie. His moon face, pencil moustache, and receding hairline give him a comical look, and his sense of humor added to it. His body, like a pear, sloped from narrow shoulders to his giant middle and sloped down again to his short, stubby legs. The odd shape of his body didn't bother him, nor did it keep him from calling attention to himself. He liked the attention.

He got his microphone hooked up while the Saints were taking batting practice. "Testing…testing…testing. One…two…three." When he got everyone's attention, he proceeded. "If anyone can't hear this announcement, please raise your hand." The crowd chuckled, but Rollie wasn't done.

"Take me out to the ball game," he sang. "Take me out to the park."

By this time the Saints had stopped batting practice and were staring up at the booth. I found an imaginary object on the floor and ducked down behind the counter, pretending to pick it up so no one could see me.

Then Rollie began giving the baseball scores in the major leagues. "We have some scores…over in the National League…the Cubs are leading the Braves 3-2 in the third…." He went on through the entire major league schedule.

After both teams finished batting practice, Rollie announced the starting lineups with great flair, emphasizing each player's nickname. "Leading off for the Purple Aces, 'Scootin' Scooter McCray. Batting second, 'Ironman' Oliver Newby. Batting third is 'Beltin' Billy Barton." Rollie drew out the first syllable of each name and then paused long enough for the crowd cheer.

"Are these their real names?" I asked Jimmy.

"No. Dad makes 'em up. He gives them new ones every game."

When the lineups were over, Jimmy came on the air just minutes before the umpire yelled, "Play ball!" He introduced himself and then me, identifying me as a sidekick, scorekeeper, and color man. I wasn't sure what those were, but I figured I'd soon find out.

Jimmy's approach to the lineups, minus the nicknames, was a little more subdued. When he finished he read a commercial for Brockman's Grocery Store, where "homegrown fruits and vegetables are hauled in fresh every day. You can't get any fresher than Brockman's."

The customers at Maddie's heard the commercial for "Maddie's Cafe, the place where good people meet for good food." Smokey's Pool Room, the Purcell Drug Store, and Tulley's Tavern all had their own commercials. Over on South Street Grandma coerced Grandpa into turning off the Cardinals to listen to their grandson and neighbor.

"Leading off for the Saints is Eddie Woodhams, the second baseman. He's batting .302 with ten stolen bases," Jimmy began. "A breeze is blowing in from left field. The outfield is playing straight-away. Here's the windup, the pitch, and….it's a called strike."

And so it went through the early innings. When batters came up for the second and third times, Jimmy began asking me to report what they had done in previous at bats. My voice quavered at first; then I began to feel more comfortable. By the sixth inning, I was feeling confident enough to offer some "color" observations. Once I predicted when a runner was going to steal. I was starting to like this radio stuff.

The last two innings were anticlimactic as the home team hung on for the win. Jimmy began signing off, "That's a wrap for tonight, folks. Don't forget to patronize our sponsors. We'll see you next week when the Purple Aces take on the Jasper Engines right here at the Sand Bowl. For Garrett Gentry, this is Jimmy Brockman, saying goodnight and good luck."

Grandma was sitting in the dining room reading a newspaper when I walked in and asked if they'd listened to the game.

"We did, and we both thought you did a nice job. I'm sure it was fun, but I bet you're tired. Tip Albee expects you up bright and early tomorrow morning."

I'd forgotten about tomorrow.

The heat and humidity were both in the 90s the day we were to finish setting out the last field of melons. It had been more than two weeks since we'd started, counting the two days we lost to rain. Tip worked only six days a week, taking Sunday off for church and a day of rest, and that was the only day off I'd had since we resumed after the rains. It had threatened rain again last night on the radio. A heavy rainstorm had hit St. Louis late in the afternoon. We figured it was heading our way.

When I awoke, the radio said the rain missed us, hitting up around Sullivan. I rode out north of town just as the sun was peeking up over the hill, casting shadows of the civil air patrol and water towers over the length of the town. By the time I reached Tip's I was already soaked in sweat. It was only going to get worse.

By five o'clock we got to the end of the last row of melons. I wasn't sure how much more my aching back could take, but as we sat on the back of the wagon as Jack drove us up to the shed, I looked back at the field and felt good about what we had just done. I saw Tip admiring it too.

"Okay, everybody off the wagon and go wash up," yelled Tip, nodding toward the hand pump in the side yard, "and then into the shed."

We took turns pumping for each other. I poured a cup of water over my head, then lathered up with Wilma Albee's lye soap and dried off on a towel she had hung on the tree. Inside the shed Tip had set up two rows of tables lined with paper plates and utensils.

"You boys get your tin cups and draw yourselves a lemonade," Tip said, "Then take your plate and let Wilma load it up for ya." Mrs. Albee gave each of us a fillet of catfish, plus big helpings of baked beans, cole slaw, and fruit salad.

When everyone was done, Tip stood up and told everyone how proud he was of us, how hard we had worked, and how glad he was that the rain had held off, but now it was okay to let it rain. He then told everyone to open the white envelope next to his plate. I opened mine and pulled out a check for $60, and under it was a five-dollar bill. I looked around, and everyone else had a check and a five -dollar bill too.

"That five's a bonus. Ya'all helped me get my crop in on time so I figured you deserved a little extra."

Now I knew why Tip was so nice to work for.

CHAPTER 14

Purcell Station shut down on Memorial Day. People decorated the cemeteries, picnicked, swam in the river, or listened to the 500-Mile Race on the radio. Since Grandpa suffered his stroke, our options were limited. Jimmy Brockman volunteered to drive us out to the cemetery just east of town on the Wheatland Pike to decorate the graves of Grandma's relatives.

Early in the morning, while the dew was fresh, Grandma cut some long-stemmed roses and irises from the bed next to the house and found the porcelain vases she'd stored last year in the wood shed. We needed four bouquets in all but she made up five in case she saw a grave that wasn't decorated. Jimmy picked us up in his dad's Packard, and Grandma and I climbed in the backseat and set two vases each on the floor between our feet. Grandpa, following family protocol of males in the front, women and children in the back, held the other one in the passenger seat.

We drove east out of town and entered the iron gate of the cemetery. It was already well-decorated when we got there, although several people were still working on it. We drove to the far northeast side, where Grandma told Jimmy to stop. There we got out and carried the vases over to a small, gray headstone. It read: "Geraldine Abel, born 1870, died 1929."

"This is my mother's," she said. Then pointing to the one beside it, she said, "And this one belongs to my father." I read the inscription: "Bartholomew Abel, born 1866, died, 1932."

The markers were partly eroded, and the chiseled letters were dark and hard to read. "Did they live in Purcell Station?" I asked.

"No, they lived in a farmhouse east of town. Lived in the same house for forty-one years, until Mom died." She bent down and placed a vase next to the graves. "She got pneumonia. They put her in the hospital and she never got out."

"How many kids did she have?"

"Well, there were three of us girls and five boys. Another girl died in infancy."

I stepped over to the other marker. "What did your father do?"

"He farmed. Raised eight kids on eighty acres. Grew our own food, canned it, and stored it in the cellar for wintertime. We had a cow, some pigs, and chickens. We chopped our own firewood."

She walked over to another grave and set a vase down beside it. I looked at the inscription: "Luellen Abel, born June 5, 1893, died June 6, 1893."

"That's Luellen. She only lived a few hours."

"Why'd she die?"

"We don't know. Most babies were born at home back then. Something went wrong, and the doctor couldn't save her."

I stared at the stone and thought of how her life had only lasted one day. I wondered why some people get to live ninety years and others only one day.

Grandma was moving over to another grave. "And over here is the grave of my grandmother."

I followed her past a row of small tombstones and saw her place a vase of roses next to a marker. I bent down to read it. "Little Leaf Whitley, born 1848, died 1911."

"Was that her real name?

"It was. She was a full-blooded Powhatan Indian."

I stared at the name. "You mean we're part Indian, too? No one ever told me that. Did you know her?"

"Yes, but not well. She lived over in Pike County, so we didn't get to visit often. We didn't have a car then. But, she was very nice. She went to common school until she was thirteen, learned English, and then raised six children."

We stood and looked at the graves in silence for a moment, and then Grandpa started to walk to the car. I could tell he was getting tired. As we passed a small marker, Grandma lagged behind and then stopped. It was one of the few tombstones left undecorated, but Grandma had come prepared. As she bent down and placed the remaining vase in front of the stone, I leaned in to see the name. It read "Rasmus Barkus."

"Whose is it?" I asked.

"That's Pudge Barkus." She stepped back and stared for a long time. "He had a hard life. Died a young man."

"Why didn't his family place any flowers on his grave?"

"Not many of 'em left. They died or moved away. Only one's left around here now. You know him as Spooks."

I rode home in silence, thinking about Spooks and the family that had left him behind, and realized there was a lot I didn't know about him. All I knew was he was big, dark-skinned, slow, and he stuttered. He was a grown man who sat with the young people in church, pushed a wheelbarrow around town, played softball in the vacant lot, got teased by the men at Dub's, and was tormented by Jesse and his friends.

When we arrived home, the women prepared the dishes for the picnic we were having with the Brockmans and Francises. I helped the men move the picnic tables under the maple tree beside the driveway.

While the women were setting the table, Jimmy and I rocked in the front porch swing, listening to the broadcast of the Indianapolis 500. Sid Collins, the lead announcer, was building up the thrilling start of the race. We listened to the playing of the National Anthem and then the singing of "Back Home in Indiana." Then Tony Hulman said, "Gentlemen, start your engines,"

I had goose bumps tingling down my spine as the cars roared out on the pace lap. Then Sid screamed, "They're dropping the green flag and the race is on! Going into the first turn...take it away Luke Walton...."

We listened to the first fifty laps before Grandma called, "Come and get it, we're ready to eat."

We hurried to the table and as we lined up to fill our plates, Grandma asked us to bow our heads in a word of thanks. When she finished and everyone said, "Amen," we all dove in. Jimmy and I did our best to keep up with Rollie on seconds and then dessert. When we were sufficiently stuffed, we excused ourselves and returned to the porch swing to hear the end of the race.

Sid Collins was talking faster now. There was a duel between Troy Ruttman and Roger Ward, and the excitement was building for the finish. Just then, I heard Louise Francis call me.

"Your mother's on the phone," she said. "Your grandmother's talked to her and she wants to say hello to you." I hurried across the driveway and took the phone from Grandma.

"Hi, Mom. How are you? How's Dad?"

"I'm fine, and he's anxious to get home, but he knows it's a long haul yet. How have you been? Have you been helping out and earning your keep?"

"Yes, when I can. I just finished working in Tip Albee's melon fields. I put on six pounds, and I've been mowing the yard and helping in the garden, and I've been to the free show on Saturday nights." I paused to catch my breath. "And Jimmy Brockman invited me over to see the shack."

"I'd say you're very privileged. Not too many people get invited to the shack."

"Have you?"

"No. I think it must be men only."

"We're listening to the race now, and then I think we're going down to the river to take a swim."

"It doesn't sound like you're running out of things to do. I'll let you get back to the race. Take care of Grandma and Grandpa for me."

"Okay. You take care of Dad."

I returned to the porch just as Troy Ruttman crossed the finish line and took the checkered flag. Afterward, Jimmy and I went over to the tables where the adults sat and played a few games of H-O-R-S-E in the driveway. We played until late afternoon, when we were all hot and sweaty; then we put on our trunks and went down to the river for a swim.

A trail ran through the sycamores and tulip poplars, worn down by years of swimmers and fishermen stomping through to the bend that flowed under the bridge.

When we arrived there were two groups of boys already there. An older group, mostly in their teens, had gathered on the bridge and were jumping and screaming as they plunged into the river. Another group of younger boys was skinny-dipping from the sand bar. Jimmy must have sensed my surprise.

"You don't bother with swim trunks unless you're planning on jumping off the bridge. Got to wear them up there, though, or you could really rack yourself up hittin' the water at that height." He gave me a knowing smile. "If you know what I mean."

I nodded to let him know I did. "Don't they care if anybody sees 'em?" I asked.

"Nah. Girls stay away from here. They go upriver on the Parson Bend sand bar where they can lie out in the sun. They'd rather do that than jump from the bridge or swing on the rope."

"Do they swim naked, too?" I asked, trying not to act too interested.

"No, they figure the boys would spy on them if they did. We checked that out, just to be sure."

"What keeps the girls from spying on the boys?"

"Because it'd be all over town the next day. They'd never hear the end of it."

The water was cool and clear. The spring rains were over, and the muddy silt from upstream rains had cleared out. We waded out over the sand bar and were halfway across with the water up to our ribs when I stepped into a hole and disappeared in over my head. Startled, I tried to find the bottom with my foot, but couldn't. I could feel the current moving me downstream, and I began thrashing around, trying to find the surface. I needed air. I started to panic. Just then, I felt a hand grab my arm and pull me up. I surfaced. Jimmy was holding me up by my arms.

"Whoa," he said. "You got sucked into a hole. This current can pull you down before you know it."

Coughing and taking deep breaths, I dog-paddled over to where I could feel the bottom with my feet and regained my balance. I hadn't told Jimmy I couldn't swim.

I caught my breath and saw we were in the middle of the river. The bridge was just upstream, and on its steel frame stood a group of boys taking turns jumping into the water. Jimmy and I stood there for a moment watching them walk out to the edge of the steel frame and drop, screaming, doubling up their knees and throwing up their arms as they hit the water with a loud splash.

I wasn't sure they saw us, but then one of them looked over and waved. Jimmy yelled, "Hey, Goose."

The boy yelled back, "Jimmy!"

"Who's that?" I asked.

"That's Goose. He's one of my teammates—except he plays. I sit on the bench. He'll be a senior next year, too."

I saw Goose looking at us. "Hey, Jimmy, who's that with you?"

"Minnie Halderman's grandson," Jimmy yelled back, and the group on the bridge stopped to look.

"Hang on, I'll be right there," Goose yelled.

He did a cannonball jump off the bridge, and when he surfaced he came up spewing water in a rooster tail pointing in our direction. He swam over until he could stand up in front of us. "Hi, I'm Al Gossert. They call me Goose."

"Hi, I'm Garrett."

"He's here for the summer," said Jimmy, "staying with the Haldermans. He's...."

"Aaaauuugggghhhh!" The scream came from the bridge. The three of us looked up and saw a group of boys jumping off, one after another, their splashes spewing up plumes like small bombs exploding in the water. Then I heard it. A passenger train was coming fast from the south. With all the yelling and splashing and carrying on, it got here before anyone knew it.

It came over the bridge, rumbling and shaking it, just as the last boy cleared the steel girder and cratered the water beneath it. When it disappeared through the trees we could hear the crossing signals in town clanging, and then it got quiet, the rumble here and gone in seconds.

"That was the Dixie Flyer," Jimmy said. "The fastest express on the tracks. Goes from Chicago to Jacksonville in twenty-five hours. We try to stay out of its way when we hear it coming."

"That was close!" I said.

"Nah, not really," said Jimmy. "That's all part of the game. They see how long they can stay up there. The last guy to jump wins."

"You mean that scream was not because they were scared?"

"Not at all," said Goose, laughing. "That was a scream of excitement. That's how they get their kicks, facing danger and beating it. It's a sport."

"If you jump before the train comes around the corner, you're called a chicken, and if you stay until it enters the bridge you're a warrior, and if you're the last to jump, you're a hero," added Jimmy.

"That's pretty scary. Has anyone ever been hit by the train?" I asked.

"No, but some have come close. It sounds closer when they go into town on Saturday night and talk about it in front of the girls," said Goose.

"Yeah," said Jimmy, "The more they tell it, the better it gets. There're some girls who think Jesse Sprowl nearly lost his leg. The story gained credibility one time when he limped up Main Street one Saturday night, bragging how the train barely nipped him."

The whooping and hollering ended, and the older boys climbed back up to the bridge and began jumping off again.

"You want to try it?" Jimmy asked.

"Not really. I don't swim that well."

"Then let's go up on the rope. That's a little tamer, and the water's not as deep.

I wasn't given a choice.

Up on the bank, a rope hung from a limb of a large sycamore tree jutting out over the water. A knot was tied in the bottom of the rope, and that's where Jimmy said I should put my feet after I push off. Jimmy showed me how to grab a hold and he pulled me back up the bank. Then running down the bank I swung out over the water. When the rope got to the end I let go, dropping into the river. It was over my head, just deep enough I could push off the bottom. I sprang up just as Goose took hold of my arm and pulled me until I touched shallow water.

"Perfect," yelled Jimmy. I'd faked an eagerness to try it, but now I wanted to do it again. Soon I joined the others in letting out screaming howls before hitting the water.

We had been there more than an hour when the whistle of another train came up from the south. It was slower than the other one, and all the boys on the bridge took their time getting out of the way. When the engine crossed the bridge we could see it was pulling a long line of box-cars. The doors were open and they were empty.

"They're stopping. They must be dropping cars on the side at the Co-op," said Goose.

Just then something caught my eye as the last car crossed the bridge. "Did you see that? Someone jumped out of that boxcar."

"There's another one," said Jimmy.

They rolled forward after they hit the ground, then waited until the train passed, got up, and brushed themselves off. After the train disappeared, another figure came walking up the tracks from the direction of Sprowl's shed. I squinted to see who it was.

"I think that's Jesse coming up to meet 'em," Jimmy said. "They must be his cousins."

"That's bad news," said Goose. "It's never any good when they're together."

The three of them joined up, then walked to the bridge where they met up with the other boys who were there jumping. Hearing what Goose said about them, I was glad we weren't up there. If his cousins were anything like Jesse, I didn't want any part of them, either.

We swung on the rope a while longer, but I wasn't having as much fun. I kept looking toward the bridge, hoping Jessse wouldn't see me. I was on the swing, dropping into the water, when suddenly Goose yelled, "Look!" He was pointing at the bridge.

I bobbed up and shook the water out of my hair to see where Goose was pointing. The group of boys had grown now, and there seemed to be a commotion.

I climbed out of the water and asked Jimmy what was going on.

"It's probably Jesse. Something's got everybody stirred up," he said. They were all standing in a circle in the middle of the bridge. It was getting louder.

"It looks like there's about to be a fight," said Goose.

We heard shouting. Then someone let out a big belly laugh, and the others must have thought something was real funny, too, for they all laughed. Then I saw an object fly in the air, and one of the boys jumped up and caught it and threw it across the circle to another boy. It looked like someone in the middle lunged for it just as that boy tossed it to someone else, and there was more laughter.

"It looks like... like...oh—uh, I think...they've got Spooks," said Goose.

A gap opened up in the circle, and we could see his bib overalls and red bandana. They were tossing his straw hat around the circle and taunting him to try to get it. Each time he lunged toward the boy holding the hat, the boy would hold it until the last second and then throw it to someone else. Spooks kept lunging for it again and again, until he began to wobble.

When one boy caught it, Spooks dove toward him, stumbled, and tackled him just as he released the hat. The two of them fell down on the cross ties and for a moment I thought they would roll off into the river. Some of the boys helped their friend up, but they let Spooks lie there as they all laughed.

Spooks got up to his knees and tried to stand up, but Jesse pushed him back down and straddled his back like he was riding a bronco.

Just then Goose yelled. "Let him alone, Jesse."

Jesse stopped and looked down at the water. The younger boys had all stopped swinging on the rope and were staring up at the bridge.

The boys on the bridge got quiet, too. His cousins moved over to the edge and looked down, like they're looking to pick a fight.

"Let him up. He's not bothering anybody," Goose yelled again.

Jesse got up off Spooks' back and stood on the side looking down. His cousin said something under his breath, and Jesse's eyes became narrow and menacing. "Why don't you come on up here and make me?" he sneered.

Jimmy and I looked at Goose. There were more of them than there were of us.

"Just give him his hat back and let him go," said Goose.

Jesse stood over Spooks a little longer to let everyone know he didn't take orders. Then he slowly stepped away, but not before giving Spooks a quick kick on the rear. He walked over to the boy holding Spooks' hat, took it out of his hand, and stood facing Goose.

"Here, if he wants his hat back he can get it himself." With that, Jesse sailed the hat out over the river. He looked at Spooks who was struggling to get up off his knees, and with his foot pushed Spooks, rolling him over and off the cross ties, screaming and plunging into the river below.

The scream stopped abruptly when Spooks hit the water, his body making a huge crater in front of us. Goose and Jimmy dove under and within seconds had a hold of him. They came up to the surface, and all I could see was the thrashing and flailing of arms and legs. Goose was under him with his arms around Spooks' barrel chest. Jimmy came up next and lifted his body into a flat position to let Goose pull Spooks to shallow water. I couldn't swim well enough to help, but I saw Spooks' hat floating down on the shoal side of the river and dog paddled after it.

They pulled Spooks ashore, and he sat slumped on the sand bar coughing and hacking and spitting up water. He looked dazed. Jimmy untied Spooks' work shoes and socks and squeezed out the water. I took a towel I'd brought from home and tried to dry Spooks' face and hair and arms.

He sat there panting. It took several minutes to get him settled down.

"I c—can't swim," he uttered.

Goose and Jimmy sat in the sand beside Spooks, exhausted.

"That guy is worthless," Goose said. "And his cousins, too." His face was red with rage. I don't know what he would have done to Jesse, but it didn't matter anyway. Jesse, his cousins, and all the other boys were gone.

We waited until we'd all caught our breath, and then we dried Spooks off and put his shoes back on for the walk up the hill. We reached Goose's pickup truck and helped Spooks into the back. Jimmy and I climbed in with him, and Goose drove up to Maddie's and turned into the back alley. We helped Spooks out of the truck and into the back door, into the room where he slept. Jimmy opened his closet and took a pair of overalls off a hook and some socks and underwear from his chest of drawers and left them on his bed. Then we left him alone and went in the café and told Maddie what happened.

It was nine o'clock and dark outside by the time Grandma finished drying the supper dishes. I was worn out from everything that had happened and ready for sleep. I went in my room to get ready for bed but, instead, came back to the kitchen and sat down. There was something on my mind.

When Grandma cleared the last cup from the drying rack, I asked, "You know what you said at the cemetery, when you put those flowers on the grave of that Barkus guy?"

"Yes. What about it?"

"Well, you said his only relative left around here was Spooks. I've been thinking, just who is Spooks?"

Grandma sat down, rested her elbows on the table, and rubbed her temples. Closing her eyes, she took a deep breath, as if trying to figure out where to start. Finally, she began.

"Well, it's late, so I'll make a long story short. You see, his mother died when he was three, and his father raised him and his twelve brothers and sisters. When his father died, Spooks was nine and he was left with an older sister. The others had all moved away or were off fighting in the war. When he was almost grown his sister married and moved to Missouri, so Spooks had no place to stay. He was not able to provide for himself, so Maddie let him live in the back room of her cafe. He's been there over twenty years now. He gets his meals there for doing odd jobs and gets a little money by doing work for people around town."

"Is that why he has that wheelbarrow?"

"Yes. He's hauling trash or moving things for people. Most of 'em give him work so they can pay him and make him feel he earned it."

"How did he get the name 'Spooks?"

"Well, with all that death and turmoil when he was young, the story goes that he'd have nightmares and get up crying and go get in bed with one of his sisters. When they asked what was wrong, he'd say, 'There's spooks in my bed.' The name stuck and he's been called that ever since."

"But why do people pick on him?"

"I guess because he is big and slow and he stutters. For some reason, some people think that's funny. But there may be more to it than that. Some probably do it because of his skin."

"What about his skin?"

"You've probably noticed it darker than most people's around here, and there's a reason." She paused. "You see, his grandfather came up north through the Underground and stopped off at Purcell Station around time of the Civil War."

"You mean the Underground Railroad?"

"That's right. He was a slave. The story goes that he had bounty hunters right on his tail when he showed up at the back door of the old Winslow house. That's up on the tracks at the north end of town, behind the baseball field. It was a stopover for the Underground."

"Is it still there?"

"What's left of it. It's abandoned now. It's that old house north of the saw mill. You may've seen it. Sometime kids get in there and smoke cigarettes and who knows what else, and some say it's haunted, but that's just kid talk. Anyway, some good people hid him and kept him out of harm's way. Then, when the war ended, he just stayed. People kinda took him in, and he ended up marrying a German girl from across the river in Gibson County. They had kids and settled a little colony of other slave descendants down the river in Gibson. Others settled here. Then they had kids, and Spooks was one of them."

"So that's why they pick on him?"

"No one ever says so, but I suspect that's part of it, along with those other reasons. Some people have a problem with that. There's prejudice everywhere and I'm sure some of it's right here in Purcell Station. But, I've discovered life is one trial after another to see who has the mettle to stand up and do the right thing, and a lot of people in this town have done that. It was the good people here who saved his grandfather's life, and there're a lot of good folks here still saving people. You see them every day doing things for Spooks, but they do good things for others, too. It's just that sometimes it's not out in the open. You'll see that yourself someday."

CHAPTER 15

June arrived and the cool current of the river never felt so good. Jimmy, Goose, and I went down every afternoon that first week, when the temperature and humidity both hovered around 95. I collected my nerve and became better at jumping off the bridge and bobbing up like an apple in a tub of water. But, the rope swing became my favorite. I learned to climb up the high bank, swing out over the water, and fly like a squirrel jumping trees. I even got to flipping over in midair before landing feet first. It made Jimmy and Goose proud that I caught on so fast, and the other boys were starting to notice, too. A couple of times Jesse came out of the trees and watched for a while before sneering about how "anybody could do that." He always left before proving it.

I didn't share any of these acrobatics with Grandma, nor did I tell her about the game of "chicken" played out on the bridge.

In the mornings I spent time in the garden, working in the yard, running errands, or using my bicycle to explore. I would ride to the top of the hill, then turn around and coast down Main Street, swerving like a downhill skier to control my speed, stopping where Main Street ended at the train depot. There I got to talking with Taylor Barth. He was a tall, friendly, white-haired man who wore a captain's cap and a green vest that made him look dignified and official.

Most of the time he spent tidying up, sweeping the floor, checking freight or baggage, and chatting with anybody who came his way. Whenever I would stop by, he was more than willing to make conversation. On those occasions I learned he had retired seven years earlier from the L & N Railroad as a brakeman. He had lost his wife three years ago to pneumonia, and his only son had been killed in the war, the big one. "Dubya, Dubya Two," he called it.

When I first heard this, we were sitting on the bench outside the station waiting for a train. My uncles had served in the war, too, and I'd heard just enough war stories to stir my curiosity. I wasn't sure how much he wanted to talk about it, so I started out in a roundabout way asking if his son had enlisted or been drafted.

"He enlisted. Walked right in to the recruitment office the day after Pearl Harbor and joined up, like about everybody else who saw what was coming."

There was a silence and I didn't know whether to go on. Finally, I didn't have to.

"He was with Patton's Third Army in France," he started, and then waited. "They got bogged down in Alsace-Lorraine outside of Metz and were running out of gas and supplies when the Germans closed in, and they had nowhere to go. He got hit with mortar. Just like that, it was over. That was August, 30th, 1944."

I could see his eyes getting watery. He shifted his legs and tugged on his cap.

"A few days later, my wife was sitting in the parlor playing the piano when someone knocked on the door. She got up to answer it and looked through the curtain and saw a man standing there in uniform, and she nearly fell to her knees. Nobody liked seeing a man in uniform standing on their front porch. She knew what he was there for."

"What was he...your son...what was he like?"

"Like most of the boys in Purcell Station. Aw, we have some bad apples, but most of 'em around here grow up and work hard and try to make something of themselves. Then some, like Jed, grow up and go to war and never come back. But he wasn't the only one. The Edsons and McGriffs and Coonrods all lost sons, too. Every one of them trying to save France."

He waited, staring at the platform. I thought he was through, but he wasn't. "All from little old Purcell Station, Indiana, on the other side of the world, trying to save France."

He raised his head and stared at the horizon toward the bottoms to the west. A long silence followed, and I began to feel uncomfortable. Then I saw his face and the redness and the glistening in his eyes. I'd heard enough to know when to stop, so I changed the subject, but just a little.

"Did Jed know my mother?"

He took a hanky out of his vest and blew his nose. "Know her? Of course!" He perked up. "They went to school together for twelve years. They were pretty close friends. Took her to the prom, if I remember right."

"Were they... uh, were they seeing each other?" I asked.

"Not like you might think. Leah was different. She had ambition and didn't let boys get in the way. She kind of held them at arm's length, but she and Jed were great friends."

"Were they still friends when Jed enlisted?"

"Right up to the end. Leah Halderman was friends with everybody. That comes from her mother. Yes, they were friends, but she was gone from here then. She'd gone off to college, got married to one of the Gentry boys from down in the bottoms—but I don't suppose I need to tell you that—and moved somewhere up north. I guess you know where. When Jed died, one of the first persons we called was your mother. She came home immediately and sat up with my wife and me until the funeral was over, and Jeb was in the grave. That's what she did, and I've never forgotten it."

I started to ask more, but the sound of a whistle coming out of the north changed the subject. Taylor rose from the bench and went in to check the schedule for the southbound local. The crossing guard came down as the train eased into the station. Taylor repositioned his cap and stood erect, waving to the engineers as the engine passed. It rolled to a stop, and the engine hissed, belched, and released a long, final hiss before falling silent.

At that moment a pickup truck wheeled into the north side of the station, sliding to a stop in the loose gravel. Bud Tate jumped out with a canvas bag slung over his shoulder and headed for the sliding door of the mail car. A man inside threw off another canvas bag and reached down to take Bud's cargo. They exchanged some friendly chatter, and then Bud picked up the other bag and walked back toward his truck, nodding to Taylor and me.

"You almost didn't make it, Bud." Taylor said.

"Yeah, you know how it is at the post office. Everybody wantin' to stop and talk. It's hard to get any work done," he said, glancing back at Taylor. "See you tomorrow."

Taylor had already begun talking to a passenger who'd just stepped off the train. He wore a suit and tie, and his hair was combed back and parted down the middle. He had two bags, one large and one small, which looked like a briefcase. I studied him. He looked familiar.

"Need some help with your bags, mister?" Taylor asked.

"No, thanks, I'm just going over there," he said, nodding toward the Purcell Hotel.

He took his bags, crossed the street, and climbed the steps to the hotel. Taylor and I stood watching as he disappeared. I felt I'd seen him somewhere: the hair, parted in the middle and slicked back, didn't fit in around here.

I asked Taylor. "Have you ever seen him before?"

"Yep! Came through here about a month ago. I remember him because not many come through here dressed like that."

"He looks like someone I've…you say a month ago? You mean about the time I got here?"

"About then, I guess." Taylor tipped his cap up and scratched his head. "Fact of the matter is he might have got here the same day. I remember he only had a briefcase and a newspaper tucked under his arm. No suitcase. I thought that was strange for someone staying in a hotel."

"Did he get here before I did?"

"If I remember right, he got in around mid afternoon, maybe on the 3:15 local. You got here later. I remember because it was almost quittin' time and no one was here to meet you."

Just then it hit me. "On the train! He was the man on my train! He was reading a newspaper, and when I mentioned Purcell Station to the lady across from me, he dropped his paper and stared at me for a long time. He just stared right through me like I'd said something wrong."

"But if he was on your train, how did he get here before you did?"

"When we got to Terre Haute, he disappeared. Then I saw him in the ticket line. He must have got on the early train. I took the 3:35."

"That would be about right. I'm sure he got here before you did."

"And I remember the ticket man said, 'You too' when I told him I wanted a ticket to Purcell Station."

"Well, that makes sense."

"Did you hear his accent? He sounded like the lady who sat across from me on the train. She was from somewhere out east, Baltimore I think. He sounded like that, too."

"Could be. He sure isn't from around here."

"I wonder what he's doing here. That odd look he gave me on the train—it sure was strange."

"Then he should fit right in around here." Taylor was smiling.

We stayed there trying to figure out the stranger until a long, slow freight train passed through. When the caboose came by, the brakeman was standing on the back platform and we exchanged waves. Then I stood up and said, "I've got to be going. I'll stop by the post office and get the mail if Mr. Tate has it sorted already."

"He'll have it sorted if nobody stops in to visit."

Bud's truck was sitting in front, and the mail bag was gone, so I figured he'd at least got that far. When I entered, a bell jingled over the door to let Bud know someone was there. I walked over to the bank of boxes and started to fiddle with the Haldermans' combination, then peeked through the glass window and noticed the box was empty. I approached the service window and saw Bud standing at a table, sorting mail.

"Hello, Garrett, if you're looking for Haldermans' mail, it ain't sorted yet."

"That's okay. I'll wait if it won't be too long."

"Shouldn't be too long, but in that case, why don't you come back here and help out?" he said, pointing to a side door that led to the back room. "It'll make your wait shorter."

I did as he said and entered the back room. The air reeked of old paper, stamp glue, and ink pads. Bud's bald head was glistening under a bare light bulb hanging from the ceiling. He was wearing a green visor like the guy at the train station in Terre Haute.

"Here, take this stack and put 'em in the boxes. The names are underneath, so be sure you get 'em in the right ones."

98

I picked up the stack and placed them where they belonged. Then I picked up another stack, and that's when I saw it. The letter was addressed to:

Minnie Halderman

Box 117

Purcell Station, Indiana

I glanced at the return address and saw the name Jake Halderman and a military address I didn't understand. It was Uncle Jake. He was in the Navy somewhere in the South Pacific, but we didn't really know where. With the war in Korea, everything was kept pretty secret. I turned to Bud and asked if I could take this home when I got through.

"Sure, and here's something else." He tossed a postcard. It was from Cleveland, Ohio, and had a picture of Lake Erie and a yacht basin on the back. I turned it over.

Dear Mom, Dad, and Garrett, This is the view from Edward's new room. He has moved from the Clinic to a convalescent center along the lake shore west of the city. He is starting his rehab program. He is glad to be out of the hospital. I think he is feeling better. We miss you. Love, Leah.

I finished my sorting and told Bud goodbye. Racing home, I rode through the back alley and ran into the kitchen.

"I got the mail," I yelled. "There's a letter from Jake and a postcard from Mom. She says dad is feeling better and has moved out of the hospital."

Grandma was standing over the stove and when she heard me shout she put down the wooden spoon. Taking the postcard, she scanned it and smiled. She then ripped open the letter from Jake and read it quietly. I watched her for signs if it was good news or bad and seeing neither, I waited nervously. Finally, she put it down and said, "Jake's coming home."

CHAPTER 16

Jesse wasn't around, but the heat spell was, and it stayed with us another week. He'd stayed out of sight since the day he pushed Spooks off the bridge. I told Skipper what happened, and she said Jesse was just smart enough to know when he'd met his match. She was referring to Goose, who had told Jesse to stop and was strong enough to back it up. Skipper and I made a point to check on Spooks every so often, just to make sure he was okay. It wasn't just Jesse we were concerned about, but his cousins too. Jesse always had more courage when they were around.

Jesse's absence freed Jimmy, Goose, and me to enjoy the swimming hole and get out of the heat. We stayed every afternoon until the shadows began to lengthen or we got hungry, whichever came first. After supper, Grandma, Grandpa, and I would go out on the front porch and listen to the radio through the open window. If the Cardinals weren't on, Grandma would tune in to her favorite station and listen to Hoagy Carmichael tunes. One of her favorites was "In the Cool, Cool, Cool of the Evening."

"*In the cool, cool of the evening, tell 'em I'll be there. In the cool, cool, cool of the evening, better save a chair...*" Grandma sat swinging and fanning herself as the scent of roses drifted over the porch. "*In the shank of the night, when the doin's are right, you can tell 'em I'll be there.*"

Grandpa started calling the evening time after supper and before dark the "shank" of the night, when everything was still and quiet and the sun was laid to rest. It became our nightly ritual. Sometimes the neighbors would join us. When they did Jimmy and I would dismiss ourselves at seven o'clock and go over to the shack for his nightly radio show.

By mid-June, he had picked up a sizeable audience and my name was getting known around town, too. I was becoming someone other than Minnie Halderman's grandson and Leah Gentry's son.

My casual evenings with Jimmy came to an end, though, when Tip asked me to help turn vines in his melon fields. I had no idea what that was until he explained that's what they do before they cultivate the melons. You take a pole with a hook on the end and walk along and turn the vines so they all run in the same direction so the tractor can plow between the rows.

It sounded like another one of those long, hot days, but when I found out Skipper was going to help, I no longer considered the heat a problem.

By Saturday, the drought brought high winds with a storm brewing in the southwest. We finished under darkening clouds shortly after noon, and not a moment too soon. Coming in at forty miles an hour, the winds were kicking up the sand until it was difficult to see the end of the field. Tip got to the end of a row just as Skip and I finished, so he drove over to us and yelled, "Hop on. You won't be able to walk in this wind."

I hung onto my straw hat with one hand and grabbed the fender with the other. The sand was blowing in my eyes, and I had to turn away from the wind. I held tight as we bounced along the sandy path until we reached the barn lot where Tip wheeled us into the open door of the packing shed. The wind howled and rattled the tin roof, shaking the rafters.

"How was that for timing, huh?" asked Tip. "It was a raw sky in the southwest. I knew it was comin.'"

He was yelling over the din of the storm, because by now large sheets of rain pelted the tin roof and sides of the shed, making it hard to hear his voice. Tip motioned for us to follow him, and he led us into a side room he kept as an office. It was quieter, although we could still hear the rain beating against the roof. He walked behind a cluttered desk and bent over a small safe sitting next to the wall. He opened it without working the combination and pulled out a drawer, taking some bills in the palm of one hand and counting them with the thumb of the other.

"Here, you've earned it," he said, stepping around the desk. "And thanks for getting done before the storm."

I counted three ten-dollar bills. We both thanked him.

"Now, how are you two going to get back to town in this storm?" he asked.

"I drove the Blue Bruise since it looked like rain," Skipper said. That's what she called the old beat-up pickup truck.

Tip pulled up a couple of cantaloupe crates and offered them as chairs. He took a seat on the swivel chair behind his desk and rolled it back far enough that he could put his feet up on his desk. The rain showed no sign of letting up. I figured this was how we were going to pass time until it did.

For the next hour, we were Tip's captive audience. We heard about the First World War and the friends he lost in it, the Great Depression and how Purcell Station had gotten through it, and about the time President Roosevelt came to Vincennes to dedicate the George Rogers Clark Memorial. He talked about the farmers down in the bottoms and how some of them had become "fifty-cent millionaires" when the oil wells started coming in, and he talked about others who'd lost their crops to drought and their farms to foreclosures in the 1930s.

When he finished, he sat staring at the top of his desk and the mess of papers strewn over it. Finally he said, "It's letting up some. I'm going out and start the Blue Bruise."

He slipped on an old rain jacket and headed into the wind and drizzle. It was several minutes before the blue pickup came sputtering around the barn and into the shed. Tip got out, leaving the motor running, and lifted my bike over the side and laid it in the bed. He patted the back fender and said, "Ya want me to follow you, just in case?"

"No, we'll be all right," Skipper said. "It's okay once it gets going."

The rain lightened up by the time we got to town, and Skipper dropped me off in the driveway.

The free show was cancelled because of the weather. We sat on the porch after supper, watching and listening to the rain, the first one in over a month. When the wind blew it to the outer edges of the porch, Grandma moved her rocker closer to the parlor window, but I stayed put, feeling the fresh mist on my skin. It felt good after my morning in the hot sun. Again the rain slowed, only to pick up again. Finally, during one of the slack periods I asked Grandma if she needed anything from the store.

Grandpa spoke up. "I don't suppose your wanting to go into town has anything to do with that fresh money burning a hole in your pocket, does it?"

"Maybe a dime for a salty dog; the rest is going in my sock drawer with the money I made last month.

"That reminds me, just which drawer is that, anyway? I searched all morning for that money, and I couldn't latch onto it."

"It's in the same drawer as those mouse traps I baited last week."

Grandma smiled. "No, I don't need anything, but you go ahead and run along." I think she thought I'd finally put Grandpa in his place.

The night was still young when I rode up Main Street and stopped in front of the Purcell Drug Store. It was packed with people getting in out of the rain. When I edged inside the front door, I headed over to the soda fountain, but there were no seats left.

The Andrews Sisters were singing on the jukebox, but I could barely hear it for the noise. As I inched my way back to the front, a stool at the counter came open, and I grabbed it. The man on my left had his back to me, but when he turned around I saw him. It was Spooks. He stared at me for a minute like he was trying to place me; then he grinned and said, "You're G-Garrett."

"Hi, Spooks."

"You h-helped me out of the w-water."

"Along with Jimmy and Goose. I'm friends with Skipper, too."

The girl working behind the counter come up, wiped the counter, and asked us what we'd have.

"I'd like a Coke and a bag of peanuts." I turned to Spooks. "You want a salty dog, too? I'm buying."

"Okay," he said. "S-Skipper's nice. One time she helped me wh—en Jesse was being m—mean to me. Sh...es not scared of Jesse."

"I know. She's nice to everybody."

The waitress came back with two bottles of Coke and two bags of peanuts. "Here you go. That'll be twenty cents."

I paid her, then shook the peanut bag a few times and put the corner of it in my mouth, biting it between my teeth and tearing it open. I let the peanuts slide into the bottle, put my thumb over the opening, and shook it until the peanuts were soaked and the pop began to fizz. Spooks watched me and then tried to do the same with his bottle. His large hands were having trouble. Some of his peanuts spilled onto the counter.

"Need some help?" I asked.

"Yeah, can't get 'em in bottle."

"Here, try it like this." I showed him how to cup his hand around the mouth of the bottle to form a chute.

He tried it, and it worked better this time. When he was done, he shook the bottle the way he'd seen me do and took a long swig, munching the peanuts as he set the bottle down.

"That's goood," he said.

We sat there munching the soggy peanuts. Then Spooks began talking, telling me about his wheel-barrow and the jobs he did for people around town. He talked about the people who were good to him: Maddie, the Francises, the Brockmans, the Manions, the Slinkers, Taylor Barth, Lady Muldoon, my grandparents, and people at church. But, he got most excited when he told me about the home run he'd hit playing softball in the vacant lot.

"I h—hit a home run, and all the kids ch—eered and slapped me on the b—back," he said, "and then they brought me in here and b—bought me a Coke.

I remembered it, when all the kids fumbled the ball and let Spooks score.

When we finished our drinks, Spooks asked me to walk outside with him. He wanted to show me his wheelbarrow. It was parallel parked in front of the drugstore between two cars. He was especially proud of the license plate attached to the handlebars. "Th—is makes it l—legal." he said.

He offered me a ride home, but I thanked him and told him maybe some other time.

It was time for the news when I got home. Jimmy was already on the air when I pushed open the door to the shack. He waved me in and motioned to the empty chair beside the desk He was speaking into the microphone and reading a clipping taken from the evening edition of the Commercial.

"Chinese forces launched their second artillery and mortar attack on T-Bone Ridge last night...." He finished the news from Korea and moved on to local news. "The county commissioners voted two-to-one last night on the contract for expanding the county jail...."

Jimmy finished reading from the stack of clippings and then paused. "And now a word from our sponsor. If you're looking for the place to get fresh meats, fruits, and vegetables, Brockman's Grocery is the place to shop." He went through the specials on smoked ham, whole fryers, and five-pound bags of potatoes.

When he finished, he resumed with the news.

"On the local scene, the Purcell Station Volunteer Fire Department will hold its annual fish fry this Friday. Everyone is invited to enjoy the festivities. There will be a raffle with numerous prizes, including an electric cattle prod from the Farm Bureau Co-op, a portable cider press from Slinker's General Store, and a burial plot at Hilltop Cemetery. Proceeds will go toward purchasing a new tanker for the department."

Jimmy took a deep breath and then added, "That's a wrap for tonight. Stay tuned for Night Lights." Jimmy placed an LP on the turntable and dropped the needle. It was Perry Como, and he would sing until sign-off at the end of the hour.

CHAPTER 17

The food and drinks at the fire department's fish fry were donated. The fish were caught in the river throughout the spring and kept frozen down at the Princeton Frozen Food Locker. A number of men contributed to this catch, including Mr. Francis, who had a favorite fishing hole upriver that he kept to himself. One time I hinted I would like to go there with him, but when he finally got around to asking me, I was working for Tip and couldn't go. I think he already knew that.

The Women's Auxiliary of the Baptist Church mixed up large vats of lemonade and iced tea. All the other churches, including the Lutherans and Catholics out in the country, brought in food, since it was their fire department, too. The Catholics also loaned their bingo boards for after-dinner entertainment.

Every summer on the last Friday of June, the fire truck was removed and parked outside, and long tables were set up inside where the food was placed. By 5:30, there were already enough people there to fill the first seating and a line had formed all the way out to the street.

Grandpa, Nub Hawkins, Tip Albee, and others who were used to eating supper at 5 o'clock, were in line toward the front. I waited until Jimmy and Goose arrived and hung around with them until getting in line. By the time we got our food there were few empty tables, so we had to take what was left and sit at a table with some farmers I'd seen in town on Saturday nights.

Shortly after we sat down, one of the farmers kept staring at Goose and Jimmy, like he was trying to place where he might have seen them. Finally, he looked at Goose and said, "You're the boy who beat us in the tourney last year, aren't you?"

The other farmers stopped talking and looked at Goose.

"I guess it depends on who you are," said Goose, although he had a pretty good idea.

"Gibault Catholic. You're the one that made that lucky shot from center court at the gun, aren't you?"

Gibault was the Catholic school "up at the city," as the locals say. As far as the citizens of Purcell Station were concerned, Goose's shot, putting Gibault out of the sectional tournament, couldn't have happened to a better team. Local fans made no secret of their dislike of the private school raiding the players from Purcell Station and other nearby towns. Private schools didn't have districts the public schools had, so they could take players regardless of where they lived. Over the years, more than one local boy had helped Gibault defeat the boys from the Station.

"Well, I wouldn't say it was lucky," said Goose. "Coach set that play up. We just did what he told us to."

"Yeah, It was good coaching and good execution," added Jimmy.

"Well, your 'execution' cost me fifty dollars," said the farmer.

"That'll teach you. Maybe you'll bet on the good guys next time." Jimmy smiled.

"I thought I did last time," he said.

"No, those were the bad guys," Jimmy said. "Goose here is money in the bank. You'd better remember that next season."

"Better yet, why don't you come up to the city and play for us next year?" the farmer said, looking at Goose. That brought out a few chuckles from the other farmers.

"Aha!" said Coach Francis. He had been sitting with Rollie Brockman at the next table. He'd gotten up to go for a glass of iced tea and had caught just enough of the conversation to hear the invitation for Goose to join the enemy next season. "My suspicions have been realized. You gentlemen have just broken a cardinal rule of the Indiana High School Athletic Association—attempting to entice an athlete to transfer schools for athletic purposes."

"Now, Coach," said the farmer, recognizing Coach Francis, "we don't do that sort of thing at Gibault."

"You won't if I turn you in," added Mr. Francis with a twinkle in his eye.

"You know we got enough city kids who can play. We don't need your boys."

"That's good to know. Does that go for all the other little towns around here, too?" asked Mr. Francis, but he was walking away smiling, not expecting an answer.

The farmer looked back at Goose. "Just forget I said that, for the record, anyway. But, if you want a good Catholic education, we might have a place for you—for purely academic reasons, of course."

"I don't suppose he'd be expected to play basketball, too, would he?" asked Jimmy.

"No, no, of course not," the farmer grinned. "Unless he wanted to."

The rest of the meal we spent replaying all last season's basketball games. Apparently the farmers had attended all of Gibault's games and many of Purcell Station's, too, and knew the names of all the players. It was after hearing Jimmy talk that one of the men said, "Hey, are you the kid who does the baseball games at the Sand Bowl on that little radio station?"

"I am. How'd you know?"

"On a clear night I can pull it in on my radio."

"You can? How far away do you live?" asked Jimmy.

"About two miles up on the highway and a mile west."

Jimmy stared at the man. "You pick it up that far away?"

"Sometimes. Don't worry, I won't turn you in. That is, if you won't turn me in for trying to recruit your friend here." He turned to his friends who were snickering.

Jimmy looked pale. He didn't want his signal to reach the highway where the wrong people might hear it. "It's a deal. Forget my station, and we'll forget what you said to Goose."

They all agreed and went back for dessert, but I could tell Jimmy was nervous.

The entertainment had already started on the open side of the parking lot. The first attraction was the basketball shooting contest. For 25 cents, a person could purchase three shots from the free throw line. If one of them went in, he shot until he missed. The person with the highest number of consecutive baskets at the end of the night won $10. The second and third most baskets won $5 and $3. There was no shortage of men and boys, plus a girl or two, who thought they could win.

A crowd had already circled around the court, and a line of contestants had formed behind the table where chances were sold. Taylor Barth manned the table, selling tickets, and Rollie Brockman stood on the court beside the free throw line holding a microphone.

"First up, we have last year's runner-up, Spike Hochmeister."

The crowd clapped politely. Spike was from the bottoms west of town and not well-connected to folks in town. He also once played for the hated Gibault Patriots. After stepping to the line, he let it fly and swished the first shot, so his string started at that point.

I was standing with Jimmy and Goose behind the basket, facing the crowd. I wondered if Skipper was there. I hadn't seen her all evening, but I knew she was coming. Scanning the crowd, I lost track of Rollie's counting until I heard, "Thirteen… fourteen…ooooh, sorry, Spike. Let's give him a hand, folks."

Several more tried to beat Spike's fourteen consecutive shots, but none made it. I could see Goose getting anxious. Finally he said, "I'm going to try it. I've hit more than that in a row before." He inched his way through the crowd and got in line behind the table. As more people finished eating, the crowd grew bigger.

I looked for Skipper, but someone else caught my eye: a man standing behind a group of boys on the far side, partially hidden. The side of his face looked familiar. I moved away from Jimmy, circling to my left to get a better look. Just as I got a glimpse, he moved slightly, and I lost him for a moment. I kept walking, and then I saw his whole face. It was the stranger from the train!

I walked back to Jimmy and nudged him. "You see that man over there?" I asked, pointing toward the bleachers. "The man in the blue shirt. See? Standing behind those boys."

"Yeah. What about 'im?"

"I was down at the depot one day talking to Taylor Barth, and this guy got off the train, carrying two bags, and went into the hotel across the street."

"What's so unusual about that?"

"Well, the way he was dressed, and his accent was different. But what's really odd is he was on the same train I took the day I came here. We'd just pulled out of Indianapolis and he heard me mention Purcell Station to the lady across from me and he acted really strange. Put down his newspaper and stared at me like I'd said something wrong. For some reason the name Purcell Station must have meant something to him. Then, I was at the depot talking to Taylor Barth the other day, and he got off the train and went across the street to the hotel. He acted like he didn't want to talk to anyone. Whatta you think he's doing here?"

Jimmy thought for a moment. "Maybe he's a revenuer."

"What would he be doing here?"

"Maybe he's interested in what Eddie Sprowl's doing in that shed down by the river," Jimmy said. "Or he could be a scout for the St. Louis Cardinals."

"Or maybe he's from the FCC," I said.

Jimmy paused, looked at me, and then at the man. "Uh-oh. I hadn't thought of that. If that farmer picked up my station across the high-way...."

"What're you going to do?"

"I don't know. I'm going to have to think about it."

I glanced back at the stranger and felt him looking in our direction. He must have been looking at Jimmy. Maybe he *was* from the FCC.

"I've gotta go. Tell Goose I went home, and he can come by later after everything's over," Jimmy said, and off he went.

I watched the stranger for a couple of minutes and then spied Skipper and her friends not five feet from him. I waved to see if I could get her attention, and finally she spied me and waved back. She said something to her friends and backed away, circling around behind the crowd.

"Hi," she said, "I've been looking for you. "I'm getting in line. Are you going to try this?"

They called her a "tomboy," and she could back it up by beating all but the most athletic of boys in town. I wasn't sure I wanted to be shown up by a girl, but I didn't see any good way out.

"I reckon. But you go first."

Goose was up next, and we got in line behind him. We watched him get his string going at 11, and then 12, 13, and then…. "He's tied the record! Now, can he break it?" shouted Rollie.

Goose extended it to eighteen before the next shot rolled off the side of the rim. "We have a new leader. Take a bow, Goose Gossert," cried Rollie.

Skipper was next. "Now, we have Skipper Manion, Purcell Station's premier athlete in a ponytail." She took the ball and launched a high-arcing shot that came down through the net without hitting the rim. The crowd cheered.

She then hit eight straight before a miss, prompting Rollie to announce, "And Skipper Manion now takes over third place." The crowd barely stopped cheering before I stepped up to take my first shot. "Next up is an outsider from all the way upstate in Wabash County, the grandson of Minnie and Conrad Halderman, Garrett Gentry."

I heard the crowd when I made my second shot after missing the first. And I heard them after each shot I made, up until I tied Skipper on the eighth shot. After that I didn't care what happened, and when the ninth shot caromed off the back of the rim I was happy.

Skipper came over, put her arm on my shoulder, and said, "Nice going." We circled behind the crowd and went into the fire station, where the ladies from church were clearing off the tables and setting them up for bingo. We each got a cup of lemonade and sat down on a bench. Skipper looked around as if looking for someone. "Where's Jimmy? I saw you with him earlier."

"He left. He thinks someone's after him. Did you see that guy standing in the crowd near you when the free throw contest started? The one in the really nice clothes?"

"Maybe. Did he have on a blue shirt?"

"Yeah, that's the stranger I told you about."

"It is? Why would he be after Jimmy?"

"Well, Jimmy found out some farmers sometimes hear his signal from across the highway. He's scared someone might have turned him in."

"So, he thinks this guy's here to check up on him?"

"Yes. But he could be here for lots of reasons, couldn't he?"

"I can think of a few."

Just then, a wild cheer went up from the crowd. Skipper and I walked back to see what the commotion was and heard Rollie announce, "Now, we have everybody's uncle…Uncle Spooks!"

"Uh-oh," said Skipper. "This isn't going to be good."

Spooks was standing at the free throw line trying to bounce the ball, but it rolled off his fingers and bounced away. A young boy picked it up and threw it back far too hard and it bounced off his hands into his forehead. A few people in the crowd thought that was funny.

"They're making fun of him," Skipper said. "If that was my little brother I'd jerk a knot in his tail right in front of everybody."

Spooks stopped trying to dribble, took the ball in both hands, and pushed it in the direction of the goal. It didn't come close. Some of the kids in the crowd jeered again.

He tried again, but the second shot only reached the pole supporting the backboard. "You got one more chance, Spooky." The voice came from the back of the circle. I looked around to see who'd yelled. Skipper saw me looking, "It's Jesse. I know that voice."

I moved over so I could see. He was standing there with his pals and they were all goading Spooks and drawing laughter from people standing around them. When Spooks took his third and final shot and it, too, missed everything, Jesse let out a whoop that rose above all the others. "Spookyman, you stink," he yelled, soaking up the laughter.

Rollie got on the microphone and announced, "That's all the contestants who've bought tickets. Is there anyone else who would like to try? Remember, all you have to do is hit nineteen to win the first prize of $10 dollars." He looked around. The crowd grew silent and looked at each other, waiting to see if anyone would step up. No one moved. Just when Rollie started, "Going once…going twice…last call…going three times…."

"Yes, sir, we have a contestant!" It was Skipper, standing right beside me. "I'm buying a ticket for Mr. Jesse Sprowl."

The crowd got quiet. Jesse's jaw dropped. His stare darted across the circle at Skipper. I figured he didn't want to be in the arena; it was more fun hooting at those who were. He looked around at the people who just a moment ago had been laughing with him. Now they were looking at him. His pals stepped back, not wanting any part of this, waiting to see what he was going to do.

All eyes were on Skipper as she came out of the crowd and up to the table. She slapped down a quarter. "This is for Jesse's ticket."

Jesse hadn't made a move. Rollie, seeing what Skipper was doing, spoke into the mic. "Let's hear it for Jesse Sprowl, folks. Let's see what the guy can do."

He revved up the crowd and got them clapping and then yelling, "Jesse! Jesse! Jesse!"

Jesse's face turned red. He looked like he'd rather be anywhere but here. Then, a man in bib overalls standing behind him gave him a little push, and he lurched forward. The crowd, thinking he was stepping up to the line, began to cheer. Now, he was at a point where he couldn't back down.

Skipper walked over to him, smiling, and handed him the ball. "Since you think Spooks is so bad, let's see what you can do."

He shot her a menacing look, but she didn't seem to care. Knowing it was too late to back out, he took the ball and dribbled it before launching his first shot.

He made the first one, giving him hope he could get out of this with dignity. But when he missed the second, he stormed off the court, pushed through the crowd, and never looked back.

The crowd jeered. I turned to Skipper, "Why'd you do that? Weren't you afraid of him?"

"Nope. He wasn't going to do anything in front of this crowd. There are other reasons, too, but that's between him and me."

Before I could ask any more questions, Rollie's voice came on over the microphone calling Skipper, Spike Hochmeister, and me, to come forward to receive our prize money. Then he called Goose to the mic and awarded him the $10 winner's prize, and the crowd applauded.

When the noise died down, Rollie announced, "Bingo is starting in front of the station. Take a seat. We have some wonderful prizes to give away tonight."

All the seats filled up within minutes. Rollie presided over the calling of letters until each game had a winner. Skipper and I watched Grandpa play for over half an hour before giving up.

"I finally got smart," Grandpa told Nub Hawkins. "I can't compete with these Catholics. They practice every Friday night."

Nub agreed, "I'll let 'em take the Lutherans' money but not mine. I'll wait and see how I do on the raffle."

The raffle lasted until 10 o'clock and Grandpa and his friends fared no better. The grand prize, a burial plot at Hilltop Cemetery went to one of the Cartiers, one of the French Catholics from up near the city. There was much speculation about what they were going to do with it since everybody knew the Catholics didn't bury their dead in a Protestant cemetery.

Finally, Rollie announced, "That's it, folks. Thanks for coming and supporting the Purcell Station Volunteer Fire Department. Because of your effort and generosity, we cleared a profit of $1,317 this year, a new record and enough for a down payment on a new tanker." The crowd let out a rousing cheer.

Goose and I helped clear the tables and chairs, and then we hurried over to Brockman's to find Jimmy. We found him in the shack, taking down his radio equipment and placing it in a trunk. WPSR was going off the air, at least until the smoke cleared, or until someone figured out exactly who the stranger was.

CHAPTER **18**

On July 3, I ate lunch then went out to the porch swing with Grandpa. Grandma came out a few minutes later but soon left. She seemed anxious.

"Is she all right?" I asked.

"Oh, I'm sure she's fine. She said something about feeling kinda funny this morning, like something's going to happen."

"Like what?"

"Nothin' in particular. Women think they got a sixth sense sometimes and think they can predict something. Not much different with men, though. I can predict when it's gonna rain by my trick knee."

"Really? Your knee tells you when it's going to rain?"

"Works every time."

"Can your knee make it rain?"

"Naw, you can't ask too much of a man's knee. If I could do that I'd get rid of this awful drought we're having."

When Grandpa talked like this he always had a gleam in his eye, and I knew he was putting me on.

"Will you tell me in advance next time it's going to rain? Just to make sure you're not listening to the weather report?"

"You'll be the first to know. You'll know before the weatherman does. Where do you think Jimmy Brockman gets his weather reports?"

"That reminds me, have you seen him lately?"

"No. I think he's been working over at the store. Come to think of it, I don't recall hearing his radio broadcasts this week."

"I think he's scared. A strange man got off the train last week and has been spied around town. Nobody seems to know who he is or why he's here. Jimmy's afraid he might be some fed looking into his radio station."

"Well, that would explain it, I reckon. You say nobody knows what this guy's up to?"

"Not really. I've seen him around, and so have a lot of other people. I stopped in Danny's Barber Shop the other day, and they were talking about him. Taylor Barth says he's seen him going in and out of the hotel, and one day he got on the train and went up to the city but came back that night. Someone else said he was up at the school asking questions of the principal. He showed up at the fish fry. I heard someone at Dub's say he was seen talking to Marshall Hopper over at the town hall. Looks kinda odd to me."

Grandma came back out on the porch and sat in her rocker. She was working on a doily, the same one she'd been working on all week.

"We're having a picnic before the parade tomorrow with the Brockmans and Francises," she said, looking at me. "I'm making ice cream and I'd like you to go over to Brockman's and get me the ingredients. Here's what I need." She handed me a piece of paper.

"Okay," I said. "I need to stop at the library anyway to return a book and get another one."

In the library I found the young adult section. It was right in front of the Norman Rockwell painting of the boy with the big hat and floppy ears, like the hat I wore at Tip's. Earlier, I had taken Skipper's suggestion and asked Miss Perkins if they had a copy of *Catcher in the Rye*, but she looked at me kinda funny and said they were out of that particular title. I wasn't sure I believed her so I asked her to put my name on a waiting list if a copy ever showed up. She said she would, but she wasn't very convincing. Since nothing ever became of it, I settled on a series of biographies. This time I selected one on Thomas Edison.

When I got home, I watched Grandma mix the ingredients, and then I turned the crank on the ice cream maker until she announced it was ready to put in the ice box. I stood at the kitchen sink and looked out the window to where Grandpa was sitting under the maple tree, alone. The afternoon sun was fading, and the shadow of our house climbed the wall of the Francises' house next door. It looked like Grandpa was falling asleep.

Inside the kitchen was a different story. Grandma was fussing around getting ready for tomorrow's picnic. She seemed almost too busy, even anxious. I thought of what Grandpa said out on the porch and wondered if women really did have a sixth sense.

I felt I was just in her way, so I picked up the ball from the bin on the back porch and walked out the back door. Just as the screen door slammed, I caught a glimpse of movement at the other end of the arbor. The tunnel was dark, but I could see the silhouette of a man coming down through it. I couldn't see his face, and I wondered why he hadn't spoken. I felt myself start to panic, so I turned to step back to the porch to say something to Grandma when the man came out of the tunnel and into the evening sunlight. I recognized him.

"Grandma! Grandma! Uncle Jake's home!"

She came out the screen door and stood, frozen, looking at her youngest son, blond and splendid in his white Navy dress uniform. He smiled, held out his arms, and lifted her up, all one hundred pounds of her, and swung her around while she sobbed. It had been a year since she had seen him.

Crying now and shaking, she waited, saying nothing until the trembling stopped. Then she leaned back and stared at his face. "Why didn't you tell me you were coming?"

He looked into her eyes with a mischievous look. "For the same reason I didn't write for the last month. I can't talk about it. Besides, I wanted to surprise you."

"Well, you sure...."

"What's going on here?" It was Grandpa, shuffling over with his cane. I had gone over to tell him Jake was home. "Who's this stranger? He looks familiar, but I can't place his name."

Jake let go of Grandma and grabbed Grandpa by the shoulders. They clutched each other, and if I didn't know better I thought I saw a tear drop down Grandpa's cheek.

"Good to see you, Dad. You been taking care of yourself?"

"As well as possible for an old man who can't see, can't hear, and can't walk.

"Good to know you've got no complaints," Jake said.

They held the hug until I thought Grandpa was losing his grip, and then they stood holding each other at arm's length while Jake started talking about his journey home.

He had disembarked in San Diego four days earlier and hopped the train to St. Louis. He'd spent the night there with an old buddy from boot camp, then boarded another train to Terre Haute, followed by a south bounder to Purcell Station. He was greeted there by Taylor Barth, who swore he wouldn't tell a soul for at least thirty minutes that Jake was in town. This gave Jake time to walk up the back alley and surprise everyone before the word got around.

We sat on the front porch until the sun fell below the tree line of the river and Grandma got chilled. Then we went in the kitchen, listening to Jake tell all he was allowed to say about his tour of duty in the South Pacific.

At noon the next day, the Fourth of July, we gathered under the maple tree by the driveway. Grandma called everybody together and asked a blessing on our troops and our country as we celebrated its anniversary and offered thanks for the Lord bringing Jake safely home from the war. We then chose our seats, being careful to sit down all together to counter what had happened last year when Rollie, all two hundred and fifty pounds of him, sat down first and almost tipped the table over on his lap.

The food, including the cherry pie a la mode, was the hit everybody thought it would be. But the biggest hit was Uncle Jake talking about his adventures in the Navy. He had been sent overseas just as WW II was winding down, arriving in time to help bring home the boys who fought and won the war in Europe.

In the shade of the maple tree, he described his first time across the Atlantic and the moment they entered the Mediterranean Sea and saw the Rock of Gibraltar, and how the sun gleamed off it like it was a beacon. He told of passing through the Panama Canal and the English Channel, the Sea of Japan, and port-hopping in the Greek Islands.

He was still talking at two o'clock when a police car turned into the driveway and stopped. Out stepped Mert Hopper, the town marshal. He was a tall, lean man maybe in his sixties, with grey hair. As he approached, he took off his hat and walked past the table where the women were sitting.

"Good afternoon, ladies," he said, and then turned to the men and added, "Gentlemen."

We all nodded, and Grandpa spoke up, "Howdy, Mert. What brings you out today?"

"Well, the word's out that Jake's back in town," he said, extending his hand toward Jake. "How you doing, son?"

Jake shook his hand. "Just fine, Marshal. Word travels fast around here, doesn't it?"

"Sure does. I just came by to tell you the Legion's going to have a float in the parade today, and they asked me to see if you'd be a part of it."

"That would be a nice gesture, but I'm not a member, Mert."

"That's okay. We're not that beholden to protocol around here. You should know that. We'd welcome you anyway. Lot of people around here look up to a guy in uniform, like the one you're wearing."

"If you're sure it's okay, I'd be honored, Mert."

"They sent me to get you, so it must be okay."

He smiled at the ladies, put on his wide brim hat, and nodded to Jake, "You need to be at the Sand Bowl at 2:30. That's where we assemble. Parade starts at 3 o'clock sharp."

"I'll be there," Jake said as Mert climbed in his car and left.

Jake stood up and started toward the house. "I'd better check myself out in the mirror. Don't want to disappoint the young ladies watching the parade."

"They don't care what you look like, as long as you're wearing a uniform," hollered Grandpa.

The women cleared off the table and went in to get ready for the parade. Jake came out the back door, and, holding the keys to the Chevy, asked Grandpa, "When's the last time you started that buggy?"

Grandpa said, "About this time last year, when you were home."

"That's what I thought. I'll take it over to the Sand Bowl and blow out the carbon for you." He entered the garage, and a minute later I heard it sputter. Finally, it kicked over. Spewing out blue exhaust, Jake backed it down the driveway.

I walked with Grandpa and Grandma. By the time we got to Main Street people had already lined the front yards up the hill and in front of the stores down the hill. Flags draped the store fronts, and young kids ran circles up and down the street, carrying little flags on wooden sticks.

As 3 o'clock approached, we heard the siren and saw Mert Hopper's 1947 Pontiac coming down the hill with its domed red light flashing on top. He always led the parade as an official street-clearing gesture and to let everyone know he was in charge. I overheard Grandpa say it was the "only thing he was in charge of, and that includes his bossy wife, Sal." She happened to be sitting with him in the shotgun seat.

Following Mert came the color guard from the American Legion, followed by the Purcell Station Marching Band led by a high-stepping Ginny Denbow. As they passed she looked over at me and smiled, causing Grandpa to turn, look around, and wisecrack, "Who's she looking at? I don't see anyone here in her league."

I saw Skipper next, marching in the front row with the other clarinets. She must have seen Ginny look over at me, because she too looked, waved, and smiled.

This time Grandpa shot me a mock look of surprise and said, "They must think you're rich. I can't think of any other reason they'd be lookin' over here."

When they had passed, Ginny halted the band between Slinker's General Store and Maddie's Cafe as the sergeant of the color guard gave the order, "Present arms!" The flag was presented, followed by the National Anthem.

Then came the float of the American Legion, with veterans from both World Wars and Korea riding on the flatbed wagon, wearing their legion hats and waving as the band played "Yankee Doodle Dandy." They stopped momentarily, and that's when I saw Uncle Jake, in his dress whites, sitting on the back. When the crowd saw him they stood up and cheered.

All my life I'd heard the stories. As a kid everyone knew Jake. He was the smiling towhead with the spirited sense of humor, who would tip your outhouse over on Halloween and come back the next day and help you put it back up. He was handsome— at least the girls and their mothers thought so—and not very humble, according to Grandma.

"He had a good time," Grandma said. "People adored him. He was always good for a laugh, but boy, was he a handful. He went to church. I made him do that, but I don't think it took."

"Coach Francis tried to get him out for the basketball team," Grandpa added, "but Jake figured he'd have to give up girls and cigarettes and just couldn't bring himself around to doing either one."

I could see he was warming up to the subject. A twinkle emerged in his eye. I sensed he didn't share Grandma's view on the difficulty of raising Jake, or else he hadn't been that involved in it. "He struggled in school. Just wasn't that interested. He's smart though. He'd have to be, to think up some of that mischief he got himself into."

"What kind of mischief?" I wanted to know.

Grandpa seemed eager to answer. "Well, there was the time I got a visit from Mert Hopper along about midnight. Seems Jake and his friends took Mabel Starks's underwear off her clothesline and strung it up on the water tower. Mabel reported it missing about the same time a member of the Civil Air Patrol, who was in the tower that night, saw it flapping in the moonlight and thought it was enemy aircraft. He called the authorities, who had just heard from Mabel, and they came out and took a look and put two and two together, and it added up to strange undergarments instead of strange aircraft. Of course, the size of Mabel and the size of the garments made identification easy."

"Did Jake get in trouble over it?" I asked.

"Trouble? He got triple jeopardy! You see, Mabel happened to be the Latin teacher at the high school, and Jake wasn't doing too good in her class. When the principal found out, he gave Jake three wallops with the paddle, and Mabel lowered his grade from a 'D' to an 'F.' Then Marshal Hopper fined him $7.50 for trespassing on government property and made him do restitution."

"What kind of restitution?"

"He had to clean the toilets in the town lockup."

"Purcell Station has a jail?"

"Well, sort of. It's in the back room of the bank. It's the only building outside the Methodist Church and school that's made of brick. They can't burn it down or carve a hole in the wall if it's brick.'

"Isn't it kind of strange to have a jail cell in a bank?"

"Why, not at all. It's real handy. They try robbin' the bank, and they're shoved right into the cell. Don't even have to take 'em outside." I got the sense Grandpa was enjoying this.

"How did they know it was Jake who did it?"

"It had to be. It was too good a prank to trust it to amateurs. Everybody in town knew it had to be Jake."

"Did that stop him from any more pranks?"

"Not a bit. He...."

A loud roar interrupted him. The parade had moved on, and something was causing quite a commotion. "It's Rollie!" said Grandma.

Rollie was playing a piano on the back of a flatbed truck. People were cheering and applauding and Rollie's round face returned a broad smile as he went right on playing "It's a Grand Old Flag."

"Rollie's one of the highlights of the parade every year," said Grandpa. "The first time he played in the parade, the driver of the truck, Burt Roemer, was waving to the crowd and not paying any attention and almost rammed the back of the fire truck, which had stopped suddenly in front of him. Rollie's piano slammed into the back of the cab just as he got to the chorus. Burt was so stunned by the sound of the crash, he floored the gas pedal and the piano shot to the back of the truck like a bullet and hung over the edge."

"What happened to Rollie?"

"His stool stopped just short of dumping him on the street, and he just kept on playing as if nothing had happened. Some men from the sidewalk jumped up to push the piano back on the bed, and he went on."

I watched, and as he came into view more people cheered. By now he was playing with a flourish, his hands rising high between chords, as he and his mustache smiled at the crowd.

A Model T Ford pickup with a sign saying "Farm Bureau Feed Store" came by, carrying young kids waving and throwing handfuls of candy to the crowd. Then came a mini-motorcycle troop from the Shriner's Club from up in the city.

A succession of politicians followed on foot: the county commissioners, the township trustee, the county clerk, and the local representative to the state legislature. "They're all out this year because it's an election year. Last year none of 'em came," said Grandpa.

A few more floats came by, followed by John Deere and Farmall tractors and a flatbed melon wagon carrying a sign that read, "Purcell Station, Watermelon Capital of the U.S.A." After it came the Purcell Station fire truck, blowing its horns and siren signaling the end of the parade. A dozen or more volunteer firemen stood on the side boards, throwing candy into the crowd.

As soon as it passed, a throng of families, kids, stray dogs, and baby buggies fell in behind the fire truck and followed the parade, trailing a long line of stragglers.

"That should do it until the fireworks," Grandpa said as he stood up. "I'm going to need a nap if I'm going to stay up for that."

The walk home was even slower than the walk over. By the time we got to the grape arbor, Grandpa needed to rest. Grandma went on ahead in the house and soon came out with two glasses of iced tea. We sat there on the bench in the tunnel and sipped while Grandpa caught his breath.

It was almost supper time when I heard the Chevy sputter up the driveway. Jake parked it under the maple tree and came over to our bench.

"How'd you like that parade?" asked Grandpa.

"Pretty easy from my seat," said Jake. "I wouldn't have wanted to be walking it though. It was hotter than the Philippines out there."

We sat there fanning ourselves until Grandma came out and said supper was ready. Afterward, Grandpa took his nap, and Jake and I sat in the swing on the front porch while Grandma sat in her rocker. For the next hour Grandma caught Jake up on all the news about Purcell Station. He asked about Jimmy Brockman's radio station, and when I offered the story about the stranger showing up at the train station and registering at the hotel, he got really interested.

"I'm not sure they'd be here looking at Jimmy's station. That seems kinda small- time for the Feds. It's gotta be something else."

After failing to come up with an answer, Jake quickly changed the subject. "How're your mom and dad?"

"I talk to Mom every Sunday over on the Francises' phone. Dad's out of the hospital and in a rehab center."

"Well, your mom's a real trouper, so your dad's in good hands. Did you know she took care of me one summer when I was about your age, after I broke both arms?"

"No. How'd you break your arms?"

"Well, it's a long story, but the short version is I 'borrowed' Rollie Brockman's motorcycle for a little joy ride. I got as far as the levee on the road to the highway and thought I'd rev it up and see how far I could land down the other side."

I glanced at Grandma, and she had her head in her hand, as if she'd lived this story too many times. "Now, Jake, you shouldn't be telling Garrett these stories. His mother wouldn't approve."

"I'm already into it, and besides, maybe it can be a lesson."

I looked back at Jake. "So, what happened?"

"I landed sideways, came down in a ditch, and tried to break the fall with my arms. Got all scratched up, cracked a rib, and broke both arms. Not something I recommend."

"What'd you do then?"

"I lay there a few minutes, until a car came from the highway, saw me, and stopped. It happened to be someone who knew me, so he took me to Doc Branham, got him out of bed, and he set my arms and patched me up. A few days later, your mom got home from college and took me under her wing, waiting on me hand and foot. She fed me, took me places, and humored me. She even tried to counsel me into changing my ways, but it didn't take."

"Did you tell her what happened?"

"Didn't have to. Everybody in town knew all about it the next day."

A silence followed as I waited and thought about the next question. "When did it take?"

"Pardon me?"

"When did it take? When did you change?"

"Oh. That didn't occur until I was in the Navy. I finally figured it out when I saw the dead and wounded coming home from the war in Europe. Some of it came to me, standing alone on the deck of a battleship in the South Pacific at midnight, staring at the stars and wondering if people in Purcell Station could see them too. As if that was the only thing linking us together, although I knew it was daytime there. It kinda made me homesick, wishing I could be home again and starting over."

Just then we heard the muted voice of Harry Carey and then Grandpa's shuffle before we saw him come through the front door. He looked sleepy. The Cardinals were playing the Cubs, and he was using the broadcast to wake himself up. I got up and offered him my seat in the swing. Grandma asked him if he still planned to go to the fireworks. He said, "What?"

When he asked her to repeat herself a second time, she noticed he didn't have his hearing aid in.

She yelled, "You forgot your hearing aids."

He answered, "I know I'm getting ready for the fireworks,"

Jake drove us to the Sand Bowl in the Chevy. The stands were almost full, but we found a spot behind the last row of bleachers. Since we had only three chairs, I said I'd go sit with any friends I could find. I looked for Jimmy and Goose but hoped I would run into Skipper instead.

I looked in the refreshment stand, but didn't see her, nor was she anywhere in the bleachers. I was about to give up when I heard my name. It came from the direction of the ball field, but I didn't see anyone. I started down the end of the bleachers along the third base line. There was a retaining wall there, and beyond it I saw her head pop up. She waved for me to come down. When I got there I looked over the wall and saw Skipper with Ginny, Sarah, and two others I didn't know.

"Hi, come on down," she said.

As I stepped over the wall Skipper said, "I'd like you to meet my cousin June and her friend Abby. They're from Ireland."

"Ireland? Aren't you a long way from home?" I asked.

"No, Ireland, Indiana. It's over near Jasper. About an hour from here."

"Oh! That Ireland." I said, pretending I'd heard of it.

"They're here for the holiday, and then we're having a slumber party at my house tonight."

June and Abby looked somewhere between my age and Skipper's. "We've heard a lot about you." June smiled.

"Really?" I asked.

"Yes, Skipper talks about you a lot. Said you have blue eyes."

"Just a minute," said Skipper. "I've told them about you and how your father is in a Cleveland hospital and about your mother and…."

"And how she thinks you're cute," interrupted June.

"I didn't say that, I just said….'

"You don't think he's cute?" continued June.

"I didn't say what I thought, I said…."

"Well, is he or isn't he cute?"

"Sure, he's cute, but I didn't dwell on it like you make it sound," said Skipper, blushing.

I felt my own face getting red as I wondered just what Skipper did say, but then came a boom, and a fiery rocket exploded in the sky above center field. The fireworks had started.

We rested on the blanket, looking up into the exploding sky. In the background we could see taillights and headlights of traffic on Highway 41, and to the north a halo hovered over the city of Vincennes. In the river bottoms to the west the gas flames of the oil wells made their own fireworks.

With each explosion came oohs and aahs from the bleachers, plus the occasional crying of a baby afraid of the loud blasts. This went on until a continuous roar erupted as a rapid burst of rockets filled the air for the grand finale. When the noise ended and people began shuffling off to their cars, Skipper invited me to go downtown with them. I went to tell Grandma, who reminded me she would be waiting up and not to be late.

We entered the Purcell Drug Store and found a table. A middle-aged woman with bleached hair came up and asked what we wanted. "Hi, Bea, I'll have an orange soda," said Skipper. The rest of us chimed in with the same.

The room was crowded with people squeezing between the tables and booths. The jukebox was playing a Frank Sinatra tune, but the noise nearly drowned it out.

When Sinatra finished his song and the Andrews Sisters came on, the front door swung open and in walked Jesse Sprowl and his posse. They looked around, surveying the room, and then Jesse smiled and said something to his friends. On the other side, Spooks was sitting at the counter with his back to us. He was sitting by himself, drinking a milkshake.

Jesse started moving among the tables, heading in the direction of Spooks. At the exact moment Spooks lifted his drink, Jesse passed behind him and bumped his arm. Instantly, Spooks spit out a mouthful of his shake, turned around, and swore loudly as Jesse and his gang laughed their way out the side door. The people at the tables behind him looked up to see a white milkshake mustache on Spooks's red face. Their laughter drowned out the Andrews Sisters. Angry and embarrassed, Spooks spit out a few more oaths and stormed out the front door.

Skipper sprung to her feet and followed him. Nobody else seemed to know what had happened; they just sat there, laughing. I followed Skipper, who had caught up with Spooks outside. She gave him her napkin and told him to sit on the curb until she got back. She then stormed up the dark street to where Jesse and his friends stood in the shadows of some trees. They were still laughing.

She screamed, "You cowards! I saw what you did."

Jesse and his friends ignored her and started further up the darkened street. Skipper followed. When they got out of earshot of everybody, Jesse suddenly stopped, turned, and faced her. His friends circled and closed in. His face was red with rage, and he spewed out a string of curse words. "I've been waiting for you." He shook and his voice quivered. He could barely get the words out.

Hiding in the dark shadows of the trees, I crept up the street behind them. My heart pounded as I stopped short and waited to see what Jesse was going to do.

"I let it go last time. I ain't this time!" he screamed. Then he stepped up, putting his face within inches of hers. One of his friends—the short, chubby one—got behind her and bent down on all fours. It was the same trick he'd pulled on me.

Jesse was talking softly now, saying something I couldn't understand. His back was to me. His friends were smirking, knowing what was coming next. I tiptoed up the sidewalk in the darkness behind him. As I got close, Skipper glanced over his shoulder and saw me coming. She timed it perfectly. Just as I leveled my shoulder into his back, she ducked. The force of my blow threw Jesse over Skipper's crouched body and onto the chubby boy who was kneeled behind her. Jesse fell over the two bodies face-first and let out a yell. He rolled over, and then I saw the blood from his nose and cheek. A film of loose sand from the sidewalk had grated the side of his face and jaw. Everyone got quiet. Jesse lifted his head, dazed, and put his hand to his bloody cheek.

The chubby boy tried to stand up, but he fell over Jesse's feet. Jesse let out another yell as the boy landed on his chest. The other boys, standing over their fallen leader, stood mute, not sure what to do.

By this time, a crowd had gathered in front of the drugstore, and Sarah and Ginny and their friends had come out to see where Skipper had gone. Skipper saw them looking up the street in our direction, so she calmly got up after Jesse's unfortunate fall, dusted the sand off her clothes, and said, "Let's go. I have to be home by ten."

We walked back, gathered Skipper's friends, and crossed the street. "What went on back there?" asked Ginny.

"Oh, nothing. Just Jesse trying to bully Spooks again," said Skipper, hoping that would put an end to it. "Let's go home."

We crossed the street and I walked with the girls to Skipper's house at the top of the hill and told them goodnight. It was past the time I promised Grandma I'd be home. I remembered she would be waiting up. I didn't want to run into Jesse again, so I took the back streets home. It was dark and still; low-lying clouds had replaced the starry sky, and the trees blocked out the street lights. I heard a car starting up over on Main Street and figured the drugstore crowd was leaving. I hoped Jesse and his friends went with them.

I used the street light at the next corner as a beacon. I had only to get up to the next corner and turn into the alley to be home. I looked ahead to see if Grandma had left the porch light on but didn't see it. It was quieter now and eerie. Something didn't seem right. I picked up my pace. I slipped into the darkness again looking for the turn into the alley. Then I thought I heard footsteps. I stepped up my pace, almost running as I glanced over my shoulder. I saw no one, so it must have been my imagination. I looked again for the alley, knowing it had to be there somewhere. I turned, but it was too soon; my knee hit the corner post of the garden fence. A sharp pain shot up my leg. Limping, I rounded the corner, and slowly feeling my way around in the dark, I headed up the alley behind the Francises' back yard. I thought it odd that I didn't hear any more footsteps until I realized the soft sand would muffle them.

Just as I passed between the barn and the garage someone jumped out of a bush in front of me. I flinched and stepped back. My heart was pounding. I started to run the other way, but I heard someone coming behind me. Then another came behind him. Within seconds, I found myself surrounded.

I heard his voice; then saw his face. Jesse, bleeding and scarred from the sand and sidewalk, bumped against me. Trembling with anger and speaking softly to keep from attracting attention, he muttered, "You think you're going to get away with that?"

I felt myself shiver. I turned away, not wanting him to sense my fear, and all I saw were faces staring back. "Get away with what?" I mumbled.

"You know what I'm talking about."

He put his hand to my neck and squeezed it, then pushed me until I fell back into someone standing behind me, who pushed me back toward Jesse. I'd seen this game played with Spooks. I looked for an opening in the circle and saw one on the side next to the garden. I bolted between the smallest boy and the chubby one I'd seen back on Main Street. I bulled my way through, then screamed as I felt the scratches on my arms and face. I'd landed in the briars of a blackberry bush.

I started to get up, but my clothes were caught. I felt blood rolling down my cheek and arms. Jesse stood over me. He kicked me in the ribs, and I let out another yell. Seconds later, a light came on above the door of the back porch. Jesse looked up, then back at me, and uttered an oath. Then he delivered one last parting kick to my back before he led his pack down the alley and into the darkness.

I lay there bleeding, caught up in the briars. I heard someone coming through the tunnel and squinted to see. I didn't want it to be Grandma.

"Garrett? Is that you?" It was Uncle Jake. He came into the alley and saw me lying in the blackberry bush. "What the…?" Then he saw my face and arms. "What happened?"

He helped me out of the briars, carefully lifting one limb at a time off my bare skin and shirt. When he got me out he stood there brushing me off; then led me down the tunnel to the back porch. I told him everything that had happened. "But I don't want you to tell Grandma or she'll get all worried."

"Tell her what? That you were walking home through the alley in the dark and fell into the blackberry bush and got all scratched up?" He winked. "Look, I know Jesse. They don't call him Jesse James for nothing. You did what was right. You came to Skipper's aid. You don't know what he'd have done if you hadn't. Now, let's go in and get you cleaned up. We'll let this be our secret."

Jake had convinced Grandma to go to bed, saying he'd stay up until I got home. We took off our shoes on the back porch and tiptoed into the kitchen. Jake then took me to the sink, cleaned up my scratches, and put some salve and Band-Aids over them. Then he whispered for me to follow him. We edged quietly out to the front porch and took a seat in the swing.

Sitting there in the dark, swinging, Jake said, "So, tell me about this stranger."

I told him what I'd seen and what I'd heard at the barber shop, Dub's, and the depot, about how this strange man often appeared at odd places and then disappeared. Jake listened and asked a lot of questions. I couldn't figure out why he was so interested.

CHAPTER 19

The Farm Bureau Feed Store sat across the tracks north of the train depot. I was on my way there to see if Grandpa was right when he said I was growing like a weed and eating them out of their life savings. I parked my bike out front by the hitching post, useless now that the John Deeres and Farmalls had taken over. They must have figured as long as Willie Lickert was still shoeing horses at his blacksmith shop up the street, they might as well keep their hitching post in case horses made a comeback.

Peadad—I didn't know his last name—was standing behind a wooden counter totaling up a customer's bill. Without looking up he grunted, "Help ya?"

"Grandpa told me to come down here and get weighed," I said as I headed to the back of the store.

"Ya know where it's at," Peadad said, still working his pencil. He was a short, round-faced man somewhere in his forties. Grandpa told me Peadad didn't go past the ninth grade, but he could recite the names of every President of the United States, what party he belonged to, and the number of terms he served.

The scale was on floor level so carts of feed and grain could be pulled onto it to be weighed. The numbers, from zero to one thousand, were in a glass-enclosed casing like that of a grandfather clock. I stepped on the platform and watched the dial creep up and finally settle. I'd put on 10 pounds. Maybe Grandpa was right.

Peadad was still writing as I thanked him and left. I rode past the depot and saw Taylor Barth out sweeping the platform so I stopped to say hello. I hadn't seen him since we saw the stranger go into the hotel.

"Hi, there, young man. I got some news…hey, what happened to you?"

"Oh, just some scratches I got from a blackberry bush. It's about healed now."

"Well, you look like you got in a cat fight. Anyway, I got some news you might be interested in."

"I hope it's good."

"Well, your mysterious stranger?" He hesitated, trying to add suspense. "Packed up and left town. Got on a train yesterday. Didn't say a word but 'thanks' when I sold him his ticket. Still don't know what he was up to."

"Well, when you sold him his ticket where was he going?"

"East Coast. Washington. Somewhere around there.'

"Then he must be a Fed."

"He just may be."

I stared at Taylor for a long time to see if he would offer any more information: then I remembered Jimmy. "I gotta go." I yelled back to Taylor, "Thanks. I'll see you soon."

"Take care now," he said. "Come visit me when you get time."

I promised I would. I liked Mr. Barth. I had ever since he sat on that bench and told me about his son Jed getting killed in the war.

Brockman's Store was nearly empty when I got there. Mrs. Brockman stood behind the counter, waiting on a lady with a small baby on her hip.

"Hi, Garrett," she said, barely looking up. She was figuring up the bill for two sacks of groceries. "What brings you in today?"

"I'm looking for Jimmy. Is he here?"

"He is. Just a minute, and I'll get him." She finished totaling the bill and giving the lady her change, then walked back to the door to the back room. "Jimmy!" she yelled. "I need you to carry Thelma's groceries out to her car."

Jimmy appeared through the door. "Afternoon, Mrs. Bartle. Let me give you a hand." He picked up the bags and, walking to the door, saw me standing over near a bucket of cinnamon balls. "Hey, Garret. Haven't seen you in a while. Where've you been?"

"I was about to say the same to you." I followed him out the door while he placed Mrs. Bartle's bags in her car. When she thanked him and drove off I said, "I have some news for you."

"It'd better be good. I feel like I've been in jail the past few weeks."

"It is. The stranger left town. I just talked to Taylor Barth, who sold him a ticket. Left for the East Coast yesterday."

Jimmy studied me a moment. "Whoa, I think the cell door just swung open. How would you like to come over to the shack tonight and celebrate?"

After Jimmy got off work at the store he went up and down Main Street, telling everybody the station would be back on that night. When I arrived at the shack he was sitting at the desk. "What's the lead story?" I asked as I closed the door behind me.

"It's got to be the mystery man. It's had the whole town buzzing. I have a quote from Taylor Barth to add some color to it."

At seven o'clock Jimmy flipped the switch and began reading the evening news. He led off with the stranger story, quoting Taylor and outlining some of the places people had reported seeing him around town and some of the theories folks had for him being here. A story on the number of stray dogs and problems they were causing in trash cans came next, followed by stories on the drought, the weather forecast, a wrap-up of the 4th of July parade, and the two-game losing streak of the Purple Aces.

When he finished, he picked up a record and set it on the turntable. "We're going to start off tonight with the Billboard Magazine No. 1 hit by Johnny Ray: 'Cry.'" He dropped the needle, and Johnny's voice came crooning over the amplifier: *"If your sweetheart sends a letter of goodbye, it's no secret you'll feel better if you cry…"*

I could tell Jimmy was his old self again. When the second verse came around, he flipped a switch and sang the lyrics himself.

"When your heartaches seem to hang around too long, and your blues keep getting bluer with each song…."

"Do you want to do the next verse?" he asked.

"No, I don't know the words."

"Here, I'll write 'em down for you."

"That's okay, I'm not very good."

"One thing about this station: you don't have to be good. You just have to know the disk jockey."

The second verse was ending when Jimmy put the mic to my face and flipped the switch. I had no choice. I hesitated, then realized if I waited too long, the next verse would start before I was through. So I sang.

Jimmy quickly flipped the switch back when I was through, just in time to catch the next verse. "That was so good they probably thought it was me," he said.

We stayed two more hours, playing and singing through a tall stack of records, running the electric train, eating cinnamon balls, and downing them with Nehi colas. It was fun hanging out with Jimmy Brockman in the shack. I sometimes forgot he was five years older.

When I came to the back door a little after nine, Jake was sitting at the kitchen table with Grandma and Grandpa, drinking coffee. They must have been listening to WPSR, because when the back door slammed behind me, Jake turned and said, "Well, look here, if it isn't the Caruso of Purcell Station himself."

I skirted the table and sat down in the open chair across from Jake. "Crusoe? Robinson Crusoe?

"Caruso, the famous Italian tenor. Boy, we've got to get you out more often. Don't you ever listen to classical music?"

"Not really." My only exposure was when my mother played the piano, but I had no idea what she was playing. "I suppose you do?"

It seemed unlikely. He had never played an instrument growing up, and he was, by all accounts, not much interested in school or any activities offered there. He was the anti-student. When I asked this question, he didn't answer. Instead, he got up and went into his bedroom just off the kitchen. In a few minutes he came back with a stack of 78 rpm records and disappeared into the dining room where the phonograph machine sat in a corner. He put on a stack of records and waited.

Soon I heard the sound of an orchestra. Jake came back in the kitchen and flopped the album cover down on the table in front of me. I looked at the picture and then the title: Vivaldi: *The Four Seasons.*

"Here's your first course in classical music. This is Antonio Vivaldi, an Italian composer. He's famous for these concertos, played here by Louis Kaufman and the New York Philharmonic Orchestra. Come on in here."

He led me into the dining room where we sat down on the sofa. He didn't bother turning on a light, so we sat there in the dark and listened while he explained the music and the mood of the changing seasons.

"When it gets to the summer, the mood changes from one of peace and tranquility to threatening north winds and then a great thunderstorm. Listen as the music changes with the oncoming storm."

Maybe it was the dark room or Jake's interpretation, but I could sense the message as the orchestra pounded its warning and then the thunder and lightning of the storm coming over the land. We sat there in the darkness until it was over, and finally I asked Jake the question I'd kept inside.

"How did you learn about this stuff? I mean, everybody's talked about how you didn't care about things like this when you were a kid."

I heard a sigh; he might have been expecting the question. Then he got serious.

"I didn't do well in school. I didn't care. I just wanted to have a good time, and I didn't care at whose expense. I'm not proud of that. It's just a fact." I heard him shift around on his end of the sofa. "I got in the Navy and found out there was a lot out there I didn't know, lots of places and people and things to learn and understand. So, I decided to make up for what I didn't do earlier. I started reading everything I could get my hands on. I took classes and just tried to soak up everything I could when I was in ports all over the world."

"How did you learn about this music?"

"Vilvaldi? Straight from the source: Italy. We were in port in Napoli, and I went ashore one day and was walking down the street, and heard this music coming from an open window of a house. It wasn't like anything I'd ever heard. I stopped and sat on the curb under a shade tree and listened. Soon, a lady came out and saw me and asked if I liked Vivaldi. And I said, 'Who?' And she proceeded to tell me, and I guess she thought I was a good listener. She invited me in to listen to some more and have a glass of wine. That's how I discovered Vivaldi."

"Is he the only one you discovered?"

"At first. Then, whenever we put in at a port, I would go sightseeing or go to the local library and find books and music and learn about some of the others. I just started filling in what I didn't know with things I was finding out. I even saw *Aida* in Rome. That's a famous opera."

"What else did you find out?"

"I got interested in the countries I visited and how they ran themselves. I read about Washington, Jefferson, Lincoln, Disraeli, Churchill, even Hitler."

"I'm reading some of those, too. Got them at the library."

"Good. Keep reading 'em. They didn't have that library when I was a kid. I probably wouldn't have used it if they had."

I heard Grandpa go out the back door for one last trip to the outhouse. Grandma poked her head in our dark room and said, "You boys going to stay up all night? We're going to bed."

"We'll be going soon," Jake said. "We'll see you in the morning."

"Good night, sleep tight," she said.

We meant to go soon. Instead, Jake and I stayed up two more hours talking. When the clock on the mantel struck midnight Jake said, "We'd better get some sleep. We can finish this another time."

When I finally got to bed, I lay there thinking about Jake and how things change and how people change. And I started thinking about how I'd be turning thirteen in a couple of months.

The radio blared through the open parlor window, but this evening it was not the St. Louis Cardinals. It was an orchestra at the International Amphitheatre in Chicago playing a lively tune while the delegates to the Republican National Convention snake danced through the aisles after the nomination of Dwight David Eisenhower for president. The music and dance had gone on for over ten minutes and showed no sign of slowing down.

"It's about time the Republicans got someone in there who can win." It was Grandpa, sitting in the swing with Jake. "Twenty years is too long for one party to be in office."

Rollie Brockman had come over from across the street and was sitting in one of the porch rockers. "Particularly if that party is the Democrats, right?" he asked.

"Particularly, those Commie lovers."

"I don't know," said Rollie, "I don't think we want a military man in the White House. We've had enough wars. I think Ike'll keep us in Korea, who knows how long."

Grandpa made no secret of his politics. "Whatta you mean? He's already promised to go over to Korea and see for himself what's going on over there. He'll get us out. What we don't want is any more of that Harry S. Truman." The middle initial sounded a lot like "ass." Jake thought that was funny and laughed out loud. I did, too, but not so anybody would know. Grandma sat in her rocker and crocheted in silence, pretending she didn't hear such vulgarity.

"Well, it all boils down to who the Democrats nominate. Kefauver looks like the front-runner, either him or Russell of Georgia," Rollie said, sounding diplomatic and neutral. "Stevenson's said he doesn't want it."

Jake stopped laughing long enough to offer his appraisal. "Whoever they elect will have to do two things: stop the war and stand tough against the Communists. The problem is these two things are opposed to each other. The war *is* against the Communists."

Grandpa was just warming up. "If they'd just let Joe McCarthy alone, he'd have weeded all those Commies out by now. The damn Democrats are soft on Communism, and they...."

"Now, Conrad, your grandson is present. You watch your language," Grandma said, this time looking up and meeting his eyes with a glare.

Jake turned to me and spoke just loud enough for Grandpa to hear: "Your grandpa thinks 'damn Democrats' is all one word."

"...they let all those spies in the government." Grandpa was ignoring us. "And then, when McCarthy exposed them they went after him."

Rollie was rocking heavily now as if warming up for an argument but couldn't get a word in. I wasn't sure if he was a Democrat or just wanting to balance out Grandpa. Jake was simply amused, and I was waiting for Grandpa to make another blunder and catch another one of Grandma's stares.

The music stopped, and the words of Dwight Eisenhower rang out from the microphone and echoed over the large audience. Grandpa stopped long enough to hear the man he hoped would be our next president, but Ike was having a hard time speaking. Every few seconds the crowd broke out in applause, and a couple of times wild cheering erupted and lasted for several minutes.

"Hear that?" Grandpa said. "That crowd's eager for a change."

We sat in silence for a moment interrupted only by the grave words of General Eisenhower and the wind chimes on Louise Francis's front porch. During the speech I thought of the thousands of people in the amphitheatre and the millions like us sitting at home listening to the general talk.

"It's too bad no one around here has a television," said Jake. "This is the first one to be televised."

"In four years there'll be some sets in town; then we can see it," said Rollie.

"Who knows who will still be around in four years," Grandpa said. "If we don't get these Commies out of office, we'll all be either dead or ruled by Stalin."

"I don't know that you could say the Democrats are soft. Didn't Roosevelt just get us in and out of World War II?" Jake asked.

"Don't get me started. Look what he gave away at Yalta. If he and Churchill had a spine we wouldn't be looking at the Commies down the end of a gun barrel now."

"If they're so soft, why did Truman get us in Korea?" Jake wanted to know.

"Because he wanted to fight the Commies over there on their turf, not ours, or so he says. What he should have done is what that Senator Taft over in Ohio said, and that's to leave everybody over there alone and stay right where we are, the hell with the rest of the world."

"Now, Conrad, I said watch your language. Little pitchers have big ears." It was Grandma again.

"I'm sure he's heard much worse," Jake said.

He was right. I'd hung around Smokey's Pool Room and Dub's D-X enough to learn all the swear words I didn't already know. But, there was no need to tell Grandma that.

"Maybe so, but he doesn't need to hear it from his Grandpa."

Grandpa must have figured with two strikes, he'd leave before he got the third one. He stood up and shuffled into the house, and shortly the radio went dead. It came back to life with sharp tweets, crackling sounds, and then the voice of the Cardinals' Harry Carey on KMOX.

Jablonski was at the plate with two outs in the second when Jimmy Brockman came across the street. "Did you listen to Ike's speech?" he asked. "He just finished."

"Didn't miss a word," Rollie chided, "except when Connie had some-thing to say that was more important."

"Which was about every other minute," added Jake.

Grandpa was back on the swing now; he started to say something but glanced at Grandma and remained quiet.

Jimmy looked at me. "Come over and help with the news. I'm doing the convention and Ike's speech, then the Helsinki Olympic Games. Lots of stuff tonight."

We went on the air at 7 p.m. sharp. As usual, Jimmy led off with a teaser as to what stories we would be covering, and then he let me read the local news. I talked about the prospects for a good melon harvest, quoting the county extension agent from the Purdue University School of Agriculture. Next, I read a story about a mysterious break-in at Tul-ley's Tavern the night before and how no money or liquor was taken but twenty-five pounds of dog food was missing. Marshal Hooper figured the thief was from out of town since all the stray dogs in town rum-maged in trashcans and the house pets ate straight from the table. I closed with the Purple Aces baseball team's fifteen-inning loss to the Darmstadt Devil Dogs.

Jimmy then did the national news, leading off with the Republican Convention in Chicago. As he did this I sidled out the door and to the front yard, just close enough to notice that Grandpa and Jake had turned off the Cardinals and were listening to Jimmy's account of the conven-tion. Every so often I could hear Grandpa saying something, but I couldn't make out what it was, although it sounded pretty emotional.

I listened until Jimmy was on to other news and then went back to the shack. He wrapped it up with an announcement that the Democra-tic Convention would be starting July 21 in the same Chicago amphithe-atre and that in the interest of balance, he would bring his perspective to WPSR at that time. Then he signed off.

When I walked back across the street Grandpa stood up and said, "I'm turning in. The Cardinals can finish this one without me."

I took his seat in the swing beside Jake. "Does grandpa really think President Truman lets Communists run the government?" I asked.

Jake took his time answering. "You have to understand, if there was one Communist in the government, your grandpa would think there are a thousand. Senator McCarthy's on a witch hunt, playing on everybody's fears. He's got everybody riled up and in a fever, accusing anybody he doesn't like of being a Communist. Nobody's proven it yet."

"But, what about the president? Is it true what Grandpa says, that he really is a bad president?"

"Well, I've met him, and I think…."

"You what? You've actually met the president? Of the United States? When?"

"When I was stationed in D.C. I was assigned to a detail on his yacht."

"The president has a yacht?"

"Yep, it's docked at the Naval Station in Washington, on the Anacostia River."

"When does he use it?"

"Well, it sits in dock most of the time, but once in a while he comes aboard and lets the crew take him out for a cruise on the Potomac and the Chesapeake Bay. He uses it to relax and get away for a while."

"And you were on his crew? How'd you get to do that?"

"Well, you have to be stationed there first, and then you have to apply, and then they check your background for clearance. If you get past that and get recommendations from your superiors, you get considered. The rest is probably luck."

"Wow, what was it like to meet him?"

"He was polite. He shook our hands when we first met and thanked us when we returned. But, we had jobs to do, and he did, too. He kept to himself and his aides most of the time. Sometimes he would come out on deck and sit in a deck chair, but only if we were in open sea."

We were sitting in darkness now, the lights in the house long gone. The swing screeched as we rocked back and forth, breaking the silence. I sat there beside Jake, who had met the president, and I wondered how anyone from Purcell Station could do that.

I couldn't sleep that night, thinking about what else he told me, which got me thinking there might be another story behind the stranger who was in town.

CHAPTER **20**

Jake sat at the oak pedestal table in the kitchen just as he had done for every meal for seventeen years before he joined the Navy. It was noon, and we were sharing a farewell meal with him before he boarded the 2:15 for Chicago, where he was to report to the Great Lakes Naval Training Center.

"How long will you be in Chicago?" Grandma asked.

"That depends. I won't know for some time. I expect to be back on the East Coast by fall, and then I'll have to make my decision."

"Decision?"

"Yep. Whether to re-up or muster out."

The last two words seemed to pique Grandma's interest. "You mean you could get out if you wanted to?"

"If I want to. After my Korean extension expires this fall, I have a choice."

"If you opt out, what will you do?" she asked. Her voice had suddenly perked up. "Will you come back home?"

"It's all up in the air. I have some ideas, but it's too soon to talk about 'em. Just trust me."

I looked at Jake with a question but couldn't get it out. He saw me and winked; I had a hunch what that meant. Last night when we sat up and talked, he mentioned he had applied to get into a new branch called Naval Intelligence. He didn't want Grandma and Grandpa to know it yet, because he might not make it. He said it's a long process, and he would have to pass through a number of hoops, including a thorough background check, to get admitted. I promised I'd keep it between us.

That's what kept me awake last night. When he said he'd have to pass a background check, I put two and two together, and connected that to the stranger. Maybe that's why he's here. Jake had brushed it off when we were talking about the stranger on the porch yesterday. Maybe he knew.

Jake sat back, taking a long sip of his ice tea.

"It's going on one o'clock," he was standing now, looking at his watch. "I'd better get things together and change."

He went to his room to finish packing his bags and change into his dress uniform. I helped Grandma clear the table, store the leftovers, and stack the dishes in the sink. Staying busy prolonged the goodbye. When we finished in the kitchen, we went out to the front porch to get some air and wait.

After carrying his bags out to the kitchen, Jake, in his dress whites, joined the rest of us and took a seat beside Grandpa on the swing. He hadn't worn the uniform since the July 4th parade, and I had forgotten how sharp he looked in it

It was another sweltering day, and there was little breeze. Grandma sat in her rocker, fanning herself. Jake and Grandpa sat mute, swinging, staring down the street toward the river bottoms in the silence that comes before a parting.

It was minutes before Jake spoke up. "Those trees down there, they've sure grown since the last time I sat here." He was pointing to a grove of river birches along Trotter's melon field.

"Lot of things have grown since you were here," said Grandma.

"Speaking of those trees, why hasn't anyone seen Eddie Sprowl lately? Jake asked. "Doesn't he ever come outta his woods down there?"

"No, and he keeps his wife outta sight, too. Who knows what he's doing back there?" Grandpa said. "Law-breakin's easier when it's done in secret."

"There's probably a good reason why he keeps her out of sight," Grandma added. "She probably knows too much." I waited for her to say more, but she just sat there, leaving me to wonder what Eddie's wife knew.

"I'd better get a move on. My train leaves in twenty minutes," Jake said, rising up out of the swing. He took a long look around, as if he wanted to remember everything as a reference for the next time he'd come home. Then he led us to the kitchen, where he picked up his suitcase, grabbed his duffle bag, and we all walked out the back door and through the grape arbor. At the end of the tunnel, Jake stopped, turned, and took a long look back at the house.

It was all downhill to the train station, and that made it a lot easier for Grandpa. I worried about the walk back, though. We arrived in plenty of time. Taylor Barth was sitting in the cage behind the counter doing some paperwork when we entered. Jake set his suitcase down and walked over to the cage just as Taylor looked up.

"Why, Jake! Don't tell me your furlough's up this quick?"

"Afraid so, Taylor. I need a ticket to Chicago."

"Coming up. I hope you got around to seein' everybody while you were here."

"Everybody I wanted to see. It doesn't take long to see everybody in Purcell Station."

"You got that right," Taylor said. "I heard lots of people say how good you looked."

"And those were just my relatives." Jake smiled.

Taylor looked up and laughed. He tore off a ticket, wrote in the destination and handed it to Jake. "Here you go. This should get you there." He pulled out his pocket watch. "Train should be here in about seven minutes, more or less."

Jake thanked him and tucked the ticket in his shirt pocket. "We might as well sit inside while we're waiting," he said, pointing to the two benches in the middle of the station. A ceiling fan overhead stirred the air and gave some relief from the heat.

Someone pulled up outside in the parking lot, and in a minute Bud Pate swung open the front door. He headed over to the cage but saw us sitting there. "Hey, there's my favorite sailor. Whatcha all dressed up for, Jake?"

"Just for you, Bud."

Growing up, Jake had been one of Bud's "buddies." As a kid, he used to hang around the post office, trying to open the combinations on people's mailboxes. Bud always knew what he was up to and would sometimes hide behind the wall of boxes and wait until Jake got one open. Then he'd reach through the back of the box just as Jake opened it and grab his hand, squeezing it until he cried "uncle."

"You stuck your hand in any mailboxes in the Navy?" Bud asked.

"That would be a federal offense, Bud, and just might get me court-martialed."

"I think it was a federal offense a few years ago in Purcell Station, too, if I remember correctly."

"Then it's a good thing you didn't catch anyone doing it," Jake said.

"By the way, how long is it before the statute of limitations runs out?" Bud asked.

"Long enough. Besides, you'd need evidence."

"Does that bone I broke in your pinky count? I could subpoena your X-ray"

Taylor was enjoying this and decided to get in. "You should have seen him sneak on the trains. He would hide out on the other side of the tracks, and when the train was starting to roll, he would jump on and ride the blinds into town. It would take at least that long for anyone to find him, and since that was the next stop anyway, he didn't care if they threw him off."

Grandpa sat listening, his dancing eyes betraying a stone face. Grandma didn't give away her thoughts, but I figured she had heard most of this before. I'm sure she was just glad it was all behind him.

The whistle came from the south. The first one was a warning to anyone who might be on the bridge. The second whistle came as it rounded the bend between the river and the station, alerting the stationmaster and any cars at the crossing. That's when Bud hustled out to his truck to get the mail bag. Jake picked up his bags, and we headed out to the platform. The train stopped and the conductor stepped off and placed a wooden box at the foot of the steps. A porter came down, took Jake's bags, and disappeared in the car.

Jake took Grandpa's hand and shook it, and then they hugged. "Take care of yourself, Dad."

Grandpa held him tight but didn't say anything, only nodding. A tear in his eye glistened in the sunlight

Jake turned to Grandma, and they hugged. "That goes for you, too. I don't know when I'll be back, but I'll write and let you know."

"You be careful," she said. "I'll be praying for you."

"I know you will. I will for you, too."

He then turned to me, grabbing me around the shoulders, and said, "Don't be a fool like I was. You have a good mind—use it." He patted me on the shoulder. "Some people are lucky to be born a Gentry, a Halderman, or a Manion; then others are not so fortunate and are born a Sprowl, but luck's only half of it. It's what you do with it that matters."

He let the words hang there a moment, looking to see if I understood.

"Thanks for staying up and talking those nights," I said. "That meant a lot to me."

He nodded and then he turned, climbed the steps, and disappeared into the car.

He sat by the window, waving, and we waved back until he was out of sight. As we turned to walk into the station, I couldn't help thinking about Taylor Barth and how it must have been the day he saw his son leave Purcell Station for the last time. I just hoped it wasn't Jake's last time.

Bud Tate had picked up the fresh mail bag and was putting it in the back of his truck when he saw us. "You walking home in this heat? It must be 110 degrees. Get in. I'll run you home."

He didn't have to beg. Grandma and Grandpa got in the cab while I climbed in the back and sat on the mail bag. The warm breeze blew past me as Bud revved it up Main Street, tooted at the men on Dub's liar's bench as we rounded the corner, and dropped us off in the driveway. We thanked him for sparing us the walk, and then Grandma went in the house to make a pitcher of iced tea. Grandpa quietly followed her. I stayed outside. I felt empty.

I wandered around the backyard, through the arbor tunnel, across the alley, and into and out of the barn. The garden where Grandma and I had spent countless hours looked green and full. I walked through the woodshed and then the garage where the old Chevy sat collecting dust.

Stopping under the maple tree beside the driveway, I saw a limb that must have been the one my mother once told me about. When she was little, her father hung a rope from it, and she would sit there and swing for hours, pumping it so high she could see the sky on the way up and the ground on the way down.

I went in the garage and pulled out one of Grandpa's old ladders, stood it against the tree, climbed up, and grabbed the limb. Pulling myself up and over it, I caught my breath as I sat there for a moment. Then I looked up and found other limbs a little higher. I climbed so high I could see the whole yard and garden and buildings below, and I just sat there. Then I began to think about my folks in Cleveland, and Uncle Jake on the train, and Mom's older brothers who had fought in the war, and Taylor Barth's son who'd died in the war, and the war going on in Korea. Then I tasted the lump of sorrow. That's what I'd called it as a little kid, when I said I could taste the sorrow in my throat.

Then I remembered something else. Back in May, when I was in the station in Indianapolis waiting for my train, I sat on a bench next to a man who was reading a newspaper. When his train arrived, he got up and left, leaving the newspaper behind. I looked around to see if anyone else was going to claim it, and when nobody did, I picked up a section of the *Indianapolis News* and on the front page saw a picture of a boy chasing a flock of pigeons that was taking flight from the War Memorial Plaza downtown. It was a warm spring day, and he was running and leaning forward with his arms stretched out like he was almost flying, trying to catch a pigeon. He looked so free and hopeful that he would catch it. The caption under the picture highlighted the "youthful exuberance and spirit of a twelve-year-old." I thought how he had only a short time left to be twelve and to chase the pigeons, and then it would be too late.

That day I took my pocketknife, cut the picture out, and stuffed it in my pocket. An hour later, I boarded my train for Purcell Station and the summer of my twelfth year, my last chance to chase the pigeons.

CHAPTER 21

The void I felt when Uncle Jake left was filled by Skipper and Jimmy. It was exciting being around Jimmy, his gadgets, the river, the Sand Bowl, and his radio station. There was always something going on. As for Skipper, I was beginning to sense a different kind of pull. So when I saw her at Brockman's and she asked if I wanted to go swimming, I didn't want to sound too eager. We agreed to meet at the depot.

I arrived before Skipper did and found Taylor Barth standing out in front talking to Lady Muldoon. I rode on past, nodding to both of them, and they waved back but went on talking.

I parked my bike beside the depot and sat on the front bench in the shade, where I could see all the way up Main Street. I glanced several times over at Lady and Taylor. They kept talking; once in a while she would smile, and Taylor would nod, and they would both laugh. Usually he would drop everything when I came up, and we'd sit and talk, and he would offer me a glass of the iced tea he kept in a thermos under his desk. I figured he was too busy today.

Skipper came coasting down Main Street, and when she saw Lady and Taylor she waved and then slid to a stop in front of me. "Do you remember what I said at the free show—about a hidden place I knew about?" she said.

I nodded.

"Well, I'm going to show you. It's the most beautiful place on the whole river."

"If it's hidden, how do you know about it?"

"I'll tell you later. Let's go."

Skipper led the way through the jungle of trees and shrubs along the river. We hurried past Eddie Sprowl's place, including the mystery shed, hoping the usual pack of stray dogs was off somewhere else. I'd heard if they got too riled up Eddie might come out with his shotgun. I was wondering if he was protecting more than just what was in his shed. I wasn't sure what Grandma meant about Eddie's wife and what else she knew. It was odd how nobody ever saw her around town—or Eddie, for that matter.

Wherever the dogs were, they didn't see us, and we didn't see them. When we reached the water, we turned right and went downriver. After about half a mile the path narrowed and we had to go single-file. No trucks or cars could have made it through here, and from the looks of it, very few people had, either. We kept hacking our way on through the brush until off in the distance I saw a large hill rising out of the low bottoms.

It looked out of place. "What's that?" I asked.

"That's Taber Hill. The story is some guy in the city—a politician with a lot of money—owns it. Nobody's allowed up there. Signs are posted saying it's off-limits."

That sounded strange, but I let it go. I remembered her talking about it at the free show. We went on another mile or more before we rounded a huge bend and came to a wide sandbar just before the river turned back around the other way. We were on the bank about ten feet above the water when Skipper stopped. She looked out over the river and said, "Well, what do you think of it?"

The river was wider here and calmer, except for birds chirping in the tall sycamores that lined the banks. There was no sign of anyone ever having been here: no litter, cans, or fire ashes; only clear, rippling water and forests all around.

"It's so far from everything."

"Yes, and there's not even a trail here, only the railroad tracks over there." She pointed across the river where the railroad curved around the bend, although it was hidden by the trees. "Nobody ever comes down here."

"I can see that, but how'd you find it?"

"It was an accident. My brother and I made a raft last summer out of some old logs we got from the sawmill."

"You came here by boat?"

"Yep. It wasn't any problem coming downstream. The current pretty much took us. We had a little problem going back, though."

We left our bikes and made a path down the embankment and onto the sandbar. We then walked out to the water's edge, laid our towels on the sand, peeled down to our swim suits, and stuck our toes in the water. I couldn't help noticing Skipper's tan, and her young woman's figure made me feel too much like a twelve-year-old. I was taller than she was, now that I'd grown so fast, and I was stronger since I began lifting bales in the hay loft, but I figured she was closer to a woman than I was a man. I wanted to get in the water before she noticed.

It was warm in the shallows, but when we waded out into the current the cooler water felt good. Skipper did a surface dive, disappeared under the water, and came up across the deep part where the current was faster. She turned, looked back at me, and smiled as if to say, "Follow me."

Jimmy had taught me to swim well enough to get by, so I dove under and followed, pulling and holding my breath until I could hold it no longer. I took one last pull with my arms and bobbed my head up out of the water. I could no longer touch the bottom, so I treaded water while looking around for Skipper. I didn't see her. Several seconds passed, and just as I was starting to think something was wrong, she bobbed up downstream.

She tilted her head back and swam away. I dove in after her. She saw me coming and did a backstroke to get away. I pulled hard and kicked and came up to her underwater, but before I could open my eyes, I touched something soft. I surfaced, and she was standing up, and then I saw where I'd touched her. I began to feel my face turn red. She pretended she didn't notice and drifted away.

We were treading water when we realized we'd drifted down the river and were heading around the bend, well past our starting point. The river was deeper here, the current was faster, and there was no sandbar on either side.

"We'd better get out of this before we get swept all the way to the Wabash," Skipper said. "There's another sand bar around the bend."

We stayed in the current, floating and letting it carry us to the next bend when we heard the sound of a train approach from the south. The tracks ran away from the river until they reached the bend. As we approached we heard a screeching noise. The train was stopping.

"There's a side switch up there," Skipper said. "It's probably pulling off to let another train pass."

It stopped. There was silence for a few minutes, and then we heard another train coming from the north. It passed, and after a few minutes when its sound was faint, the north bounder started up again. We could hear the jerk of each freight car as the engine tugged it, leaving behind the silence of the river.

Skipper and I floated and dog-paddled, letting the current take us to the bend. When we got even with the sandbar and could feel the bottom with our feet, we walked up the gritty slope to the shore. Just as we stepped out, Skipper stopped and grabbed my arm. She froze.

"Did you hear that?"

"Hear what?"

"Wait." She looked out across the river toward the railroad. I turned and searched the banks, listening.

"I heard someone talking," she said, "And I think I smell smoke."

"Where?"

"Over there!" She pointed to a faint trail of smoke rising above the shrubs. "Someone's there," she said. "But nobody ever comes down this far."

"How would they get here? There're no path here."

"The only way would be by the railroad."

We stood there, not knowing whether to stay or run. Finally, Skipper said, "Let's go see!"

We waded out to the current and dove in, crossing it as it took us at an angle to the other side. There was no sandbar on that side, and the water was deep along the bank. When we reached it we found a log that had fallen down the embankment and toppled into the river. We grabbed it and climbed up into the thicket of shrubs and trees. We stopped and listened.

"It's coming from there." She was pointing toward the tracks.

Skipper led as we moved from tree to tree until we saw the tracks rising high to keep trains above the spring floods. The trail of smoke came from a trestle over a dry creek bed. We walked up through it until the voices grew louder. Stopping behind a mulberry bush along the bank, we parted the branches and saw them: five men huddled around a fire. They were cooking something.

I looked at Skipper and started to ask....

"Shhh! They're hobos," she whispered.

"How do you know?"

"I've seen them in town before," she whispered. "They hang out behind Maddie's Café or the hotel after hours and look for food. They hop the trains— ride the boxcars—and set up camps where people won't bother them."

Skipper let go of the branches to keep us hidden. After a while she whispered, "They're usually harmless, unless they get to drinking."

"You think they're drinking now?"

She parted the branches again and stared into the camp. "There're some bottles lying around, so somebody has. They can probably get all they want pretty cheap up the tracks."

"You mean Eddie Sprowl's shed?"

"Could be."

One of the men stood up and looked out toward our direction. He took a few steps, stretched, let out a loud belch, walked over to a clump of shrubs, and began to fiddle with the buttons on his pants.

"Let's get out of here," Skipper said. We hunched over and took quick steps down a small ravine toward the river. We found the log and slid down into the water, crossing the current the way we had come. When we reached the sandbar on the other side, we looked back to see if anyone was following us. Seeing no one, we walked upriver on the sandbar until it ended. There we entered the thicket of dense forest and brush, forging a path where there wasn't one before. It was slow going, but better than trying to swim upstream in the current and safer from the eyes of strangers.

We found our clothes on the sandbar where we'd left them, got dressed, got back on our bikes, and started riding back through the wooded path. In the heavy sand the pedaling was hard, and for some reason I couldn't get up any speed. I was pushing much harder than I had coming out. I noticed Skipper was having the same problem.

"What's wrong? I can't get going," she said.

I looked down and saw the problem. "Check your tires. Mine are flat."

She stopped. Hers were, too. "Someone's been here," she said. "And I bet I know who. Whose house did we pass to get here?"

"Jesse's."

"It has to be."

We pushed the bicycles through the forest, and when we got even with the Sprowl place the stray dogs were back. When they came snipping at our heels, Skipper grabbed a stick and poked it at the nose of the lead dog, and it vanished.

I looked around for Jesse.

"He's probably hiding somewhere, laughing at us," Skipper said.

We followed the tracks back to the depot, then pushed our bikes on up Main Street to Dub's D-X station. Dub brought out the air hose and aired up our tires while Jasper McCauley and his loafing friends made sport of our troubles. Then, by a stroke of luck, Jasper's wife stood, hands on hips, calling him from the middle of Main Street to come home and water her daisies. That turned all the attention to Jasper as he slumped his shoulders and meekly plodded up the street to a wife waiting with folded arms.

Tired, hungry, and put out with Jesse, Skipper and I parted at the corner, but not before she asked if I was free tomorrow.

"I think so. Why?"

"I'm taking the train up to town tomorrow, and I thought you might want to go with me."

"Sure. Why're you going?"

"There's a book I need to pick up at the county library, plus there's a lot to do there. We can make a day of it."

"Okay, I just remembered I have a book to pick up there, too. What time?"

"Train leaves at 9:54. I'll see you at the station. There's a lot of history up there. I'll take you on a tour."

CHAPTER 22

O n my way to the station I stopped at the library to ask if my name had come up yet on *Catcher in the Rye*. Miss Perkins frowned when I asked, but she said she would check and then disappeared in the back room. While waiting, I looked around the biography section to see if they had any books about the Navy. I found a book on Admiral David Farragut and another one on Pearl Harbor. I was looking through them when Miss Perkins came back and said, "It looks like it's still checked out, sorry."

She didn't look sorry to me, but I thanked her anyway and asked her to check out the book on Pearl Harbor for me. Her sorrow seemed to disappear then, and she looked pleased with my new book selection.

I headed down Main Street toward the depot. Just as I walked by Slinker's General Store, the door swung open and Spooks barged out and almost ran into me.

"Hi, Spooks," I said.

"Hi G—Garrett." He started to pick up his wheelbarrow but stopped and said, "Y-you saved my hat." He took his cap off and held it out for me to see. He pounded his fist in it, shaping it before putting it back on his head. "T—thanks for getting my h-hat."

"That's okay, Spooks. I'm glad I could reach it."

"Jesse's mean."

"I know Spooks. Have you seen him lately?"

"No. I s—stay away from him."

"Good. If you see him, you should let Skipper or me know, okay?"

"Okay."

He picked up his wheelbarrow and followed me down to the station. I didn't know why until I got to the platform and saw Taylor Barth. He explained that Bud Tate had sprained his ankle playing softball at the vacant lot and had hired Spooks to meet the afternoon mail train and take the mail bag up to the post office.

Spooks was standing there smiling when Taylor explained all this, so I said, "That's a pretty big job, Spooks. A lot of people are going to...."

But Spooks was already pushing his wheelbarrow over to the tracks before I could finish. A train was coming. When it slowed down and the mail bag landed on the platform, Spooks got it, flung it aboard his wheelbarrow, and was on his way up the street before the train was out of sight.

Inside, Taylor was on the telephone. I waited for him to hang up, and when he greeted me, I asked if I could leave my library book there for the day. He nodded, and then I asked him how much a ticket to Vincennes cost.

"One-way or round-trip?"

"Round-trip, unless you're trying to get rid of me."

"Let me think about that." He paused, then added, "Nah. I wouldn't have anybody to talk to if you left."

"Then make it round-trip."

"That'll be twenty-five cents for you. You got big plans for today?"

"Yep, going to the city. How much is it for everybody else?"

"About twenty -five cents."

"Oh. I thought maybe I was getting a discount, since I'm a regular around here."

"There's a difference between a regular and a regular paying customer, which, if my memory serves me you are not."

Just then, Skipper swung open the front door, greeted us, and asked Taylor for a ticket for "uptown."

"Right over here." He walked behind the counter and stamped out two tickets just as a whistle blew. The train was waiting. We told Taylor we'd see him this evening, handed our tickets to the conductor, and boarded.

Soon we were coming into the outskirts of the city, passing businesses and warehouses, then houses with kids playing out in the yards. They waved when they saw us with our noses pressed against the window. The houses were bigger and older in the middle part of town. "This is where the founders settled. Some people call them 'Blue Bloods,'" Skipper said. "People around here will tell you about it, too. They're proud of their history."

As the train slowed to approach the station, we came to a clearing and the depot came in sight. A passenger train on the Baltimore and Ohio had already stopped, and its passengers were off milling around. A young boy was hawking newspapers up and down the platform. When we pulled to a stop and got off, Skipper informed me that Red Skelton had sold newspapers here as a young boy.

"My father told me that, too," I said. "I listen to his radio show all the time."

"Now he has a television show, too. I've been trying to get my father to buy a TV, but he says he doesn't want to be the first one in Purcell Station to have one."

"Have you ever seen one?"

"I saw one once in the window of an appliance store uptown. People were watching a basketball game on it. It was fifteen degrees in February, and they were standing on the sidewalk, watching the game through the window."

We were walking down Washington Avenue toward downtown when Skipper stopped in front of a brick building. "We're here. It's bigger than our library, so I hope they have it."

I was nervous, but Skipper seemed sure of herself. I followed her to the front desk. A lady with gray hair pulled up in a bun was standing behind the counter typing something on an old Remington. One of the keys kept sticking, and she was getting frustrated. She didn't seem to notice us, and when Skipper turned around and gave me a look, I nodded that maybe we should just go. Skipper didn't respond but turned back to watch the lady type.

Finally, she ripped the paper out of the typewriter as if she were either glad that was over or so mad she was going to quit. She lowered her head and peered at us over the glasses that were sliding down her nose, then waited as if it was our turn to talk.

Skipper took the hint. "Excuse me, ma'am, but could you tell us if *Catcher in the Rye* is on file?"

The lady looked first at Skipper, then me, then back at Skipper. "You can check for yourself on the shelf right over there. It's listed alphabetically by author." She pointed to stacks near the back wall.

She wasn't going out of her way to help, but I didn't think she was going to frown on us borrowing the book like Miss Perkins did, either. We found the stacks that led us to the "S's," and we found Salinger.

"Look!" said Skipper. "There's a copy." She picked it up and held it open to the dust cover so we could read it.

Finally, I said, "Let's go. I'm getting nervous."

She closed the book, and we walked back to the front desk, where she laid it on the counter and waited. The librarian was in the back cubicle but saw us, gave us an exasperated look, and came forward, taking her time to let us know we were putting her out. Skipper laid her card out on top of the book and the lady took it and examined it. She looked at Skipper and then at me, like we should feel guilty or something, then finally opened the book, stamped the due date in the back, and gave Skipper her card back.

"Thank you, ma'am." Skipper tucked the book under her arm, and we left.

"I can't believe we got it," I said as we walked down Seventh Street toward the court house.

"I've heard some libraries have banned it or lend it only to adults," Skipper said. "But, if you act like you know what you're doing, they think you're older."

We were in front of the courthouse. Skipper motioned for me to cross the street, where she led me to a grassy lawn and a cluster of trees and shrubs. She looked around to see if anyone was looking, then crept into a lilac bush and disappeared. When she came out, she was without the book.

"I'm hiding the book in there so we won't have to carry it all day. We'll come back and get it on the way home."

We walked to Main Street and turned toward the river. The street was crowded with shoppers and people going to lunch. Skipper asked if I was hungry and I said I was, so she led us to the lunch counter at the Kresge

Five and Ten Cent Store. We took a seat at the counter and ordered two ham and cheese sandwiches and two chocolate milkshakes, to go."

By the time our order came there were people waiting for a seat, so we got up, paid our bill, and went up Main toward the river, where we found a bench in a shaded, grassy park and sat down to eat. When we finished, Skipper told me to follow her. We crossed Vigo Street when I suddenly stopped and looked ahead.

Skipper saw me staring at the end of the street. "It's the oldest cathedral in Indiana," she said, describing a church unlike any I'd ever seen before. "Next to it is the first library built in the state, and beside it is the state's first university." They were two brick buildings, worn but showing their age well. "Over there," she said, pointing to a large, limestone rotunda, "is the George Rogers Clark Memorial. And in front of it is the Lincoln Memorial Bridge."

I took it all in as we walked across the street and up to the front of the cathedral. "The Old Cathedral dates back to 1749, but this building was put up in 1826," she added. "It's open, if you want to go inside."

It was quiet and dark inside, except for some candles and some light coming in through the stained glass windows along the sides. We walked up the center aisle, but stopped when we saw some people sitting in the pews down near the front. Instead, Skipper motioned for me to follow her to the outside aisle where we walked along the wall to a door beside the altar. She stopped and whispered, pointing to the murals behind the altar. "The middle one is *The Crucifixion*. It was painted in 1870."

I looked in awe. "How'd you know this stuff? You're not Catholic."

"Mostly from field trips at school and reading about it. My parents also have friends who belong here."

She motioned for me to follow her through the small door and down a narrow stairway into a lower level. "These are crypts. Some of the bishops from the early years of the church are buried here."

I walked along the wall and saw the names: Brute, de la Hailandiere, Bazin, and de St. Palais. Above the crypt of Brute sat a statue of the Virgin Mary. "That was brought over from France in 1838," said Skipper.

Skipper was not done. We walked out the side exit of the cathedral and onto the grounds of the George Rogers Clark Memorial. "It's a national monument. President Roosevelt came here in 1936 to dedicate it." I remembered Tip telling us that.

It was a large, round structure surrounded by limestone pillars, with steps leading up to the entrance. Inside we heard the echo of someone talking in a monotone and found a tour guide leading a small group of tourists in a description of the murals that surrounded the rotunda. We joined them and heard a brief history of Clark's defeat of the British in 1779.

When the tour ended, we walked out onto the Memorial Terrace and then across the lawn to the Lincoln Memorial Bridge. Walking up the steps, we came to a wall that overlooked the river and the memorial grounds, and there we took a seat. A stone monument told us this was where Abe Lincoln crossed the Wabash in 1830 when he moved to Illinois. He was twenty-one years old

When we stood up, Skipper said, "We've got time to go see Grouseland. It was the home of William Henry Harrison. We can take a short-cut if we take the levee."

The levee ran north along the river and past some of the city's oldest homes.

"These homes were built by the French," Skipper said. "They came here from Louisiana and Canada, and a lot of their descendants still live here. You can look in the phone book and still see the French names."

"Were all the settlers French?" I asked.

"No, the British came in and took over, so a lot of local people came from England, too. At first the French and British didn't get along."

"Do they now?"

"Oh, for the most part. There's still a few who have their noses in the air, but nobody pays much attention to 'em. It's kind of like the Catholics and the Lutherans and the Baptists back in Purcell Station. They get along, but they keep their distance, too."

We walked past a row of old brick homes with white columns and railings above on the balconies. "These homes closest to the river are the oldest. That's because the first settlers came by boat. If you go a few blocks away, they're different."

We came to an opening, and there stood the two-story brick mansion called Grouseland. It had tall, white columns on its front porch and a balcony above it.

"Before Harrison became president, he was the president of the Indiana Territory. Its capital was here." We went inside and Skipper gave me a quick tour of the rooms, using what she had heard when she had taken field trips there in school. When we were finished, she looked at her watch and said, "We have about an hour to kill before our train leaves. We can go downtown. There's one more place I'd like to take you."

We took side streets this time, walking through the narrow streets laid out in a northeast-southwest angle. "It's like the cities and towns in France," Skipper said. "It's even named after a town in France."

"Does that mean this place is more French than English?"

"It depends on whether you ask a Frenchman or an Englishman." She smiled.

We reached Main Street and turned the corner. It was still crowded. We walked another block, past stores and shops, until Skipper said, "Turn in here."

I looked for a door but only saw a narrow hallway recessed between two stores.

"In here." She led me into the dark passage, through a heavy door, and up a long, narrow set of stairs. At the top she opened another door, over which a sign read, "No one under the age of sixteen."

"Are you sure we can go in here?" I asked.

"They don't check. I've been here before."

As the door swung open, I heard the sound of clacking billiard balls and the den of people talking. Music played in the background. We stepped around the corner and into a smoke-filled room. I counted four pool tables in the front, and they were all busy. A boy in a tee shirt with a pack of cigarettes twisted in the sleeve stood chalking his cue stick. He yelled, "Rack'em up, Mack," and an elderly man, smoking a cigar, came out of the crowd, bent over the table with a wooden triangle, and racked up a new game.

"Don't mind this," she said, gesturing to the group of boys and young men sizing up shots or leaning against the wall with cigarettes dangling from their mouths. She motioned toward a soda fountain in the back, and I followed. A row of stools lined the counter, and a set of booths sat along the opposite wall. It was noisy. A song started up on the juke box as we wove our way through the mob. I noticed they were all male.

"Why aren't there any girls in here?" I asked.

"I guess it's an unwritten rule. Nothing official, but most girls wouldn't want to come in and get leered at. Anyway, I've been here, and they've never thrown me out."

"Aren't you afraid they'll leer at you?"

"Mother always says if a girl conducts herself right and demands respect, she'll get respect. I've never had a problem here before."

"How'd you know about this?"

"My brother, Patrick. All the kids come here between sessions of the basketball tournament, when they're killing time before the night games. He brought me here then. I think it was so crowded they didn't even notice I was a girl."

"Have you been here since then?"

"Only a couple of times, but always with Patrick. They have the best sodas in town. As long as a girl has money, they don't seem to mind."

I looked around and felt the stare of some of the older guys. I wasn't sure if that meant they didn't like her being here or that they were looking at her with other ideas.

Skipper asked me what I wanted and then stepped up to an opening at the counter between two boys on stools and ordered two chocolate sodas. One of the boys said something to her that I couldn't hear. She must not have liked his tone so she stepped back and ignored him. A jukebox was playing a Teresa Brewer hit, "Till I Waltz Again with You."

Our order came, and after we paid for it we moved over to the middle to get out of the way. We stood there sipping our drinks because there was no place to sit. If Skipper could sense the number of boys staring at her, she didn't let on. I noticed, though, and I started to feel a need to protect her—but that was funny, because what could I do? I was too young even to be in there. Everyone was older and bigger. They probably figured I was her kid brother.

The jukebox stopped, and things got quiet until Doris Day came on singing, "A Guy is a Guy."

When the noise resumed, a muscular boy in a tee shirt and jeans pushed his way through the crowd and came face to face with Skipper. Taking a long draw on his cigarette and letting the smoke out slowly, he said, "Hi, baby, would you like to dance?"

Skipper carefully took a long sip on her straw, studying the bottom of her nearly empty glass and finally said, "No, thank you. I don't know you."

He must have sensed the looks of the others, because he put the cigarette in the corner of his mouth and let it dangle like he'd seen Bogart in Casablanca. "That's no problem," he muttered. "My name's Kirk. I guess you know yours."

He smiled and looked around at the other boys, who, he seemed sure, were now watching and waiting to see how cool he was. A voice in the back yelled, "Smooth move, Kirklin! Smoooth!"

Ignoring him, Skipper turned to say something to me, and he must have felt his prey getting away from him, so he grabbed her by the arm. She jerked it free and stepped back just as I reached for his arm and held it. I let go as soon as she was free, but I already knew the consequences. He looked at me and then at her and asked, "Is this your little brother?"

"No, he's my boyfriend."

I flinched. Not only was I surprised, but I immediately knew I might have to face something in front of all these strangers that I was not capable of carrying out.

"Oh, is he?" Kirk smirked, moving to within inches of my face. He reminded me of those Marine posters found in post offices and government buildings. He contorted his face into a scowl. I felt myself cowering, yet I tried to stand erect and meet him eye to eye. He was a head taller, a good fifty pounds heavier, and he had friends. I had only Skipper.

Much to my surprise, that was enough.

Skipper stepped closer, just in case he tried something. Then she lowered her voice and whispered in Kirk's ear, so the others couldn't hear. "I do know my name, and I think you do, too. It's Manion." She waited. "As in Jack Manion."

He stopped staring at me and turned to look at her. His scowl softened, like he was thinking, and I could see the muscles in his face relax. He just looked at Skipper, and didn't say anything.

"Now, my boyfriend and I have a train to catch. I think you owe us an apology."

He looked around to see who was watching. Then turning toward Skipper, but looking at the floor, he nearly whispered, "I didn't mean anything by it. I was just showing off."

It was as close as he could come to an apology in front of his friends, but it got us out of the room, down the stairs, and into the street.

We were a block down Main Street before I caught my breath. "What was that all about? How'd we get out of there alive?"

"My father always says that everything that goes around comes around."

"What's that supposed to mean?"

"Well, I played a hunch, and it worked. When he was showing off to his friends, one of them yelled 'Smooth move, Kirklin.' Did you hear that?"

"Yeah, something like that."

"Well, a few years ago, Dad helped a guy who had been in trouble with the law. He had a big family to support, and after spending time in prison nobody would give him a job. Dad heard about him and was told he was a pretty good mechanic, so Dad gave him a job. His name's Kirklin, and he turned out to be a pretty good worker. I knew he had a son about nineteen or so, and I took a chance this might be him. There aren't many Kirklins around here. It's not English, and it's sure not French. When I told him my name I studied his face, and I knew he recognized it. I figured then we were going to be okay."

We came to the corner of Seventh Street and turned toward the courthouse. "You're amazing, Skipper." I couldn't think how to thank her for getting us out of there.

At the court house she crawled into the lilac bush, then came out with J. D. Salinger tucked under her arm and a smile on her face. "Now, let's get to the station before we miss the train."

We caught the 5:15 southbound local as it was pulling out. Taylor Barth was waiting for us when we stepped off the train, my book on Pearl Harbor under his arm. "I didn't want you to forget this," he said as he handed it to me. "I was afraid you two got lost. It's kinda late."

"It was a pretty full day," I said, and left it at that.

"Here, you take this, too," Skipper said as she handed me the Salinger book. "I've already read it."

I walked up Main Street with Skipper, hiding Salinger under my book on Pearl Harbor. When we got to Dub's corner, Skipper and I parted, promising to get together again before Tip called us to the melon fields.

When I got home Grandma asked, "Did you enjoy your day in the city?"

"I did, and Skipper was a good guide. She sure knows her history. And I got a book at the library. It's on Pearl Harbor." I was preparing her for the amount of time I might spend reading in the next few days.

"Your Uncle Jake read that. He said it's one reason he wanted to join the Navy."

"Maybe I will, too, after I read it."

"You'd better think about college first. You need to continue what your mother started."

"I know. I want to go to Indiana. They're supposed to have a really good basketball team this year—maybe win the national championship."

"Well, there's a lot more there than basketball. You keep reading those books you're checking out. It'll help you in college."

I assured her I would. I was beginning to feel guilty about the one I was hiding.

After supper, when the neighbors gathered on their porches to swing and chat or listen to the radio, I shot baskets in the driveway. I followed up with Jimmy and the radio show at seven, then told Grandma and Grandpa goodnight. It was nine o'clock. I closed my bedroom door, turned on the bedside light, opened my new library book, and read:

If you really want to hear about it, the first thing you'll probably want to know is where I was born and what my lousy childhood was like....

CHAPTER **23**

The corn, tomatoes, and potatoes were coming in quickly, and Grandma needed help in the garden. I rose early every morning for a week and helped bring in the harvest before the sun got too hot. Grandma began canning the tomatoes in her pressure cooker and putting them into quart jars. It was my job to pick, peel, and cut them up; then when they were cooked, in jars, and cooled, I carried them to the cellar.

By the end of the week, the cellar was full and we had given the neighbors all the vegetables they could use. Grandma then gave Spooks a job hauling more vegetables to give to Reverend Snyder, Lady Muldoon, and Taylor Barth. I rode my bike along with him to make sure Jesse or his friends didn't try to sabotage his wheelbarrow like they did the week before. When Skipper and I got back home from our train trip, we found out some of Jesse's buddies had dumped Spooks' load of garbage on the railroad just as he was crossing the tracks. A train came along a few minutes later and spewed it all over the station platform.

Luckily, today we didn't run into Jesse. He'd sometimes disappear for days at a time, and there were rumors that when things got hot he'd go down to Patoka to visit his cousins. That may have explained the reports out of Patoka last week that vandals had hung a cross in the front yard of a Negro family who had just moved there from Princeton. The Patoka town marshal was seen walking out of Mert Hopper's office the next day, so people figured Jesse was a suspect.

It was early afternoon when I left Spooks at Dub's D-X and saw the Blue Bruise sitting a block down the street in front of Slinker's General Store. I thought Skipper might be there, and sure enough, just then she came out to get in the truck.

"Hey, Skip," I yelled. She stopped and waited for me to catch up. I started down the street, and just as I got in front of Brockman's Grocery, a car roared up beside me and slid to a stop. A lady with two small kids in the backseat quickly jumped out and ran into the store. She left her car door open and the motor running. She must have left something in the store. I hesitated for a moment, thinking she'd come right back out. Seconds passed, so I looked in the store window to see if I could see her. Just as I turned back around, her car started moving down the hill. I ran after it. I grabbed the door and tried to jump into the driver's seat, but the door swung around and knocked me off balance. I fell to the ground. The car was picking up speed and heading down the middle of the street.

A lady on the sidewalk in front of the bank saw it and yelled, "Help! Somebody!" She waved her arms and shouted, "There're kids in there."

A couple of young boys riding their bicycles up the hill swerved to get out of its way. I heard one yell, "There's nobody driving!"

It was heading toward the depot. I thought of Taylor Barth and those kids in the backseat. I ran down the street yelling, "Help! Help!"

Skipper, standing beside her truck, heard me yell. She climbed in her truck and, just as the car reached her, she pulled into the street, as the car crashed into her rear bumper, bounced, and hit it again. With the force of the car pushing against the Blue Bruise, Skipper slowed it down and brought it under control. She eased it to a stop no more than fifty feet from the depot.

I was still running down the street along with a number of other witnesses who had heard the commotion and emptied the stores and businesses. The cook and two waitresses from the Purcell Hotel dining room were coming down the steps to see what happened. When I got there, Skipper was already out of the truck and opening the doors to check on the two kids in the backseat. They were crying. Skipper took the little girl, picked her up, and held her.

"It's okay," she said. "It's all over now. It's okay."

Taylor Barth had come out of the depot and was trying to figure out what the commotion was all about. As bystanders explained to Taylor what had happened, Rollie Brockman drove up in his Packard and jumped out. A lady swung open his passenger side door and ran up to the car. Shaking, she lifted her sobbing little boy. "I'm sorry, honey. I'm so sorry. Are you okay?" She turned to Skipper, who was still holding the little girl, and she put her arm around both kids and held them while they cried.

By this time quite a crowd had gathered. The car and truck were still blocking the street, and three cars coming from across the tracks had stopped. Several cars had come down the street and were stacked up behind the accident. A siren sounded, and I saw its flashing red lights inching along the curb to get around the parked cars. It was Mert Hopper. He got out, wearing his uniform and pistol belt, and quickly took charge.

"Anybody hurt?" He looked at the two children, who had stopped crying now.

The mother said, "Only their feelings, Mert. They're okay. It was all my fault."

"What happened, anyway?" he asked, looking at the bumper of the car to see if it was damaged.

"Like I said, it was all my fault. I'd forgotten my purse at Brockman's and turned around to go back and get it. I was so anxious, I guess I left my car running and in neutral."

Mert looked around to assess any damage while she was talking, and when she was through he asked if anyone else witnessed this. When nobody spoke up I said, "I saw it."

Mert turned around to see who was speaking. "Want to tell me what happened next, Garrett?"

"Well, when I saw it moving, I tried to run and catch up to it. I got almost in the door, but it swung around and knocked me backward. I got up, but by then it was too late. It was heading down the hill. Skipper was down in front of Maddie's and saw it, and she jumped in her truck and let it crash into the Blue Bruise. Then she just eased it to a stop."

Mert looked at Skipper and asked, "Is that right, Skipper? That how it happened?"

"That's about it. But if Garrett hadn't yelled at me seconds before, I wouldn't have had time to do anything."

Mert looked at me and back at Skipper. "Looks like you both get some credit. That could've been a real disaster."

I heard people in the crowd muttering something I couldn't understand, and then someone started clapping. Soon the rest picked it up. There must have been a hundred people standing there clapping.

Mert turned around and faced the mother. "You're lucky, Maggie. I guess you've learned a lesson."

"I swear, Mert. I'll never do that again." She turned to Skipper and then to me. "I don't know how to thank you both. You saved my children."

Mert asked Skipper to pull her truck over so traffic could get through. He helped the lady and her children back in her car and let her go. Rollie Brockman, who seldom went anywhere without a pocket full of candy, reached in the car and gave each child a lollipop. They let go of their mother and stopped whimpering.

When the traffic started moving again and the crowd began to disperse, Mert walked over to Skipper and me as we stood beside the Blue Bruise. He had a somber look on his face as he flipped through the pages of what looked like a ticket book. He took a pen out of his vest pocket and, looking down at the book, said, "I need to see your driver's license."

Skipper looked at Mert, then she looked at me and back at him. She fidgeted. Several seconds passed. Mert was still studying his book. Finally, Skipper said, "You know I don't …."

Then Mert burst forth with a loud hyena laugh that startled Taylor Barth standing in the doorway of the depot fifty feet away. "I got you there for a minute, didn't I?"

He put the book and pen away and smiled. "You be careful now. If you take that thing out on the highway and the state boys get you, you're on your own. Don't come to me for help."

"Thanks, I know that."

Skipper and I got in the Blue Bruise, drove up the hill to her house, and told her mother what happened. Her father was at work in the garage, so when we finished telling her mother, we walked three blocks down to the garage to tell him. He was in his office finishing a phone call, so he motioned for us to take a seat. I looked around the room and studied the dozen or so plaques lining the walls, showing awards he had received. When he hung up he leaned back in his swivel chair and put his hands behind his head. "So, we have a couple of heroes here I understand."

"You've heard?" Skipper asked.

"The whole town's heard. Once a siren goes off, things get around."

"I should've known. Are you upset?"

"No, not as long as you're doing something worthwhile." Then he looked at me and said, "And I hear you had a part in this, too."

I was sitting up straight, shaking. I had only met Mr. Manion once, weeks ago. He was always so busy running his garage and farm. "I really didn't do much, sir, just got Skipper's attention. She did the rest."

"Now, you're probably being too modest. I hear you and Skipper have spent a lot of time together."

"That's right, we have. She's shown me all around town."

"Well, she talks about you a lot. I know your mother and father and I understand why she'd like your company. If my daughter grows up to be like your mother, I'd be very proud."

"Thank you. I think she's pretty special already." I felt myself blush and didn't want to look in her direction, so I found a plaque on the wall over Mr. Manion's shoulder and studied it. I was starting to feel uncomfortable when a mechanic came in from the garage and asked Mr. Manion to come look at something on a car he was working on. I quickly agreed when Skipper asked if I wanted to go home and tell my grandparents what had happened.

We came in the back door to the kitchen, but we didn't see anyone, so we went out to the front porch. There sat Grandma, Grandpa, Rollie, and Jimmy Brockman.

"Here they are. The heroes!" Jimmy announced.

"You've already heard?" I asked.

"We got the word firsthand from Rollie," Grandma said.

After Rollie told and retold the story, getting every detail right and maybe adding a little, Skipper and I came out looking even better. By the time it got around town a few times, my part had expanded to include running down the hill and reaching into the car to steer it from side-swiping cars parked on both sides of the street and Skipper having to weave her truck down the hill, avoiding pedestrians and stray dogs.

That night, Jimmy's radio broadcast featured Skipper and me as guests. It was our chance to set the story straight and head off the wild tales that had grown with every rehashing of our story. We tried, but in the days that followed the people of Purcell Station, hungry for good news in a time of war, wanted little to do with the truth. They liked their own version better.

CHAPTER 24

O n Saturday morning Grandma said I needed a haircut. I didn't think I did, but I didn't object. I liked the company in Danny's barbershop, and I'd stopped in there a few times just to listen to the stories and any gossip I could catch about the stranger in town. One story had him waiting there to get a haircut and then leaving, without saying a word, before Danny called his number. They figured he was just there to get some information. There were a lot of other theories about him, but not much in the way of facts.

Grandpa said a person could get a real education at Danny's on Saturdays among all the characters from out of town, so I went. Now that the stranger was gone again and the runaway car incident was dying down, I wanted to hear what was left to talk about.

There were nine chairs with padded seats and armrests and only one barber chair. That usually meant a pretty long wait, but not as long as you'd think, because most of the chairs were occupied by men coming in to loaf and hear themselves talk.

There was only one chair left when I walked in. Danny was in the midst of giving a shave to a guy in bib overalls and work boots. He held his straight razor to the man's neck and without looking up said, "Hi, Garrett."

"Hi, Mr. Pickett," I said. I still couldn't call him by his first name, although most of the kids my age did. "How many ahead of me?"

"Oh, by the time you sort out the chaff, about three, maybe four."

I took the only seat available, between Mert Hooper, who addressed me with a "Hi, Tiger, flagged down any cars lately?" and a guy I'd never seen before. I immediately thought of the stranger, but then I realized it wasn't him. He wore pressed slacks and what Grandma calls Sunday go-to-meeting shoes, unlike the other men, who wore mostly overalls, jeans, and work boots. He sported a stylish moustache and bushy hair parted down the middle. He looked like the men I'd seen in my father's old college yearbook, the kind who called themselves by their initials rather than their first names.

I soon realized I'd entered in the middle of a conversation.

"I'd say it's going to go on the third ballot, at least. I don't think they'll get it done before then," the slick dresser said. His accent didn't sound local.

I couldn't figure out what they were talking about until Danny, who was steaming the neck of the man in the chair with a hot towel, picked up on the conversation. "Well, if Kefauver doesn't win it on the first ballot, he'll not win it at all."

I'd heard Grandpa complaining all week about the Democratic Convention going on in Chicago. He refused to listen to it on the radio as he had done with the Republican Convention, but he did read about it in the newspaper when he thought no one was looking. I walked in and caught him once and heard him mumble something under his breath, but he quickly turned to the sports section and started talking about the Cardinals.

If Grandpa didn't want to dwell on the Democrats, the men in the barber shop did. The well-dressed man next to me spoke with authority: "Stevenson says he doesn't want it, but after that speech last night, there's gonna be a lot of support to draft him."

"Well, I don't see how they can make a man run for president if he doesn't want to." It was Mert Hooper on my right, talking to the stranger on my left.

"If the people call, you have to serve," said Danny. His left hand was holding his comb on the customer's head while his right hand held his scissors pointing straight up, as if the haircut could wait.

"Maybe they should just forget both of 'em and take that guy Russell down in Georgia." The speaker was a man down on the end who hadn't said a word until now.

The stranger leaned forward to see who was talking and said, "In that case why don't they take Harriman? He'd have the support of the East Coast."

"Forget the East Coast," said the man in the barber chair.

"Stu's right," said Mert. "We don't want Russell or Kefauver, either one. Some of those Southerners are still mad they lost the Civil War."

"Well, it's clear to me," said Stu. He was just getting up after Danny removed the apron and shook it. "We need someone from the Midwest. Someone who knows what the farmers need. That's why I like Stevenson. He's from just across the river."

"He's from Illinois, all right, upstate Illinois. Those upstate politicians don't give a pig's gut about the farmers," Mert said.

"Besides, if Stevenson doesn't want it, you can't make him take it," the man on the end said.

Stu got out of the chair and gave Danny a dollar and told him to keep the change. On the way out, he turned to the group and added, "Maybe Stevenson's just playing hard to get. It's like when you're courting a lady. She's more desirable if she plays hard to get."

"What would you know about courtin' ladies, Stu?" said the quiet guy sitting by the door.

"About as much as he knows about politics," said Mert Hopper.

"I guess we all can't be as enlightened as you people," Stu said as he flung his arm at the whole lot and walked out the door.

"Next!" yelled Danny. An older man sitting near the back of the room got up and ambled to the chair. Danny sharpened his razor on the strap hanging from his chair as the old man took his seat.

"What'll it be, Sylvester, shave and a cut?"

"Just a little trim this time. Gotta go to a wedding tomorrow."

"We'll fix you right up," said Danny. "Whose wedding is it?"

"Mine."

"Yours? Since when did you start courtin' the ladies?"

"Lady. Just one. One's enough."

"You can say that again," said the guy by the front door. "Of course, for some men, one's too many." He looked around to see a reaction and heard someone snicker.

"Are you going to tell us who the lucky lady is, or do we have to guess?" asked Danny.

"Audrey Landis. You probably don't know her. She's from over in Pike County. Met her through my cousin, about three years ago."

"Is she as old as you, or are you robbing the cradle?" asked Mert.

"Now, do ya think I'd marry someone as old as me?"

The man in the back jumped in, "I don't know, Sy. You sure she's not just after your money?"

"If so, she's in for a big surprise."

Danny put the apron over Sy and tied it behind his neck. He started massaging his head and then combed it down. "Now, how do you want this cut, since it's your wedding tomorrow? You want your ears stuck out or just a trim?"

"Better just make it a trim. That way if you butcher me, you'll have a little left to make corrections."

There were two more customers before it was my turn, and next belonged to the stranger on my left. When he stood and walked over to the chair I noticed the other men staring at him. He sat down carefully, crossed his legs just above the knee, and held up his chin so Danny could fasten the apron strip around his neck. From the distinguished way he went about settling into the chair, I think he knew he was being watched.

Danny didn't ask him what he wanted, so I figured he was a regular who wasn't getting married tomorrow. As Danny ran the comb through the bushy hair, combing it away from the middle in both directions, he asked, "So, what's going on up at the state house? Any news on the school project?"

"We're working on it, trying to get the funding past the state tax board. Should know something by fall." He had his back to us and was looking at himself in the mirror. I saw him glance over at our wall to see if we were paying attention.

Danny went on. "The natives are getting restless. They want that new gym. We're supposed to have a pretty good team the next three or four years, and they've outgrown that old cracker box."

"No doubt, no doubt, and that's on the agenda. But everybody wants something, and we just have to sort out the priorities." He was trying to be diplomatic.

"Just don't forget what we sent you up there for, Duke," said the man in the back. "You got elected by no more votes than what this town delivered." He was smiling, but his tone told me he meant it, too.

By now I'd figured out the well-dressed man was a state representative and the local population felt he owed them something. He was watching closely in the mirror as Danny snipped the hair pulled through the comb, as if every hair was important to the overall affect.

"Yeah, that's what they say over in Hazelton, too. And in Petersburg, and all the rest. Everybody's got something they want, and I owe it to them." He smirked. "But you boys all know me and what I'll try to do."

"That's what worries us, Duke," said the man in the back. "We know you all too well." That brought out a few more snickers.

Just then two young boys, about six or seven years old, entered and took the two remaining seats. Their mother followed and said to Danny, "I'm leaving them off. They need a buzz. I'll be back. How soon should they be ready?"

Danny looked at the row of chairs that were now filled and asked, "How many are waiting for haircuts?" Six hands went up including the two boys.

"About an hour, depending on how much hair Elmer has under that cap."

"Okay, I'll be back."

The two boys sat down and watched Danny finish Duke's haircut and shave. When Danny took the apron off and gave it a shake, Duke stood and gave himself a once- over in the mirror. He must have liked what he saw, because he pulled two dollars out of his wallet and told Danny to keep the change, even though a shave and haircut was only $1.25.

Danny was well into the next customer when the door swung open and in swaggered a large man in cowboy boots, spurs, and a ten-gallon Stetson. He wore holsters with pearl-handled pistols on each hip, a purple rhinestone shirt, and a bolo tie. His hair stuck out the back of his hat in a ponytail.

"Howdy, Tex," said Danny. "You come in here to get that horse's tail whacked off, or you just here to spread the manure?"

"I ain't lettin' you touch that hair. It took me five years to grow it long enough to please the ladies, so I ain't gonna let you ruin it."

"What ladies would that be, Rip?" asked Mert.

"All of 'em and any of 'em. They all like to run their fingers through it."

"I sure hope they wash their hands afterward," said Mert.

Tex took the only vacant seat next to the two young boys. The oldest one looked at his guns and then up at Tex and asked, "Why did he call you Rip?"

"That's my nickname."

"Is Tex your real name?"

"No, that's a nickname, too."

"Why do you have two nicknames?"

"Actually, I have three."

"What's the other one?"

"Bullet."

"How did you get three nicknames?"

"Got two of 'em in the war. I was a paratrooper in the war, so they called me Rip, for ripcord. You know the thing that unleashes a parachute?"

"I guess. How did you get the name Bullet?"

"Well, to make a long story short, I got that fighting the Germans. You see, they were firing wooden bullets at us, and I got wounded." A few snickers were uttered along the wall. "Got it right in the legs and arms. See this?" he said, showing off a scar on his right bicep. "That's one of my scars." He pulled up his pants leg and pointed to a mark on his calf. And that's another one. Those Germans were firing wooden bullets, and I got hit so many times I'm still picking out the splinters."

A couple of men down the line guffawed at this, and Danny cleared his throat, fighting off a smile. I wondered how many times Danny had heard this story.

"Why do they call you Tex?"

"Why do you think? Look't me. Don't I look like a Tex?"

"You look like a guy I saw in a movie once. His name was Tex. He was a cowboy."

The men waiting must have thought that was funny; they let out a whoop and cackled like hens. "He's a cowboy all right—a drugstore cowboy," said the man in the back.

Tex shot them a look. "I've got a million stories I could tell about the war, but this isn't the time or place," he said, looking down the row of waiting customers. "Just let it suffice to say my war record speaks for itself."

"If it could get a word in edgewise." Mert snickered.

The little boy asked, "Why do you wear those guns? There're no Germans around here, are there?"

"Of course, we have Germans, but they're peaceful Germans. I wear these guns in case Mert Hopper needs help keepin' the town free of riffraff."

"Does it help?"

"Do ya see any riffraff around here?"

"I dunno. What's riffraff?"

"Well, if you don't know what that means, there must not be any around here. Ain't that right, Mert?"

"If you say so, Tex. It's all because of you and those six-shooters."

The boys looked impressed. They sat quietly, staring at Tex for a moment. Finally the older one asked, "Can I touch one of those guns?"

"Sure," said Tex as he eased one out of the holster. "Now, hold it like this. Careful now, but don't worry, there's no ammo in it, just blanks."

The boy carefully took it in his hand and slipped his index finger into the trigger casing. "Now, don't point it at anybody, even though it's not loaded," said Tex.

The boy raised the gun and held it up in front of his nose, eyed down the barrel, then pointed it at the large mirror along the opposite wall. Danny had his back to him and was shaving Mert's neck when it exploded. The boy pulled the trigger thinking there was nothing in it, causing Danny to slice a sizeable gash in the neck of Mert Hopper.

"Whoa there!" yelled Tex. He took the gun back immediately and put it in his holster. The boy, his eyes large as quarters, slinked back in his chair and watched as Danny took a damp towel and tried to stop the bleeding on Mert's neck.

When the bleeding continued after more wet towels were applied, Danny said, "Someone run down and get Doc Branham. Tell 'im what happened."

The man they called Elmer opened the door and was gone in a second. Danny continued to work on the cut while Tex and the others took turns wetting down clean towels and mopping the floor of spilled blood. The boy who'd fired the blank was now slumped back in his chair, sobbing.

Alarm spread on Main Street when people heard a gunshot and saw Elmer running down the street to get Doc Branham. A crowd gathered in front of the barber shop to peer into the window. The poker game at Smokey's Pool Room next door broke up, and with the exception of the winner, who stayed to guard his money, the five losers, looking for an excuse to quit, were all out in the street bringing the newcomers up to speed on what had happened.

In no time, a rumor spread that a killer had fled Danny's Barber Shop and was armed and dangerous. This was prompted by the testimony of the credible but myopic Gertrude Winslow, a Methodist, who breathlessly explained, "I was across the street and heard a shot and saw a man run out of Danny's and down the street." The story gained even more credibility when they learned the wounded was no other than Mert Hopper, the town marshal.

"It's no telling how many enemies he has, upholding the law like he does," a woman on the sidewalk said.

Upon hearing the rumor, the mother of the two boys rushed to Danny's, flung open the door, and seeing her boy crying thought he'd been caught in the crossfire and wounded. She knelt down and held him.

"Oh, Jonnie, are you hurt? Where does it hurt?" When she saw no wounds, she stood and asked, "Are you okay? What happened?"

A car pulled up out front, and the crowd parted to let Doc Branham through. He walked in deliberately, carrying his black bag, and Danny waved him over to the barber chair to inspect Mert's neck. Doc opened his bag, took out some ointments and salve and gauze, and began to work. Tex took the mother aside and explained to her what had happened.

"You mean you let him play with your gun?"

"It wasn't loaded. Just blanks, Cheryl," said Tex.

"You mean it was just the noise that caused Mert's injury? Not a bullet?"

"That's right. He didn't do anything wrong. It was my fault, if anyone's to blame."

"I thought he'd been shot. People were saying there was a shooting and a man ran away. I was scared to death."

Tex stood there, shifting on one leg and then the other. "I guess we're lucky, aren't we? Sometimes the fiction is worse than the truth."

"Oh, really? If anyone should know, it's you. I bet you were telling him one of your tall tales, weren't you?"

"You could say that."

"Tex, you'd better tone those stories down a bit. A little less fiction and a little more truth."

"I'll work on it," said Tex, without a lot of conviction.

Mert walked out on his own two feet after Doc fixed him up, and I finally got my haircut. When I got home Grandma asked me where I'd been.

"Just at Danny's getting a haircut."

"It takes two hours to get a haircut?"

"Not exactly. But it takes a while to see everything that goes on there."

"What does that mean?"

"Well, do you know a guy who calls himself Tex?"

"I do, and I think I know why you took so long."

"Did he really go to war and fight the Germans?"

"Not unless you count the Lutherans out at St. Croix Hill. I doubt if he's ever been past the next county. But there's something else you might want to know: Sometimes Tex acts with the Old Town Players. That's a civic theater in Vincennes. Sometimes he has trouble realizing when the play is over."

CHAPTER 25

All week I stayed up late, reading my forbidden book. On Friday night, I read about Holden Caulfield's trip to New York City until I couldn't stay awake any longer. It was mid-morning before I got up. Grandma was scrubbing floors and didn't want anybody "underfoot." She had already talked Don Francis into taking Grandpa fishing with him down the river. I took a quarter from my dresser and went over to Main Street, leaving Grandma with her floors to scrub. When I passed Dub's, a group of boys and men were playing softball in the vacant lot. As I walked along the sidewalk one of the men yelled, "Hey, Garrett, come on down. We need an outfielder."

The game stopped, and they all turned to see if I was coming. I jumped off the sidewalk and jogged over to the infield. A man threw me a mitt, and I asked, "Where do I play?"

He was a middle-aged man I'd seen sitting out in front of Dub's several times. When I turned to go to my position, I heard the second baseman call him "Dad."

I jogged out to center field and noticed how it sloped up an incline to the grease rack at Dub's. Right field ended at the back door of Mert Hopper's house. I wondered what a ball through his kitchen window would cost.

I surveyed my team and counted thirteen. Best I could tell, the other team had more, but I quickly found out some of them, two heavyset men in particular, only played offense. If they were lucky enough to get a hit, they had a designated runner, usually under the age of six. They really didn't need me, but some of the older men seemed to welcome any newcomer; it meant they had less ground to cover.

The game was to go until four o'clock, and whoever was ahead then won. When Dub blew his truck horn at 4 o'clock, nobody knew the score so both sides claimed victory. After the customary celebration, I jumped up on the sidewalk among the spectators and was surprised to see Skipper with Ginny and Sarah.

I asked her if she was working for Tip on Monday.

"Yes. What about you?"

"Yep. He's picking me up at six in his truck." I turned to Sarah. "Are you pitching melons, too?"

"No, I'm starting a new job at Slinker's, filling in for Mrs. Slinker while she's having an operation."

"Tell him what you told me," Skipper said.

"Oh, you mean about the basement? When I was at Slinker's yesterday, he showed me around the store, and I found out they have a bomb shelter down in the basement. It's pretty neat. You guys want to see it?"

"Can we go down there?" Ginny asked.

"Sure, you can go anywhere at Slinker's."

I had been in Slinker's several times but never in the basement. There was a balcony around the main floor, but I'd never gone up there, either. As we walked in, a little buzzer went off to announce someone entered. We looked around but couldn't find Mr. Slinker, so we walked through the rows of shelves to the back of the store.

"Follow me," said Sarah. She led us to a stairway in the back corner that led up to the balcony. The wooden steps creaked as we walked up, and at the top we followed Sarah to a small room in the back. The door was open, and inside was a large wooden desk cluttered with papers, boxes, magazines, and dirty dishes. Sitting behind this mess with his feet up on his deck was Mr. Slinker. He was looking at a magazine but put it down when we entered.

"Hi, girls," he said. "Oh, you too, Garrett. You kids looking for trouble? You came to the right place."

"No, we're just nosing around. Care if we go down to the shelter?" asked Sarah.

"Hey, that's a secret."

"Not a very well-kept secret," Ginny said.

"Well, it's just for my friends, in case the Russians drop the bomb."

"Why would you want to waste that whole shelter on just two people?" asked Skipper.

"Ah, very cute. I can tell you're your old man's little girl." He snorted. Then, turning to face me, he said, "Garrett, how do ya put up with such smart-alecks?"

"It's all I can stand, sir," I said.

Sarah ignored both comments. "Well, I'm going to show them around. Is that okay?"

"Hop to it. Just don't disturb the rats and vipers I keep down there. I haven't fed them today. They're probably hungry."

The girls looked at each other and rolled their eyes.

Sarah let Skipper lead the way down the dark stairway. At the bottom she slowly pushed open the door, and we heard its rusty hinges squeak. We tiptoed through the door into the dark, damp room and fumbled around for a light. I finally found a light cord hanging from the ceiling and pulled it. A dim bulb lit up the room just enough for us to make out what was in there.

Sarah walked into the middle, tiptoeing as if she didn't want to scare any rats or other varmints that might be lurking in the shadows. The rest of us followed. We listened for tiny feet. After hearing and seeing nothing, we relaxed and looked around the room at the shelves. They were covered with canned goods, boxes of crackers and cereals, water canisters, first-aid kits, flashlights, batteries, pillows, and clothing. Leaning against another wall were folding cots, blankets, and two folding tables. In the corner was something that looked like a portable toilet.

The girls were looking at the cans of food as I walked across the room to inspect a dark recess in the far corner. It was partially hidden by some shelves which blocked the light from the ceiling bulb. It was dark and musty-smelling. I reached out and felt the cold concrete, running my fingers along the wall until I touched something odd. I squinted to make out the shape of it. It looked circular, but it seemed like it was mounted on a different surface. I touched it with both hands and tapped it with my knuckles. It sounded hollow.

I went back to where the girls stood and picked up a flashlight. "Do you think this works?"

"Why?" asked Skipper.

"I've found something over in that corner. I want to see what it is."

I pushed on the switch. Nothing happened. "Can you hand me those batteries?" I asked. I put the batteries in and got the flashlight working. When I walked over to the corner, the girls, now curious, followed. I shined the light on the wooden object I had touched and saw it was a round metal plate mounted on a wooden door.

As soon as we saw it, I heard Sarah gasp. I looked around and caught a funny look in Skipper's eyes.

"What?" I asked.

The girls looked at each other, hesitating as if they didn't know whether to answer or not. Ginny turned and walked away, and Sarah followed.

"I think we'd better get out of here," said Ginny.

I looked at Skipper, who had not budged but stood with me as the other two started upstairs. "We're going," said Sarah. "I work for him now."

They left. I was getting nervous. "Should we go, too?"

Skipper looked at the stairs and put her finger to her lips, shushing me to be quiet. She shook her head no.

"I need to tell you something, but first we need to open this door."

I wasn't sure. "What if we get caught?"

Ignoring my question, Skipper lifted the latch and pulled. It creaked, and she stopped, listening for footsteps up above. Then she pulled again and cracked the door open so that we could squeeze through. As we stepped in she took the flashlight and shined it around the walls. The room was smaller than the first one. There were rows of chairs around each wall. Above them was a rack of pegs mounted on the walls about head high, and on each peg was a black metal helmet hanging by a strap.

"What's all this?" I whispered.

Skipper put her finger to her lips, "Shh."

She waited, thinking she heard something. Neither of us moved for several seconds, until we were sure it was clear. It was then I turned around and saw on the wall beside the door something that looked like a chart. I touched Skipper's shoulder and pointed to it. She shined the light on it, and I could see words written in some kind of script. Just then we heard footsteps upstairs, and this time there was no mistake. Skipper and I quickly squeezed back out the door and pulled it shut, trying not to let it squeak. We put the flashlight back on the shelf. There was no time to remove the batteries. Someone was coming down the stairs.

"You still down there?" It was Mr. Slinker.

Skipper spoke up: "Yes, we're coming up. We were just looking over all the stuff you have down here."

"Well, I was getting worried some rats got ya." The footsteps stopped.

We turned out the light, and I followed Skipper up the stairs. The sunlight beaming in the front windows nearly blinded us as we made our way to the front door. Mr. Slinker stood nearby.

"Thanks, Mr. Slinker," Skipper said. "We got out alive. That's more than I can say for those rats."

"Thanks for taking care of 'em for me," Slinker shot back.

When we got outside Ginny and Sarah were gone. We walked back up the street and were well out of earshot of Slinker's General Store when I asked Skipper, "You going to tell me what we saw back there?"

We were up to the Baptist Church, and she motioned me over to the picnic table, away from the street. She looked around to make sure we were alone.

"All I know is that there is this group called The Black Helmet Society. It's supposed to be a secret. People seem to know about it, but they don't talk about it. It's a mystery who they are and what they do, but there are a lot of theories and people have their suspicions. The members must be sworn to secrecy, so not much is known about them."

"Do people know about the room we were just in?"

"I don't think so. That's why we needed to get out of there. I'm sure we weren't supposed to see it."

"Are we going to be in trouble?"

"I hope not. Mr. Slinker didn't see us in there. I have a feeling the less we know, the better off we'll be, so let's not tell anyone we were in there, okay?"

"Okay, but now I'll wonder...."

"So do a lot of people. I have a feeling someday it's all going to come out." She started back toward the sidewalk. "I know I didn't answer your questions, but that's all I know. Remember, not a word about this!"

We walked to the sidewalk, and I looked down the street to be sure Mr. Slinker was not following us. "I hope he doesn't look for finger-prints."

"Now you're getting paranoid," said Skipper. "If we don't tell anyone what we saw we'll be all right. She stood up. "I have to go now. I'll see you at the free show tonight."

I sat on the porch after supper and listened to Grandpa rant on about the Cardinals, which he favored, and the Democrats, which he didn't. Grandma joined us in her rocking chair after finishing up in the kitchen. She was darning some of grandpa's socks.

"Have you ever really explored Slinker's?" I asked her. "I mean upstairs and downstairs."

"Yes, I've been upstairs a few times. I can't say I've ever been in the basement."

"Well, Sarah is going to be working there next week, and she took us on a tour."

"That's nice. What did you find down there?"

"Mr. Slinker's made it into a bomb shelter. He's got all kinds of stuff stored in there."

I looked at Grandpa to see if he was paying attention and if he showed any interest in the basement, or the Black Helmets, or the room they met in. So far, none of this seemed to interest him.

"He has? I wonder why he thinks anyone would want to bomb Purcell Station," Grandma asked.

"How could they bomb Purcell Station? We have a crack Civil Air Patrol tower on the lookout for enemy aircraft." Grandpa was listening after all.

"Did you know there was a bomb shelter down there?" I asked. I left it open for either of them to answer.

"No, I didn't," said Grandma. "But I'm not surprised at anything Boots Slinker does."

I really wanted to hear from Grandpa. If he was a Black Helmet, then he'd know about the shelter. "Did you Grandpa?"

He cleared his throat and let out a cough. "I'd heard something about it once. Been a while, though."

He didn't really say he'd seen it, but he didn't deny it either.

We talked on until it was getting dark, when I walked over to the free show. The cartoons were just starting when I spotted Skipper and her friends on their blanket.

I sat down beside her and leaned back on the pillow she brought for me. Not another word was said about the afternoon's excursion. I kept my word and watched the show, but my mind was in Slinker's basement.

CHAPTER 26

Whatever was going on in Slinker's basement had raised a lot of questions, and nobody seemed to know or want to share the answers. Grandma sensed something was on my mind, so she asked me about it.

I didn't want to get into it, so I told her, "I've been thinking about Jesse and what he did to Spooks down at the railroad crossing." It wasn't a lie, but it wasn't the whole truth, either. "When Skipper and I are out at Tip's, who's going to look out for him?"

"Maybe you won't have to worry about him. Have you seen the newspaper?"

"No. Why?"

"Three boys got thrown in the Gibson County jail night before last for attacking a man outside a tavern down there. Here, take a look." There it was, on the front page. "One of them was Jesse, and the other two were his cousins. It said they waited for the guy to come outside and they jumped him. He tried to fight back, and they beat him up. Now he's in the hospital."

I quickly read the rest of the story. "What's going to happen to them now?"

"I have a feeling they're gonna be in jail a while."

"I guess that's why I haven't seen him."

"That's not unusual. Sometimes he disappears for days on end. People figured it was because of the beatings his dad gave him. Guess he's too big for that now, so he runs off and causes trouble with his cousins."

"His dad beats him?"

"I'm sure he does. He'd get tanked up on his own liquor. I suspect that's why you never see Jesse's mother, either. If nobody sees any bruises, they can't say it happened."

I realized that's why the Sprowl place was guarded by all those dogs. I wanted to tell Skipper what happened, so I tore the story out of the paper and rode up to Manion's Garage where I found Skipper under a Chevy pickup, changing the oil filter. She climbed out from under it, wiped her hands on a rag, and I showed her the story.

"That's good news for Spooks," she said.

"At least for a while," I said. "Are you about done under that truck?"

"Just finished. Why?"

"Let's go outside. I wanna talk about something."

She told the mechanic she was leaving, and we went out the side door and down the street.

"I've been thinking about the Black Helmets," I said. "I can't get them off my mind. Why is it so secret."

"Well, you're probably not going to get a lot of information from anybody who knows."

"Are they good guys?"

"We'd have to see them actually doing something to know that."

"Okay, where do they do what they do? Is it just in that room in Slinker's basement?"

"Uh, I don't think so. I think there're other places, too."

"How do you know?"

She waited, looked around, and then went on. "I'll tell you something if you promise not to tell."

"I promise."

"You remember the time Patrick and I took that long raft trip down the river last summer?"

"Past the hobo camp?"

"Yes. I've never told anyone this, but before we started back upstream, we tied up the raft and hiked through the trees up around Taber Hill. We wanted to see what's up there."

"Did you find out?"

"Uh-uh, I think so. It's surrounded by trees and guarded by the steep hillside. When Patrick and I were hiking through the trees, we heard gunshots coming from the direction of the hill. We thought it was some-one poaching until we heard a volley and then more rounds going off. We thought that was strange, so we waited. Then we heard more shots. We climbed up through the trees and up the steep hill until we reached the top and could see out into a large opening."

"What'd you see?"

We were sitting on the wall in front of the Baptist Church. Skipper looked across the street to be sure the men sitting at Dub's couldn't hear.

"Instead of me telling you about it, why not go see it?"

"Really? Isn't it a long way from here?"

"It is if you go by the river, but I know a shortcut." She looked at her watch. "Ride down to the depot while I go home and get my bike. I'll meet you there in ten minutes."

"But, won't we get in trouble?"

"Not if we don't get caught."

I was sitting on the bench outside the depot with Taylor when I heard a loud motor and saw Skipper come down the street in the Blue Bruise.

"I thought you were riding your bike," I said.

"I am. Throw your bike in the back with mine. We'll need it."

I saw Taylor scratching his head as we drove off toward the highway.

"What's going on?" I asked. "You can't drive on the highway."

"We're turning up here," she said, pointing to the levee. When we reached the top she stopped, then turned and followed tracks that had been worn on the top of the levee. Somebody had been here before.

"People drive up here when they go fishing downstream, but I think other people drive it, too, until it ends at the foot of the hills. That's as far as we can go in the truck. We'll have to bike the rest of the way. There's no way a truck can get through the jungle between here and the hill.

"What about the bikes? Can they get through?"

"Only to the hill. We'll have to leave them and walk up. It's too steep."

When we got to the end of the levee, Skipper found a clearing in the trees, turned the truck around, and pointed it back toward town. "Just in case we have to get out of here fast," she explained.

We pedaled our bikes through the trees and brush, fighting off limbs and briars. It took us another fifteen minutes to reach the area where it got so steep we couldn't ride any further. We parked our bikes and started climbing the hill, grabbing branches to pull ourselves up as we went. Every so often Skipper would stop, hold up her hand, and listen.

When we heard nothing, we continued climbing. The hill was steep, and the briars were scratching my arms, causing them to bleed, but I was too nervous and excited to stop.

When we reached the top, Skipper motioned for me to stand behind her. She walked up behind a tree and waited, looking around. Then she stepped out and told me to follow her. I did, and there in front of us was a large open field. The thick grass had been freshly mowed. It looked about the size of two football fields and just as flat, but there were structures scattered all around.

"Those are obstacle courses," said Skipper. "The time Patrick and I were up here they were doing maneuvers over them and shooting at those targets over there."

She pointed to the end of the field where cutout figures of soldiers were propped up as targets. On one side of the field long ropes hung from racks, and on another side a moat-like ditch ran in front of a wall. The wall had spikes on it to use in climbing. Two ropes strung between telephone poles stood about thirty yards apart and about ten feet off the ground. "They were hanging from those ropes and hand walking to the other side," she said.

A shed with a tin roof and bars over the windows stood off to the side. Beside it stood a pole where an American flag flapped in the breeze, and under it hung a red flag with a black helmet embroidered on it.

"What's in the shed?" I asked.

Skipper shrugged. "Let's find out."

We didn't see anyone, so we edged out into the opening and waited. When we were sure no one was around, we took off running toward the shed. I got there first and, hugging the wall, slowly edged my way to the small window by the door. Skipper watched me for any expression. I looked in. It was dark inside except for light from the two side windows.

I cupped my hands around my face, blocking out the sunlight, and tried to make out an object on the other side of the room. It sat in front of a side window, and all I could see was its rounded silhouette. Around it I could see racks of rifles and what looked like boxes of ammunition. A wooden crate held something that looked like hand grenades. A row of helmets hung on the opposite wall. They were black and had a red "BH" on the sides. There was a large table in the middle, and at the end of it sat the object I was trying to make out. I motioned Skipper to come over, and she put her face to the window beside me.

I whispered, "What *is* that?"

Just then, it moved. I saw it and jumped back the same time Skipper did.

"Go!" She whispered, grabbing my arm. We ducked behind the shed and ran as fast as we could into the nearest trees. Just when we got to the woods I glanced over my shoulder and saw a man come around the building, looking in our direction. We wove our way through the trees until we were out of sight and then stopped behind a large oak tree and watched. His face was shielded by sunglasses, and a cap was pulled down over his eyes. He was wearing fatigues and boots, and a rifle was slung over his shoulder. He was holding something in his hand.

I was shaking now. I backed away from Skipper so she wouldn't feel me tremble. We had a small opening where we could see him without him seeing us, but he was walking in our direction. He seemed to be doing something with the object in his hand, and I thought of the hand grenades. Then he put it up to his cheek. He looked like he was talking to someone, but we couldn't see anyone around.

"It's a walkie-talkie," Skipper whispered. "He must be calling for help."

"Wow! Let's get out of here," I said.

"Okay, but our bikes are on the other side. We'll have to get over there somehow."

"I'll follow you."

We walked carefully, making sure we didn't step on any branches or twigs that would snap and give our position away. Darting between trees, we stopped every so often to see if we were being followed. We were circling the open field, deep in the woods, heading toward our bikes when Skipper stopped, held up her hand, and waited. We stood there for several seconds.

"Run!" yelled Skipper. She grabbed my arm and pulled as she took off toward our bikes. Then I heard it, too: the sound of a motor coming from the levee. "Uh -oh, they're going to see the truck," Skipper said. "Quick, we've gotta get there first."

She led the way toward the river, far from where we came in. We were running through the brush, getting slapped in the face and arms with branches. Skipper stumbled and fell over a fallen log. I tripped over her; then pulled her up. We reached the steepest part of the hill where we jumped down, sliding in the loose dirt.

The sound of the motor stopped, so we knew whoever it was had to be on foot. Our bikes were at the bottom of the hill. Finally, we reached them, jumped on, and rode through the underbrush toward the river. We were in new terrain, trying to keep from making any noise. So far we hadn't seen anyone, but we could feel them. We were lucky they didn't have any dogs with them.

When we caught sight of the Blue Bruise, we hid and waited. When it looked all clear, we dashed up to it, threw our bikes in the back, and jumped in. Skipper was about to start it up when she noticed a piece of paper stuck in the windshield wiper. She got out, grabbed it, and brought it back into the cab.

She read it out loud: "We know who you are. Forget what you saw here."

We both looked around, shaking as she started the truck and slowly edged away. Just then I turned around and saw a black pickup truck hidden off to the side in a clump of trees. I didn't wait to see if anyone was in it.

"Go!" I said. Skipper stepped on the gas and threw up a trail of rocks and dirt as we sped out of the clearing. On the levee we were going so fast I thought we might veer off and roll down the embankment. I kept looking back to see if anyone was following us, but we were throwing up so much dust I couldn't see. We reached the pavement and turned toward town. My nerves were shot by the time we crossed the tracks and passed the depot. Taylor was sitting on the bench talking to Lady Muldoon. He waved, and I waved back as if nothing had happened.

Driving up Main Street, we checked our mirrors to see if we were being followed.

"That was close," Skipper said. "I'm going to park this thing and keep it out of sight for a while. It's good we're going to be working at Tip's. Nobody will bother us out there.

She dropped me off at home and we agreed not to talk about what we had seen. "The Black Helmets have two reasons to be after us now," Skipper said.

I was watching out the kitchen window when I heard the rumble of Tip's truck coming down the street. I bounded down the steps, gave a quick wave to Tip, and jumped in the back where two older boys sat on a bale of straw. I knew one of them as Raymond and the other they called Augie. I had seen them both around town at the softball games and at the swimming hole.

When we picked up Skipper, she climbed up and sat down against a bale, casually as if yesterday's trip to Tabor Hill had never happened. The ride out to Tip's was cool and breezy in the back of the truck, but an angry sun was rising over the eastern hills and the sand would be hot on our feet. At least at Tip's we'd be safe from whoever saw us at Taber Hill.

When we arrived at the packing shed, Tip pulled the tractor up, and we all climbed in the wagon for the bumpy ride out to the field. Tip assigned each of us a row, and he worked alongside us so he could check on the ripeness of the melons.

The sun was already beating down and heading to 95 degrees, according to WPSR. This wasn't going to be an easy day. We worked for more than an hour getting the first wagon loaded and another hour unloading it in the packing shed. By noon, we were on our third wagon when Tip told us to break for lunch. Thirty minutes under a shade tree in Tip's front yard and plenty to drink got me going for the afternoon, but I wasn't sure how long I would last. The heat was coming up through my shoes from the hot sand and soaking my socks. The bandana I remembered to bring was stuck to my neck.

I looked around and saw Skipper stopping to wipe her brow with her sleeve. She smiled, but then went right back to work. It wasn't the first time I'd seen her looking at me. She must have thought I might die out here. Augie and Raymond weren't looking much better.

It wasn't until we finished unloading the third load of the afternoon that Tip pulled the tractor into the shed and shut it off.

"We got a truck coming in tomorrow morning," he announced. "Guy's gonna take 'em up to Chicago. We'll load it up first thing in the morning and then go back out. The next load's going to Detroit on Wednesday. No rest for the wicked."

I was hot, tired, and hungry. The thought of doing this again tomorrow was almost too much. Then I remembered yesterday and realized this was a lot safer.

"Get yourself a drink and rest a minute. Then hop in the truck, and I'll run you all back to town," Tip said. "You can all take a melon with you if you want."

After a drink and then pouring a cup of water over our heads, we each picked out a melon and climbed in the back of Tip's truck. I sprawled out on one of the straw bales on the way home, and if it weren't for the hot sun I could've fallen asleep. My muscles ached, and the soft straw felt good to my stretched-out back. Skipper sat next to me, and I thought her eyes were closed, until she punched me in the ribs. I looked up. She was pointing to the pickup truck that was following us. It was black.

CHAPTER **27**

Cleveland

The wind came off Lake Erie, flapping the rigging of the sails on the schooners docked at the marina below. The sleek white yachts moored in the leeward side of the breakwater sat bobbing like apples in a barrel. It was early afternoon and the wind had kicked up to fifteen knots just as Edward Gentry rose from his bed to take his afternoon lap around the "square." The square was the shape of the ground floor of the Lakeside Rehabilitation Center and the course his physical therapist laid out for him to walk three times a day.

Leah Gentry entered just as he swung his thin legs over the side of the bed. "Wait until I help you," she said. "You heard what the therapist said."

She helped lift him off the side of the bed until he could grab his walker, then they made their way out the door and down the hall. As he approached the nurse's station he cleared his throat to alert Abilene he was on the loose. She had grey hair, a winsome smile, and a sense of humor that matched his own, and she ran the station with an iron hand and a hearty laugh. Hearing his cue, she said, "Round two, huh?" referring to Edward's second lap of the day.

"You're keeping track?" Edward asked.

"Somebody's got to keep an eye on you." She went about her paperwork without looking up. "Just to make yourself useful, I should give you the mail and let you deliver it while you're making your rounds. It'd save me time."

Edward stopped, leaning on his walker. "You know what they say about rain, sleet, and snow, and the mail? Well, they didn't say anything about a sore back."

"What? You can't carry a mailbag over your shoulder?"

"Maybe, if you want me in here another six weeks."

"In that case, you're off the hook. Don't know that we could put up with you another six weeks."

"How about another three? The doc thinks I might be able to leave then." He started down the hall but stopped and turned back to Abilene. "You know, you're gonna miss me when I'm gone."

Abilene smiled and waited until he was out of earshot, then turned to another nurse and said. "He's right. He's like a magnet. His room is the only place the staff hangs out in when they have some free time."

Edward and Leah completed their round stopping to say a few words to patients they'd gotten to know along the way. When they returned Edward sat back on his bed and looked out the window. The walk left him winded. He leaned back on his bed and stretched his legs out. His voice weak and strained, he asked, "Would you crank it up to raise my legs?"

When it was where he wanted it, he waved his arm to let her know. Leah saw his eyes were getting heavy, so she went to the window and drew the curtains to lessen the glare from the lake. When he drifted off, she tiptoed out of the room and to the inn next door where she was staying, giving her the break she needed.

When she rose from her own nap and walked back to Edward's room an hour later, he was awake and sitting up in his bed. The curtains were open, and he was watching a tugboat pushing a line of barges out on Lake Erie. It was heading east, probably to Cleveland or Erie. He figured it came through Detroit and the upper Great Lakes, maybe Thunder Bay or Sault Ste. Marie. Either way, the wind was behind it, and it was making good time.

Leah entered in the middle of these thoughts. "How'd you sleep?"

"Like a baby," he answered.

She sat in the only chair and looked out the window. Edward lay on his back and started lifting his leg and slowly lowering it. Then he did the same with the other leg, doing what his therapist showed him.

Soon, Abilene came charging into the room. "You've got mail. I had to deliver it myself, since I couldn't get my favorite patient to do it." She handed Leah two letters. One looked like a bill from the hospital, and the other had a return address of Purcell Station, Indiana.

"Looks like a good one and a bad one," said Abilene. "Although I try not to be too nosy."

"Really? What do they say?" asked Edward.

"Now, how would I know?" Abilene said as she left the room.

Leah laid the bill aside and tore open the envelope. Edward turned to Leah. "What is it?" Leah unfolded it and said, "It's from Garrett." She read it aloud:

> *Dear Mom and Dad,*
>
> *I hope Dad is getting better and will be able to come home soon. I'm having a good time and am learning a lot. I'm pitching melons now for Tip Albee, and my back is sore, so I guess Dad and I have a lot in common.*
>
> *Uncle Jake is gone, but I had a good time sitting up late at night and listening to him. He's lived an exciting life, and he got me thinking about things. I guess I could say the same things about Purcell Station.*
>
> *I'm finding out there are some secrets in this town. Skipper and I came across a hideout of a mysterious group called "The Society of Black Helmets." Have you heard of them? I've tried to find out who they are and what they do, but it's hard to get any information. I'm beginning to see there's more going on around here than I thought.*
>
> *Anyway, I'm going to miss this place and the people, but I look forward to next month when I can see you again. Take care. I love you.*
>
> *Garrett*

Leah folded the letter, put it in her purse, and sat quietly on the bed. Finally, she spoke: "I hope no one saw them there."

She looked at Edward. He was staring out the window, but he didn't seem to see the lake. He seemed far away.

A minute passed. Then Edward said, "If they did, I know who I can call."

CHAPTER **28**

I was on my way up the hill to meet Jimmy when I heard a vehicle behind me. I nearly wrecked when I turned around and saw a black pickup. I swerved out of its way and onto the sidewalk and watched as it passed. The passenger, a bearded man in a baseball cap, stared as they went by. It was the second black pickup I'd seen since Skipper and I came home from Taber Hill, and both times I felt I was being watched. The first one, which had followed us in from Tip's, had stopped in front of Slinker's and two guys had gotten out and gone inside. They'd looked at us when we went past. I was starting to think twice about going out alone, but I figured I'd be safe at the Civil Defense Tower.

It sat on the hill above the town just north of the water tower and two blocks from Skipper's house. All summer I'd heard talk about the tower and how they fought the Cold War there, so it held a certain mystery. Skipper once asked if I wanted to go up, but I begged off. I didn't tell her I was scared of heights.

It was my first day off since Tip told us he wouldn't need us anymore. The trucks to Chicago and Detroit and other cities were coming around less frequently now. I wasn't too disappointed; there were other things I wanted to do, and Labor Day was going to be here soon enough. Other than the free show, where I went to help Skipper keep an eye on Spooks and Jesse, the past few weeks had been about work and church on Sunday, and one memorable Sunday dinner.

Grandma had invited Reverend Snyder over for dinner after church, which she does occasionally. She also invited the Francises, the Brockmans, and Spooks. She asked Spooks to come over early to help set it up, but the real reason she wanted him there was to prepare him in case they ran out of fried chicken. Spooks had a reputation for being a big eater, and it wasn't beyond him to say so if he thought someone else was getting what he considered his share.

Spooks was collecting the chairs and setting them up to the table when Grandma told him, "Now Spooks, I want you to understand something. We're having fried chicken, and I know how you like fried chicken, and I know you're hungry. But, if it gets down to where there is one last piece left, you're not to take it. You let the preacher have it. If he doesn't take it after a while, then you can have it. If he takes it and you're still hungry, I'll get up and fry you an egg. Do you understand?"

"You g…got my…word, Minnie."

"Just remember, don't say anything. If he takes the last piece, I'll fix you an egg."

Spooks was working on his plate, having seconds on mashed potatoes, gravy, and green beans. The chicken plate was making its second trip around the table, and Spooks was eyeing it as it passed Rollie, who stabbed a second breast with his fork. Mr. Francis took a leg and passed the last piece on to Reverend Snyder. By then Spooks, sitting with his fork upright in his fist, got very interested and watched the reverend closely.

Reverend Snyder hesitated, holding the plate in front of him. "I shouldn't," he said, just before he stabbed it with his fork and dropped it on his plate.

Grandma looked at Spooks, who was eyeing the preacher, and put her finger to her lips. But it was too late.

"Put the skillet on, Minnie, the damn preacher just took the last piece of chicken," blurted Spooks as he sat eyeing the chicken on the preacher's plate. It was the first time I'd heard Spooks speak without stuttering.

It got real quiet after that, as everyone stared first at Spooks and then at the reverend. Grandma slowly rose from her seat, walked around behind Spooks, and whispered something in his ear. He then got up and followed her out of the kitchen and into the parlor, where the door closed behind them. After dinner, when the guests were all sitting out on the front porch, Spooks got his egg.

The Air Patrol tower stood about four stories high. A set of steep wooden ladders worked their way past three landings to an opening in the floor at the top. I let Jimmy go first and then I followed, trying not to look down. Halfway up the second ladder I seized the sides of the ladder and froze. Jimmy had reached the next landing and started up the third ladder when he looked down and saw I wasn't moving.

"You doing okay?" he asked.

"Yeah, I think so. I just got a little winded." I didn't want him to know.

I got myself together and reached the next landing just as Jimmy got to the top, opened the trap door, and climbed through into the cabin. I managed to reach the opening and followed him in.

The room was square and had windows on three sides. On the fourth wall wooden pegs held several sets of binoculars, and next to them hung a large, mounted corkboard with pictures and drawings of various aircraft, both enemy and friendly. Under each picture the name and national origin of the craft was listed. On the left was a chart with a list of names running down several columns. I recognized some of them.

"What are these numbers beside each person's name?"

"That's how many planes they've identified. If they identify five planes and record them, they get a badge. For every five they identify, they get another rung on their badges."

"When do they do this?"

"Any time they can. It's open all day, every day. People come and go."

"Is it mostly adults?"

"Nope. Anybody. Females, kids."

"Why do they do it?"

"It's patriotic. You never know when the Russians are coming. That's why there's a bomb shelter under the tower."

"There's a bomb shelter here, too?"

"Yep, and it's stocked and ready to go."

I studied the chart again. "Is your name up here?"

"Look over here. It's in this column. This shows I've received five rungs or twenty five scores."

"Is that good?"

"Well, look down here. How many names have more than me?"

I scanned the chart. "Just two?"

"Look and see who they are."

I followed down the list and saw Rollie Brockman's name. "Your father? He does this, too?"

"You'd be surprised who all comes up here. Keep looking."

I looked down the column, searching for a number higher than Jimmy's twenty-five and Rollie's twenty-seven. Finally, I came to number twenty-eight and followed it with my finger across the left side of the page. There it was: Jesse Sprowl!

I looked at Jimmy.

"He's sneaky about it. Waits until no one's here. He doesn't like people to know."

"Wow! He doesn't seem like the kind."

"A lot of people thought that, but he has an eye for looking at a picture and seeing that same shape in a plane. He has problems when he tries to read the names, but he's really good with the pictures. And he's real interested in airplanes."

I thought about the run-ins I'd had with Jesse. This just didn't add up.

I moved over to a window, trying to comprehend all this, when I heard the sound of a motor. The thought of a black pickup entered my mind.

"Here, take a look at this." Jimmy was looking northwest. "I can see the water tower at St. Francisville, Illinois." He handed me the binoculars, and I was looking through them when the motor I heard got louder.

"Put them on that plane up there," said Jimmy. He was pointing at a small plane flying over Highway 41. That was the noise I heard.

"Now get a good look and remember the details. Look at the shape, wings over or under, that sort of thing. See if you can pick up the numbers and letters on the fuselage."

I squinted and studied the shape. "Its wings are over. I can't see the numbers, maybe a five and a three...."

"Okay, now put those down and remember the shape and look on the chart. See if you can find one that looks like it."

I looked up and down the figures on the chart and finally saw an American make that looked like it might be a match. I pointed. "I think it's this one."

"Eureka! Good choice. It's a two-seater Piper Cub. Belongs to Wib Waldrup, a farmer down in the bottoms."

"You can identify the plane and its owner, too?"

"Sometimes. There aren't many around here who own airplanes. I've seen Wib up there so many times I could almost tell him by the sound of the motor."

We hung the binoculars up, and I looked down the list to see more names: Tate, Barth, Barkus, Snyder, Hawkins, Dexter, Eckert, and Begley.

"This is like the softball games over on Main Street."

"How's that?" asked Jimmy.

"They're both open to anybody who wants to play."

"I guess so. There's not much that's exclusive around here."

I mulled that over a moment when a thought suddenly occurred to me. "Are you sure about that?"

"Whatta you mean?"

"What about the Black Helmets? Aren't they exclusive?"

"You know about them?"

"I've heard some talk. I don't really know much." I didn't want to break my promise to Skipper about our trips to Slinker's basement and Tabor Hill.

Jimmy studied me for a moment. "I don't know much, either. I'm just surprised you'd heard of them."

"It seems like there are a lot of secrets around here."

"Maybe not among ourselves, but to outsiders."

"Is that why you can have a radio station without a license, and everybody knows about it but the feds?"

"Maybe, and why a few other things go on around here that aren't exactly legal."

It was the first time I'd heard someone say what I had been thinking. I had a lot of questions, but I walked away and took another loop around the room. I searched the sky for more planes, but we'd pretty much seen everything there was to see, and I was already thinking about the trip down. It was one thing climbing up, another thing climbing down backward. "I'm ready to go if you are," I said.

I went first, since Jimmy had to shut the trap door. It was a lot harder going down, but I made it without looking at the ground. We mounted our bikes and rode down the hill. Jimmy didn't ask why I suggested we take a back street, but then he wasn't hiding from black pickup trucks, either.

CHAPTER 29

The Sand Bowl and baseball took my mind off black trucks, strangers, and Jesse Sprowl for a while, and it was good to be on the radio again.

Rollie Brockman was in rare form, inspired by the size of the crowd for the Jasper game, throwing in personal tidbits, such as, "Coming to bat for the Purple Aces is Shuuuuugg Willlllett, the proud papa of a brand new baby boy, number three, if you're keeping score. Shug is 0 for 2 tonight, but batting 3 for 3 at home." The crowd gave Shug a standing ovation. He proceeded to strike out on four pitches, but no one seemed to care. They figured he'd been up all night.

After the third inning Rollie announced that there were "scouts on the premises tonight from two major league teams." Of course, he didn't identify the teams or his source, but it gave everyone cause to search the stands for slick-looking outsiders. I looked around for the mysterious stranger but didn't find him.

In the fifth inning, I heard the whistle of a southbound train and saw its headlight coming down the track past the left field fence. Both the leftfielder and centerfielder turned to look as they awaited the next pitch. It was a long, loud freighter, and its clatter stayed with us, drowning out Rollie's announcement of the next batter. When it passed I looked beyond the tracks into the darkness and saw the headlights of cars on Highway 41. Somewhere beyond there was my father's boyhood farm.

We'd go there in the summers, and on starlit nights I would look east and see the bright lights of the Sand Bowl on the Purcell Station hillside and beg my father to take me to the game. On those rare occasions I got to go, my heart would pound as we neared the town and drove up the hill into the parking lot and paid our admission. We would bring our cushions, find a seat on the concrete bleachers, and listen to the sounds of bats cracking out fly balls during batting practice.

The smell of popcorn and hotdogs would make me hungry, even though I had just had supper an hour earlier. Dad always made me wait until the fifth inning. Then he'd give me a dime, and I'd go up to the refreshment booth behind the stands. It was there when I was nine that I first saw her. She was working the booth with two women, and when it was my turn to order she came to the counter and asked what I wanted. I stood there shifting my weight, just looking at her, and for a moment I forgot. Then I remembered: "A Nehi and popcorn, please."

She turned to go back to the cooler as I watched her. She looked to be about twelve. When she came back she saw me staring at her, so she smiled.

"That'll be ten cents."

I opened my sweating hand for her and she took the money. "You're not from here are you?" she asked.

"No, not really, I guess…." It was the best I could do under the circumstances. She was pretty, and I was nervous. "I was, but I'm not now. We moved away when I was two weeks old."

"Well, that counts, I guess." She smiled as she handed me my order. I wanted to keep talking, but when she turned away I blurted, "My parents were from here." But, I guess she knew that if I was born here.

Just then, I'd felt the presence of a man standing behind me, and she asked him what he wanted. As I took my popcorn and Nehi and turned to go back to my seat, I heard him say, "Hi, Skip." I looked around but didn't see anyone who looked like a Skip.

The game went eleven innings, and when the last out was made Jimmy asked me to give the wrap-up statistics. When I finished and Jimmy signed off, we started packing up the equipment. Then I saw Skipper in the refreshment booth helping her mother clean up. She saw me and gave me a big "Hi, Garrett," and a smile, and this time there was no one waiting behind me. "Are you coming down to the drugstore?"

I looked at Jimmy for an answer. "Maybe, if we get done in time," he said.

We took our time packing the car to let the traffic clear out. When we finished, Jimmy suggested we take the stuff over to the shack and unload it before going downtown. He didn't want to do it later and wake his grandmother.

We backed the Packard up to the Brockmans' garage, carried the equipment around to the shack, and set it up for tomorrow's broadcast. By the time we finished, it was past eleven o'clock, and Rollie had come home and gone to bed. Grandma had told me she would leave the back door open. Lately, she'd given up waiting for me since I always got home on time. We got back in the car and headed for Main Street.

"It's late," Jimmy said, "But we'll drive by and see if anybody's still there."

When we rounded the corner only two cars remained parked along the curb. Jimmy slowed to a crawl as we passed the drugstore and looked in. Only one table was occupied; Skipper and the others were gone. A couple walked along the sidewalk with their backs to us, but otherwise the street was quiet. We drove down the hill, past Tulley's, where a few cars were parked out in front, and we could hear music blaring from the jukebox inside. Maddie's Café was already closed and the neon light turned off. A night light hung from the ceiling in back, casting ghostly shadows on the wall.

Jimmy kept driving down the darkened street, past Lady Muldoon's picket fence. When he got to the bottom, he turned right at the depot and drove parallel to the tracks. A low-lying cloud floated by and blocked the light of the full moon, leaving the street light on the corner to show us where to cross the tracks.

Jimmy said, "I don't feel like going home yet. Let's make a run to Payton's."

We turned, crossed the railroad track, and headed west toward the highway. Payton's Truck Stop and Diner was located on the highway about a mile from the Purcell Station turnoff. It stayed open all night and served as a stop off for truckers driving all-nighters out of Chicago and points south.

"I'm thirsty. Eleven innings and all that talking gave me a dry mouth," Jimmy said.

As we crossed the levee, I looked up at the moon shining through eerie breaks in the clouds. It reminded me of Halloween and witches riding through the sky on brooms. We drove along the side of the levee until the road curved right and we approached the highway. Traffic was sparse now as midnight approached. Far off, we could see the lights of Payton's as we came to a stop at the dark intersection. A lone semi came from our left, and Jimmy could have beaten it, but he waited just to be safe. We were in no hurry since Payton's stayed open all night, and we were pretty sure the folks back home were sound asleep.

The windows of the Packard were open trying to capture what little breeze the night air had to offer. We could hear the sound of crickets coming from the ditch and the fence row beyond it. The semi was taking its time grunting up the highway under what sounded like a heavy load. Jimmy waited patiently, tapping his fingers on the steering wheel and staring at the truck. As it approached the struggling motor got louder, and I covered my ears as it got even with us. The Packard shook in the semi's draft as it passed within feet of our front bumper. Then it was silent.

Suddenly, I heard something behind me. Jimmy jerked his head around and looked at me with wide eyes. Just then, the dome light went on. I flinched. I barely caught an image, but before I could make it out, the door slammed and the light went off again. We both strained to see who got in, but the only light we had came from the dashboard, and the back of the seat blocked it. All we saw was a shadow.

"Just turn around and start driving," said the voice, raspy and slurred. He leaned forward and reached out with his hand just far enough to let the instrument panel light shine on it. He held a gun.

My body stiffened. I looked at Jimmy. He looked straight ahead, not wanting to give the gunman a reason to use his weapon. Jimmy did as ordered and started driving. "Where t-to?" he managed to get out.

"Just start driving that way." He pointed north. "I'll tell you when to stop. And if you try anything, I got this gun pointed at your head."

I shivered and felt like I was going to wet my pants. Out of the corner of my eye I saw Jimmy looking in the rearview mirror, and after a while I noticed that whenever a car approached from the other direction and shined its lights on us, Jimmy looked up at the mirror again.

We were going toward Vincennes. The man in the back was quiet. I started getting crazy ideas about where he was taking us and what he was planning to do with us. Then I thought of Grandma and what she was going to say when I didn't come home. What about Mom and Dad? What if I never came home? Why did we have to go to Payton's, anyway? If the game hadn't gone extra innings and we'd gotten to the drug store before it closed, we'd be home in bed by now.

I glanced toward Jimmy, wondering what he was thinking. Then I noticed the farther we went the more we seemed to be slowing down. The speedometer showed we were barely going forty miles an hour. I wondered what was going on.

I was staring at the road, afraid to move, when I saw Jimmy's left arm move. He lifted his hand and took hold of the window crank. Then he began rolling up his window, so slowly it was barely noticeable. About halfway up he stopped, pointed at my door, and motioned for me to crank my window up, too.

I put my hand on the handle and started turning, moving my window up slowly. Jimmy continued turning his, and after several minutes both windows were closed. It was eerily quiet now, and I was afraid the gunman would notice.

We listened for any movement in the backseat, but it was silent. Then Jimmy, looking in the rearview mirror, slowly lifted his right hand and put it on the knob that controlled the heater. He left it there for a while, waiting for any reaction from the man with the gun. Getting none, he turned the heat on its highest level and put the fan on low.

Jimmy was up to something. I just hoped it wasn't going to get us shot. We were getting closer to town, and he was going even slower now. The traffic had thinned out, only a few trucks still running. If only we could spot a state trooper.

It was getting warm in the car, and I was beginning to sweat. Moments before, I'd had chills, and now the sweat was dripping off my forehead and upper lip. I saw Jimmy wipe his brow with his wrist and knew he was feeling it, too.

Just as the lights of the city were getting closer, a noise from the backseat startled me, and I jerked my head sideways, looking at Jimmy. He stared back. He was smiling.

Then I heard it again and realized the man in back was snoring. Jimmy glanced at the mirror just as a car went by and looked at the man's face. Then he put his index finger to his lips to tell me to be quiet.

In the city the street lights shined in the car as we drove through intersections. I was afraid the lights would wake the man up. Jimmy must have thought so too because he was driving faster now, through stop signs and red lights. I realized he was hoping to get stopped by the police, but this time of night none were around. We drove up Sixth Street to the downtown business district. Everything was closed. No one was on the street. Jimmy turned right on Busserson Street and then to Seventh and then Eighth Street where he pulled up in front of a two-story stone building. Over the door a sign read "Knox County Sheriff."

He looked around in the backseat and saw the man with his head flung back against the seat, his mouth open, snoring, his hand still holding the gun. I knew any movement or noise could jolt him awake and cause him to start shooting.

Jimmy left the motor running and motioned for me to roll down my window. He didn't want me to use the door and make the dome light go on. He then whispered, "Climb out… slow. Get the sheriff."

With my window open I put my feet in the seat, turned my back to the window, and pushed myself backward out of the car, spun around, and stepped lightly onto the sidewalk. Then I edged away, watching what was going on behind me. The thought of getting shot in the back went through my mind. Once away from the car, I sneaked up to the jail and opened the door. Jimmy stayed in the car with the motor running, hoping the gunman would stay asleep just a moment longer. It took less than a minute for the sheriff and a deputy to come out. One of them circled around in the darkness behind the car, and the other one approached from the side. They made me stay in the jail office, where I watched from a window.

As they sidled up to the car, Jimmy motioned for them to come ahead, that it was okay. When they got to the open window, the sheriff looked in and saw the man was still asleep. He then reached in through the window, leaning in so far his feet left the ground, and grabbed a hold of the pistol and very slowly removed it from the man's limp hand. Once he had it secured, he motioned for the deputy to take one side of the car and he took the other. Then they opened the doors, leaned in, and pounced on the sleeping man.

He was jolted out of his sleep so fast he had little time to resist. The cops had the cuffs on him within seconds and were ordering him out of the car. They stood him up spread-eagle and searched him. Then they steered him into the station, past where I was waiting, and into a cell. Jimmy followed them in, and once the prisoner was secured and out of sight, the sheriff asked Jimmy and me to take a seat.

"You boys are lucky you're alive. You want to tell us what happened, Jimmy?"

I was surprised the sheriff knew Jimmy's name.

"Well, we stopped at the Purcell Station turnoff on our way to Payton's, and this guy opened the back door, got in, pulled a gun, and said to start driving."

"That's all he said, just start driving?"

"Oh, he added that he'd kill us if we tried anything."

"So, what happened between then and when you pulled up here?"

"Well, after a while I smelled liquor on him, and I figured he was pretty tanked up. So I rolled up the windows and cranked up the heater and let it get real hot in there, hoping he'd fall asleep, and he did. We heard him snore."

The sheriff looked at the deputy and shook his head. "Rollie Brockman always said his kid was smart as a whip. I guess it's not bragging if you can back it up."

The deputy looked at Jimmy. "What would you've done if he hadn't fallen asleep by the time you got here?"

"I don't know. I was trying to break the law to get someone to stop me, but you guys must have been in here playing euchre or something."

The sheriff let out a belly laugh proportionate to his huge midsection. "Now we got a comedian on our hands. You sound like your old man."

I was glad they knew Rollie Brockman. When Jimmy said that I thought we were going to jail for insulting the police.

"Speaking of Rollie, I think it's time to give him a call and tell him his kid's out chasing down crooks and insulting the cops."

Jimmy sat up. "Do you have to? Couldn't we just go on home and tell him ourselves?"

"What? And me miss a chance to wake up your old man and tell him his kid's in jail?"

"But, we're not really in jail."

"Right, but before you think about leaving, we have to fill out a report on this incident."

"We do? Can't you just let us go?"

"No can do. We've got a criminal here, guilty of kidnapping and a lot of other stuff, and we have to go by the book if we're going to prosecute him, so sit back and relax. You're not done here yet."

The sheriff walked over to his desk, took out a book, and started writing. "Now, if you want to make a phone call…."

"That sounds like we're the criminals," Jimmy said.

"Or I can make the call and scare your father out of his wits. Either way, one of us has to do it. What if he's pacing the floor, wondering where you are?"

I realized that was probably what Grandma was doing right now. If she woke up and saw the kitchen light still on and knew I wasn't in yet, she'd panic. I looked at Jimmy. "Maybe you better call. I don't want them all worried about us."

"Okay. I'll do it for you."

The sheriff led him to a phone in the next room, and Jimmy went in and disappeared. He came out a few minutes later, flopped down in a chair, and said, "He's better now. He woke up and saw the car was still out, and went across the street and saw the kitchen light on and knew you weren't home, either. He didn't wake Minnie because he didn't want to worry her. He said if we get home before she finds out, he'll go over with you to explain what happened."

I was glad to know she hadn't missed me yet.

The sheriff kept us fifteen more minutes while he filled out his report. "There," he said. "That should do it. You'll read all about it in the papers tomorrow."

We were out the door by the time the sheriff finished talking. It was past two a.m. and we were exhausted. On the way home Jimmy rolled down the windows and let the cool night air keep us awake. We talked all the way home, playing it back and wondering what would've happened if we'd made the wrong move.

When we got home Rollie was waiting up on the front porch. He didn't want us coming in the house and waking Mrs. Brockman. He met us in the driveway and said he'd walk over with me and explain to Grandma what happened.

"Do you have to? Why don't I just go over and go to bed? She'd never know."

"Whoa! That's what you think. Don't you think she ever reads the paper? Don't you think everybody in Purcell Station will know all about this by tomorrow?"

"This is going to be in the paper?"

"You bet. I don't know how you do it. You seem like such a quiet young man, and then you go help stop a runaway car and now catch a kidnapper."

We crossed the street and went in the back door and into the kitchen. There was Grandma, sitting at the table reading her Bible. She looked up when Rollie came in; then she saw me.

"I didn't know you kept such late hours," she said as she closed her Bible.

Rollie pulled up a chair, and I took one, too. He proceeded to tell Grandma the whole story, and when he was through, she got up, tucked her house coat around her neck, and said, "I knew the Lord wouldn't let anything happen to you." Then she thanked Rollie, gave me a hug, and went to bed. Rollie winked at me as he eased out the door and disappeared in the dark night.

CHAPTER **30**

They don't play softball in the vacant lot on Saturdays in August. Instead the farmers set up tents and tables there and sell their harvest of fruits, vegetables, and melons to people in Purcell Station and surrounding towns, causing the nearest thing to a traffic jam that Purcell Station will probably ever see.

It was just before noon when I wandered over to see it for myself. I didn't expect anyone to know about last night's experience, since the newspaper wouldn't be out until mid-afternoon. When I walked past the drugstore I found out I was wrong.

"Hey, Garrett, I heard about last night." It was Ginny Denbow.

"How'd you know?"

"Skipper told me. She heard it from her Dad, who talked to Sheriff Boykin."

She was coming out the door followed by Sarah Begley. "What was it like? Did you think you were gonna die?"

I looked around and felt the stares of others who were within earshot. I had no desire to play hero because I'd come so close to dying. "It was really Jimmy," I said. "He did it."

"Were you scared?" asked a boy who had joined the crowd.

"Yeah, really scared. He had a gun."

I stood there trying to answer questions for a few more uncomfortable minutes, and then heard a car come up and stop next to the sidewalk.

Out of the door jumped Skipper. She saw me and smiled. "Hi, you want to go inside and have a seat?"

We found a booth in the corner and sat down. Sarah and Ginny stood outside, still talking among the crowd who wanted to know what all happened last night.

"I got the story from the Sheriff through Dad," Skipper said. "The Sheriff said you and Jimmy pulled off something really smart. Not many people would've thought of that."

"Well, it was Jimmy's idea. I just went along. I didn't have any choice."

"You had to be really careful getting out of the car without waking the guy up. After all, he had a gun."

"I guess you can do a lot of things when you're scared."

We sat there, going over the whole story until I got tired talking about it, so I changed the subject. "I have to go. Maybe I'll see you at the free show tonight."

I wanted to get away from the crowd, and I knew where I wanted to go. I took the back streets to avoid the traffic. Taylor Barth was sitting on the bench on the shady side of the depot when I rode into the parking lot. Lady Muldoon sitting beside him.

"Hey there, young man. I hear you made the news again last night," he said.

"Wasn't much I did. How'd you hear about it, anyway?"

"Hard to keep it a secret around here. Lady here got it from some lady up the street who got it from a lady further up the street, and pretty soon it's all the way down here." He smiled

"If it weren't for people like me, you wouldn't know anything," Lady retorted. "Just be glad I filter some of it before it gets to you."

Taylor winked at me with the eye Lady couldn't see. He was enjoying Lady Muldoon's spunk. I was beginning to think something was going on here, and knowing what all Taylor had gone through the past few years, I hoped I was right.

We sat for a while longer, and I rushed through the questions about the night before and corrected the exaggerations. By the time the story had worked its way down the street to Taylor, Jimmy had swerved the car so violently that our gun-toting passenger conked his head on the door frame and lay unconscious all the way to the police station where Jimmy disarmed him, and we both hauled his limp body in a fireman's carry all the way to his waiting cell.

I tried to set the record straight; then I got up and started to go when Taylor said, "Look up!

"Where?"

"Over there," he said, pointing across the street. "That guy coming out of the hotel."

A man was standing at the top of the steps of the hotel, holding a briefcase. When he turned toward us, I saw who he was.

"What's he doing back here?"

"Probably whatever he was doing the first time he was here. Maybe he didn't get finished."

"I'd like to know what he's up to. I thought everyone knew everything here."

"Maybe we'd better put Lady here on the case," said Taylor. "She and her friends could probably sniff it out."

"All right, that's enough," she said, but she was smiling. "I'm no worse than you. You sit here at the foot of the Main Street like a sentry at the palace and watch everything and everybody who comes to town— those who get off the train, and those who go into the hotel, and you say I'm a busybody? And then you point out a stranger at the hotel, and you're baffled because you don't know his story? What nerve!"

Taylor was chuckling now, knowing he was riling her up. I figured it was time for me to go. I looked once more at the stranger. It was too late in the season for him to be a melon buyer, and a major league scout wouldn't be visiting when the Purple Aces were on a two-game road trip. If he was a revenuer it shouldn't take two visits to find out Eddie Sprowl might be making moonshine back in the woods across the tracks. It must be about Uncle Jake and the Navy.

I started to mount my bike when the sound of a south bounder brought down the crossing guards.

"It's the 3:52," said Taylor, standing up and checking his pocket watch. "It's dropping off the newspapers."

I followed him around the depot as the train slowed to a stop. A porter threw down a bundle of papers and waved at Taylor. We waited for any passengers, but none got off.

"No peddlers or snake oil salesmen today," said Taylor. "They probably heard how a couple of our finest citizens took the law into their own hands last night and decided they'd move on down the line."

"Maybe they heard about how you watch everything they do and tell everything you know." Lady Muldoon had followed us around to the platform, bound to get the last word in with Taylor. "I've got to be going now," she said, turning to walk up the street, "Some of us have more important things to do than sit around and gossip."

Before Taylor could think of a comeback, two boys on bicycles came charging onto the platform and sliding to a stop in front of the newspaper bag.

"Hi, Hokie, Rod. You boys got here just in time. I was just getting ready to burn these in that trash can." Taylor looked into their eyes for a reaction. They didn't disappoint him.

"Let's see...." said Rod, looking skyward to count in his head. "One hundred and ten newspapers at 3 cents apiece.... That would be three dollars and thirty cents, and we wouldn't have to pass any of these papers."

"In that case, I'll let you go ahead and pass'em. I wouldn't want you to get something for nothing." They had already started sorting and folding the papers and putting them into separate bags.

Grandpa and I were sitting on the front porch when Rod came by on his bike and flung the *Evening Commercial* onto the steps. He glanced at me and waved; apparently recognizing me from the train platform, then threw the Brockmans' paper toward their porch and rode down the hill.

I handed the paper to Grandpa, who was sitting in the swing. He unfolded it to the front page and read silently. I waited to see if he saw anything about last night. When Grandma came out to call us to supper, Grandpa said, "Wait. You'll want to hear this."

It was on the right hand column of the front page. He read it aloud:

PURCELL STATION—A gun-toting fugitive kidnapped two local youths at the junction of Highway 41 and Purcell Road last night and ordered them to drive north. Before they reached Vincennes, the youths noted their captor had fallen asleep and were able to deliver him to the county sheriff's department, where he was taken into custody.

The two boys, Jimmy Brockman, 17, and Garrett Gentry, 12, used their wits to induce sleep when they smelled alcohol on the gunman's breath. They closed the windows, turned up the heat, and drove around, waiting for their captor to fall asleep. When they heard him snoring, they carefully drove up to the sheriff's department and while Brockman sat idling the motor, Gentry quietly slipped out of the car window and ran into the sheriff's office.

Sheriff Boykin and Deputy Wagner then came out and surrounded the car, disarmed the suspect, and took him into custody.

"Those boys did a smart thing and brought in a dangerous man without any bloodshed," said the sheriff. "They should be commended for using their wits in defusing a very dangerous situation."

The sheriff identified the man as Jackson Laroche, 37, and his last known address was New Orleans, Louisiana.

There were many questions left unanswered by the time the Commercial went to press. Further investigation will be conducted by the sheriff's department to determine the motive and how Mr. Laroche happened to be in the area and under the influence of alcohol.

Grandma said, "I'll need to cut that out and send it to Leah. I'll write her tomorrow and explain it all. I don't want her to hear about it from someone who doesn't know what they're talking about."

Grandpa put the paper down, looked at me, and said, "There's a fine line between a hero and a dead man."

He didn't need to tell me. I'd been thinking the same thing.

We went inside and sat down to supper. As she always does, Grandma said grace, and this time she added in an extra phrase, thanking the Lord for sparing our lives. At the end we all said, "Amen," including Grandpa. It was the first time I'd heard him say it.

Neither Jimmy nor I knew we would be the subject of Reverend Snyder's sermon at church Sunday morning. We both sat rigid in the back with the other young people as Reverend Snyder talked about the Lord watching over His flock.

"Those who receive the protection of the Lord are His sheep. They are the ones who follow His guidance, even in the face of danger, those who trust in His protection no matter the situation. We find this in Psalms 23, verses 1-6, but we also see it in the lives of our brethren right here in Purcell Station. Two nights ago, the Lord gave two of our young people the courage and wherewithal to endure and overcome the evil intentions of a man who had strayed from the flock. The Lord guided them to safety and to justice for their captor. By being obedient to the ways of the Lord, they were able to fear no evil, and therein lies a lesson for us all. We must prepare our hearts and place confidence in the Lord, and if we do we shall fear no evil."

When he finished silence fell over the congregation, and I felt their stares. The last two days had been a whirl of emotions. The ordeal itself, the retelling of it to friends, then reading about it in the newspaper, and now having it used in the Sunday sermon was overwhelming.

The silence was broken by the sudden piano introduction of the closing hymn. The congregation stood as Reverend Snyder led us in "God Will Take Care of You."

> Be not dismayed whatever betide,
> God will take care of you.
> Beneath His wings of love abide
> God will take care of you."

After Reverend Snyder gave the benediction, the congregation filed out of the pews and hung around in the aisles talking. The young crowd sitting in the back wasted little time moving into the vestibule and then outside. There we stood milling around as we did every Sunday. In a few moments the adults came out the door, and soon Jimmy and I were surrounded, receiving well-wishes and hugs from the women and firm handshakes from the men

After the crowd dispersed, Grandma and I were walking home when she put her arm around me. "You know, the Lord works in mysterious ways. Sometimes He sends us signals." She paused to let me think about that for a minute. Then she added, "Have you given any thought to the ministry?"

CHAPTER 31

I was in the middle of Holden Caulfield's three days in New York City, the part where he encountered his sister Phoebe and told her he was thinking of going to Colorado. I managed with a flashlight and the sheets pulled over my head so Grandma wouldn't know what I was doing. It didn't seem like a book she'd want me reading, especially if she was thinking of me in terms of the ministry.

It was 10 o'clock when she went to bed, and the clock beside my bed now showed 11:25, so I figured she'd be sound asleep by now. I read a while longer and then heard Grandpa get up to make the first of his two trips to the outhouse. I was never sure he made it all the way, but the sound of the screen door snapping shut let me know he at least got outside. I had these trips timed from past experience and knew the first stop was just before midnight. The next would be around 3 a.m. If everything went okay, I'd be back by then.

When he was back in bed and snoring again, I turned off my light and waited. I kept both the south and west windows open to catch any sound and breeze the night offered. The moon peeked through the leaves of the redbud tree outside the south window. Out the other window I could see the street light from the corner shining through the rose trellis.

I lay there staring out at the moonlight, listening, and thinking maybe something had happened. Once, the quiet was interrupted by the sound of a coyote coming from the river, or was it Sprowls' dogs barking? Then I heard a grating like a stick rubbing against my screen. I sat upright and stared into the darkness. When I saw her silhouette down below the trellis, I opened the screen and whispered, "Just a second."

I pulled on my pants and shirt and slipped on my shoes. I tucked two spare pillows under my sheet and fluffed it up to make it look like I was still asleep. Opening the screen, I sat on the window sill, swung my legs over the side, and lowered my feet onto the top rung of the trellis. I turned around and closed the screen, then slowly climbed down the trellis, using it as a ladder.

"Ouch!" I yelled. I felt a sharp prick on my leg. A branch from one of the roses had worked itself inside my pants leg. Before I could remove it, I felt it scratch my shin, and then I felt the cold trickle of blood running down my ankle.

"Shh. What's the matter?" Skipper whispered.

"I'm bleeding. A thorn got caught in my leg."

I jumped down, and when I hit the ground Skipper took her flashlight and looked at my wound. "This is going to give us away when Grandma sees the blood on my pants," I said.

"Come here," she said. She led me around the house and back to the alley to the outhouse. She opened the door and went inside, coming out with a wad of toilet paper.

"Here," she said, folding it into a pad and placing it against my bleeding shin. "Hold it on until I get back."

She disappeared into the woodshed and came out with some binder twine Grandpa kept there for various purposes. She then wrapped it several times around the pad and my shin. "There that should keep it off your pants."

We took baby steps down the alley, inching our way toward the railroad, holding onto each other to keep from stepping in a hole and falling. The line of sheds, trees, and outhouses along the alley formed a boundary, keeping us on track.

As we reached the corner and stood under a street light I saw Skipper was carrying something over her outside shoulder. It was some kind of bag attached to a shoulder strap.

"What's that?" I asked.

"It's insurance. You'll see in a minute,"

We continued down to Depot Street and turned left just before we reached the railroad. When the street ended into a dirt lane, we crossed over the railroad tracks toward the river, past Sprowl's hidden compound. We hadn't gone more than fifty feet when I heard them coming. The pack of dogs flew out of trees surrounding Sprowl's fortress and into our path, barking and raising all kinds of commotion. I was waiting for the flood light on Sprowl's back shed to come on and Eddie himself to appear with a shotgun, when suddenly the barking stopped.

Skipper was bending down and scattering stuff from her bag on the ground.

"What are you doing?" I asked.

"I'm giving these guys something to eat."

When she finished, she took her flashlight and shined it on the buffet she had carried in a plastic liner in her shoulder bag.

"Where'd you get that?" I looked around and saw slabs of meat, mashed potatoes, corn, and chicken noodles.

"Maddie's," Skipper said. "It's leftovers from her plate lunch menu. She gave me everything she couldn't put in tomorrow's stew."

"Geeze, how did you think of that?"

"I figured they'd hear us coming and make all kinds of racket, so I asked Maddie for whatever she could spare. They're always hungry. I figured this would quiet them down."

"Well, it worked. You're a genius."

"Not really." She laughed. "It doesn't take that much to outsmart Sprowl's dogs, but we better get out of here before they finish and start up again."

We walked along the tracks until we got to the river, and then we turned downstream along a narrow lane. The tall sycamores and cottonwoods covered us, blocking out the moonlight.

Half an hour later, we came to the bend where Skipper and I discovered the hobo camp a month ago. There, the lane ended, leaving us a narrow path on which we had to walk single file. We were deep in the underbrush, ducking under limbs and fighting off the swishing bushes that flipped us in the face and arms.

I slapped a mosquito that landed on my neck and another one on my arm. Skipper must have heard me. "It's really swampy through here because of the floods," she said. "Some of these mosquitoes get as big as horse flies."

"They must like me. I've been waving them off, but they're still biting."

"Just hang on a little longer. We're almost there."

We'd come over two miles since we left the railroad and Sprowl's dogs, and now the thicket was wearing me down. I was beginning to wonder if it was worth it and how we were ever going to get back before Grandpa's next trip outside.

"We're almost there, I think," said Skipper.

We waded on through the marshy ground and heavy foliage another hundred yards before Skipper slowed to a stop. "It should be about right...." I came up from behind her and stood looking over her shoulder. She shined a light on it, and there it was. "Here."

It was bigger and taller than I expected. "They built it high to keep it dry from the floods," Skipper said. "You can see the water marks. That's how high the water got up last spring."

She shined the light on the poles rising high in the air to the tin hut, then moved the flashlight up the ladder and onto a small landing in front of the door. Without saying a word, she let it shine on the emblem. It was a black helmet.

There was no sign, just the emblem. I studied it for a moment and then asked, "Do you think anybody's in there?"

"No, we'd probably hear them if they were. I've heard they chant and say oaths and stuff like that."

"Do you think it's locked?"

"Probably don't need to. Nobody could find it."

I stopped. The thought came to me: how did she know this was here?

She was already moving toward the ladder. I followed. She reached the bottom step and turned around to speak when something caught her eye.

"I...." She stopped, looking beyond me toward the path we'd just taken. She turned off her flashlight. "Shh!" she whispered. I froze. "Did you hear that?"

We stood still, listening, watching, and then we saw it: a flash of light moving among the bushes and trees from the only path out of here. Then we heard the cracking of footsteps on twigs and the movement of branches and limbs.

"Quick, move!"

Skipper led me through the dark trees to the bank of the river where we knelt down in the brush. Cascading ripples in the river drowned out any noise we might have made. We crouched in behind our cover and waited. At least whoever it was didn't bring dogs with him.

The light got bigger as it approached the clearing, and when it came through the last of the ground cover, we saw the silhouette of a man carrying a lantern. He stopped out in the clearing and shined the light on the side of the hut. He stood there, looking at the black helmet, then looked around as if he expected to find someone watching.

Not seeing anyone, he stepped forward, measuring his steps, and then started up the ladder. He paused halfway up and shined his light on the ground, making sure he didn't have company. Then he finished his climb and stood on the landing. He put his hand on the doorknob and turned it, pushing the door open slightly. Then he waited. A moment later he pushed the door all the way open and shined the lantern in.

Skipper and I watched him disappear inside the hut. I could feel my heart pounding in my chest and in my temples. I was getting eaten alive by mosquitoes, and the gnats were swarming around my head.

"I think we'd better take a chance and run for it," I said.

"No, it's too risky, and besides, something isn't right."

"Whatta you mean?"

"This doesn't add up. If this man was a member he wouldn't have to be sneaking around."

"Maybe he's one of the hobos from the camp."

"I doubt it?" Skipper said. "They usually don't bother anybody or mess with people's stuff. No, I think it's someone else."

"Like a cop?"

"Maybe."

It was nearing two hours since we'd left home and would take that long to get back. I was beginning to think this wasn't such a good idea. It was my fault. I'd talked Skipper into it after we discovered the Black Helmet room in Slinker's basement and then their training grounds on Tabor Hill. I'd raised a lot of questions about this place, and I begged her to show it to me. It was her idea to do it at night. She thought it was too risky in the daytime.

I let her pick the night, and now I was wondering how she knew the Black Helmets wouldn't be meeting here tonight. I was almost afraid to ask, but I wanted to know. "Skipper, you seem to know…."

"Shhh!" she whispered. She put her finger to her lips and looked up at the landing. The door was opening, casting a light out toward the trees. I thought he must have heard our whispers and was coming out to look for us, but the light was swinging and in all directions. He froze there for a moment, looking around, and then he stepped out and pulled the door closed behind him. It looked like he took something out of his breast pocket and wiped the doorknob with it.

Climbing down the ladder, I saw he had some papers tucked under his arm and he was having problems holding them. He stopped a couple of times to regroup, but second time he dropped the lantern. It bounced off one of the steps and fell to the ground, causing the light to flicker and go out.

We could hear him utter an oath, and then he was shuffling around in the dark trying to find the lantern.

"What if he can't find it?" I asked.

"I don't know. We can't lend him ours, that's for sure."

"I know. It's just, if he's stuck here, so are we. We couldn't use our light to get home. He'd see us."

We were mulling that over when we saw the man strike a match and get down on the ground, searching. He finally found it behind one of the poles and struck another match to re-light it. I let out a deep breath and watched him gather up his papers and make his way toward the path that led back to town.

We waited long enough to let him get away so he couldn't see or hear us, then we came out into the opening. It was nearing 3 a.m., and I knew Grandma would be up. It was already too late to be home. We stood looking at the hut.

"Have you ever been inside?" I asked.

"No."

"Then how did you know it was here?"

Skipper looked me in the eye, and I thought she was going to answer. Instead she walked over to a log that had fallen on the bank of the river and sat down, leaving a place for me to sit too. She sat there for a whole minute, and then she spoke.

"I know you've got a lot of questions, and there's something I need to tell you. I found out some stuff I'm not supposed to know." She waited as if thinking how she wanted to go on. "Do you remember when you first came to town and went to the free show that first Saturday night, and Jesse was making fun of Spooks in front of all those kids?"

"Yes, and you stepped in and put a stop to it."

"Well, did you ever wonder why Jesse let me do it?"

"It's been a mystery to me ever since," I said. "I mean, he could've stomped you into the ground, but he let you back him down."

"Well, there's a reason. No one knows this but my parents, and I want to keep it between us. It happened when I was in the sixth grade. Jesse was, too, except he was three years older. He'd been held back twice, and he still couldn't read much above second grade. One day Mrs. Larwell, our teacher, took me aside and asked me to work with Jesse. She put us in the cloak room, just off our classroom, and she'd check on us to see if Jesse was working. One day he was goofing off, and Mrs. Larwell told him he was going to have to stay after school, and she asked if I could stay and help him. I said I could, and we were working when Mrs. Larwell got called out of the room to go to the office to take a phone call."

Skipper was holding her head in her palms, staring at the ground. I wasn't sure I wanted to know the rest.

"When we were alone, Jesse dropped his book, and when he picked it up he put his hand under my dress and...put his other hand over my mouth." She stopped. I waited for her to continue. "He pushed me over and landed on top of me and...he tried...I've...I've tried to forget...."

"What did you do?"

"He was on top of me, and I couldn't breathe. I managed to free my arm and I slapped him up the side of his head and almost burst his ear drum. He rolled over and grabbed his ear and wailed in pain. Then I heard the footsteps. Mrs. Larwell wore those high-heeled shoes and on the wood floor you could hear her coming. I got up and told Jesse to get up and quit whimpering. When Mrs. Larwell came back, I didn't say anything. I didn't want her to feel it was her fault for being out of the room. Instead, I went home and told my parents."

"What did they say?"

"My mother was really upset. She wanted to report it to the sheriff, but my father was pretty calm. He told Mom not to call the sheriff—that he'd take care of it."

"What did you want them to do?"

"I didn't want to make a big issue out of it. I'd always felt kinda sorry for Jesse, knowing what he had to live with, but I couldn't let him get away with it, either. When my dad said he'd take care of it that was okay with me."

"Did you know what he meant by that?"

"Not then, but I think I do now."

"What do you mean?"

"Over the years I've put two and two together, and I figured out my father knew how things got done in Purcell Station."

"And how is that?"

"I'm sure he knew about the Black Helmets. I don't know if he's in it or not, but I think he knew that if he put them on to what Jesse did, they'd take care of it, and I think they did."

"What did they do?"

"I don't know. For all I know they brought or lured him out here and scared the devil out of him. They do all those chants and rituals and mysterious stuff, and they have weapons and who knows what else. I think people are scared of them. There're all kinds of stories about what they can do to someone. Whatever they did, it worked. He changed, at least around me. It didn't change his bullying toward Spooks or others, including you, but it did with me."

I sat there, thinking about what Skipper said. Then I asked, "Who else have the Black Helmets dealt with?"

"Well, there's the story about Spike Bolton."

"Who's that? What happened?"

"He was a drunk who beat his wife, until one night he sent his wife to the hospital with a broken nose and two black eyes. The next day he suddenly disappeared, and when he resurfaced a few days later he'd found religion. There was a lot of speculation, and the story went around that the Black Helmets took care of him. Whatever it was, he got sober and hasn't had a drop of liquor since. He even takes his wife to church every Sunday."

"Are there others, too?"

"Yes, but I don't want to go into it now."

I sat studying Skipper's face, needing to know something else. Finally, I asked, "How did you know this club house was here? You've not answered that."

"No, I haven't, but I can." She turned to straddle the log and face me. "Do you remember when I told you about the raft my brother and I made last summer?"

"Yeah."

"Well, I didn't tell you what else happened that day. We were floating around the bend in the current, and it was quiet. Once the river straightened out the current took us over to this side of the bank, where we heard what sounded like chanting coming from the woods right here. We didn't expect anybody to be out here, since it was so far away from everything, so we tied up to a tree and climbed up the bank to the place we were just hiding. That's when we found this hut. We saw the emblem. We'd heard whispers about them, and now we had proof."

"What did you do when you saw it?"

"We got scared. We heard the chanting and shouts and ran back to the raft. We knew we shouldn't be there."

"So, besides chanting and taking care of things, what else do they do?"

"You know how the Civil Defense people up in the tower vow to fight communism, and they patrol the skies for enemy planes? Well, from what I can figure out, the Black Helmets must do the same kind of thing on the ground."

"They fight communists?"

"Communists and any other enemy of the people. Why else would they have that training ground up on Tabor Hill? It's probably to prepare them to fight any enemy, those from outside, or those among us."

"Do you mean an enemy could be anybody who breaks the law or hurts someone?"

"Maybe."

"So if someone has a problem, the Black Helmets take care of it?"

"I'm just guessing, but I think they do things that nobody else can."

We sat there in silence for a moment; then finally I asked, "Do you think anybody has ever been up there, besides them? I nodded at the hut.

"No," she said pointing the flashlight on the emblem and holding it there. I'm sure it would be risky if they got caught."

A minute passed. It was already too late to get home before Grandpa's trip outside.

"Let's go," I said. "I wanna know what that man saw in there."

Skipper stood and shined the flashlight in my face. "If we do, you have to promise never to tell anyone."

"I promise. Besides, I wouldn't want them to find out."

She studied my eyes to see if I was telling the truth. Then she led the way, letting the light shine on the rungs as we slowly started up the ladder. At the landing she waited for me to catch up and then gently turned the doorknob. Pushing open the door, we tiptoed in and Skipper circled the light around the walls.

On the wall opposite the door hung a large board with charts and lists tacked on it. In front of it was a wooden table with four rows of chairs facing it. There were no windows, but there were hatches on opposite walls that opened up and could be propped open to let in light and air.

I closed the door behind us. I didn't want the stranger to come back and surprise us.

"Look!" Skipper was pointing to the front wall. She shined the light on a poster. It read:

***PLEDGE OF THE BLACK HELMETS OF AMERICA.

Having been awarded the rank of _____ in unit _____ of the Black Helmets of America, I pledge loyalty and allegiance in the service of the people of the United States of America.

I give my word of honor that I will obey all reasonable commands of my superior officers and that I will keep secret all matters pertaining to the organization and its officers; that I will seek to protect all citizens regardless of race, national origin, or religion against all aggression, whether it be communist, other foreign, or domestic in nature; that I will be true and loyal to the organization and its officers: and that I will endeavor to be a good, law-abiding citizen of the United States and uphold the mores of my local community.

Signed: _____
B.H. No. _____ Recommended by _____ of Unit _____
Witnessed by _____ of Unit _____
Dated this _____ Day of _____ 1952

I walked over to a corner where a small table held a stack of pamphlets. I picked one up and it read: *Official Handbook: Black Helmets of America.* I leafed through its table of contents and saw listed the articles of its constitution. It outlined the number of divisions and units and the officers designated to each unit. There were no names listed.

"I think we'd better get out of here," I said.

Skipper was looking through a stack of documents on Communist and Nazi propaganda tactics. She nodded but kept on reading. I looked around the room, but without a light I couldn't see anything that caught my attention. I was moving toward another wall when I bumped into a chair and sent it crashing to the floor. The noise caused Skipper to jump and let out a small shriek

"It's just a chair," I said. I picked it up.

"Okay, let's go."

Just as we reached the door, we both stopped. Skipper grabbed my arm and froze. We listened. It sounded like footsteps, then twigs breaking under feet. We waited.

We listened for feet coming up the ladder. After a few minutes, Skipper stepped toward the door and turned the knob. She cracked the door and peered through the darkness. She put her ear to the opening and waited.

"Maybe it was an animal," I whispered.

"I'm going to shine a light and see what happens," she said.

She pointed the light into the clearing around the hut, but we saw nothing unusual. Then she moved it to the brush area we'd hid in earlier. Nothing came to light, but then we heard a slight movement, and just then a pair of red eyes peered through the brush and stayed there. It stayed there until another pair appeared on the other side of the shrubs. And then another.

I walked out on the landing and took a chance. I'd heard how they freeze in the headlights. I took my foot and kicked the tin wall of the hut. My guess was right as the three deer took off running toward the river, and we got out of there.

The way home went faster. I was hot and tired and didn't care much if I got slapped in the face with branches or tree limbs. At one point we saw a light across the river, and we stopped and listened. We heard the faint sound of voices.

"It's the hobo camp. It's their campfire," Skipper said.

We waited to see if we could see anyone. "Are you sure it wasn't one of them?" I asked.

"I'm sure. First of all, how would he get across the river? The guy we saw wasn't all wet from swimming across."

"That's true."

"Whoever it was, he was looking for something."

We began walking again. We reached the railroad and sneaked past Sprowl's hideway, avoiding his dogs, and soon we were trudging up the back alley we had come down nearly four hours ago.

Skipper and I parted at the alley behind the woodshed. I was tired and sore from the mosquito bites and the scabs from the scratches on my leg. It was itching, so I ripped off the toilet paper bandage Skipper had put together and threw it in the barrel Grandma used for trash. I told Skipper goodnight.

"See you tomorrow. I have a feeling we'll be catching up on our sleep most of the morning," she said.

She disappeared through the alley. I came around the woodshed, down the arbor, and around to my back bedroom window. I was careful this time climbing up the trellis and avoiding the thorns. At the top rung I leaned in, pushed open the screen, and waited. Then I climbed in, slowly closed the screen behind me, and got undressed. The clock on my table told me it was 4 a.m.

I slept until 10 o'clock, and when I came into the kitchen to eat breakfast, Grandma wondered if I'd had a bad night. "You woke me up last night," she said.

My heart leapt. I stopped with a mouth full of cereal and stared at her. "I did?"

"Yes, you must have had a bad dream. You were yelling something. I couldn't make out what it was."

"Oh, maybe I did," I said.

CHAPTER 32

Two days had passed since our night trip down the river. When I saw Skipper in front of Slinker's General Store I yelled, "Skip! Wait up."

I crossed the street behind a red Farmall pulling two wagons filled with melons. It was headed down Main to the tracks, where a row of boxcars waited on side rails for the last of the late crop.

"I was just going in to see Sarah," Skipper said. "She's working today. Want to come?"

"Sure."

A pickup truck with two men inside came up the hill, and when they got even with us they looked over and stared like they were going to say something. Ever since we found the note on the windshield of the Blue Bruise, I'd been on the lookout for men in pickup trucks, even those that were not black. Our trips to Slinker's basement, Taber Hill, and now the clubhouse down the river made me paranoid. I was afraid what might happen if the Black Helmets found out we'd been to all three.

Skipper waited for me to cross and then looked around to be sure we were alone. "Did you get in without waking anyone?" she asked.

"Yes, but when I got up yesterday morning I thought I'd been caught. Grandma asked if I had a bad night. She said I was yelling in my sleep and must have had a nightmare. "How about you?"

"I attracted a few stray dogs in the alley, but they fizzled out by the time I got home. My only problem was the next morning. Dad woke me to go out to the farm and help him shoo in a heifer that got out through a hole in the fence."

"What time was that?"

"About 6:30. I had two and a half hours sleep."

"What did you do?"

"I waited until dad went to the garage, and I went in the barn and fell asleep on some bales of straw up in the loft. I didn't wake up until noon."

"We were lucky."

We were standing on the sidewalk in front of Slinker's front door. A voice came from behind us. "Hey, you two. What're you doing out here?" It was Sarah. She had just stepped out the front door.

"Just on our way to see you," said Skipper. "You busy?"

"I'm just taking a break. It's slow now, but you should've seen it this morning. There must've been twenty-five or thirty people in here the first hour. It's funny, they were all men."

"Must've been good for business." Skipper said.

"That's what's so strange," said Sarah. "None of them bought anything. They milled around, and every once in a while some of them would go in the back room to Slinker's office. The others just stood around. I'd ask them if I could help them, and they said no, that they were just looking."

"That *is* odd," said Skipper.

"It is. When all of them finished going in the back room, they just kind of disappeared. Some stood around on the sidewalk talking, but they didn't stay long."

"How were they acting?" Skipper asked.

"They were real serious. No joking around or anything. It was strange how they appeared so suddenly and then disappeared just as fast."

"Did you know any of them?" Skipper asked.

"I recognized some of them, their faces anyway, but most of them I didn't know. Usually not that many strange people come through here. But I did hear one of them call another one Duke."

"Duke?" I asked. "What did he look like?"

"He was dressed up—kind of distinguished looking—polished shoes. Had thick bushy hair. He wasn't like the rest of them."

"That's what I thought," I said. "That sounds like the guy I saw in the barber shop a while back. He's some kind of big shot, I think. A politician. I wonder what he was doing here?"

"I don't know, but he sure stood out," Sara said.

Just then a truck stopped in front of Slinker's and two men got out. They looked our way and then entered the store.

Sarah stood up. "I gotta go. I don't want Mr. Slinker to wonder where I am, although he's been holed up in his office all day, talking on the phone."

Skipper and I told her goodbye and headed up Main Street. When we reached Smokey's, we saw Jesse shooting a game with Pee Wee. I'm sure he saw us, and I was afraid he'd come out and say something, but he just leaned over the table with his cigarette dangling out of the corner of his mouth and smashed the ball into the pocket. Then he stood up, took a long drag, and flicked the butt on the floor.

"I'm getting nervous, trying to dodge both Jesse and black pickup trucks, and now that guy from last night," I said.

"Don't worry about Jesse, and as for those men in the black pickup, if they wanted us they'd have gotten us by now. I think they just wanted to scare us," said Skipper. "And the guy last night didn't see us, so that's nothing to worry about."

"I hope so, but it still makes me nervous."

I got home just in time for supper, and when it was over and the dishes done, Grandpa and I carried on in the swing on the front porch. Jimmy Brockman came over and joined us. As the sun was sinking over the sycamores and river birches Rollie came over, walking up the front steps and asking, "Did you get your paper tonight?"

"Not yet," Grandpa said. "Did you? That little booger's getting later every day."

Jimmy said, "I just talked to Louise and they didn't get theirs either. I think I'll ride down to the station and see what the problem is."

"I'll go with you," I said.

We coasted down to the tracks, pulled up at the depot, and tried the door. It was locked. Taylor Barth had already left. We walked around the platform and looked for the papers but didn't see them.

"The boys must've picked 'em up. Let's go find 'em," Jimmy said. We rode up Main and turned right on Second Street, and there we saw Hokie Grimes on his bicycle. Jimmy yelled, "Hi, Hoke what's the problem? Why're you just now getting 'em out?"

Hokie stopped, put one foot down to hold up his bike, and reached into his bag. "It's all at the bottom of the page, Jimmy. You can read it for yourself." He unfolded a copy and handed it to Jimmy. "Here, you can take yours now, too," he said as he handed me another paper.

I looked on the bottom of the front page, and in the left hand corner there was a small square that read:

Due to the nature of the late-breaking headline story, we apologize for the delay in the delivery of your evening newspaper. We held the deadline over to get the full details of the story in order to keep our readers informed of an important local development. We hope our readers understand. Thank you for your patience.

I quickly flipped the paper over and saw the headline stretching across the top of the page: CAPTURED KIDNAPPER, HIJACKER WANTED FOR MURDER IN NEW ORLEANS

Jimmy read it the same time and let out a yelp. "Whoa, hang on. Wait till you hear this." He paused; then read on. "It's a good thing we didn't know this at the time." He read the story out loud as Hokie sat on his bike listening. I followed, reading along in my copy:

Police learned today the fugitive who hijacked a car and kidnapped two Purcell Station youths last month is wanted for murder and armed robbery in New Orleans, Louisiana.

Sheriff Clyde Boykin released the results of an investigation to determine why lone gunman, Jackson Laroche, 37, hijacked a car driven by Jimmy Brockman and his passenger Garrett Gentry at the junction of Purcell Station Road and Highway 41 last July.

The youths successfully delivered the fugitive to local police when they suspected he was heavily sedated with alcohol and induced him to fall asleep, whereby they turned him over to the sheriff. The boys were publicly acclaimed for their bravery and alert action in bringing the suspect into custody.

Police have uncovered the circuitous route the fugitive took to avoid capture for more than two weeks. He apparently traveled by rail, hopping freight trains and hiding in hobo camps scattered along railroads where few questions are ever asked.

They have determined he stopped in a secluded camp on White River between Hazelton and Purcell Station. He stayed there three days before leaving in the night to walk the tracks to Purcell Station, where he gained access to a large amount of hard liquor from a suspected bootlegger just outside of the town.

After becoming inebriated, he apparently walked along the top of the levee to the highway junction, where he waited in darkness until he could ambush an unsuspecting motorist. It was there he pulled a gun on the two youths and ordered them to drive northbound to an undetermined location. Police believe that destination was Chicago, where the suspect is thought to have lived previously.

They also discovered he is currently wanted on numerous warrants in Detroit and Carson City, Nevada. Laroche is accused of murdering a young couple who gave him a ride while hitchhiking along Highway 90 northeast of New Orleans when his car broke down. Their bodies, stripped of all personal effects, were found two days later along a lagoon near Biloxi, Mississippi.

Laroche is currently in custody in Vincennes until New Orleans officials arrive to transport him to Louisiana to stand trial. The investigation continues to determine if other states have warrants out for his arrest.

"You mean you were in a car with that murderer?" asked Hokie. "You coulda got killed!"

"Hoke, that's already crossed my mind," said Jimmy. He folded the paper and tucked it under his arm. "Come on, Garrett, let's take the news home. This is gonna upset your grandma."

We rode back up the street, and I was glad no one had read the story yet, because I didn't want to be reminded again how lucky we were to be alive. Grandpa and Rollie were still on the porch when we came into the yard. Mr. Francis was in his yard and saw us pull up with newspapers.

"Where'd you get those, Jimmy?" he asked. "I don't know why they're so late."

"We went down to the depot and found Hokie on Second Street, so we stopped him and got ours. Sorry, I didn't think to get yours."

"That's okay. Probably nothing in it, anyway," he said as he walked up the steps and sat in the rocker.

"There is tonight," Jimmy said. "Here, take a look." He handed his copy to Mr. Francis and the other copy to Grandpa and Rollie.

They read in silence. When they finished they sat looking at Jimmy and then at me. Grandpa spoke first. "Do you boys know how close…?"

Jimmy broke in. "We came to dying?"

Grandma came out the door and heard the last of part. "Who's dying?"

"Oh, nothing. We were just talking about a story we saw in the paper," Grandpa said. "You might want to read it."

He handed her the paper and waited. As she read it, her arm began to shake. When she was through, she laid it aside and said, "The Lord was watching over you."

Grandma never mentioned it again, at least to me. But, I can't say that for the rest of Purcell Station. Everywhere Jimmy and I went we were asked if we knew how lucky we were. Then we were asked one more time to tell them all the details.

CHAPTER 33

I was on my way to the post office to pick up the mail. The fuss over the gunman incident had died down somewhat, so Grandma's attention focused on receiving a letter from Jake. He usually wrote every week, two weeks at most, but it had been more than a month, and she wasn't sure whether he was in the States or in the Pacific. The news from Korea was getting worse, and I could tell she was afraid he might be going back.

Bud Tate was in the back counting letters when I entered. He looked up under his visor to see who came in. "Well, look who's here. How 'ya doin,' stranger?"

"Fine. I came to see if Uncle Jake sent a letter today."

"Haven't found one yet, but I'm not through sorting," he said. "I read about you in the paper, but I hadn't seen you for so long I figured you'd gone back up north where it's safe."

"Not yet, but it won't be long. You sure you haven't missed it? We haven't heard from him for a long time."

"Let me look in the dead letter file." He swiveled his chair and leaned back. "I throw every tenth letter in there just for meanness."

He pretended to look in the round cardboard tub sitting behind him, stirring papers up with his hand. "Not here, but I'll keep a lookout for ya."

"Thanks, I'll check back again. Grandma's pretty worried."

"Oh, he's probably on a secret mission someplace that he can't talk about."

"You're probably right." I let the screen door slam behind me.

I crossed Main Street and saw there was no softball game in the vacant lot. This must be the dog days of summer I'd heard people talk about. Only two old men sat on the bench in front of Dub's; one of them had his eyes closed and was snorting, working up to a full-blown snore. Dub was busy under the grease rack, changing the oil on a truck.

Coming up the alley, I turned into the arbor to report the bad news to Grandma. The arbor was thick with grapes, big, round, purple ones. I pulled one off the vine and tested it. It was sour but juicy. Then I gathered a few more in my hand and walked into the back porch.

Grandma was in the middle of canning tomatoes but stopped when she heard the screen door slam. "Any news?" she asked.

She saw my empty hand and the other holding the grapes and got her answer. I shook my head to verify it.

"Well, we'll just keep hoping."

She had already turned to her pressure cooker and was loosening the top. She stood over the stove, her shoulders slumped. She didn't say another word about Jake, but she didn't have too. I could tell what she was thinking.

I thought about him, too, and the nights we'd stayed up and talked. I walked out the back door and sat under the maple tree, and then I felt a little sourness in my throat. I wasn't sure if it was the grapes or something else.

I looked at the garden across the alley. Large red tomatoes hung from the vines, but only brown stalks remained of the sweet corn. Holes lay in the ground where the potatoes used to grow, and the lettuce, radishes, and onions had dried up and withered. Behind the barn strawberries had turned brown, and stalks of asparagus and rhubarb had turned woody. I wandered down the rows to the line of fruit trees. The limbs of the peach and pear trees sagged with fruit, nearly touching the ground. These and the tomatoes were all that was left. The season was changing.

I left the garden and strolled down the alley, past the woodshed and outhouse, down the hill outside my bedroom window. I came to the trellis I'd used as my ladder that night and inspected the thorns that had scarred my shin. I wondered what Grandma knew and if I'd get caught the next time.

I went around to the front porch. The swing was empty now. Grandpa was taking his afternoon nap. I took a seat. It was quiet. I wondered where everyone was. I was sensing the end of something; I wasn't sure what.

CHAPTER **34**

T he next-to-last free show of the summer started at dusk, just as it had every Saturday night all summer, only this time it fell on the day that set a record high temperature of 101 degrees. Grandpa sat on the porch and fanned himself most of the afternoon, trying to catch what little southwestern breeze came over the bend of the river. By supper time the temperature was still over a hundred, and the radio said it would stay in the lower 80s most of the night.

I finished supper well before dark and went over to the vacant lot to stake out our spot. There seemed to be a larger crowd in town, probably because it was in the lull between melon season and the corn and soybean harvest. Their numbers forced us to crowd in close to make room, and that created even more body heat.

I met up with Skipper and Sarah in front of Dub's and asked if they'd like to go get a drink first, since the cartoons were just starting. They did.

We edged our way into the door of the drugstore, weaved through the crowd to the counter, and waited. After ordering three R.C.'s we made our way back through the crowd. When we reached the door and stepped out on the sidewalk, we nearly bumped into two brawny boys I didn't recognize. One of them was talking to the chubby, freckled-faced boy they called Pee Wee, the boy who helped Jesse push me to the ground my first day in town last spring.

As we edged past them I heard Pee Wee talking. "I don't know whur he's at. He's usually here for the show. Did ya check his house?"

I motioned for Skipper and Sarah to wait. I wanted to hear this.

"He ain't there," said the tallest boy. He wore bib overalls with no shirt underneath. His arms looked like Willie Lickert's, the blacksmith, only dirtier. From the smell of his armpits, he hadn't bothered with a Saturday-night bath. He also smelled of liquor.

"Well, if I see 'im I'll tell him you're looking for 'im," said Pee Wee. "Whata you want him for?"

The other boy, who had stringy hair and long sideburns, spoke up. "Ain't none of your business. Let's just say we have a little business lined up down in Hazelton."

"What kind of business?"

"A man's business and none of yours."

"Who said I'm not a man?"

"You don't look like no man to me, dough boy," said the first boy. "Now, why don't you go nosin' around and try to find Jesse and tell 'em his cousin Earl is looking for 'em."

Pee Wee turned to leave. "I'll tell'im if I find him." We watched him wander up Main and cross the street toward the vacant lot, where we lost him in the crowd.

"Those guys are Jesse's cousins, and that's Pee Wee Harding," said Skipper. "He started hanging around Jesse in grade school to keep kids from teasing him. Nobody teased him in front of Jesse. Except Jesse, of course. He treated him like a dog, but he wouldn't let anybody else treat him like one."

The two boys milled around the sidewalk, their eyes searching the crowd. The one called Earl looked agitated, and I heard him muttering some oath under his breath as they disappeared inside Maddie's. They reappeared a minute later and stood outside Slinker's General Store.

It was getting dark and the cartoons were ending, so we weaved our way through the crowd and took our places on the quilt to watch the show. After the cartoons were over the Movietone News came on, showing the latest from the front in Korea. Fighting was intense around the thirty-eighth parallel, with rockets and flares lighting up the night skies. It made me think about Uncle Jake. I woke up last night sweating on my pillow after a bad dream where Jake was on a ship off the coast of Korea, getting bombarded with missiles.

The news wrapped up on a happier note with a look at the pennant races in both leagues. The Dodgers beat the Giants 10-8 and Gil Hodges hit a home run for the Dodgers.

"That's the guy who once played here at the Sand Bowl," I informed Skipper. "Don Francis struck him out."

"Maybe Don Francis should be pitching for the Giants," said Sarah. "Looks like they need a pitcher."

The Yankees' highlights showed Joe DiMaggio hitting a long fly to centerfield and pulling up when he saw his brother Dom catch it for Boston. It looked like the Yankees and Dodgers would be meeting in the World Series.

"I'm for the Dodgers," I told Skipper. "They're the underdogs, and I'm always for the underdogs."

"Me, too," she said. "That's why I'm worried about Pee Wee and Jesse's cousins."

"Whatta you mean?"

"Well, did you see the way they talked down to Pee Wee? I'd say he's an underdog, too—has been all his life—and I don't think they're done with him yet."

"Whatta you think they're going to do?"

"I don't know. I wish I knew why they wanted Jesse."

The movie *Sunset Boulevard* started, and we sat down to watch William Holden and Gloria Swanson in one of last summer's popular movies. I settled back with my head on a pillow, but I noticed Skipper seemed restless. About ten minutes into the show, she leaned over and whispered, "I'm going to find them."

"Who?" I asked.

"Those boys. I think they're up to something." She stood up and, bending over so not to block the view of others, scuttled back to the wall along the sidewalk. I watched until she reached the street.

"I'll be back," I told Ginny and Sarah.

The street and sidewalks were still crowded. I caught up with Skipper. "I'm coming, too."

"Okay, I'm gonna find out what they want with Jesse."

We walked along the north side of Main, looking in every building that was open. We checked out the hotel down by the tracks, then crossed the street and came back up the hill on the other side of the street. We stepped inside Maddie's and Slinker's, came past Danny's barbershop, and stopped in front of Smokey's Pool Room. We stepped inside and looked through the open archway to the back room where the poker game was going on. I sneaked a quick look around the corner. The men in the poker games didn't like people getting too nosy.

We walked past the crowd sitting on the sidewalk and then on past Dub's, where the usual crowd occupied the liar's bench.

"Let's go down the alley behind the movie screen," said Skipper. "Sometimes kids hang out back there."

Behind Dub's we turned down the alley and edged our way behind Brockman's Grocery. Then we stopped. There standing outside the back door of Smokey's stood the outline of three people. They were arguing about something. It was dark except for the light coming through the back screen door. Skipper put her finger to her lips and motioned me to follow. We came up behind a tree, just close enough to hear them talking.

"I'm tellin' ya, time's wasting." It was Big Earl. He sounded angry.

"I can't find him. I looked everywhere. If we can't find him I'll take his place," said Pee Wee.

"Ha! The Scranton brothers would probably laugh at ya." Big Earl sneered.

"Who're the Scranton brothers?" asked Pee Wee.

"Let's just say it involves the honor of a girl, and they're trying to dishonor her."

"Whatta you think, Butch? Ya think Pee Wee's up to it?"

"If we don't find Jesse, and if he wants to prove he's a man, I say let's take 'im," said Butch.

"Maybe, but he'd better not be extra baggage," said Big Earl.

Skipper leaned into my ear and whispered, "We can't let'm take Pee Wee. He doesn't know what he's getting into."

"How are you gonna stop them?"

"Follow me."

Skipper stepped out of the shadow of the tree toward the three boys. I saw Big Earl flinch when he saw her. "What the...?" he said.

Skipper walked into the light coming from Smokey's back door so they could see her. "Are you the guys who are looking for Jesse?" Skipper spoke up. "I heard you talking in front of the drugstore a while ago."

Earl waited until he could get a good look. "Could be. What's it to ya?" He stood with his thumbs hooked onto the straps of his bib overalls and rocked back on his heels. His chest swelled up when he saw it was a girl.

"I think I know where he might be."

"Oh yeah, where's that?" Earl eyed Skipper up and down.

"I think he might be down on the river. He goes night fishing down around Thompson's Bend."

"You think so, huh? And how we supposed to find him?" asked Big Earl.

"Just cross the tracks and follow the path along the river downstream. The bend's about 500 yards below the bridge. You look like you can find your way around."

"You got that right." Earl wasn't about to let on he might not know where he was going. "Come on, Butch, let's get movin'. This girl better know what she's talkin' about. I ain't up for no wild goose chase."

Pee Wee stepped up. "Can I come, too? I can help find 'im."

"We don't need you now, and we sure don't need no pipsqueak like you taggin' along," said Butch.

"But I can fight just as well as Jesse can. We always have each other's backs."

"We get Jesse, we don't need you," said Butch. "You got it? Now beat it."

They turned away and headed down the alley. When they were out of sight, Skipper looked at Pee Wee. "You don't need them, Pee Wee," she said. "You shouldn't beg them like that."

Pee Wee shifted his feet. "I know, but Jesse'd be proud if he knew I went in his place and helped beat up on those Spangle brothers."

"See, you don't even know their names, and you have no business with these yahoos. Who knows if they're even telling the truth?"

Pee Wee looked down at the ground. "It's just that I don't want Jesse gettin' mad at me and think I chickened out."

"Jesse can think anything he wants. How do you even know Jesse would've gone with them?"

"They said he was their cousin. I bet he'd a gone." Pee Wee was sounding less sure of himself.

"There's something you need to know about Jesse," said Skipper. "He picks his fights. He avoids any fight he knows he can't win. It's time you understood that. He's not the big hero you think he is."

"If Jesse thinks I chickened out, will you tell 'im I tried, but they wouldn't let me?"

"Let's see if Jesse even goes with them. Maybe he'll turn them down, too, if they can even find him."

"Naw, Jesse'll go if they find him." Pee Wee was convinced.

"We'll see," said Skipper

Pee Wee stood there. His pathetic begging to go with the boys made me feel sorry for him. I put my hand on his shoulder and asked, "You wanna come sit with us and watch the rest of the movie?"

"Yeah, Pee Wee," said Skipper. Come on and watch the show. We got a big bag of popcorn. I bet you're hungry."

"Oh, all right. I ain't got nothin' better to do." He also didn't want to appear too eager. "But if they come back without Jesse, I'm going with them."

We found the quilt and sat down with Sarah and Ginny, who looked surprised to see Pee Wee Harding. Skipper scooped up a bowl full of popcorn and handed it to Pee Wee. The movie was well into the middle of the plot, and I was trying to piece together what was happening with little luck. Pee Wee seemed content to eat popcorn.

When he finished his second bowl, he brushed off his buttery hands and announced. "I'm thirsty."

"You have any money, Pee Wee?" asked Skipper.

"Ain't got none. I gave it to Big Earl."

"You gave him your money?"

"He asked for it."

"What did you give him?"

"A buck-fifty," Pee Wee said.

"You just handed over your money to two strangers? Why?"

"He said he'd beat me up if I didn't."

"Pee Wee, did you really think they'd beat you up in front of all these people?"

"Wudn't in front of nobody. It was in back of Smokey's."

"Was that right before we came up and found you with those guys?"

"Uh-uh."

"They took your money, and you still begged to go with them?"

"I didn't want them to think I was scared."

"Come with me. I'll go with you to get a drink." I followed as she led him through the stretched-out bodies on blankets. Skipper paid for his drink, and then we walked up the street in the shadows of the maple trees.

"Pee Wee, you can't beg people to be your friend. You have to earn their respect first. As long as you hang around Jesse and people like his cousins, you're never going to get their respect. Do you understand?"

"But Jesse's the only friend I got."

"Jesse's no friend. He uses you. Look, what would you do if Jesse died tonight? What would you do for a friend then?" asked Skipper.

"I dunno. Jesse ain't dying tonight, so I don't have to think about it."

"Maybe so, but you still don't need to do his bidding for him or his cousins." I could tell Skipper was frustrated trying to talk sense into Pee Wee. "Let's go finish the movie," she said.

We stayed until it ended, but it wasn't until the next morning that I found out the movie wasn't all that ended that night.

CHAPTER 35

The movie had lasted later than usual, and then I walked Skipper up the hill to her house. We sat on the front porch in the swing and talked for almost another hour when I realized it was going on twelve. I jumped off the porch and ran down Main Street. The street was quiet. The stores and restaurants were locked up and dark. The only person I saw was Spooks pushing his wheelbarrow cattycorner across Third and Main, carrying the garbage from Maddie's Café and the drugstore. He did this every weekend after the big crowds left. The proprietors didn't want to attract rats by letting their garbage sit around until Monday.

When I turned the corner at Dub's, I heard a siren off in the distance toward the highway, but I kept on walking home without giving it another thought.

I fell asleep just after midnight. At nine o'clock I was awakened by the ringing of the church bells. Grandma had already left, so I ate a quick bowl of Cheerios, ran down Fourth Street and up the church steps, and slid into a back pew with the other kids. The organ was just into the first hymn and people were standing. I took out a hymnal and looked down the pew to see who was there and noticed no one was singing. Some were staring straight ahead; others were whispering. Something didn't seem right.

Skipper sat at the other end of the pew next to Spooks, who was in his usual seat by the window. He was saying something to her. He seemed excited and a little agitated. Skipper turned and saw me looking at her, and it was then I noticed a tear falling down her cheek. She gave me a look as if searching for some kind of reaction. I stared back and held out my hands, palms up, asking, "What?"

She arched her eyebrows. My blank look told her I had no idea what was going on. She started sidling down the pew in front of the others. "You haven't heard have you?" she whispered.

"Heard what?"

"What happened last night."

"What happened?"

She waved her arm toward the door. "Let's go out there." We went out the door at the back of the sanctuary and into the belfry, where we were alone.

"Those two boys," she began, then paused. "Those boys looking for Jesse?"

"Yes, what about them?"

"They came over the levee...about midnight..." She sucked in deep breaths, waited, then began again. "It's horrible...they got airborne...lost control...and flipped over in the backwater pond."

"They what? Are they...?

"No," Skipper said. "The fire department...pulled them... out of the water early this morning."

I stared past Skipper through the open door to the street, where life was going on. Two people I'd just spoken to last night were dead. No sooner had it sunk in when another thought hit me, sending my heart pounding. "Did they have Jesse with them?"

"They didn't find any other body."

"What happened to him? Didn't they find him?"

"That's what I'd like to know. Wherever he was, he was lucky."

"What about Pee Wee? Do you realize you saved his life last night?"

"Maybe, but maybe Jesse saved his life."

"Jesse? What do you mean?

"Jesse was the decoy that sent them searching and forgetting Pee Wee."

"Decoy? How?"

"I gave them some bad information," Skipper said.

"You did? On Purpose?"

The hymn ended, and it got quiet inside. "We'd better get back in there before someone comes through here."

We struggled through the rest of the hymns and Scripture reading, and then everyone was dismissed to their classes. When Mr. Carmony, our teacher, began our class with a prayer, he prayed for the boys in the accident. When finished, the lesson he had prepared was set aside, and the rest of the hour centered on the incident and how the choices we make always have consequences.

Stunned, I sat through Sunday School, and when the church service started Reverend Snyder prayed for the boys and their families and friends and the "terrible tragedy that happened outside Purcell Station last night." I sat through the sermon but heard little of it. Instead, I kept thinking about Pee Wee and Jesse and how fate and chance play into what happens.

When church ended people stood around talking in front of the building. Someone said it was the first traffic fatality in Purcell Station in thirty years. Rumors flew around town most of the day, and it wasn't until Monday afternoon's newspaper came out that some of the questions were answered. A front-page story in the *Commercial* read:

HIGH SPEED CAUSE OF DEATH OF TWO PATOKA YOUTHS

Two Patoka youths drowned when their speeding car careened off the Purcell Station levee and landed in a backwater pond last night.

Earl Ratterman, 19, and Edwin "Butch" Pulliam, 18, swerved to avoid a motorcycle rider approaching the peak of the levee from the other direction and landed upside-down in ten feet of water. Police say speed was a factor in the accident. They are performing a toxicology exam to see if alcohol was involved.

The accident occurred about midnight and was witnessed by Cletus "Spooks" Barkus, a trash collector who alerted the Purcell Station Volunteer Fire Department.

The rider of the motorcycle, Rollie Brockman, 49, was unaware of the accident until he heard the sirens. He explained he was returning from a run to a truck stop on highway 41. "I saw a blur coming over the levee and lost sight of it as I came down my side. I didn't know it went off the road," he said.

Relatives of the two boys in Patoka said they were involved in a feud with a group of youths in that town and were going to Purcell Station to find "reinforcements," which they apparently failed to do. No other bodies were found.

That night, Jimmy asked me to help him with his radio broadcast after learning I had met the two victims just hours before their deaths. At seven o'clock he read the news almost verbatim as it appeared in the newspaper, and then he introduced me to shed some light on what the boys were doing in Purcell Station and who they were looking for.

I told how Skipper and I first saw them outside the drugstore and then again behind Smokey's Pool Room. I told them who the boys were looking for and what Skipper told them, but I left out the part about Pee Wee wanting to go in Jesse's place. He didn't need more reasons for people to tease him. When we were finished, Jimmy gave the rest of the news and began playing the records he'd selected for the night.

Skipper came over the next day. I was in the barn and didn't hear her come in and climb up the ladder to the loft. I was standing there holding a bale of straw over my head when I heard her voice. "Hey, Garrett!"

I dropped the bale and turned around. "Warn me next time. I almost dropped this on my head. What's up?"

"I need to talk to you."

"Okay." I wiped the sweat off my face, sat down on a bale, and motioned her to sit next to me.

She sat down and waited; then she began. "Yesterday, you asked me what kind of bad information I gave Jesse's cousins, so I want to explain."

"Good! I've been wondering."

"Well, here's what happened. I sent them down the river, but I really didn't think he was there. I didn't know where he was, but if he was fishing he always goes up the river to Sparkman's Slough."

"How do you know that?"

"I know more about Jesse than you think. I've wanted to tell you this for a long time, but I couldn't. Can you keep a secret? I mean it. You can't tell anyone."

"I promise."

"Well, you know how he's been spending time up in the tower identifying planes?"

"Uh-uh, I saw his name on the board."

"Well, he's always wanted to learn to fly, but he knew he could never pass the test if he couldn't read. So, one day he asked me to help him. He's real self-conscious about it. He didn't want anyone to know."

"You helped him after what he did to you in sixth grade?"

"We talked about that. I know he feels bad about it. In his own odd way he's let me know he's sorry, and I told him I forgave him."

I leaned back on a bale and put my hands behind my head, thinking about how Skipper could be so forgiving.

Finally, I asked, "But, how did you know he was fishing last night?"

"I didn't, but after spending a lot of time reading with him, he's opened up a lot to me. He told me he'd been going out at night and bringing in some good-sized catfish up at the slough. That gave me the idea he *might* be fishing. I thought sending his cousins the wrong direction was a good way to get them away from both Jesse and Pee Wee."

"Well, it worked. How do you think so fast like that?"

"I don't know. Reverend Snyder thinks it was divine guidance."

"I'm sure Grandma would say so, too."

We sat there talking about fate and how it worked. Finally I said, "So, tell me how you've been helping him read?"

"Well, we meet three times a week...."

"Where?" I interrupted.

"In a back room of the library. It's an old storage room. Nobody ever goes back there. It has a back door to the alley. Jesse goes in there, and I come in the front and wander around until nobody is looking, and then I go in the back. I take a primer from the library with me, and I have him follow me as I read to him. Then I have him read back to me. He takes the book home with him and practices and brings it back, and we do it again."

"Does he take it seriously?"

"Yes. He really wants to get it, but he doesn't want anyone to know. I tell him there's no shame in people knowing, but he's not buying it."

"So, did you meet him this morning?"

"That's what else I came to tell you. He came in and started asking me about Saturday night. He wanted to know all about it and what Earl and Butch wanted and what I told them."

"Did he tell you where he was that night?"

"That's what's weird. You know the old Winslow House up along the tracks on the north side? The one kids say is haunted?"

"Yeah. You can see it from the Sand Bowl, right?"

"That's the one, the Underground Railroad house. Well, it's been abandoned for fifty years or so, and it's boarded up. Jesse told me he's been trying to get away from his father because on Saturday nights he gets all liquored up and beats him, so he's been going up there and taking a lantern and his books and sleeping there on Saturday nights."

"So, he wasn't fishing after all?"

"No, he was reading. I know it's hard to believe. But, here's what else. This morning all he wanted to talk about was his cousins and how I sent them in the wrong direction, and how lucky he was they didn't find him. Then I told him about Pee Wee and how he begged to go in Jesse's place and how he would've been killed if he had, and you know what? Jesse got real quiet. I told him Pee Wee follows him and wants to be liked, and instead he treats Pee Wee like he's dirt."

"What'd he say?'"

"He just listened, like he was thinking about it. Then he said, 'I guess I owe you, or I'd have ended up in the pond, too.' I told him he owes Pee Wee something, too, like being decent to him. I said, 'Here's a guy who offered to go in your place because he wanted you to think he was just as tough as you think you are, and he would be dead now. And if they had found you, you'd both be dead.'"

"Did Jesse have anything to say?"

"He just sat there, staring at the floor. When I finished saying all I had to say, I tried to get him to read, but he just sat there. Pretty soon he said, 'I've gotta go.' He stood up, tucked the book under his arm, and sneaked out the back door. Then he turned back and thanked me. It was the first time he'd ever done that."

CHAPTER 36

Summer was fading. Labor Day was just six days away, then it would be off to the north and the start of school. Jimmy and I called the last game of the season at the Sand Bowl with the Purple Aces playing a barnstorming Negro team out of Mobile. It was one of their annual stops up Highway 41 on their way to Detroit, where they played in a semi-pro tournament. It drew a good crowd who knew from past years to appreciate the team's skill and entertaining high jinks.

The Bay Stockings, as they were called, warmed up with a fast game of pepper down the first baseline with four players lined up fielding short grounders and flipping the ball behind their backs, juggling, and pulling sleight-of-hand tricks with the ball. The crowd rose to its feet, clapping.

When the game started, Rollie Brockman announced each visiting player, adding bits of information as to what major league teams he may or may not have played for. The Stockings continued to dazzle the crowd with their clowning and daring base-running, and by the seventh inning stretch the Stockings led 14 to 1. When the game ended to a rousing ovation, Jimmy wrapped up the broadcast and thanked the crowd for listening throughout the summer.

We packed up and stopped by the drugstore, where Jimmy and I found an empty booth. After we were served I saw Skipper and Ginny sitting at a table and talking to a boy who was standing with his back to us. I didn't think anything of it, until he turned sideways and I saw his face. It was Jesse. Then I saw who was standing on the other side of him: Pee Wee Harding. I didn't see any of Jesse's usual posse.

I thought that was strange, but something stranger happened the next day. Jimmy, Goose, and I joined a number of boys at the river, trying to wring out the last days of freedom before school started. The August sun was bearing down late in the afternoon when I noticed two men walking through the trees on the river bank, heading downstream. I thought they were going to join us for a swim, but they kept on walking. A few minutes later, when I saw two more men following in the same direction, I started putting two and two together. I didn't say anything to Jimmy or Goose because I'd promised Skipper I'd keep it quiet. I know Jimmy saw the second group, too.

I couldn't wait to tell Skipper, so when it was time to go home for supper, I told Jimmy, "I've gotta go. I promised I'd be home by 5:30."

I climbed out and dried off, slipped on my shorts and shirt, and stared right at three more men not twenty feet away. They saw me and ignored me, soberly walking downstream like the others.

When supper was over and we were sitting on the front porch, I was getting antsy and I told Grandma I was going downtown. I jumped over the porch railing and rode over to Dub's, where I was greeted by the crew.

"You captured any gunmen lately?" asked a man smoking a cigar.

"Naw, he's too busy with that girl up on the hill," said a guy they called Homer. "He's a ladies' man, just like his uncle Jake."

I stopped in the doorway. "You all sure know a lot about everybody's business," I said. "Are you sure this isn't a sewing circle?"

That drew a hearty laugh from Dub, who walked out just in time. "I guess he told you, didn't he? What can I do for you, Garrett?"

"I'd like a salty dog. Make it two, please."

"Coming up. Say, speaking of your uncle Jake, have you heard any word from him yet?"

"Not yet. We think he must be somewhere he can't talk about."

"Probably so. The war's getting worse every day. I hope he's okay."

Dub took my change and handed me two bags of peanuts. "Help yourself to the pop," he said.

I put the bottles in the basket on the handlebars and rode to the top of the hill.

I rang the doorbell and waited until her mother answered. "Hi, Garrett. She's out back in the hammock reading. Go on around. She'll be glad to see you."

Skipper was lying on her side, facing the other way, so I sneaked up and slapped her on the shoulder.

She flinched. "Oh! Hi. I was expecting you."

She sat up and motioned for me to sit beside her. I handed her a salty dog.

"You were expecting me? Why?"

"Because I think I know why you're here, but you tell me first."

"It's about what I saw down at the river this afternoon."

"Well," she said, "that's why I was expecting you. You're going to tell me you saw some suspicious men making their way down through the trees and brush, aren't you?"

"How'd you know?"

"I've heard some rumors. There're all kinds of funny things going on. A newspaper reporter was in town last night asking questions. I heard about it this morning from Bud Tate at the post office. It's got a lot of people nervous."

"What kind of questions?"

"About the Black Helmets. Those men you saw—you know where they were going. They must've heard about the reporter snooping around and called a meeting. They must think someone's getting too nosy."

"If they are, what do you think will happen?"

"I reckon it depends on what they've been up to and whether it's something illegal," Skipper said. "Either way, some people are getting antsy. I saw some men talking at Slinker's when I stopped in to get stuff for my dad this morning, just like that time when Sarah was working there. They were almost whispering, and they kept looking over their shoulders. I also noticed a lot of cars with license plates from Gibson and Pike Counties. That's unusual for a Monday. Saturday's when everybody comes to town."

"But why would those men go down by the river when they could just meet in Slinker's basement?"

"Maybe that's too conspicuous. In the daylight it's easier to hide down the river."

CHAPTER 37

Grandpa suggested I take one last inventory of my growth spurt before I returned home, so I waited until Friday to ride down to the Farm Bureau and ask Peadad if I could use the scales.

"Sure, if you don't mind unloading those feed bags," he said.

There were at least ten fifty-pound bags stacked on top of the floor scales. "Where do you want them?"

"Just set them on there," he said, pointing to a four-wheeled cart on rubber tires.

I lifted each one and placed it on the cart. Peadad was waiting on a customer, and when he gave the man back his change and receipt he saw I was finished.

"That was fast. I guess you're not the little pipsqueak you were when you got here."

"That's what I'm here for, to see how much I weigh." I stepped on the scales, and Peadad came over to verify it. The needle stopped wiggling, and Peadad stuck his nose up to get his bifocals just right. "Uh, a buck thirty-six. Now, let's take a look at your height."

He stood next to the framing pole where he had measured my height in May and placed a yardstick over my head, leveled it, then placed a mark on the pole. I stepped away and he measured from my first mark.

"Well, it looks like you've grown just over two inches since May. And you've put on, let's see…. "You've put on sixteen pounds. What have they been feeding you, hay?"

"No, but I have been lifting some of it. Actually, straw, but it's almost the same. Grandpa has some in his barn loft, and I go up there every day and throw them around. Then I go out in the driveway and shoot baskets with Mr. Francis. He's been putting me through drills, and my jump shot is looking better."

"Maybe you should stay here year round. You might make something of yourself." He was going over to the cart I'd loaded with feed. He tried to pull it, but it wouldn't budge. "Would you mind pulling this over to the loading dock? By the way, when are you going back?"

"Next Tuesday, the day after Labor Day."

"Well, in case I don't see you again, it's been nice having you around. Be sure and tell your momma and daddy 'hi' for me. Your dad and his daddy used to buy seed corn here."

"Thanks, I will, and thanks for letting me use your scales." I got on my bike.

"Glad to help."

I swung by the depot on the way back and saw Taylor Barth standing on the platform. He was talking to a man dressed in a suit with his back to me. I hadn't seen Taylor for a while, so I slowed down, hoping he would see me pull up. Instead, he kept talking to the man, so I parked my bike and walked over to one of the benches in front of the building that faced the tracks. I was there for almost five minutes when I heard the whistle of a northbound train. It tooted, warning any swimmers, then came around the bend of the river and slowed into the station. The traveler picked up his suitcase and waited for the train to come to a stop. As he approached the steps he turned around to say something to Taylor, and then I saw who he was. It was the mystery man.

I stood beside Taylor as the train started up and pulled out of the station, then I turned to him and asked, "Have you figured him out, yet?"

"Beats me. Never gave his name. He came back last night and went straight to the hotel. The only other time I saw him was when he walked up Main Street and came back an hour or so later."

"So, that's the third time he's been here?"

"Guess that's right."

I was getting on my bike to leave when Taylor said, "Suppose you'll be going back home soon."

256

"Next week."

"You leaving the way you came?"

"Yes sir."

"Then I'll see you before you go."

"Yes, sir."

He stood staring at me blankly. "Kinda hate to see you go."

"I kinda hate to go." We looked at each other a second, and then I got on my bike and rode off. I started up the hill past Lady Muldoon's and saw her sitting on her front porch. She saw me and waved, so I stopped in front of her fence.

"How're you doing, Miss Muldoon?" I yelled.

"I'm doing fine, Garrett. Where have you been? It's been a while."

"I worked for Tip Albee for a while. Other than that, I've been soaking up the culture." I laughed. I'd heard Mr. Francis use that term a number of times when he explained to his wife where he'd been. I think it was a cover for his trips to the horse races in Evansville.

Lady stepped off her porch and came to the fence. "Well, that's nice. Heaven knows there's plenty around here to soak up." She took a handkerchief and mopped her brow. "I've been sitting there almost the whole afternoon. It's so hot in the house, and the breeze is nice on the porch. If you want to come sit a spell I might find some ice cream and some blueberries." She smiled, and I could tell she expected a yes. I didn't want to disappoint her.

"Sure, if it's no trouble," I said as I opened the gate.

"No trouble at all. Wait on the porch and entertain Killer while I'm gone."

She left, and Killer jumped up in the swing beside me, hanging his face in my lap. Now that the summer was almost over he'd decided to become my friend.

Lady came out with two bowls of ice cream and blueberries. Killer sniffed my bowl and gave me a mournful look like he was expecting me to share it. I ignored him, so he sulked to the other end of the swing.

"So, Taylor and I were just talking about you the other day," Lady was saying. "He said he hadn't seen you for so long he thought you'd gone home."

"I just stopped down at the station a moment ago and talked to him. He's right. I hadn't been around much. I've been kinda occupied." Then something occurred to me. "You say you've been out here most of the afternoon?"

"The whole afternoon. It's too hot in the house."

"Well, when I stopped to see Taylor while ago, he was talking to a man. It was the same man who was here before, the one everybody's trying to find out who he is. Taylor said he walked up Main and then came back an hour or so later. You didn't happen to see him, did you?"

"Was he in a dark suit and tie?"

"Yes. Shouldn't be too many people dressed like that here."

"I saw him," she said.

"Did you see where he went?"

"Sure did. He went in Slinker's store. He came out about 50 minutes later."

"You timed him?"

"Not intentionally. The short cake I'm baking did, though. I'd just set my clock before he walked by. When the alarm went off, I came back out on the porch just as he was walking back."

"What do you think he was doing all that time in Slinker's?"

"I haven't the slightest idea. I just report what I see."

I remembered what Skipper told me about the reporter snooping around. "You don't think he could be a newspaper reporter, do you?"

"No. They don't dress that fancy. This guy was from somewhere else. But, I did hear there's been one nosing around."

"What do you think the reporter was looking for?"

"Could be anything. There's all kinds of fodder for an enterprising reporter around here."

That didn't tell me anything. If she knew anything about the Black Helmets she sure wasn't letting on. When I finished my ice cream I stood up to go.

"Thanks for the dessert. I have to go now, but I'll stop and say goodbye before I leave."

"You do that. Maybe I'll have a little treat for you to take on the train."

I rode off past Slinker's and was tempted to stop and go inside, but I didn't know what I'd do in there. I couldn't just go in and ask Mr. Slinker what that man was doing there. Instead, I decided to stop at the post office and see if Bud Tate had the mail sorted yet. Monday being a holiday, this might be the last mail delivery before I go back up north.

Bud was standing behind the metal boxes stuffing them with mail when I saw his eyes squinting through the tiny glass door of box 127. As I approached Grandma's box I heard Bud's voice: "Hi, Garrett. You got mail!"

He stepped over to the window, thumbed through a fist full of mail, and peeled off two letters. "Two today. Looks like your folks haven't forgotten they left you here." He handed me a letter that had a Cleveland postmark and my mother's handwriting on it. "And here's another one. No return address on it. Looks like it's from Suitland, Maryland. You know anybody from there?"

"Don't think so. Let me see." I held it up to the light. "Maybe Grandma does."

I turned to leave but then called back. "Thanks for everything Mr. Tate. I may not see you before I leave."

"If that's the case, you have a nice trip and tell your folks hello for me. I'll be looking for your letters coming through here. Not that I'm nosy."

"Good. I'll be writing often. May even write to some friends I made here, too."

"I bet you will—one in particular." Bud smiled.

I took the letters home and found Grandma and Grandpa sitting on the benches under the grape arbor peeling tomatoes for canning.

"I got the mail," I said. "We got two letters—one from Mom and another one with no return address."

Grandma wiped her hands on a rag and mopped the sweat off her brow with her sleeve. She opened the one from Mom and read it to herself while Grandpa and I watched her face for some expression. When she finished, she put it down and summarized: "She said they are leaving for home tomorrow and that Edward's really getting anxious. He's walking two miles a day and is feeling much better. He's looking forward to getting the school year started. She said they can hardly wait to see Garrett and see how much he has grown." Grandma looked at me and added, "It won't be a total surprise. I've been updating them from time to time. I hope that doesn't spoil it for you."

"It won't. Peadad just measured me. I'm even taller than Skipper now," I said. "What about the other letter?"

She slipped her paring knife in the flap, sliced it open, and took out the small slip of paper. She read it aloud.

"Dear Mom and Dad,

Sorry I haven't written sooner. I can't tell you everything that has happened, but I can tell you that I have passed the training and background check for a special assignment in Navel Intelligence. I won't be able to tell you where I am and what I am doing, but trust that I will be okay. This means that I have re-upped for another tour of duty. It is what I really want to do. Give my regards to Garrett, and tell him someday I will have even more stories to tell. Take care of yourselves now, and don't worry about me.

"Your son, Jake."

Grandma reread the letter to herself, as if she might have missed something, and then folded it back up in the envelope and walked in the house. Grandpa and I followed and watched as she put it in a cigar box that had Jake's name on it.

"At least we know now." It was all she said before walking back out the door. Grandpa sat beside her. They sat peeling tomatoes in silence.

CHAPTER **38**

A hint of fall came on the Sunday of Labor Day weekend and the cooler night air stayed around into the mid-morning. I left for church early knowing it would be the last time I would get to see some of the people before I went home. Also, there was going to be a baptism down at the river right after church, and I didn't think that was a time to visit.

I'd never see a baptism like this before, where the congregation meets on the river bank and the preacher submerges the person being baptized. Back home we baptized by sprinkling, so I asked Grandma why they did it this way.

"It comes from the Book of John," she explained. "Baptists believe in using what they call 'living waters,' that is, flowing waters from a stream or river. In Romans, Chapter 6, believers are said to be buried and transformed or raised to a new life in Christ, and baptism by immersion is our way of carrying out this transformation."

"Can anybody watch?" I asked, since I didn't belong to this church.

"Yes, you don't have to be a member. We believe that by conducting it in public, it's a witness that all believers can identify with. There may be others there who aren't members of this church, either."

Sunday school started with the singing, announcements, and Scripture lesson, followed by dismissal to the classes. After Sunday school ended the church service started immediately, and most of the congregation stayed. A few left, including Spooks, who always had trouble sitting through two hours on the hard pews. Skipper and I took the space in the back row by the window, the one Spooks vacated. From there we could look out and see him across the street at Dub's, sitting with the liars and drinking a Coke. His wheelbarrow was left at home. Spooks didn't work on Sunday.

Reverend Snyder gave a brief sermon on redemption, tying it in with the baptism that would follow after the service. After the singing of the last hymn and the benediction, Reverend Snyder gave instructions to the congregation as to where the baptism would take place. We were dismissed and told to reassemble in twenty minutes just upstream from the railroad bridge.

Don and Louise Francis offered Grandma and me a ride. We boarded his Chevy and drove through the river bottoms to where the pavement ended and parked under a clump of sycamores. Walking through the heavy sand, we came to the water's edge where we joined a group already there.

"Who's getting baptized, today?" I asked Grandma.

"The Getlings," she said. "They're new. They've only been here for little over a month. Moved in from down in the Wabash bottoms."

"Is that all?"

Grandma paused. "No, there's someone else, but you wouldn't know her."

We reached the river and stood with the congregation in a semicircle along the shore facing the water. Reverend Snyder had changed out of his suit and into cotton pants and shirt. He was barefooted. He called the congregation to order with a prayer and then told why we were gathered there. He explained that Baptists believed in baptism by immersion "as Jesus was baptized by John in the River Jordan as seen in Matthew 28:13-17."

He then motioned for Thomas Getling and his wife, Gertrude, to come forward. They were dressed in white robes. They walked into the water up to their waists and stood before Reverend Snyder. He took Mrs. Getling's hand first and had her turn to the shore; then he introduced her to the congregation. Saying she had professed her belief in Christ and had desired to be baptized in His name, he then placed a hand behind her, leaned her back, and immersed her, saying, "I baptize you in the name of the Father, Son, and the Holy Spirit." He then paraphrased Romans 6: 3-4: "As Christ was raised from the dead by the glory of the Father, that we too might walk in newness of life."

He then took the hand of Mr. Getling and, after introducing him to the congregation, immersed him in the water and repeated the liturgy. When he finished and Mr. Getling ascended the shore to join his wife, a woman in a white robe appeared from out of the crowd and waded into the water. She had her back to the shore, and all I could see was her grey hair. Her steps were slow and unsteady. She seemed elderly or crippled, I wasn't sure.

Reverend Snyder reached out to ease her into the deeper water. When she reached waist depth, he slowly steered her around to face the congregation. A gust of wind blew her hair over her eyes, and she took her thin hand and pushed it back. Then I saw her face. Her forehead was deeply lined and hollow. Pasty cheeks gave her a haggard look. Her eyes were dark and sunken, like someone tired and worn. I looked at her sad eyes and remembered what my father said about everyone having a story to tell. I wondered what her story was.

"I would like to introduce to you a new member of our congregation, who comes today to profess her belief in Christ as her Savior and express her desire to be baptized in His name: Flossie Sprowl."

I wasn't sure I heard correctly, so I turned to Grandma and whispered, "Did he say Sprowl?"

She put her finger to her lips to remind me we were witnessing a solemn ceremony, but then she nodded yes.

"Jesse's grandmother?" I asked quietly.

Grandma shook her head no. She glanced at the blank look on my face and whispered, "Mother."

"Jesse's mother? That's Jesse's mother?"

Grandma nodded, putting her finger to her mouth again to tell me to be quiet. I'd heard Jesse's mother might be kept captive in her own home, and after looking at her, I believed that was possible. She was so sad looking and beaten down and worn.

I stared at her in disbelief.

After Reverend Snyder introduced her he repeated the baptism ritual and lowered her into the water as he did the others. When she came up out of the water, her hair was swept back and the sun shined on her face, and for a moment I sensed a softening of the lines in her face. Then when he repeated the line from Romans 6:3-4, saying, "Like Christ, we too might walk in newness of life," I was sure I saw a faint smile as she leaned her head back, her eyes closed, as if she was seeing something inside her mind.

Flossie Sprowl continued to smile as she swayed to the music and listened to Reverend Snyder lead the congregation in a closing hymn:

> *River, wash over me, cleanse and make me new*
> *Bathe me, refresh me, and fill me anew.*

We were standing in a circle surrounding the three newly baptized members. As we sang I slowly moved around to the side and behind everyone to get a better look at Mrs. Sprowl. I had imagined all summer how she might look, and never would I have believed it would be like this. As I moved, I saw a face a lot different than the one I'd seen minutes ago. She was smiling and singing, holding tightly to the hand of Reverend Snyder while the other hand reached upward toward the sky. The words came flowing out of her mouth like she had been released from bondage:

> *Spirit, watch over me*
> *Lead me to Jesus' feet*
> *Cause me to worship and fill me anew*
> *Spirit, watch over me.*

When the hymn ended, the congregation closed in, laying hands on the newly baptized and welcoming them into the spirituality of the congregation. I waited my turn and lined up to shake their hands, and when I got to Mrs. Sprowl I took her hand and told her I was glad to meet her. Then I told her I knew her son, Jesse.

She squeezed my hand and thanked me, then looked over my shoulder as if she was looking for someone.

As people were leaving, I walked up the river bank toward Mr. Francis's car. I held the door open for Grandma and Mrs. Francis, and before

I got in I turned to look one more time at Mrs. Sprowl. As she was walking up the bank with the others she strayed and drifted over toward a clump of lilac bushes. When she got close I saw someone step out of the shadows, and then I saw them talking. I got in the car and closed the door. Mr. Francis backed it up to turn around, and I got a better angle; that's when I saw who she was talking to. Jesse had been there, too.

It was late afternoon when I got a chance to talk to Grandma without anyone around. She and Louise Francis spent the afternoon under the maple tree by the driveway while Mr. Francis put me through our daily basketball routine before taking his fishing pole down to the river. Grandpa watched for a while then went in the house for his afternoon nap. I waited for Louise to go answer her ringing phone, and then I followed Grandma into the kitchen and asked her what I'd been wondering about all afternoon.

"How did Flossie Sprowl become baptized? I've never seen her at church?"

Grandma pulled out a chair, sat down, and motioned me to do the same. "Sometimes there are unusual circumstances," she said. "You see, Flossie used to come to church a long time ago, before she married Eddie. After they got married, she just kind of disappeared. Soon she was saddled with all those kids and needed to stay home and take care of them."

"You mean she has other kids besides Jesse?"

"Yes, four others. Three boys and a girl. The boys all joined the Army as soon as they were old enough. The girl, Sadie, ran off with a migrant worker. None of them could wait to get out of the house."

"Why?"

"Eddie got to drinking. Some people figured he was abusing them. That's probably why Flossie became a recluse. She had no place to go. She had to stay home for Jesse. It still wasn't enough, but at least they both survived."

"Couldn't she do anything about it?"

"Maybe, but it took a long time to get up the courage."

"How'd she get the courage?"

"It wasn't by herself."

"Then who helped her?"

"Jesse."

"Jesse? He helped her? After all these years?"

"That's what his mother told Reverend Snyder. He shared it with me and some of the elders so we'd understand why she was going to be baptized."

"But why'd he let her be baptized if she wasn't in the church?"

"Well, after Jesse helped liberate her, she came to Reverend Snyder and told him the whole story of her life with Eddie. She started meeting with him and talking about returning to church, and she asked him if he would baptize her. She wasn't ready yet. She wanted time to get healthy and cleanse her soul first. She also didn't want to come out in public and rile Eddie up again, either. She had to wait until it was safe. When they both thought she was ready, they proceeded. That's what we witnessed today."

I sat there thinking about Jesse. First, he was up in the tower identifying planes; then meeting secretly with Skipper to learn how to read; and now I'm hearing he helped his mother get out from under the heavy hand of his father. And I just saw him down at the river witnessing her baptism.

My head was spinning. "None of this seems possible."

"Well, I think there's a lesson in all this. In order to grow sometimes you have to be tested. It's not just Jesse. Look at your Uncle Jake. Even you and Jimmy that night with the gunman, or you and Skipper with the runaway car. Or remember how Skipper used her wits to deal with that Kirklin boy at the pool room up at the city? That's what I'm talking about. It's like there are little checkpoints along our path that God puts there to test our mettle, to see what we're made of. Some people pass that test, some don't, and for others it takes a little more time. I'm willing to bet something happened in Jesse's life that turned it all around for him, and that's where he got his courage to stand up to his father."

"But why was he so mean to everybody else?"

"Probably because of the way his father treated him and his mother. He took it out on others. What's important now is what happens next."

CHAPTER 39

There was no skinny-dipping on Labor Day. The river was alive with mothers, fathers and kids. They were swinging from the tree rope, jumping from the railroad bridge, floating on inner tubes, or basking in the sun on the sand bar. The older kids had the bridge and the rope, the younger ones the inner tubes. Neither bothered the other.

I came with Skipper. I wanted to squeeze every minute of my last day of the summer with her. On the way I met her at her father's garage where we picked up two inner tubes and aired them up. When we arrived at the river, there must have been a hundred people already there.

Skipper took a blanket and a small ice chest out of the basket on her handle bars, and I took both inner tubes. We waded out into water, holding the blanket and ice chest over her head until we reached the sand bar on the other shore. We were downriver by ourselves a hundred yards below all the noise and activity, and it was quiet enough we could hear the water rippling over the shallows. We spread our blanket and stretched out, grabbing the sun's last rays of summer.

The autumn warmth felt good on my body and made me wish summer would never end. I looked over at Skipper with her dark tan and blonde hair and had another reason I didn't want summer to end. But, tomorrow I would be boarding the train for the long ride home.

I looked at Skipper and broke the silence. "It's hard to believe in two days I'll be sitting in school with my nose in a book, three hundred miles from here."

"I know, it's kind of sad. It's been fun." She was staring off in the distance. Finally, she said, "Speaking of books, have you finished *Catcher in the Rye* yet?"

"I was going to tell you. I finished it last week."

"So, what did you think of Holden?"

I watched a cloud moving between us and the sun. "Well, for one thing, I think he was afraid of growing up," I said.

"What about his dream of catching children from falling over the cliff?"

"I think he thought the rye field was a place kids could romp about and play and be happy. Kind of like Purcell Station...and...."

"Like Purcell Station?" she interrupted. "Be serious. What do you mean by that?" She was sitting up now, laughing.

"Well, I mean, look around. Don't you see people romping and playing? I think it's like that rye field."

"And just how?"

"While I haven't been most places, I've been here long enough to see people have a lot of fun. They play together here at the river and at the softball game over on Main Street. It goes on and on and includes everybody, and if somebody gets a hit or scores a run, both sides cheer. Where else do you see that? And people here look out for each other. I heard my grandma say, 'people here don't have much, but they have each other.' That's something. She also talked about how when a war comes along they give their young men to the cause and band together to help each other out. And when someone goes too far wrong, they have their ways of bringing them back in."

"Are you thinking about our town's little secret?"

"Could be, except I'm not supposed to know about it."

"Me neither. Now, let's get back to my question. If Holden protects the children from falling off the cliff, what's he protecting them from? What's below the cliff?"

"Holden thinks if they go over the cliff they become adults, and he doesn't want kids to grow up and be like them."

"So, Holden protects the kids, and you say Purcell Station is like the rye field. So, does that mean the Black Helmets are like Holden in the rye field protecting people from something?"

"Maybe. Holden doesn't want to become an adult. I can understand that. I've been thinking a lot about that lately, too."

"You mean giving up your childhood?"

"What I mean is I'll be thirteen two days after I get home, and I'll never be twelve again, and I think twelve is a pretty good time."

Skipper sat smiling and shaking her head. "In that case, I think we'd better make the most of these last days of your twelfth year." She stood up. "How about let's get in these inner tubes and see where the current takes us."

That was fine with me. I was getting too far ahead of myself. We threw the inner tubes in the water and drifted into the current.

The August river was slow and meandering, having pooled with the scarcity of rain. We floated down and around the bend out of sight of the others. It was quiet now, away from the crowd and into the tall sycamores lining both sides of the river bank. We floated for half an hour, listening to the cardinals and robins chirping and fluttering in the trees. A red-tailed hawk flew over the treetops on the north side, and the birds got quiet.

I rested my head on the back of the inner tube and stared at the blue sky. I glanced at Skipper and saw she had her eyes closed and a smile on her face. Neither of us said anything for several minutes. After a while, we came up to a sandbar and Skipper broke the silence. "Remember this?"

"Where we swam that day?"

"Yes. Remember what we saw?"

We drifted close to the sand bar until our inner tubes scraped the bottom, and then we stood up. "Over there?" I asked, pointing through the thick brush and trees toward the railroad.

"Yeah. Let's see if it's still there."

We pulled our inner tubes up on the sandbar and made our way into the brush. When we reached an opening we stopped. Up ahead we saw the small stream crossing under the railroad, and there it was: the hobo camp. We saw the smoldering of a fire that had been left to die and the clutter of tin cans thrown aside in piles. On the ground under the trestle lay a man asleep and snoring. His head was propped up on a bag that looked like it was stuffed with clothing. There was no one else in sight at the moment, but there were bottles and evidence others had been there.

"I think the railroad detectives have been watching them closer since that gunman came through here. The one you captured single-handedly," Skipper teased.

"Oh, I had some help on that."

"Well, I suppose Jimmy gets a little credit."

"I was thinking of someone else."

"Who? There was only you and Jimmy."

"I'm not so sure. If it wasn't for the fact the guy had too much to drink, we'd have never pulled it off. I think we have a bootlegger to thank for that," I said. "Otherwise it could have turned out a lot different."

I could see Skipper thinking that through. "So, here's a guy doing something illegal, and it turns into something good...."

"It's sort of like the Black Helmets, isn't it? I mean, from what we know they have good intentions, but...."

"Questionable means?" Skipper interrupted.

"Yeah, I guess so. We really don't know, but why would they keep it so secret if it wasn't?"

"I imagine that's what everyone wants to know."

We walked back to our inner tubes. Sitting down in the shallow water we pushed off into the current when Skipper said, "You know, it's not that far from here. Let's go past their club house, just to see if anybody's there. We can be quiet and stay out of sight."

"I don't know. I wouldn't want to get caught snooping around there. Besides, I have to be back. They're having a big supper for me tonight."

"We've got time. It's not that far."

I let her talk me into it. We let the current take us down the bend close to the clubhouse. We couldn't see it from the water, but we found the fallen tree on the bank that we'd hid behind that night.

We stopped in the shallow water and dragged our feet into the sand for an anchor. We waited and listened, then climbed up the fallen log far enough that we could see the roof.

"Do you think we know any of the Black Helmets?" I asked.

Skipper held up her hand as if she was listening to something, and then, after I figured she had forgotten my question, she answered. "I think so."

"You do? Who?"

"I talked to one the other day. I've been waiting to tell you."

"You did? Who?"

She smiled and then waited. "You won't believe it, but do you know the story about Flossie Sprowl and how she came to be baptized yesterday?"

"Yes. Grandma told me. How'd you know about it?"

"I got it from the source."

"What source?"

"Jesse. He told me all about it in the back room of the library. I knew she was going to see the preacher and was going to be baptized, and I knew why it was happening."

"Jesse told you about stopping his dad from beating his mother?"

"That's not the way it happened exactly."

"That's what Grandma told me."

"It's partly right, but Jesse had tried to stop his dad before, and it never worked."

"Why'd it work this time?"

"Because Jesse came home one night wearing a Black Helmet." Skipper looked at me and paused. "And he wasn't alone."

"Huh?" I stared at Skipper. "Whatta you mean?"

"Jesse told me he turned eighteen last month and he did something he'd wanted to do for a long time: he joined the Black Helmets. And that's when everything changed.

When his dad saw Jesse step through the door one night, wearing that insignia, and saw a posse in uniform waiting outside in the darkness, he knew it was over. Jesse didn't say exactly, but I got the impression they took his father up on Tabor Hill that night, where he had to face the ritual of the Black Helmets. I've heard if anyone is taken up on the Hill and has to face the regiment, they get religion pretty fast. If Eddie Sprowl would have done anything to Jesse or his mother after that, he would've been run out of town. In fact, he may already be gone."

My head was swirling. I had a lot of questions. "Then if that's true, why didn't the Black Helmets do something a long time ago?"

"Eddie hid everything back in the woods, so they had no proof until Jesse joined them and filled them in. Apparently they only get involved when someone asks for help or when some evil is so obvious they can't ignore it. Eddie kept his wife out of sight so nobody would know."

"But how'd Jesse get in the Black Helmets? Aren't they strict about who they let in?"

"They are. That's what's odd about this. Jesse met all their qualifications. He passed their physical tests and basic training up on Tabor Hill; memorized their creed and constitution, took the oath, passed the probationary period, and promised to live up to their principles and purposes. He did everything they asked him to do."

I sat there, trying to take this all in. "What got into him?" I asked.

"When he asked me to help him learn to read, I saw a different side of him. I think he just got tired of his dad's abuse. But, the real turning point was when he saw how close he came to dying with his cousins. Plus, I have a feeling that without them he didn't feel so brave anymore."

"So, now his mother gets a new life because of him?"

"That's pretty much it. I guess you should never underestimate anyone. Sometimes what you see is just a front."

"But, how did he learn their constitution and creed and oath and all that stuff if he couldn't read?"

"That's what we've been studying for the past month in the back room of the library."

"You knew this all along, and you never told me?"

"I kept my promise to Jesse. He asked me not to tell. I think it was because he thought he might fail and would be embarrassed if anyone knew."

"Wow, I never knew a bully would worry about failing."

"I think everybody worries about failing, especially bullies."

I sat silent for a moment, thinking how things aren't always as they seem. I'd feared Jesse and avoided him all summer, and all this time he wasn't what everybody thought.

"You should have a star in heaven, Skipper, for what you did."

"No, not me: Jesse. He decided on his own. Maybe he had it in him all the time and just didn't know it."

"You sound like my grandmother. Sometimes the good comes out, sometimes the bad. Is there anything else that got into him?"

"Maybe. Do you remember that book I brought home on the train that day? *Of Mice and Men?*"

"Yeah, you said you got it for someone else."

"Well, I got it for him, and he's been reading it. It's about a guy named Lennie and how people always picked on him for being slow, and it has a tragic ending, kinda like Jesse's cousins. I think it made him think about people who are different."

"People like Spooks and Pee Wee?"

"Uh-uh."

CHAPTER 40

We drifted back out into the shallows. The clubhouse of the Black Helmets was quiet and out of our sight now. In a few minutes I realized the line of trees on the other side of the river had put us in the shade. "Look where the sun is. We'd better start heading back. We're having a big dinner tonight. I can't be late."

We stretched out over the front of the inner tubes and started paddling and kicking. It didn't take long before we realized we weren't making good time going upstream. We'd come a couple of hundred yards and were near the hobo camp.

"This isn't going to work," Skipper said. "Maybe we should go over on the railroad and walk it back to town. It'll be faster."

We came up on the sandbar and carried our inner tubes through the brush and up to the raised tracks. As we approached, we heard the sound of a train whistle signaling the crossing just out of Hazelton. A minute later we saw it coming around the bend at an unusually slow speed. We stayed back in the bushes, waiting to see what it was going to do. The engine passed us and came to a stop, and then it started backing up. As it did, the rails switched so that it backed up on a second set of tracks where a line of empty boxcars was sitting.

"They're backing up to hook onto those boxcars," Skipper said. "They park them here before dropping them off at the Farm Co-op."

"You mean in Purcell Station?" I asked.

"That's where they usually take them."

"Well, how about…?"

"Hopping in and getting home really quick? Is that what you're thinking?"

"Why not? It beats walking."

"But what if I'm wrong and they don't stop there?" she asked.

I started to answer when we heard a voice from the brush. "It's okay. It'll stop there."

Skipper and I jumped. We looked around, and standing at the edge of some bushes was a man in tattered shirt and crumpled pants. He had a white beard and wore a rumpled straw hat. He was holding a tin cup with something dark spilling out of it.

"What?" asked Skipper.

"It's okay. They drop 'em off in Purcell Station. I've ridden them before. They park 'em here until they need 'em up there."

It was the man we'd seen earlier sleeping in the hobo camp.

"You've ridden them?" Skipper asked.

"Many times. I know when they're coming and where they're going. Been doing it a long time."

The train had backed into the empty cars, and we could hear the couplings connect all down the line. When it was completed, it moved slowly forward, and the sound of the pull cascaded again down the line until the last car was moving. Skipper and I looked at each other and had the same idea. We ran up to an open car and threw our inner tubes in. She jumped up and grabbed the floor with both hands. I took her ankles and pushed her the rest of the way up. Then she leaned over and held out both her hands. I grabbed a hold and, running alongside, jumped and threw one leg up and over. She pulled until I was inside the door.

Once safely in, we waved at the man, and he waved back. The train was picking up speed as we sat there giggling at our daring move. We watched the river and its foliage passing quickly out the door on one side and the rolling melon fields on the other. Then I remembered something. "Did I ever tell you," I said to Skipper, "this is how my father used to come home from college, riding the rails in a boxcar?"

"No, you didn't."

"Not only that, he once rode all the way to North Dakota and back in a boxcar."

"Really? Why'd he do that?"

"It's a long story, but it's how he met my mom."

"I'd like to hear that sometime."

"Maybe you will."

It took only minutes to get back to where we had started five hours ago. The train slowed as we crossed the bridge, and we looked down at the swimmers in the river. A group of boys dogpaddled in a circle in front of the bridge, looking up at the train, having jumped just seconds ahead of it.

The old man was right. The train dropped the empty boxcars on the side rails next to the Farm Co-op; then it stayed on the switch, idling its engine. Skipper and I grabbed our inner tubes and jumped down.

"They must be waiting for another train," Skipper said. We started back to the river to retrieve our picnic basket and bikes.

The river was alive and noisy when we climbed down the bank and to paddle down to the sandbar where we'd left our stuff. I saw Jimmy and Goose lying against the bank, partly in the water, watching some kids fling themselves off the rope swing into the river.

"Hey, you two. Where you been all day?" asked Jimmy.

We sat down on the sand and told them where we went and how we got back. I was telling them the story about the hobo and the boxcar when I looked up at the bridge.

"Who's that on the bridge?" I asked. They all turned to look.

There among all the boys jumping off the steel frame was a man pushing something across the bridge. He was moving slowly on the bumpy cross ties as if he was pushing a heavy load. He was struggling as he got near the middle, where the boys stood waiting.

"That looks like Spooks," I said. "What's he doing?"

Goose was standing up now. "We'd better get up there."

We swam across the river toward the bank leading up to the bridge. Goose was strongest, so he got there first. I kept looking up at the bridge. Spooks was near the middle now and the boys were circling around him. I remembered the time Jesse pushed Spooks off the bridge.

Just then, I heard the sound that scared me. The next thing I knew everybody was jumping off the bridge into the river. It was the whistle of a north bounder, the one the other train was waiting for back at the switch.

"Oh-uh, I hope that's not the Dixie Flyer," yelled Jimmy. "Quick, we gotta go."

I heard yelling coming from the bridge. All the boys were jumping off and thrashing around in the water, looking up. On the bridge I saw two figures. I knew one of them was Spooks. The other one was behind a girder, and I couldn't make him out.

I heard Skipper yell, "Hurry, Goose. It's coming."

Goose was climbing up the steep embankment toward the bridge. I heard one more blast of the whistle, and then I saw it coming fast around the bend, a hundred yards from the bridge. I saw Spooks holding his wheelbarrow, staring straight at the oncoming train, frozen. Everybody in the water had stopped and was watching from below. Someone yelled, "Jump!"

But he didn't. He stood there, holding his wheelbarrow, staring at the train. It was on the bridge now, only seconds away. People were yelling. I didn't want to see what was going to happen next. Skipper grabbed me and screamed as she buried her head in my neck. I clutched her and looked down, not wanting to look. The train sped through the bridge, and Skipper and I shook, holding onto each other, hearing the screams that were soon drowned out by the earth-shaking noise of the train.

Then it was quiet. No one moved. No one spoke. I looked at Skipper. She was crying. We stood there trembling, holding each other, frozen the way Spooks had stood moments ago when facing the train on the bridge.

Soon I heard splashing and then shouting, and I looked up to see a wheelbarrow crumpled and floating in the river. I went numb. I didn't want to think of where Spooks's body might be. But, the commotion was coming from somewhere else. Over to the right a group of boys and men below the bridge were flailing around in the water, stirring up quite a commotion. I saw them pulling, tugging, moving over to the shallows, and lifting someone onto the sand. Then someone was pounding on him and I heard a voice yell, "Get Doc Branham. Hurry!" A boy jumped on a bike and took off toward town.

Skipper saw this too, and started swimming upstream toward the crowd. I followed. We waded out of the water and up on the sandbar where the crowd had gathered. There was Spooks lying on the sand, coughing and sputtering, his eyes bugged out in shock. He was gasping for air.

I looked around for Jimmy, but something caught my eye on the slope going up to the bridge. It was Goose, climbing up to the railroad. He seemed to be in a hurry. Jimmy was chasing after him. They reached the tracks and then ran onto the bridge. Then I saw where they were going. In the middle of the bridge a body was dangling from the rails, upside down. It wasn't moving.

"Don't look," I said to Skipper.

I turned back just as Goose got to the dangling body and reached for the man's arms. Jimmy arrived right afterward, and they both took hold and tugged, slowly lifting him up. The crowd below had turned away from Spooks and was staring up at the bridge. They were quiet again, not knowing who was hanging there.

Goose and Jimmy struggled. Goose had to step down and out on the I-beam frame along the outside of the bridge and lift while Jimmy tried to free the man's foot from the cross tie. After several minutes, they finally lifted him over onto the cross ties and stretched him out.

"Stay here with Spooks," I told Skipper. "I'm going up."

I ran up the hill and the embankment just as Doc Branham came down the path with his black bag. I pointed to where Spooks was lying, and he went down to tend to him.

I reached the bridge and ran out to Goose and Jimmy, and then I saw who it was. He was unconscious, but breathing. Jimmy was taking off his shoe, the one that had saved Jesse's life.

"What happened?" I asked.

"He saw Spooks just standing there staring at the train, so he lunged and pulled him off the track. There's no room to stand except on the steel frame, and he couldn't get Spooks on it in time, so he pushed him into the water. It was the only chance he had," said Goose.

"But how...?"

"The train was right on him. It looked like he tried to jump onto the I-beam, but his foot must have slipped and got caught between the ties. When he fell he hit his head on the beam, and it must have knocked him out. He's lucky. If it hadn't been for his foot getting caught he probably would have fallen unconscious into the water and drowned."

Goose pointed to a bloody crease on the other side of his head. It was oozing bright red, and the sight was making me squeamish, but I couldn't help thinking how Jesse risked his life to save Spooks. Things were getting crazier by the day.

But something was still kinda funny about this whole thing. I had another question. Everybody on the bridge had on swimsuits and was jumping off the bridge. Why was Jesse dressed in street clothes and shoes? I didn't ask because I figured no one there knew the answer.

Doc Branham finished checking out Spooks and came up to the bridge to tend to Jesse. He opened his bag and gave Jesse smelling salts, then he took out dressing and worked on the gash on Jesse's head. We all watched when Jesse's head jerked and he opened his eyes. He looked at the four of us and then at the bridge.

"What happened?" he mumbled.

"You're alive and on the bridge," said Jimmy. "You dodged a train and helped somebody else dodge it, too."

Jesse looked around, like he was wondering if he was really here or just dreaming. "Whurr's Spooks?" he asked.

"Spooks is okay," said Doc Branham. "And you're going to be, too. Now, let's get you off this bridge and up to the office, where I can work on that ankle before another train comes along and takes us all out."

We carried him to the back of Goose's pickup truck and then helped Spooks up the bank and into the truck, too. Goose drove off with Jesse and Spooks sitting side by side on the tailgate of the truck, up the hill to Doc's office, where he finished cleaning them up and mending a tender ankle.

CHAPTER 41

They were all gathered under the maple tree by the driveway when we arrived. Three picnic tables had been pushed together, and table cloths and place settings were arranged. A side table held the dishes each family brought to share. When Grandma saw me ride into the backyard she was on the back porch.

"Where've you been?"

"It's a long story, and you're not going to believe it."

"Oh, hi, Skipper," she said when she realized I was not alone. "We're about ready to eat. Would you like to join us? It's Garrett's farewell party."

She glanced at me. "Sure, if it's not too much trouble. I'd have to change clothes and let my mom know, though."

"Why don't you ride on up and tell her? We'll start as soon as you get back."

"Okay, I'll hurry."

I followed Grandma into the house and washed up, then went to my room and changed into clean clothes. Grandma asked me to help her carry dishes from the kitchen. When I returned with a platter of fried chicken, a black Ford sedan pulled up in the driveway, and out of the driver's side stepped Reverend Snyder. I thought he was alone, but then the door on the other side opened and out stepped Taylor Barth. He then turned around, opened the back door, and held it for Lady Muldoon.

I wasn't aware this many people had been invited.

"Who else are we waiting for?" I asked.

Just then the Brockmans' Packard turned into the driveway. Jimmy got out of the driver's side. From the other side came Spooks, walking even slower than usual and looking a little haggard. He was also carrying a large box.

"I b—brought something," he said. He had a wide smile on his face.

Grandma took the box and opened it. "Why, Spooks, what a nice cake. Did you make it yourself?"

"M—Maddie made it for us. Sh-ee said it's for Garrett."

Louise came over to Spooks, put her arm around him, and said, "That's real nice of you, Spooks. Was this your idea?"

"Y—yes. I like Ga…rett. He's…nice to me."

I walked over to Spooks and gave him a hug. "Thanks, Spooks," I said.

Grandma took the cake and put it at the end of the food table next to the tub of homemade ice cream. The food was all in place, and everybody was standing around ready to eat, but Skipper hadn't come back yet.

Grandma was ready to call everybody to order and ask Reverend Snyder to give the blessing when Skipper came wheeling down the tunnel and stopping under the maple tree.

"Sorry I'm late. I hope I didn't keep you all waiting," she said.

"Not at all," Grandma assured her. "We're just getting ready to sit down."

We had just bowed our heads when I noticed something. Skipper was wearing the same clothes she had on before she went home to change. Didn't she say she was going to change? Why did she take so long? Where did she go if she didn't go home?

When Reverend Snyder finished and everybody said "Amen" Spooks already had his fork in hand and aimed toward the plate of fried chicken. He must have remembered how it turned out the last time he ate chicken with Reverend Snyder. He also seemed to have a hardy appetite after his eventful afternoon.

As soon as everybody began eating Grandma asked Jimmy to tell the "long story" as to why we were so late. Jimmy took his time and finished just as the main course ended.

The sun was setting across the Wabash bottoms, and the September night air came filtering through the trees surrounding the house. The ladies collected the dishes and cleared the table for dessert plates as the stories began to fly.

I had listened to everybody and realized what a full summer it had been. "What was the highlight of summer, Garrett?" Mr. Francis asked. "You surely have something that stands out."

I looked up and down the table and stopped at Skipper. I couldn't say what I wanted to say. "It wasn't just one thing. It was all good. I had no idea it would be the best ever."

There was a silence as people sat there remembering. Then a voice broke the spell. "Me, too." It was Skipper. "It's been the best summer for me, too."

We all looked at her and waited for her to say more, but she blushed and looked around at all the eyes on her. Then I blushed.

Grandma saved her. "Is everybody ready for some cake and ice cream?"

"I am," said Spooks.

Louise dipped the ice cream, and everybody passed the desserts around the table. Afterward we sat there long after darkness had fallen, under the stars and a half-moon, reminiscing as the summer ended and fall began. Rollie and Don Francis talked about the upcoming basketball season and how the talk at the barbershop was already expressing high expectations.

I walked over to the table where the rest were sitting, poured myself a large glass of iced tea, and slumped down in a lounge chair. Hearing talk about the basketball season made me think of my own season. I would be home by tomorrow night and in school a day later. My basketball practices would be starting in October. Coach Barrett would be glad to see how much I'd grown and how much stronger I was, but he'd really be surprised when he saw how much I've learned from Mr. Francis.

It was after nine o'clock when the ladies started picking up the glasses and taking up the tablecloths. Grandpa was already snoring in his lounge chair, a hint that the party was over. Taylor and Lady stood up and thanked everybody for having them over, and Spooks gladly accepted Grandma's request that he take the leftover cake back home with him. The Brockmans and Francises said their goodbyes, and those who didn't plan on seeing me off tomorrow gave me a long hug and their best wishes for the new school year. Jimmy said he was going over to the shack and going on the air to broadcast the news and all that happened at the river today.

"You want to come too," he asked me. "News is always better when eyewitnesses report it."

"Just for a while. Then I need to pack for tomorrow."

Spooks came up to me and gave me a big bear hug, nearly squeezing the wind out of me. "I'll see you at the station t—tomorrow."

"Good. I'll see you then, Spooks. I'm glad you're okay," I said.

Rollie led Spooks to his car to drive him to his room behind Maddie's Café. When he drove out of sight, I realized Skipper was standing beside me.

After she told everyone goodnight, we walked up the tunnel. When we got out of earshot and into the dark alley, she said, "I'll see you later. Don't get caught."

CHAPTER **42**

I t was quiet at midnight in Purcell Station. The end of the summer was official, and the beginning of the next season had arrived: the season that changes people's lives— the beginning of school; the start of the harvest season down in the bottoms; or the time when a childhood ends and something else begins. I packed my suitcase and bathed after I got back from Jimmy's radio show and before going to bed. I told Grandma I wanted to get plenty of rest before my trip home. We sat up and talked, sensing the changes that tomorrow would bring, and then at 10 o'clock, an hour past Grandpa's bedtime, we turned in.

The cool night air had a hint of fall as it jostled my curtains over the west window. The quilt was too much, so I kicked it off and left the sheet over me to ward off the chill. I fell asleep immediately, knowing it would be deep and brief before the alarm went off. I stuck it under my pillow next to my head so they wouldn't hear it, just as I had done the time before. Two hours later I jumped when it sounded right next to my ear, and I quickly reached to turn it off. I waited without moving to see if there was any sound from their bedroom. I heard Grandpa snoring.

I dressed in the dark and waited before I raised the screen. The flashlight I kept on the bedside table nearly rolled off when I bumped it. I flashed it on the rose trellis to find the top rung. The roses had grown since last time and nearly covered the slats beneath them. I slipped on the pair of Grandpa's thick cotton work gloves I'd found hanging in the woodshed to ward off the thorns. I reached out and grabbed the top of the trellis as my foot found a lower rung, and I shifted my weight and pushed myself out the window. I closed the screen to keep the bugs out, climbed down the trellis, and jumped to the ground.

In the darkness I could hear the crickets and the howling of a wolf or maybe somebody's hounds. I felt my way behind the house and through the grape arbor where there was no moonlight and went into the alley, hoping I wouldn't arouse Poop Deck. I turned up Fourth Street to Main and continued up to the top of the hill. There were no lights in the stores or homes. I walked as quietly as I could in the darkness. I didn't want to stir any dogs that might wake the neighborhood.

When I reached the top of the hill, I turned into the yard behind the garage. I circled around it until I came to the hammock

"Hi," she said. "I've been waiting."

She slid out of the hammock, took my hand, and guided me through the shrubs to the alley and up to the road. There was a street light shining brightly at the corner. "Let's go this way," she said, and led me through the neighbor's yard and under some trees where it was dark. We turned north and walked out in the street another two hundred yards until we were there.

"Are you afraid?" she asked me.

"I'm over that," I said. "I've been up there a few times with Jimmy."

"Good. Let me go first. I could do this blindfolded."

"Do you think it's unlocked?" I asked. Even though I'd gotten over most of my fear of heights, I didn't want to climb up and find out it was locked

"It always is. No reason why it wouldn't be now."

She took my flashlight and started up the ladder. When we got to the first landing I paused and looked at the trucks over on the highway to the west. It was not so bad this time. I followed Skipper up two more flights, and then we reached the deck. The door was unlocked. She flashed the light around to make sure no one was there.

"I heard Mert Hopper came up here one night and caught a couple of kids necking," she said.

"What was he doing here at night?"

"I don't know. Maybe he'd heard a rumor or something."

"Do you think he'd come here tonight?"

"No. School starts tomorrow. Nobody would think of coming up here tonight."

"Except us."

"Except us," she repeated. She took my hand, and we walked over to the window along the west wall. "But this isn't just any night."

We stood there looking north and west toward the bottoms and watched the cars and trucks up and down Highway 41. It was a steady stream of red taillights heading north and headlights going south. "I didn't know so many people went somewhere this time of night," I said.

"Truckers like it at night. There's less traffic." She dropped my hand and rested her elbows on the windowsill, staring at the traffic. "Just think, that road goes all the way from Miami to Copper Harbor, Wisconsin."

I stood there, thinking about that, staring at the lights on the long highway. Finally, Skipper broke the silence. "Let's go out on the deck. We can see better from there."

The door opened to the north, and when we stepped out we went to the east side of the deck, where we stood above the tree tops, looking into the moonlit hills and the barren fields of the melon farms. The farmers would soon be disking it all up and sowing it in rye for the winter.

The moon lit our faces, and it was then I noticed the shadowed features of Skipper's face, the profile of her nose and chin and perfect cheekbones. She lifted her head upward and smiled at the stars, and a shiver ran down my spine. I'd dreamed of my last night in Purcell Station for weeks, and I wanted it to be one I'd remember. I found out she was thinking the same thing.

"I think we should spend your last night just by ourselves," she had said. All summer long I'd felt that Skipper and I were somehow kindred souls, but not until she said that did I think she may have felt so, too.

I'd told her I had an idea, trying not to sound too eager. "Let's go out that last night and climb the tower. I bet it's something to see up there at night."

"I'd already thought of that," she'd said. So here we were on the top of Purcell Station the last night of summer.

Skipper took my hand and pulled me around the other side of the deck, the south side. There we could see the street light in front of her house and her bedroom window. "If you see a light go on in my house, don't even tell me," she said. "It means I've been caught."

I didn't want to think about that. I didn't want her to get in trouble, nor did I want the night to end. Sometime soon, I would have to help her climb back into the window, and I knew it would be the last time I would see her this summer.

We walked around the corner and back to the west side of the deck, looking out over the highway again. Then we stopped and Skipper said, "Wait here." She disappeared into the tower and came out a moment later with two cushions from the swivel chair. She propped them up against the back of the wall, and motioned for me to sit down. We sat on the deck and leaned back, slumped against the pillows, and stared out at the bottomland and the traffic on the highway.

For a while neither of us said anything. We just looked at the cars and trucks going somewhere and the sky and the stars twinkling in the darkness. I leaned back, my shoulders and head propped against the cushion. I pulled my knees up and was staring up at the Big Dipper when I felt Skipper move. She shifted her body and placed her cushion closer to mine, and I felt her shoulder touching mine. I didn't move, not knowing if it was intentional, and then she took her hand and placed it over my hand, and I realized it was.

"Oh! Did you see that?" she asked.

"See what?"

"A shooting star. It was over there." She pointed to a spot in the western sky.

"I missed it. Sorry."

"Don't be. There's probably going to be another one."

I searched the sky for another one, but several minutes lapsed and none appeared. I was starting to feel my body shiver. I wasn't sure if it was the cool night air or the thought of my last night with Skipper.

"How many stars do you see?" I asked, trying to break the silence.

"Billions, I'm guessing. Planets, too." There was a playful lilt to her voice, and I was thankful for it.

"Do you think anybody lives on them?"

"Probably." She paused and then added, "Do you know there are supposed to be millions of galaxies and trillions of planets? It's staggering, isn't it, to think about it?"

That didn't help my shivering any. I had always had trouble comprehending the nature of the universe.

"It's more than I can understand," I said. "It's like when I watch the ants in the driveway. I think how small they are in all that sand. It's kind of how people are in the universe."

"It's overwhelming when you think about it," she whispered.

"Yes, and I have trouble understanding how it started and where it'll all end…the beginnings and endings.""

"What do you mean, end?'

"Well, you know how in school they teach that one time people thought the earth was flat? And that sailors were afraid if they went too far out to sea, they would just drop off the earth?"

"Yeah, and then Ericson, Magellon, and others came along and proved it wrong."

"Yes, and now we know it's round, but what about the universe?"

"What about it?"

"Well, if I point this flashlight straight up, how far does it go? Where does it end?"

"Who said it will end?" she asked. "Maybe it goes into infinity."

"Well, if it does, then I don't understand infinity. In infinity, how high is up? Does it end?"

"What do you think?"

"I don't know, but I became so confused about it once I finally started crying and my mother asked what was wrong and I told her."

"What did she say?"

"She said she thinks we humans shouldn't be concerned, that it's in the mind of God. She says, and these are her words, 'When it's in a realm so immense, so universal, that it's beyond our comprehension, then it's in the mind of God only.'"

"Then what are you worried about? If it is beyond human consciousness, do you think you're going to figure it out?"

"No, not really, but I shiver thinking about it."

"Well, it's been a mystery for centuries, even longer, and if humans have never been able to understand it, we're not going to tonight. Now, how about we talk about something more down-to-earth?"

Skipper moved closer to me and took her hand and rubbed my arm the way my mother did when I asked her these same questions years ago.

I waited until I stopped shaking. "Okay. I have a question," I said. "Last night, you said you were going to go change clothes and tell your mom where you were going. But, you came back dressed in the same clothes, and you were late. Why?"

"I figured you'd be asking about that." She shifted and sat up, facing me. "I have a confession to make."

"Another one? Is this anything like the one you made about the Black Helmets and Jesse?"

"No, but it's close. You know when you, Jimmy, and Goose carried Jesse to Goose's truck and took him up to Doc's office?"

"Yes, what about it?"

"Well, I saw that Jesse was dressed in street clothes, and I heard Goose say that his shoes were what saved his life. I thought that was kind of strange he'd be on the bridge dressed like that."

"I did, too."

"Well, I found out why. Last night I was supposed to meet Jesse in the back room of the library for his reading lesson. I left you with the excuse I was going home to change clothes. Instead, I went to see if Jesse would show up. I waited, and finally he came in. He was on crutches and looked white as a ghost. He was really shaken up from the incident and wanted to talk about it. When he finished, I asked him why he was up on the bridge if he wasn't swimming or jumping with his friends."

"What did he say?"

"He said he was in his dad's shed down by the railroad when he looked out and saw Spooks on the tracks pushing his wheelbarrow toward the bridge. He knew his old buddies were up there and, knowing how he'd bullied Spooks earlier, thought something like that might happen again. So he followed Spooks, and when Spooks got to the bridge Jesse saw the gang of boys standing there. Then he heard the train. He knew it was the Dixie Flyer, so he started running. When he got to the bridge Spooks was just standing there, not moving. All the others were jumping into the river. Jesse reached Spooks just as the train entered the bridge. He had less than three seconds to decide. He knew the people in the water would save Spooks, so he pushed him over the railing and into the river. Just as he was about to be hit, Jesse tried to leap onto the steel girder, but his foot slipped and he fell. He said he woke up when Doc was bandaging his cuts. That's when he learned his shoe got wedged in between the ties."

"So, that's where you were last night."

"Yes. I didn't have time to go home to change clothes or to tell Mom."

I sat there, trying to sort this all out. "So, Jesse's gone from a bully to membership in the Black Helmets, and freeing his mother from his father's abuse, and now saving the life of the person he used to bully."

Skipper looked up and smiled. "You see, there are some earthly things that are kinda hard to understand, too. That's one of them." She squeezed my hand.

After a moment I asked, "What do you think's going to happen to Jesse now?"

"All I know is that he wants to fly, and he's willing to do whatever it takes to get there. I told him I'd keep tutoring him this winter if he wants me to, and he thanked me and said he did. He wants to get a GED certificate someday and learn aviation."

"Do you think he can do it?"

"My father knows some people. One of them is Wib Waldroup, a farmer down in the bottoms. He has an airplane, a Piper Cub, and he said when Jesse finishes his GED he'll take him up and let him see how he gets along. Then, if all goes well, he'll take him to George Field over in Illinois and get him started."

"You mean, after what Jesse did to you in sixth grade, your dad's still willing to help him learn to fly?"

"Yes. It's called forgiveness. We've talked at lot since then, and I've convinced him Jesse is worth saving. Besides, he believes in second chances. He gave Ross Kirklin one, and it turned out pretty well."

We were lying against the cushions, still looking into the dark night. I wanted this night to be special, and it was, but I was hearing so much my head was starting to spin. I turned to Skipper. "You know, I'm starting to believe in miracles."

"Miracles are mysteries. They're all around us you know."

"Like the Black Helmets?" I said.

"That's one, for sure. And the guy who came into town three times and disappeared before anyone knew why he was here," she said. "That's another one."

We sat there, staring into the sky, and then I thought of something else. "Here's another question. How can the whole town play a softball game that never ends? They don't even keep score, and if they did, it would probably be ten thousand to ten thousand and one by now."

"Maybe that's the beauty of it. As long as they don't keep score, nobody loses."

I was pondering the game that never ended, and then I thought of the summer that was about to end. "You remember when I said I have trouble with the beginnings and endings of things?"

"Yes."

"Well, I don't want to think about the end of the summer—for a lot of reasons."

"Like what, for example?" Skipper asked.

"I told you this once before. It's just that twelve is a really good age, and it's kind of sad I'll never be this age again. I want to hold on to it as long as I can. It's like the end of something, and the beginning of something else, and I'm not sure what that is."

"I know. I liked being twelve, too, but I also liked being thirteen, fourteen, and fifteen. I don't think you should worry about what comes next. You're not the same as you were when you came here. You were shy and quiet and bashful. Now look at you and what you've seen and done. If you ask me, you're ready."

I didn't say anything. We were looking into the darkness and the stars and the lights on the highway. Finally, she asked, "What other reasons do you not want the summer to end?"

I knew this was coming. I knew what I wanted to say, but didn't know if I should. "Tonight, I have to say goodbye to everything I've come to like." I waited; then added, "Including you."

I was glad it was dark. A cloud had come between us and the moon. She couldn't see my face, and I couldn't see hers.

"You mean that?" she asked. She didn't laugh. In fact, her voice was tender and affectionate.

"Yeah, I mean it."

She leaned against my shoulder and rubbed my arm again. "That's nice of you to say. It's hard for me to say goodbye, too."

More silence. "You know something?" I asked. "My grandma never says, 'goodbye.' She just leaves out the 'good' and says, 'bye.'"

"Why does she do that?"

"Because she thinks that 'good' means 'for good,' and she doesn't think people ever part for good. She thinks we'll all be together again."

"Then let's do that, too. I'll say, 'bye,' to you, and you can say, 'bye,' to me, and maybe we'll see each other again."

She moved before she could feel the shiver of my body. Then she slowly stood and took me by the arm, pulling me up and out of my trance. "We have to go now," she said. "It's almost two o'clock and I have school tomorrow, and you have a long ride home."

She put her arm around me, and I slipped mine around her, and we leaned against the railing, looking down at the town beneath us. Street lights fluttered between tree limbs below, and stars flickered in the heavens above, and the moon shined on our faces. And my heart pounded as she kissed me on the cheek.

CHAPTER **43**

They were waiting for me in the kitchen. My suitcase sat by the back door. I told them I left something in my bedroom and I'd be right back. I took the envelope out of the drawer of the night table and checked inside. There were five twenties and a note inside. I sealed it, slipped into their bedroom, and lifted Grandma's pillow and hid it underneath. The note was to let them know how much I appreciated all they'd done for me. The money didn't come close to covering the cost of my keep.

When I got up in the morning I'd gone out to the garage and took down one of the old license plates Grandpa had nailed to the wall, then went into the woodshed and found a strand of old baling wire. I took some snips and clipped off two long pieces and stuck them down my pants leg. The license plate I tucked under my shirt and slipped it under my belt.

We left the house, Grandma, Grandpa and I walking out the back door and through the grape arbor toward the alley, the same way I had entered four months ago from the other direction. It was the same tunnel Uncle Jake had come down through the shadows and appeared in the bright sunlight in his white Navy bell-bottoms. It was the same arbor whose shade Grandma and Grandpa sat under in the heat of summer, cutting and peeling tomatoes for canning and squeezing juice from the grapes for jelly. It was the same tunnel I had walked and rode through countless times, going downtown and coming back with goods and news and stories.

As I carried my suitcase through it this morning, following Grandpa with his shuffle and Grandma at his side, I tasted that lump again in my throat. This was a passage, more than a walk; I could sense it. My mother always said people don't stay too long in one place. We keep moving and growing and changing. By the end of the day, I'd be in another place and see my mother and father for the first time in four months.

When we reached the alley, I checked my shirt pocket to see if I still had the letter my mother had sent me last week. In it she had quoted Hemingway and said my dad's back would be stronger now, "for when man is broken afterward he becomes stronger in the broken places." I knew she was talking about more than a broken back.

When we got to the end of the alley we turned up Third Street to Main and then left to go down to the station. It was quiet now; the kids were in school. We passed the drugstore and Maddie's Café, the bank, Brockman's Grocery, Danny's Barber Shop, Smokey's Pool Room, and Slinker's General Store.

It was here I said, "You go on. I want to stop in and say goodbye to Mr. Slinker."

They looked at me a moment and then said okay and continued down the hill toward the depot. I went in the door and stopped in the back, where the hardware was located. Mr. Slinker came out of the back room, saw me, and said, "Hi, Garrett, what can I do for you?"

"Hi, Mr. Slinker." I pointed and asked, "I was just wondering how much this one cost?"

"That one's about $18.95. Kinda high, but it's the Cadillac model. Got a cheaper one over here, only $14.95. Hey, aren't you going home today? How you gonna get this on the train?"

I figured he was going to ask me that. "Oh, I'm not taking it on the train. I'm giving it to a friend."

He studied me for a minute, stroking his chin. Then he smiled, like something just occurred to him. "How about if I let you have the Cadillac for, let's say, $15? I bet that friend would like the classy one."

"I think you're right. I'll take it." I reached in my pocket, took the last of my twenties, and handed it to him. He went to the cash register and brought me back a five, and then he smiled, "You want me to wrap it for you, since it's a gift?"

I laughed. "You'd need a lot of wrapping paper to wrap a wheelbarrow. But if you have some wire cutters, I'd like to borrow them for a minute."

"Got a pair right here." He reached behind the counter and pulled out a drawer. "Here, these should do."

He watched me pull up my shirt and remove the old license plate. Then I held my leg out real straight and asked, "Could you pull those wires out of my pants leg? I have to hold 'em straight."

He bent down and pulled out the two long pieces of wire. "You think of everything, don't you? I bet this person's going to like this new machine."

"I hope so. He had an accident with his old one yesterday."

"So I heard."

I threaded the wires through the plate's top holes, bent them, and then hooked the other ends around the handles down by the tub and twisted them tight.

"There, that should hold it," I said. "Thanks. I have to hurry now. My train's gonna be here soon."

"Thank you, too, Garrett. You're a good young man. Stop in and see me next time you're in town."

"I will." I wheeled out of Slinkers, and next stop was Maddie's Café. I left the wheelbarrow on the sidewalk and went inside. Maddie was behind the counter, and when she asked me what I'd have, I said, "I just need to ask you a question."

"Fire away. Say, don't you leave soon?"

"Yes, I'm leaving in just a few minutes, but I have to know something first. When Spooks almost got hit by that train yesterday, what was he carrying in his wheelbarrow? I'd never seen him take it on the track like that before."

Maddie stared at me a moment and then came around the counter and took a seat on a stool.

"It's all my fault. I was trying to be nice." She rubbed her temples, and a frown came across her face. "I knew everybody was down at the river enjoying the last day of summer, and I just felt like sending them all a treat, kind of a celebration. I said something about it to Spooks, and he said, "Salty dogs." That's his favorite. I loaded up some cases of Nehis and several boxes of peanuts and sent him on his way. He was so happy…going to surprise all those people." She kept rubbing her temples and staring at the floor. "I felt so bad when I heard what happened. And to boot, he lost his wheelbarrow. Spooks is lost without it. He can't work without his wheelbarrow. It's all my fault."

Her voice cracked, and I saw her eyes glisten. I thought any minute she was going to break down and sob. As she finished I stood and walked toward the door. "Come here," I said. "I have something to show you."

She followed me to the front door, and there she saw the brand-new wheelbarrow, complete with a license plate mounted on the handles. "You got that for Spooks?" She circled it, then looked at me and smiled.

"Yes, ma'am. You think he'll like it?

"Oh, my goodness, he'll love it. He's going to be so happy. Garrett, you just earned a star in your crown." She took hold of my arms, pulling me toward her, and wrapped her arms around me. I felt her shaking.

I told her I had to hurry, that my train was coming soon, and as we said our goodbyes I saw a tear fall down her cheek. I hurried down the hill, pushing the new wheelbarrow past Lady Muldoon's where Killer came to the fence, but I didn't see her anywhere. I got to the depot just as Grandma and Grandpa walked in. They didn't see me coming, so I pushed the wheelbarrow around to the side and left it. I entered the front door where Taylor Barth was waiting.

"Hi, Garrett. I've been expecting you," he said. "I got your ticket right here." Then he said, "Hi, Minnie, Conrad. I bet you're gonna miss this fella when he gets on that train."

"We sure will," Grandma said. "It's been nice having him around. Keeps us thinking young."

"You can say that again," Taylor said. "He's been good company around here, too. One of the best visitors I've ever had."

While they were talking I handed Taylor the money for my ticket. I paid for it with the money I had left from working for Tip.

"Train should be here in about…." Taylor looked at the clock on the wall. "Eleven minutes, more or less."

Just then the door swung open and Lady Muldoon walked in. "Hi, Garrett, Minnie, Connie." She looked at me and said, "I bet you thought I'd forgotten I promised you a treat to take with you, didn't you?"

I started to answer, but she interrupted. "Well, I didn't." She reached in a paper bag and pulled out a canister with a red bow wrapped around it. "I almost didn't get them baked in time. They're still hot."

I took the canister, pulled up the lid, and smelled the hot oatmeal cookies. "Thank you, Miss Muldoon. These're my favorite. You didn't have to do this."

"Oh, yes I did. A promise is a promise. Now, I want you to have a nice trip home, but before you do, it's your turn to make a promise." She stood next to me, and I realized how much taller I was now. "You have to promise you'll come and see me and Killer next time you're in town."

"You can count on it. I promise."

"Good. I'm holding you to that,"

Grandpa shuffled over to the wooden benches in the middle of the room and sat down. I stayed standing, wondering where Spooks was. He said he'd be here to say goodbye. I looked at the clock: six minutes left. I didn't want to sit. I'd be sitting for the next five or six hours. I paced the floor, looking out the window and up Main Street, wondering where he was. Finally, I saw him coming. He looked different not pushing his wheelbarrow. He was slumped over, like he'd lost his best friend. I waited until he got in the door.

"Howdy, Spooks. How ya doing?" asked Taylor. "Boy, are we all glad you made it through that thing yesterday."

Grandma stood up, went over to Spooks, and gave him a hug. "Thanks for coming, Spooks. It's nice of you."

Grandpa said, "Sorry about your wheelbarrow. I forgot to ask you last night what you were hauling in it."

I didn't hear the answer. I'd gone outside to bring the wheelbarrow around to the back door where we would exit to go to the train. When I opened the door, I picked up my suitcase and said, "We better get out there. It's about time."

They all followed me out to the platform. Spooks came out last, and that's when he saw the wheelbarrow. He walked around it, then bent over and studied it. "Whose is…?

I interrupted. "Pick it up, Spooks, and see if it fits your hands."

He reached down, wrapped his large hands around the wooden handles, and slowly picked it up. He rolled it forward and then back, and then forward. He set it down and walked around it. A big grin came across his face. He'd realized it was his.

"It's g—got a rubber tire!" he shouted. His old wheelbarrow had a steel wheel on the front, the kind you could hear grinding down the pavement a block away.

"Hey, now you can sneak up on people, Spooks," Grandpa said. "They can't hear you coming."

Spooks came back to the handles and picked it up again. "It has a l— license plate on it, too!" He smiled and circled it several more times.

Grandma looked at me and came around behind the group. She took hold of my arm and whispered in my ear. "That's a wonderful thing you did. You don't know how much that will mean to him."

"Thanks," I whispered. "But, thank Tip. He made it possible. I couldn't think of anything better to spend it on."

Lady Muldoon and Taylor both came up and told me how nice it was that Spooks could carry on his business now.

Then I heard the whistle. The train was coming across the bridge where yesterday Spooks and Jesse had almost died together. I reached down for my suitcase, and with the others following, I walked over to the platform as the train groaned to a stop. The conductor stepped down and placed the stool on the ground. He reached for my suitcase, and I turned and hugged, first Grandma, making sure I only said, "Bye," then Grandpa. We'd said our main farewells last night. Then it was Lady, Taylor, and finally Spooks.

He gripped me with his huge arms and said into my ear, "Th-anks. You're a nice f—friend."

I held him too and said, "You're a good man, Spooks. You taught me a lot this summer." I let go, stepped back, and saw his wet eyes. "Bye now, Spooks."

I boarded the train and took a seat on the station side of the aisle. The seats were empty now. Labor Day had passed. As we started up and left the station, I sat by the window and waved until they were out of sight.

We passed through the intersection just north of the station. The crossing guards were down, and a gray sedan sat idling. A young mother sat behind the wheel with a child beside her. He waved, and I waved back. Then as we moved north out of town we passed the

Winslow House, where Spooks's grandfather was saved by the Underground Railroad, and where Jessse found refuge from his father's abuse. As we passed I looked up the hill and saw the school and the baseball field behind it, and I thought of all the baseball games I'd covered on the radio there with Jimmy. I thought of Skipper and her friends and the popcorn and salty dogs and kids chasing foul balls. And then it was gone, and there was nothing but fields—gently rolling, sandy, melon fields, where kids like me worked sweating, aching, planting, pitching, and turning vines. Now they were bare, waiting for the rye to come up for the winter.

I moved across the aisle into an empty seat and looked west. There in the distance I saw the big white barn of the Gentry farm and the flat ground that stretched for miles west to the Wabash, to Illinois. I saw the sprinkling of new oil derricks that had sprung up in the past year or so, although there would not be any on the Gentry farm. My father's father had seen to that. He thought a man should work for his reward.

I looked back to the east again at the sandy hills where my mother's family was rooted, and I knew they would always have what they had there, even if they moved away or left to fight in the war. And I knew the history of the Wabash bottoms would always be a part of those of us carrying the name Gentry. Now I was astride the two of them, going back home, a part of me in both places.

I leaned back in my seat and reclined it as far back as it would go and closed my eyes. Then I heard, "Next stop, Vincennes." I sat up and looked out the window. We were slowing down through the city streets, and then we came to an opening and pulled into the station.

I shook my head to clear it and looked out the window. People were milling around the platform. The train came to a stop, and then there was a brief silence before I heard footsteps of someone coming up the aisle to get a seat. I opened my window to get some air, and that's when I heard it.

"Extra! Read all about it," yelled a young boy.

I stood and looked out the window, trying to catch a glimpse of the headline the boy was holding up. A group of people crowded around him, snapping up papers and blocking my view. When the crowd dwindled, he held up the paper again and started yelling, "Extra! Read all about it. The Black Helmets exposed!"

I bolted up the aisle and down the steps, came up with a nickel, and handed it to the boy. He handed me the paper just as the conductor yelled, "All aboard."

The train was moving as I jumped on the steps and grabbed the railing. I moved down the aisle and found my seat. We were moving quickly out of the station when I opened the paper and saw the headlines:

Black Helmets Under Investigation.

Beneath it a sub-headline read: *FBI Probe Nearing Conclusion.*
I read the front-page story:

> *A secret paramilitary society headquartered at Purcell Station has been under investigation by the Federal Bureau of Investigation over the past four months. The probe came as a result of a federal indictment against a similar organization in Detroit and Chicago called "The Black Legion."*
>
> *These affiliates have been described as "hooded terrorists" and were feared to be an offshoot of the Ku Klux Klan. Another group, known as "The Mystic Order of the Black Snakes," is also a part of the sweeping F.B.I investigation of paramilitary organizations that have proliferated throughout the Midwest.*
>
> *In response to the probe, Boots Slinker of Purcell Station and National Commander of the Black Helmets of America, said, "There is absolutely no connection between the Black Helmets and the Black Legion or the Black Snakes. We are vigorously opposed to such organizations."*
>
> *The Black Helmets, whose national headquarters is in Purcell Station, has affiliations in Wisconsin, New York, Kentucky, Mississippi, and Illinois, according to Slinker.*
>
> *Slinker went on to defend his organization, saying, "Our purpose is to protect all Americans, regardless of race, color, or creed, against the threat of Communism, Nazism, and all terrorist groups. If any branches of these terrorists' organizations are found in our locality, we will volunteer to assist authorities in helping rid our area of such poison."*
>
> *Although information about the Black Helmets, a highly secret order, is difficult to obtain, they are believed to have a national*

membership of over 11,000, with 55 belonging to the founding chapter in Purcell Station.

Interviews with folks in the area reveal that there may be more to the unit's purposes than those stated by Commander Slinker.

"They run that town," said Eddie Sprowl, a former resident. "Anybody who doesn't think there's law and order there doesn't know the Black Helmets."

Others offered a different view. "They perform community service. I don't know what this place would be like if we didn't have them," said Bud Tate, the local postmaster.

The investigation's final report will be forthcoming shortly, said a source from the Washington headquarters of Director of the FBI J. Edgar Hoover.

Sheriff Clyde Boykin says his office has had the Black Helmets under observation for some time and feels, "They have passed our scrutiny and have proven to be a valuable community asset."

I put the paper down and stared out the window. We were going north. Mom said we had to keep moving. She also said not all mysteries are the province of the human mind to solve, but I guess that means some of them are. I leaned my head on the back of the seat and smiled and thought of Skipper, knowing that tonight she, too, would finally know the mystery of the suspicious man who'd kept us guessing all summer.

We were going fast now, out of town and into the rolling countryside, past the melon fields where the crops once stood. The season was over. I reached into my pocket and pulled out my billfold. In the side pocket I found the clipping I'd saved from the newspaper at the station in Indianapolis back in May. I unfolded it and studied the picture; then I read the caption, about the twelve year old boy chasing the pigeons, trying to catch them before it was too late.

ACKNOWLEDGEMENTS

When the first draft of this book was well underway, I set up a visit with three natives of Knox County, Indiana, whom I had known only vaguely. Meeting at the Vincennes home of Jackie Worland, present also were Bill Amers and his wife Betty. We spent the better part of two hours as they reminisced about life in the town of my ancestors, on which this book is based. Then, Jackie dropped a bombshell. She asked me if I had ever heard of the "Black Helmets." I hadn't.

She left the room and came back a few minutes later with a thick scrapbook and placed it on the coffee table in front of me. For the next half hour we went through the pictures, stories, and newspaper clippings of the "real" Black Helmets of America, a secret society founded in Knox County in the 1930's. It had attracted national media attention, in addition to the FBI, and speculation was rampant as to what its motives and practices were. Jackie offered firsthand knowledge from stories she had heard as a child. It was at the end that she revealed her father had been the National Commander of the BHA.

Their mystery was intriguing, and I realized my book had taken on a whole new direction. Bill and I hurried down to the Knox County Library before it closed to make copies of the clippings and pictures. The Black Helmets became an integral part of my story, along with other stories Jackie, Bill, and Betty shared that night. To them, I owe a deep debt of gratitude.

Equally important was the help offered by Jeff Palmer, another native whose family is the model for two characters in the book. Jeff's critiques of early drafts were on target, and his suggestions gave the story a sense of authenticity. His contributions to background material were enhanced with his sharing of the book *Pappy*, authored by his late father, Don Palmer, Sr. I owe them both my deep appreciation.

For his expertise in editing the manuscript I thank Dr. Dennis Hensley, a prolific author and Director of the Professional Writing Program at Taylor University. His comments and encouragement and his eye for detail kept me focused and inspired. My gratitude also goes out to Nancy Baxter, Senior Editor at Hawthorne Publishing, whose critique of my manuscript let me know I had a story worth telling.

My thanks go out also to my writing colleagues at the University of Iowa Summer Writing Festival, the Midwest Writers Conference at Ball State University, and the creative writing classes in the Continuing Studies Program at Indiana University. Their thoughtful analyses and encouragement were invaluable.

Special thanks go out to Mike and Betsy Walsh for the time, effort, and thought they put into one of my drafts. Our friendship endures even after I made them labor through an arduous, overdone, early draft that barely resembles the work inside these pages. Others whom I want to thank are the "Ladies of the Club:" my name for the book club of Helen Hollingsworth, Susan Nowlin, Sharon Finley, Sheri Curry, Judy Shettleroe, and Lois Sparks. Their patience with early drafts of the opening chapter gave me direction in what worked and what didn't. I also owe author James Alexander Thom and former Indiana University librarians Caroline Benedict and Betty Jarboe my gratitude for the gracious comments they provided on the opening chapters. Their resumes made those comments compelling.

On a more personal level, my wife Teresa has been both my harshest critic and my greatest booster, both of which I needed, offering many perspectives that missed my eye completely. Her patience had a lot to do with my perseverance. She also gave me the freedom to write, often in large chunks of time, while she took care of all the other things our household required. For this I am ever grateful.

Finally, she and I are fortunate to have a family of whom we are very proud. They are grown now, but their encouragement and inspiration were instrumental in my undertaking of this project. To Darin, Shannon, Kevin, David, and Kate, all talented in their own way, I thank you for your interest in what I was doing down in the basement all that time. In the end, it is all about family.

Dale Glenn